Between the Waves and the Stars

and the Stars

A NOVEL BY **B.P. LYNCH**

ALDEBARAN CREATIVE LLC

New York

Published by Aldebaran Creative LLC
Staten Island, New York

Library of Congress Control Number: 2025914685
ISBN (Paperback): 979-8-9990499-0-2
ISBN (eBook): 979-8-9990499-1-9

First Edition

Cover art, illustrations, and interior design by B.P. Lynch
Printed in the United States of America

Aldebaran Creative is an independent publisher dedicated to fiction, poetry, and visual storytelling with heart.

To the boy who dreamed,
and the people who helped him along the way.

1

The ocean had always been everything to me. When I was a kid, it was straight up magical. I'd sit in the shallows, letting the waves bury my legs in the sand. Back then, the ocean didn't expect anything from me. It was just there, a place to play, to enjoy, to forget the rest of the world.

As I got older, it stopped being just a playground. It became something to master. First skimboarding, then boogie boarding, and finally surfing—each one felt like leveling up. I wiped out more times than I could count, the board slamming into me or the waves swallowing me whole. It was frustrating, and more than a bit humbling, but that first wave I actually caught? It wasn't pretty or anything, but it was *everything*. It was only a little knee-high, but I got the timing right and popped up. My legs were shaky and knees were bent all wrong, but for about six seconds with Rafe and Avery cheering me on? I felt like I could do anything.

But the ocean isn't all thrills and victories. Sometimes it just feels different, heavier, like it's holding a mirror up to me. Sometimes when I look at it, I don't just see the water. I see myself. I see the kid building sandcastles with my dad, with the sun shining all golden and bright... back when everything felt simple. And I see the teenager sitting alone on the same stretch of sand after my dad died, sand slipping through my fingers in the wind, wondering how the same waves could still roll in like nothing had changed.

Like the whole fucking world hadn't just changed.

Three years later, there I was, out on my mint green Chilli Popper board, bobbing with swells that barely rose. The whole vibe was off, the timing was off—not just in the water, but in me. I kept running loops in my head, second-guessing every thought, every move.

I stared out at that blank line where the hazy pink of the sky met the deep blue of the Pacific. I'd surfed this beach hundreds of times, stared out at that line hundreds more. Sure it was no Malibu, but it was *ours*. It was familiar… and yet that familiarity was starting to feel a whole lot less comfortable—a whole lot more like a cage.

I was both lost and trapped, being left behind by my friends who would be heading off on their next big adventure at the end of summer. And me? I had nothing lined up. Not a single damn thing.

It had only been a week since I graduated high school and everyone in the Class of 2024 seemed to have a plan. College, internships, jobs… they were all moving forward and figuring out their lives.

But me?

I was just… here. Floating. Waiting for something in the water to shift… waiting for a wave to break.

I wasn't sure if it was it the ocean making me feel like this, or if the ocean was just reflecting what was already inside me. Maybe it was both. Maybe it didn't matter.

I took a deep breath and held it for a few seconds before letting it out slowly. It was a trick my guidance counselor had taught me. It was supposed to help when things felt… too much. Lately, I found myself using it a lot… and found it working less and less.

I lost track of time as set after set of disappointing waves passed me. A pair of seagulls squawked overhead. Against the streaks of orange and yellow pushing out the soft pinks as the sun climbed higher above the palm tree skyline of Venice Beach, I squinted up at them as they circled me like vultures. What were they waiting for?

"Kiiikooo," Rafe's voice sliced through my thoughts. He stretched out the syllables of my name, making it sound like a song. "How's it going, fam?"

I replied with a weak "heh" that barely qualified as a chuckle. "It's not going much of anywhere," I replied, scooping a handful of water and tossing it over the nose of my board.

"Hey, Kiko, you gotta chill, my dude. Like my abuela always says, '*La paciencia es una virtud*'" he said in an exaggerated accent, laying it on thick. "Patience is a virtue. We can't make the waves come faster. They'll get here when they're ready. We just gotta ride them when they do."

The smallest hint of a smile tugged at the corner of my mouth as I shook my head. Rafe was always able to drop Spanish into conversations like it was nothing. I could follow along, but I never felt confident speaking it back. He also had a grandma saying for literally everything.

"Yeah, yeah," I replied. "Abuelita's wisdom and all that. But right now, I think I need a bit more than patience. I need some actual waves."

Rafe clicked his tongue dramatically. "Don't be disrespecting Abuelita Rosa like that," he said, laughing and fake-offended. "She *knows* things, man. Whoa, whoa! Like remember what happened last time you didn't listen to her?"

"Oh, we're going there now?" I laughed.

Rafe threw up his hands acting all innocent. "Hey, I'm not going anywhere. I'm just saying—she warned you about those sketchy street tacos from that truck on Overland, and you were all, 'What's the worst that could happen?' You remember that?"

"Yeah, I remember" I groaned. "The regular guy wasn't there, and I just figured—"

"Oh yeah, you figured all right," Rafe interrupted, that stupid grin of his going wide. It was the kind of grin that made you want to knock it right off his face. So I let my intrusive thoughts win and scooped up a handful of water and launched it at him, hitting him square in the face. He froze for a second, then cracked up laughing.

"Oh, it's like that?" he said, sweeping his arm in a dramatic arc and sending a massive splash back at me, soaking my chest and face.

For a moment, we weren't just two people drifting through an awkward in-between phase of life. It was like something hit pause on everything in my head—the worries, the overthinking, the weird emptiness I couldn't shake. It was just the two of us, laughing and splashing like we were twelve again. There were no deadlines, no expectations, no future to figure out. Just this moment.

Our hands locked together in this dumb one-arm wrestling game we'd been playing forever, where we try to push the other one off his board. It wasn't really about strength, but more like muscle memory at this point. It was ritual. Just this low-key flex, proof of all the hours we spent out here. Getting older, screwing up and laughing… through most of it at least.

Rafe's shaggy curls were dripping, and the sun sparkled off the gold chain and cross pendant around his neck. Sure it wasn't real gold, but Rafe wore it like it was. He had this confidence that made anything he did work—like right now.

He had this cocky spark in his eyes, the kind that was giving "watch me pull some amazing move" energy.

He moved first—as usual—pushing forward. I countered without thinking, trying to shove him backwards while also trying to hold my balance steady. The rocking of the waves only added to the challenge as our boards wobbled beneath us. The ocean was not helping.

We were laughing again as we struggled. It wasn't just about the game. That laugh was everything—every inside joke, every stupid memory we'd stacked up over the years. It was the kind of laugh you couldn't fake, the kind that comes from years of friendship, when you know someone's got your back no matter what.

Well… at least I hoped he did.

Finally, Rafe made this over-the-top move, tipping his board way too far, and splashing into the water. I didn't even try to fight it and gravity wasn't asking. He pulled me in right after him.

The water was cold—typical for June—and slapped me in the face as I went under. When I popped back up, Rafe was already laughing his head off like he won. Like it was all part of his plan.

We floated there for a minute with our boards drifting next to us. Not talking, just breathing. The sky above us looked like it was trying too hard to be pretty. Like someone cranked up the saturation on the sky in Photoshop or turned on some Instagram filter.

Rafe was just floating there… being Rafe. That solid and constant friend I've had for years—without a thought in his head. And I won't lie, for half a second, my brain finally shut up.

This was the stuff that mattered—not the big plans or the pressure to figure it all out. Worrying about timelines and the future or the how-the-hell-do-I-grow-up question. Just these random, perfect moments with someone who just *gets* you—or in this case—as close as I let anyone get.

"Wave Whisperer! Where you been hiding?" Rafe shouted like he had no volume control—because he didn't.

I hadn't even seen Avery paddling up. Her purple-tipped hair was pulled back, but a few strands were flying loose as she paddled, totally unbothered. She moved like she'd been surfing since birth, which actually, wasn't even a stretch. Where Rafe and I had spent middle school eating sand and barely staying upright, Avery had already been shredding. Her dad was a local surf legend, and Avery? She was the rightful heir to that throne.

"Are you two just gonna float there all day, or are we actually gonna catch something?" she called out, playful but with that competitive edge that made you want to prove her wrong, even if you knew you couldn't.

"Relax," Rafe said. "I'm teaching Kiko about patience!"

Avery snorted with a full-on eye roll included. "Patience?" she said, spinning to face me. "C'mon, Kiko. Don't let him brainwash you with one of his grandma's proverbs again."

"You're not wrong," I said with a laugh as Rafe grasped his chest in mock betrayal.

"Why's everyone always clowning on Abuela?" he demanded, throwing his hands up like a cartoon character.

"Sorry, not sorry, Rafael," Avery shot back with a wink. "Life's too short to wait around for perfect conditions. These waves are calling my name, and they're not about to wait for you two."

Her brown eyes shifted to the water, scanning it like it was doing something only she could see. Avery didn't need some app on her phone or whatever to track the swells. She just *knew*. One wave caught her attention, and without another word, she was paddling, smooth and fast, dropping in like the ocean was working with her.

It wasn't even a big wave, but Avery didn't need some monster to look epic. She made pretty much anything work. As the wave stood up, she popped up clean with zero hesitation. She made a smooth bottom turn and then drove down the line with total control. She wasn't flashy or anything but that's what made her style that much more impressive. It was just… pure instinct.

Rafe and I just watched, both of us quiet for once. We had no jokes, no shade. Just the awe that came with watching Avery Maddox in her element.

She wasn't just good; she was *next level*. There was no hesitation, no wasted movement. It was obvious why she people called her "Wave Whisperer." She wasn't just another surfer out here; she was a force of nature.

I glanced over at Rafe, and, yeah, he was gone. His eyes were locked on her like she was the only thing that existed in the water, the kind of look that made you want to wave a hand in front of his stare. There was this glint in his eye… and that stupid little half-smile tugging at the corner of his mouth. I knew *that* look. It wasn't just admiration—it was definitely something more.

But watching his smile seemed to drain my own.

"She's absolutely killing it out there," Rafe said, clapping a hand on my shoulder. "I gotta get me some of this."

I just sighed as he paddled off. I wasn't quite sure if he was talking about the wave… or something else.

I hung back, letting the lineup open up in front of me as the others joined in. Clean sets were rolling through, but I was still scanning for the one.

Avery and Rafe were out there, hooting and calling each other into waves. They were hyping each other up like they were in their own world.

And it definitely seemed like they were.

The longer I floated, the more I felt like I didn't belong in that world. Like they'd shifted into something new, something that didn't include me. The way they moved together, the way their smiles looked different now—quieter... closer.

It stirred something in me that was sharp and uncomfortable. I don't know, maybe jealousy? Or maybe it was just that weird realization that everything between us was changing.

That our trio was becoming a duo.

And where did that leave me?

Avery and Rafe had this energy now, this momentum like they were already moving on to the next big thing. Meanwhile, all those feelings came rushing back. I was still here, stuck, floating in the same place, waiting for a wave that might never come.

I stared out at the horizon again, trying to feel it—the rhythm, the timing, the connection I used to have. But nothing. Every wave still felt off, but I knew deep down it wasn't the ocean. I was way too stuck in my own head.

"What am I even doing here?" I mumbled.

The sun was climbing higher now, throwing everything into sharp focus. The beach was waking up—joggers, umbrellas, kids already running circles around their parents. The noise of it all felt weirdly far away, even as it grew louder. I couldn't shake the feeling that I didn't fit, like everyone else was in on something I wasn't. Out in the lineup, Rafe and Avery were laughing, catching waves like they were choreographed just for them. Watching them only made that heaviness settle deeper.

With a sigh, I turned my board toward the shore and started paddling back.

"Yo, Kiko! Where you going, dude?" Rafe called out after me, all loud and teasing.

"I gotta get to work!" I replied.

"You don't even have a job!" he shouted, cracking up.

I smirked over my shoulder. He wasn't wrong—I'd quit my frozen yogurt gig a month ago and hadn't exactly been hustling to find another. "Even more reason to go then!"

Once I hit shallow water, I hopped off, undid my leash, and pinched the water out of my nose. I hauled my board onto the beach, and let the sun bake the salt off my skin for a minute, trying to shake off the restlessness clinging to me.

Rafe and Avery weren't far behind, dripping water and still riding the high of their last wave.

"Come on, fam, don't bail now," Rafe said, flicking water from his hair and grinning like the whole day was laid out for us.

"Yeah, we're just getting started," Avery added, shaking her purple-tipped hair.

I hesitated, caught between wanting to lose myself in their energy and this pull to be alone. Something about today felt… off. Like if I stayed, I'd just bring them down with me.

I forced a smile and started walking up the beach, my board under my arm.

"Maybe next time," I said, more to myself than to them.

"Stoner Plaza tonight?" Rafe called.

"Maybe," I called back, keeping it vague. It wasn't a no, though it wasn't a yes either, but if I was being honest it was definitely more to the "no" side.

I headed over to my stuff, peeling off my wetsuit. My board shorts were loud as hell, with bright blues and oranges that looked like they belonged in a '90s music video. I pulled on my hoodie next, my go-to light-blue tie-dye one. It was oversized and soft, like wrapping myself in a piece of sky after being in the water.

I pulled on my Dodgers cap, backwards as always. My hair was getting long again, brushing my shoulders in a way that made Ma roll her eyes every time she saw it.

I grabbed my phone—an old iPhone with a cracked screen Rafe gave me when he upgraded. It was hanging on by a thread, but it still worked… mostly. I unlocked it, pressing the 3 in my code a little harder to make it take. Nothing. No calls, no texts.

Not quite sure what I was expecting, I just left the only people who ever texted me besides Ma. But I still felt some strange disappointment. I grabbed my backpack and slung it over one shoulder. It had also seen better days, frayed at the edges, but still holding on, which was more than I could say about a lot of things lately. Then I picked up my skateboard—scratched to hell, grip tape worn smooth in some spots, but my absolute ride-or-die on land. It wasn't just a board. It was like a part of me, something that always kept me moving forward, even when

I wasn't sure where I was going.

With everything in hand, I started making my way up to the boardwalk. Once I hit the solid ground of the path heading to the boardwalk, I dropped my board onto the concrete, stepped on, and gave it a push, feeling the familiar rumble of wheels against the ground.

I pulled out my phone again and untangled my wired headphones with my free hand. Yeah, I know, ancient tech, but try hunting down a lost AirPod in the bowl at the skatepark. If I'm being honest though? There's no way I could afford the wireless ones anyway.

I opened Spotify and tapped my playlist, "Kiko's Mix." The opening riff of *Riptide* by Vance Joy kicked in, soft and easy, just as I rolled past the usual chaos of the boardwalk. Street performers, tourists, vendors— it was all noise in the background as I rolled on, letting the music drown out everything else.

Away from the ocean, everything felt different—louder, busier, alive in a way the waves hadn't been. On my board, I could disappear into it all, just another face rolling through. It was still early, with most of the shops still closed, but the most diehard street performers were already hustling, and a couple dudes were already working out at Muscle Beach.

Venice always had its own rhythm, loud, messy, and constant.

I pushed off and headed inland, weaving through the small groups of people on the sidewalks. I took my usual route up Windward Avenue, passing my favorite mural: Touch of Venice. The black-and-white artwork sprawled across the side of a hotel. I glanced at it as I rolled by, but had to swerve last minute to avoid a gray Prius sticking too far out of its parking spot. Typical.

The famous VENICE sign hung overhead, strung between two buildings like a postcard. A trio of girls was posing underneath it, one of them holding up a peace sign while the others struck influencer-worthy poses. I ducked around them, carving past the roundabout and dodging a green Culver City bus that felt way too close for comfort.

The steady clack of my wheels against the pavement kept me grounded.

The further I got from the beach, the more the vibe shifted. The tourists thinned out, replaced by locals—joggers, people heading to work, an older guy sipping coffee outside a café with his dog. Everyone was in their own little world, and I slipped through it all, gliding between the sidewalk and the street, dodging cars and bikes without breaking my rhythm.

This route was second nature by now. A twenty-minute ride I could probably do blindfolded. First was Centennial Park, wedged awkwardly between the split lanes of Venice Boulevard. Then came the overpriced organic grocery store I definitely couldn't afford, and then a tiny electric car dealership with glossy, futuristic cars I couldn't even imagine ever being able to afford.

By the time I passed the firehouse on Shell Avenue, I knew I was getting close. The side streets started to get quieter, lined with those palm trees that made everything look straight out of a movie. I turned onto Victoria Avenue, the wheels of my board humming against the pavement as I cruised past the mission-style church that marked the halfway point.

The air smelled faintly of jasmine from someone's overgrown garden, mixing with the smell of salt on my body. It was still early, the light just starting to soften, and for a moment, the ride felt easy, like maybe I could lose myself in the motion and let everything else fade into the background.

My playlist hummed in my ears, a mix of chill tracks that didn't fit into any one vibe—just songs that felt right. It was the kind of playlist you threw together late at night and never stopped adding to. I was halfway through track five when I hit Lincoln Boulevard, weaving through traffic like it was part of the game.

A few more blocks, and I turned down the alley behind the houses across from the middle school. That middle school was where it all started, where I first met Rafe and Avery. Back then, I was just some awkward kid with a yard sale board and no clue what I was doing.

Now? Well, not much had changed.

But at least I wasn't doing it alone.

I rolled up to Rafe's backyard gate and kicked my board into my hand. The old wooden latch creaked as I pushed it open and I ducked into the shed to stash the Chilli Popper.

When I stepped back out, I felt lighter without the board weighing me down. I dropped my skateboard back onto the pavement, gave it a push and took off.

The streets became my playground—clean Ollies over sidewalk cracks, a kickflip that snapped perfectly under my feet. With every spin of the wheels, the weight in my chest loosened. Benson Boone was hitting the chorus in my ears, and I couldn't resist adding a little air guitar.

I weaved through the neighborhood, looping around the middle school until I hit Venice Boulevard.

That's when I saw it—the orange 33 bus pulling away from the curb.

No way was I waiting for the next one.

I leaned forward, pushing harder, the sound of my wheels slamming against the concrete picking up speed. Every movement was crisp. My board felt like it was flying, humming under me like it wanted this just as bad.

I zigzagged past slow walkers, cut into the street when it was clear, dodged a trash can, then a cracked-up sidewalk panel that nearly sent me flying.

By the time I reached the next stop in front of the high school, the bus was just pulling in. I kicked my board up, grabbed it, and hopped on— breathless, heart pounding. The driver didn't even look up as I swiped my TAP card against the reader.

I headed straight for the back, dropping into one of the vinyl seats near the door. They'd swapped out the old, disgusting fabric ones after the pandemic, but the weird plasticky smell still lingered. I rested my board across my knees and leaned against the window, staring out at the passing streets.

The bus rattled along, and the adrenaline faded, replaced by that familiar weight that crept back in whenever I slowed down. It was my reflection in the window that got me. Man, did I look tired, like someone trying to hold it together while the rest of the world sped past.

We rumbled under the 405, just as my playlist got rudely interrupted by a notification chime. I groaned and pulled out my phone, the cracked screen lighting up and showing a tiny Gmail icon in the top corner.

An email? Weird.

I unlocked it, tapped the app, and squinted suspiciously at the subject line: "Interview."

"Enrique Rodriguez," it started.

I rolled my eyes. My full name—of course.

"Thank you for submitting your application. I'd like to interview you for the barista position. I'm pleased to see you have prior experience. If you could stop by the shop sometime this week, that would be great! I'm here every day from 7 AM-5 PM. Look forward to speaking with you soon! —Neil."

I snorted. "Wow. Thanks, Ma. Real subtle."

There was zero mystery about who submitted that application. She was the only one who insisted on calling me Enrique. Plus, "prior experience?" Unless you count making instant coffee at 6 a.m. with too much creamer, Neil was in for a healthy cup of disappointment.

I looked out the window, letting Venice Boulevard distract me. Same old scene: dry cleaners with faded posters curling at the edges, tattoo parlors flashing neon "OPEN" signs, laundromats where people stared blankly at spinning washers like they were waiting for answers. It was all familiar and comfortably boring.

But then my eyes flicked back to my phone. The email still sat there, bold and demanding, like it was waiting for me to make some kind of life-changing decision. A barista job? Me? I couldn't even make cereal without spilling milk. How was I supposed to froth it?

I stared at the "Reply" button, my finger hovering like I was about to do something bold. I should've said yes. A paycheck wouldn't hurt, and maybe it'd get my mom off my back for five minutes.

But the longer I sat there, the heavier it felt.

My gut was saying "nah," and I wasn't in a mood to fight it.

With a sigh, I locked my phone and shoved it back in my pocket.

"Yeah, nope," I muttered, leaning my head against the window.

The bus rumbled on, Venice rolling past outside, same as always. The email could wait. Or maybe it couldn't. Either way, I wasn't ready to deal with it.

I leaned back against the bus seat, head pressed against the window, staring at the city blurring past. Graffiti-covered walls, random shops, people just vibing through their day—it all rushed by like some low-budget music video. The steady rumble of the bus underneath was weirdly calming, almost enough to drown out the overthinking spiral happening in my brain. Almost.

The bus jerked to a stop—my stop—and I grabbed my board, sliding past a guy blasting TikTok videos on full volume. Stepping off, I took a deep breath. The pull of home was there, familiar and safe. The ocean hadn't given me what I needed today, so it was time for Plan B: my room. My little escape, where I could just exist without anyone or anything judging me.

I dropped my board onto the pavement, gave it a quick kick, and started rolling. The wheels hummed against the concrete, and for the first time all day, my head felt a little less crowded. Skating always did that. It was like therapy, but cheaper—and, okay, riskier, but still worth it. The rhythm of pushing off and coasting, weaving around cracks and potholes, made everything feel lighter. Like for those few minutes, I wasn't stuck. I was just... moving.

I still didn't know what to do about the job thing—or any of the other "get your life together" stuff lurking in the back of my head. That could wait. Right now, it was just me, my board, and the sound of my wheels cutting through the noise. That was all I needed. For now, at least.

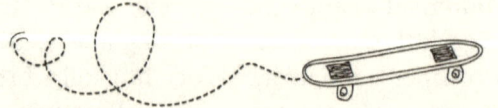

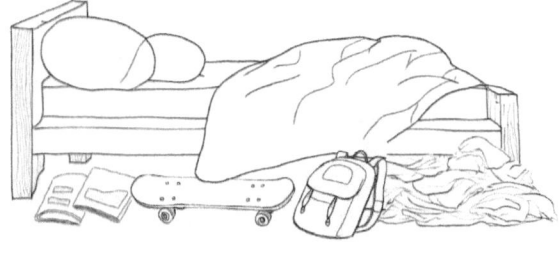

2

I didn't meet up with them that night, even though I usually liked the nights at Stoner Plaza. They were chill, laid back. No photographers in your face like at Venice Skatepark. Still, I just wasn't feeling it… and that feeling carried into the next day, so I skipped the beach and just stuck to the streets of my neighborhood.

It was Father's Day, which I guess you could say was not a great day in the Rodriguez household—at least not in the past three years. Part of me wanted to be anywhere but home, but the other part wanted to just stay in my room all day.

It was around lunchtime when I rolled up to those six steps that led to the walkway down the side of my apartment building. A few years back, they'd given the place a facelift with some dark gray paint, modern-looking railings, and even better lighting fixtures. It definitely looked better now, almost trendy—from the outside at least. Some of the first-floor neighbors had tried to put their own spin on things—potted plants, mini herb gardens, even a string of fairy lights someone had looped around their railing. It was cute, I guess. But inside? It was the same old place with the same old vibe. Paint couldn't fix everything.

I carried my board up the steps and dropped it onto the walkway. I rolled past the doors and stairwells that led to the second-floor apartments until I got to the last stairway. Our apartment was on the right, directly across from Mr. and Mrs. Navarro's place. Both doors were exactly the same, the plain brown original paint, like they ran out of the trendy gray by the time they got to the stairways. I guess you can't see them from the street so who cares right?

The locks were original, too. Ours was super stubborn, the kind of lock that needed a whole ritual to open. I slid the key in and gave it my usual jiggle-twist combo until I finally heard the click.

That's when Bandit lost his mind. His barking just exploded from the other side of the door along with the sound of his little paws skittering across the floor. The second I opened it, he launched himself at me. His tail was wagging so fast I thought he might knock himself over, and he yipped like I'd been gone for years instead of just a couple of hours.

"Hey, hey, calm down, buddy," I said, crouching down as he jumped up on my legs. I scratched behind his ears, and he leaned into me like I was the best thing to happen all day and honestly? That kind of love was hard to argue with. For a second, it even made me forget about the rest of the day and how aimless it felt. How the ocean hadn't worked its usual magic. Bandit didn't care about any of that. I was here and that was enough.

"Alright, Bandit, let's get you out," I sighed, slipping his harness onto him and clipping his leash on. He practically exploded with excitement like he couldn't wait another second. I rolled my eyes, but couldn't fight the smile. I could never fight the smile long enough with him.

We stepped outside, and Bandit was on a hundred, nose to the ground, tail wagging. We turned left, like always, heading uphill toward the quieter streets. The other direction was all noise—cars, the gas station, people yelling at each other which was not exactly the vibe I was going for today. This way was definitely better: a couple of low-key apartment buildings, then tree-lined streets with ranch-style houses—those mid-century kind you see on TV.

Bandit was locked in, sniffing every lamppost, every patch of grass, every crack in the sidewalk. I let him do his thing, tugging him forward every so often when he got too into whatever smell he'd discovered. Watching him, it was hard not to laugh—he made everything look so new and exciting, like the same old walk we took every day was a whole adventure.

We'd made it halfway through when Bandit suddenly froze. His ears shot up, and his little body went rigid as he gave this low growl.

"What now?" I muttered, following his stare.

Across the street, this massive German shepherd was strolling by with its owner.

Bandit went off. Barking like he was ready to throw down with his chest all puffed up, acting like he was ten times bigger than his fifteen-pound self.

"Dude, relax," I said, holding the leash tight. But Bandit wasn't hearing it. He probably thought he was protecting me. He was my ride or die after all, but if he thought he was taking the German shepherd... he was definitely going to do more dying than riding.

"Chill, dude," I said with a laugh, gently pulling on Bandit's leash. "You do realize he could eat you as a snack, right?"

I crouched down to his level, rubbing the sides of his head like I was trying to knock some sense into him. "Yeah, is that what you want to be? My little taquito? My little chicken nugget?" I said in the dumbest baby voice I could manage.

Bandit's ears flicked back for half a second, like he might have been listening—then he went right back to barking his tiny lungs out in full defiance mode.

Meanwhile, the German shepherd couldn't have cared less. It gave a lazy wag of its tail, its owner barely glancing over, and the two of them strolled off like Bandit wasn't out here challenging the world.

"Alright, Bandit. You're my hero. Let's keep it moving," I said, tugging the leash.

Bandit hesitated, then strutted forward like he'd won the standoff. I shook my head, laughing under my breath. Little dude had no idea how small he was, and honestly? I straight up loved that about him.

After the walk, Bandit and I headed back to the apartment. I kicked my sneakers off by the door, letting them land wherever, and undid Bandit's harness. He bolted toward the living room, in search of his favorite chew toy, then flopped on the couch like the tiny king he was.

I headed to the room I shared with Mateo, pushing the door open with my foot. It was pretty easy to guess that two completely different people lived in there.

Mateo's side was perfect. Bed made, desk clear, everything lined up all nice and neat. Above his bed, the glow-in-the-dark stars Dad put up when we were kids still stretched across the ceiling, forming constellations that hadn't budged in years—except for the ones that would sometimes fall down.

The walls on his side were covered with these space posters—galaxies, nebulas, and all that NASA stuff he was obsessed with. He also had these model planes, perfectly painted and suspended by fishing line like they were frozen mid-flight. His whole vibe screamed "future astronaut" or "engineering prodigy." Sure it was impressive, but it was also kinda intimidating.

My side?

Total disaster zone.

I propped my skateboard against the wall next to a stack of surf mags, and on top of a pile of clothes I wasn't sure were clean or not. I flopped onto my half-made bed—which is half better than it usually was.

Above it, my own posters were a random mix of indie bands, old skaters, and surf legends taped up in whatever way felt right at the time. Organized chaos, I liked to call it. Mateo called it a nightmare.

My all-time favorite poster was this black-and-white shot of Jay Adams from the legendary Z-Boys crew, mid-grind on the edge of a pool, with this dog totally stealing the spotlight in an epic photobomb. It was so raw and cool, like it captured the vibe of what skating was all about back then—just pure rebellion and fun. I had another one of Jay grinding a different pool, flipping off the camera like a total savage—but yeah, Mom vetoed that one real quick. She wasn't about the "bad influence," even though the Z-Boys basically invented skateboarding as it is today. Honestly, every time I looked at that poster, it felt like a time machine. Iconic.

I glanced at the stars above Mateo's bed, the ones Dad had stuck up there years ago. When we were kids, they used to cover the whole ceiling, but after… everything happened three years ago, I couldn't stare up at them any more. I had to be the man of the house and all that. I didn't have time to stare at glowing stars and pretend things hadn't changed.

But Mateo? I knew why he hadn't taken them down, even though he was about to start high school. They weren't just for decoration. Those stars were a piece of Dad, still hanging around—even though he wasn't. Sometimes, late at night, I'd catch Mateo staring up at them, his face all serious like he was having some deep conversation with the universe. It felt heavy. I knew he was carrying something we never really talked about.

Every once in a while, he'd try to bring it up. Like, *actually* bring it up. But I always shut it down. I'd make a joke, change the subject, anything to avoid going there. It wasn't that I didn't miss Dad. I did—*a lot*. I just… didn't know how to say it. Keeping it bottled up felt easier, even if it wasn't.

So I never said anything about the stars on his side. I figured I'd let him keep looking up at them even if I couldn't. Let him keep having whatever silent conversation he had, that I couldn't out loud.

The stars were a quiet reminder of what we had—and what we didn't anymore.

And that didn't quite feel like enough, but it would have to be.

The room vibrated, that low hum of freeway traffic on the 10, spiced up with a truck making that annoying sound they always make, shaking everything for a second. Mateo's planes swung gently on their strings, rocking like they were trying to fly away. These were the perks of living right next to one of the busiest highways in the country. I barely noticed it most days. It kinda fades into the background mostly—but you could never exactly fully ignore it, either.

Bandit clicked into the room, tail wagging like he owned the place, and I guess he did. He jumped up onto my bed without hesitation and curled up against my side, letting out this dramatic sigh like his work here was done. I reached over, scratched behind his ears, and felt him melt into my arm.

When I unlocked my phone with my other hand, there were two messages waiting for me. I hadn't even heard them come in on the walk.

Wave Whisperer 🏄   13 min ago
Hey Keeks. You ok?

Rafe (My BFF 👑**)**   15 min ago
Dude. Last night was sick. Even Zay and his crew showed up. Missed you. Wanna meet up?

I always smirked at the name Rafe had given himself in my phone. He'd set it to "My BFF" years ago, complete with the crown emoji, and I never bothered to change it. It was so him. Normally, it would've earned a quick reply, maybe even a dumb meme, but not today.

I knew why they were texting. Checking in on me. Trying to distract me. No doubt I appreciated it, but I swiped away the notifications without opening them. Like I said, easier to just not deal with it.

So I just went back to doomscrolling through my phone with that empty feeling in my chest, until my thumb hovered over *that* app—the hookup one with the yellow icon that basically screams "this will end in emotional damage." I don't even know why I keep it. I'm not the hookup type. Every time I've tried to just talk to guys on there, it just left me feeling weird and disconnected, like I was borrowing someone else's life for a second, then crashing back into mine. But still, sometimes I'd open it just to scroll. Just to see who's out there.

I've pretty much always been into dudes. I didn't have some big coming-out-to-myself moment—it was just always there. I remember this brief middle school era where I thought maybe I was into girls too, like I was trying to be open or whatever, but it never really stuck. Since high school, it's been basically all dudes. There's no grand philosophy behind it—it just is. Sometimes I feel lowkey guilty, like I'm letting down the bi kids or erasing options or whatever, but honestly? I like what I like. Simple as that.

I tapped it open without really thinking, and there it was—the usual grid of torsos and thirst traps. Everyone flexing like they were auditioning for one of those reality shows. I started tapping through profiles, not looking for anything in particular. Just... curiosity, I guess. There was one guy—Steve, 23, curly hair, wore glasses in his pic, which somehow made him look both soft and smart. Not like the others. He had this nice smile that felt real, not like he practiced it in front of the mirror a hundred times. I stared at his profile for a second longer than I meant to, trying to picture what it'd even be like to meet someone. To sit across from a guy like that, maybe hold hands, maybe kiss. I wouldn't even know how to do it. I've never kissed a guy. Never been in a relationship. No one even knows really—not my friends, not my family. And the thought of them finding out makes my stomach twist in ways I don't really have the words for.

Rafe would probably crack so many jokes. Or *would* he? Maybe he would stop making the jokes he already makes and we'd drift apart. If he's even cool with having a gay best friend to begin with.

Then there's Ma and her church group. Definitely wouldn't go over well there. Would she be ashamed of me? Would Grandma? Mateo? He's always looked up to me so much, so I couldn't shake the feeling that I'd let him down.

I sat there with Steve's profile open, pretending for half a second that maybe I could message him, say something normal, something flirty but not cringe. But my brain short-circuited, like always, and I closed the app instead. My finger drifted over to Gmail.

Neil's email from the day before was still there, staring back at me. Being all formal and polite:

"Thank you for submitting your application. I'd like
to interview you for the barista position..."

I reread it for what felt like the hundredth time, and my brain was still spinning. What could Ma have even put on the application? "World's Most Average Son. Loves skating, surfing, and *possibly* knows what a latte is." Yeah, right. It also wasn't hard to guess this wasn't the only job app she'd sent in "on my behalf."

She meant well—she always did—but it still hit me in the gut. Mom had been holding everything together for us since... well, since everything changed. And here I was, skating through life, literally and figuratively. I knew I could be doing more. That thought weighed on me harder than I liked to admit.

My finger hovered over the reply button, but I still couldn't bring myself to type anything. Instead, I hit the home button and Googled Gautier's Gourmet Café. The first link was their Instagram page, so I clicked.

The screen lit up with pictures of drinks that looked more like art than coffee. Bright pinks, greens, blues—even one that was pitch black. Some were topped with whipped cream, others had berries or nuts, and one had crushed graham crackers.

"So we have a coffee shop with no actual coffee?" I muttered, as I kept scrolling through the feed that was definitely giving sensory overload.

Bandit, who was sprawled next to me, let out a dramatic sigh.

"Yeah, same, dude," I said as I rubbed the back of his neck.

I went back to the search results and tapped on their Postmates menu. The basics were there—lattes, cappuccinos, cold brews, espressos —but then it got weird. Matcha this and turmeric that, and whatever a cortado was.

"What even *is* an espresso tonic?" I asked, holding my phone out like Bandit might have the answer. He just tilted his head and looked back at me like he was trying to process it.

"Yeah, I don't know either," I said, laughing as I shook my head and went back to scrolling.

Finally, I pulled up the map that showed a pin on Wilshire in Beverly Hills. Of course—the fancy location explains the fancy drinks. I checked the route—15 minutes by bus, plus about five on my board at each end. Could be worse.

I opened the email again but this time my finger hesitated over the reply button as my mouth twisted up.

"Well, Neil," I muttered, "get ready to meet 'Enrique,' the world's most clueless barista candidate."

I just let out a sigh and started typing. I guess a job was a job, even if it came wrapped in a mom's overbearing love and a rainbow of overpriced drinks.

3

I stopped just around the corner from Gautier's Gourmet Cafe. I was gripping my skateboard like it was some kind of shield. It had been five days since I replied to Neil's email. I set the interview for Friday to give myself time to prepare—or so I said. The truth was that I was just procrastinating… as usual.

My "interview outfit" was a last-minute mashup of a black button-down, olive chinos, and my all-black Vans Old Skools. It was formal but not formal enough—like I was cosplaying someone who had their life together. But watching all the Wilshire people walk by, looking all polished and effortless, just made me feel even more out of place. I couldn't shake the feeling that there was no way I was gonna fit in here.

I checked my reflection in the mirror of a post office truck that was parked along the red curb at the corner. I tugged at the button-down, somehow realizing for the first time that it looked a little rumpled.

Tuck it in? Would that make me look like I cared—or just more cringe?

I decided to go with tucked-in, hoping it would hide the wrinkles better, but let's just say that my reflection wasn't exactly reassuring. Even after a rushed shower and an epic battle with my hair to try to tame it even a little and make it lie flat, I still looked like… plain old me —a little rough around the edges.

"Welp," I said, "Here goes nothing."

It was more to convince myself than anything else. I took a deep breath that didn't help, stepped out of hiding, and rounded the corner… straight into a locked glass door with a sign that said "Use Other Door" with an arrow that pointed towards the parking lot.

Smooth, Kiko.

After fumbling my way to the right door—because, of course, there were two and I somehow picked the wrong one—I finally stepped inside.

The place was just as extra as their Instagram made it out to be. The sleek counters, the glass pastry case, and the fancy drink setup was giving "we charge $15 for a latte."

A bald man—who at first glance I thought was Stanley Tucci—stood behind the counter. His round glasses were perched on the edge of his nose as he tapped away at the register's touchscreen. He didn't even glance up as I walked in.

"What'll it be?" he asked. His voice was straight-up razor sharp, like, zero patience with his finger hovering over the register.

"Uh," I started, my voice coming out way shakier than I wanted. "I'm actually looking for Neil."

That at least got him to look up. His eyes traveled over me slowly, starting with my rumpled shirt—should've gone untucked—lingering on my chinos, and finally landing on my skateboard. I felt like I was being x-rayed.

"And who might you be?" he asked, his tone skeptical, like he already regretted asking.

"I'm Kiko—um, Enrique—Rodriguez," I stammered. "I mean, I'm Enrique Rodriguez, but my friends call me Kiko."

Real smooth.

"*You're* Enrique Rodriguez?" he said. His eyebrows shot up, and he gave me a quick once-over again, like he was trying to put together how this—skateboard, rumpled shirt, the whole vibe—lined up with whatever polished LinkedIn version of "Enrique" my mom must've hyped up in the application.

I swallowed hard, and I could swear the gulp was loud enough to hear, as I clutched my board a little tighter.

This was off to a fantastic start. I should just run now.

"Oh, sweetie, relax," Neil said, like he could literally clock me calculating how fast I could escape. "I don't bite."

My face immediately went hot. Now I was both awkward *and* embarrassed.

"*I* am Neil," he said, stressing the "I" like he was performing some type of Shakespeare. He extended his hand across the counter. He was rocking a floral shirt with the sleeves rolled perfectly above his wrists, like he came straight out of a vintage fashion TikTok.

"Come. Take a seat over there," he said, pointing over my shoulder.

I turned to look, taking in the rest of the coffee shop as I walked over to the table he pointed at. The cafe looked straight out of an influencer's feed—clean lines, warm wood vibes, and just enough greenery to make it feel fancy but not fake.

The seating? Totally Pinterest-core. Plush green and tan chairs were scattered around small tables, and there was a row of counter seats along the big windows right next to the door, probably prime real estate for people-watching. The giant windows onto Wilshire let in a ton of natural light. The hanging glass lights? Very minimalist aesthetic, like they were designed to get compliments without stealing too much attention.

It was *definitely* the kind of place where people dropped bank on some coffee without even blinking—and honestly, I wasn't sure if I was cool enough to be here.

As soon as we sat, Neil's energy shifted into a more "let's get serious" vibe, but his eyes softened like he'd decided I wasn't a total disaster after all—or at least was gonna give me a chance. It was enough to keep me from taking off out the front door, which, honestly? Felt like a win at this point.

"Alright, let's get the basics out of the way," Neil said, leaning back like he was on autopilot. It made me wonder how many people he interviewed for this position. "You're over 18, legally allowed to work in the U.S.?"

"Yes and yes," I replied, pretty confidently.

Solid start. So far so good.

"Good," Neil said, tapping his pen on the clipboard. "No drugs, no felonies, no deep dark secrets that'll pop up and make me regret hiring you?"

"Nope—I mean, no," I said quickly, catching myself before I could sound too casual. He raised an eyebrow for a second, which made me think he *might* have taken my correction as a lie, before he shrugged like he'd heard worse.

Then came the hard ones. "Alright," Neil said, sitting forward slightly. "So you're experienced with coffee?"

Panic hit immediately as my brain scrambled back to the barista TikToks and tutorials I'd been cramming on the bus ride over like it was finals week. All the buzzwords—"latte art," "espresso extraction," "milk steaming"—swirled in my head, but none of them helped convince me I knew what I was doing.

I cleared my throat, totally trying to play it cool. "Yeah, totally. I've always loved coffee," I said carefully, hoping he wouldn't press me too hard.

Neil just raised an eyebrow as he sat back slightly. "Uh-huh," he said. His tone was definitely skeptical. "Let me guess—you can order a caramel macchiato, and that's about the extent of your expertise?"

My stomach dropped, because clearly he saw straight through whatever Ma wrote about me in the application and whatever bullshit I was trying to serve up here, but before I could say anything, Neil waved it off.

"Don't worry about it. It's not rocket science. What I care about is the passion. Customers want more than just coffee—they want an experience."

"Totally," I said, nodding like I wasn't still spiraling inside. "It's all about the vibe."

Neil just kinda stared at me—which I gotta say was way more intimidating than him asking any of the questions.

"Alright, next question. How do you handle stress? This place gets slammed during peak hours—lines out the door, people snapping at you, and the espresso machine breaking down right when you need it most."

I thought about the chaos of skate comps, the adrenaline of trying to land a trick while everyone watched, or those late-night group projects where I had to pull it all together last second, because God knows Rafe wasn't gonna do it.

"I'm pretty good under pressure," I said, nodding. "I just stay focused, take it one thing at a time, and don't let it get to me."

Neil just nodded again, tapping his pen against the clipboard. "Can you tell me about a time you had to deal with a difficult customer or situation? How'd you handle it?"

My brain short-circuited for a second. The first thing that came to mind was my last job at this frozen yogurt place on Santa Monica Boulevard that shall go unnamed. Let's just say, I was definitely never winning employee of the year there. Man, I probably couldn't win employee of the hour even when I was working by myself. My last day, I tossed my apron on the counter and peaced out with both middle fingers in the air. Yeah, probably not the story Neil was looking for with this question.

Instead, I went with something safer: the time I broke up a fight at the skate park. I explained how I got the two guys to chill out before someone ended up chucking their board at someone's head.

Neil tilted his head slightly as his expression went back into stealth mode. "Uh-huh," he said, dragging the word out just enough to make me second-guess everything I'd just said.

Yeah, I was regretting bringing up the skate park and was trying to think of a better answer when he moved on.

"Alright," he continued. "What do you think makes for great customer service?" He waved his pen around at the cafe behind him. "Specifically in a place like this?"

"Uh…" I stalled, desperately trying to put together a semi-coherent answer. "Being quick, I guess? Like, getting orders right?"

Neil pursed his lips, giving me this unimpressed look. Clearly, I was *not* nailing it. Nope. I was definitely going down in flames.

"And, uh… being friendly?" I added. Why was I saying everything like a question? "Like, smiling at people and stuff."

Smiling at people… and… stuff…

He sighed lightly, crossing one arm over his chest and propping his chin on his other hand, index finger pressing into his cheek. It was the kind of look someone gives you when they're deciding if you're worth their time. And yeah—my confidence left the chat.

"As far as actual experience…" Neil said. "Your resume was… well, let's call it minimalist."

I nodded like I knew exactly what he was talking about, but I hadn't even seen the resume. Thanks, Ma.

"Well," I started, scrambling for something—*anything*. "I've picked up a little experience here and there…"

Neil leaned back slightly, the look on his face shifting to "I'm already over this."

Not good at all.

I took a deep breath and just went for it. "Okay," I said. "The truth is I have no *actual* barista experience, but I can pick things up very fast, and if you give me a chance I'll do my best to not disappoint you."

Neil's eyes narrowed slightly, and for a second, I thought I was done. Then he smiled—just a little—and leaned forward. "You know what?" he said, his voice softer and his stare a little less intimidating. "I appreciate the honesty—finally. So let me ask you this: what's your availability?"

"Availability?" I repeated. Yeah that caught me totally off guard. Like, we were actually talking shifts? Like, I hadn't completely bombed this interview?

"Yes… as in when can you work?" Neil said, rolling his hand that was giving *get on with it, kid.*

"Oh, uh... totally open," I said, trying to sound casual but reliable. My brain was still processing the fact that I hadn't crashed and burned yet.

"Great. Alright then, Enrique," Neil said, clapping his hands. "We'll see you on Monday. Ricky over there will be showing you the ropes. Don't let the whole intimidating exterior fool you. He is a wizard with coffee, but he's also really patient training the new ones."

I followed Neil's nod toward the register, and—oh. That's Ricky? Yeah, "intimidating exterior" was putting it mildly. Ricky looked like the lead in some Netflix rom-com. Tall, with a perfectly fitted shirt that basically screamed I have a gym membership. Even the black apron couldn't hide the fact that the dude was built. His hair was slicked back with one annoyingly perfect curl falling onto his forehead like he was auditioning for the role of "Hot Barista Hero." And that jawline? Straight up unfair. Like he wasn't just here to brew coffee, but instead to casually destroy everyone else's self-esteem.

"Enrique?" Neil's voice snapped me out of my very unproductive— and embarrasing—spiral.

I flinched, spinning back toward him. "Sorry, what?" I said, trying to act like I hadn't just been completely distracted.

"Oh, I get it," he said with a little chuckle. "He has that effect on people. But, for what it's worth, Ricky only has eyes for the ladies."

"Uh, no. It's not that—I wasn't—" I was full on stammering like my mouth forgot how to speak. My face had gone full-on red alert. "I just... got distracted. Sorry."

"No worries," Neil said with a chuckle, breaking the tension like it was nothing. "Be here by 1 p.m. It's after the lunch rush—perfect for training. We'll go over the paperwork, all that fun stuff. You'll start at $17.50 an hour, plus tips. And trust me, you're gonna want to wear dark pants. Coffee gets everywhere."

I nodded, my brain jumping from "decent pay" to "wait, I actually got the job?" then to "$17.50 an hour, plus tips?" Definitely more than I made slinging froyo. Not bad at all.

My eyes darted around the cafe again. I was trying to imagine myself actually working here. It was modern, polished, and had this low-key energy that felt alive but not in an overwhelming kind of way. The people here, though were a totally different vibe. They looked like they had places to be, important calls to make, or just had lives that were way more put together than mine. Even the employees—my new coworkers—just had this focus like they were born to pour lattes with flawless foam hearts.

I tried to picture myself fitting into all of it—me, in one of those slick black aprons, slinging drinks and chatting with customers like I actually knew what I was doing. Like, could I actually blend in here? Would I look like Ricky, who could quite possibly be an actual superhero moonlighting as a barista? Not a chance in hell. Would I look like a total fraud the second I stepped behind the counter? Almost certainly.

Still, there was something kind of exciting about the idea, like maybe I stood a chance of making it work and figuring out how to belong here.

"Thanks, Neil, you won't regret it. I'll see you Monday," I said, my voice a mix of gratitude and mild panic. This was happening. For real.

I turned to leave, but Neil called after me. "Hey, grab yourself a coffee before you head out. And take this." He handed me my very own black apron, the same one Ricky was rocking like a fashion statement, but I knew there was no way I could make it look *that* good. "It's yours now. Welcome to the team."

I took the apron, the fabric feeling heavier than it should. I nodded, swallowing the lump in my throat. "Thanks," I said again, gripping the apron like it was some kind of golden ticket.

Holding the apron in one hand—a literal what-have-I-gotten-myself-into moment—I made my way toward the counter. And, of course, standing there in all his cinematic glory was Ricky. How was he out here looking like a walking thirst trap? Like one of those guys who doesn't even realize he's the main character in every room he steps into. There was this glint in his eye that I couldn't really describe. My stomach did this tiny flip.

"Uh, yeah, can I get uh…" I started, my voice trailing off as I pretended to scan the menu overhead. "An iced coffee?"

Ricky just kinda looked at me with one of those perfect eyebrows raised, like he already clocked me playing it safe. "That's it? Going for the classic, huh?"

I laughed nervously. "Yeah, just keeping it simple for now. Can I, uh… add caramel?"

"Whoa, killer," Ricky said. "Don't get *too* adventurous on me." His smirk widened into a grin. "I got you."

I laughed again, more genuinely this time. Something about him made it easy—like his confidence wasn't just effortless, it was contagious. As he started prepping the drink, he threw a glance over his shoulder. "So you're the new guy?"

"Yeah," I said, adjusting the apron in my hands like it wasn't making me sweat. "I'm Kiko."

"Well, Kiko, enjoy this one while you can," Ricky said, turning back to the counter. "Because pretty soon, you're gonna be making your own drinks."

I smiled. This guy wasn't just *intimidatingly* good-looking—he was actually pretty chill. He slid the drink across the counter, adding a compostable straw, but then he leaned in, his voice dropping like he was about to share some top-tier classified info.

"I'm going to let you in on a secret about this place," he said, motioning me closer.

I leaned in, curious.

"Those cookies right there?" he said, pointing to the glass case on the counter next to the register, "They won't just ruin your diet. They'll ruin every cookie you'll ever eat after. Like, no cap, they're the best in LA. Maybe even the West Coast."

I snorted, glancing at the case. The cookies were stacked up next to these huge croissants and different types of danishes, and, yeah, they looked pretty fire—huge chocolate chunks, golden edges, and maybe walnuts?

"Try one if you don't believe me," Ricky said, eyebrows raising in a playful dare.

I shook my head, laughing as I took a sip of my iced coffee. It was good, but the easy back-and-forth with Ricky? That felt even better.

"C'mon... it's on me," Ricky said, snagging the top cookie with a pair of silver tongs. He paused, holding it just above the bag, raising his eyebrows.

"Alright, bet," I said, trying not to laugh. "We'll see how good these are."

Ricky dropped the cookie into the bag with a satisfied smirk, set it on the counter, and held out a fist like it was the most natural thing in the world. "Welcome to the team, Kiko. You're gonna crush it."

I bumped his fist, feeling this unexpected wave of... I don't know, like belonging or something. The whole vibe felt so easy, like Ricky wasn't just being polite—he actually meant it. For the first time all day, I didn't feel like I was totally out of place. Maybe this could work. Maybe this wasn't just the start of a job—it was the start of something better.

Grabbing the bag, I slid the cookie into my backpack for the bus ride home, though I already knew it probably wouldn't make it that far. Ricky went back to his thing behind the counter, and I walked out feeling lighter.

Iced coffee in hand, I finally stepped out of the coffee shop and dropped my board to the ground. I gave it a push, and started cruising towards the street, still trying to process how I just walked out of there with a job. As I got to the end of the sidewalk someone rounded the corner of the building... and I barely stopped in time to avoid running straight into him.

"Easy there, skater boy," the guy said with a laugh, as he jumped back.

He looked about my age, maybe a little older, and he was dressed in clothes that screamed effortlessly cool— perfectly tailored, with just enough style to make me feel like I hadn't tried hard enough today. His designer sunglasses were massive, but he slid them down just enough to reveal these brown eyes that were—well I don't want to get too corny so let's just say they were nice. His whole energy was confident, like he knew he was a vibe and didn't have to try to prove it.

"You're in quite a rush," he said.

"My bad," I managed as I felt this stupid grin spreading on my face. I could feel my heart picking up speed. "I should watch where I'm going."

"Yes," he purred. "You might miss something."

There was something about the way he said it—casual but like more —that made my stomach flip in a way I wasn't used to. Before I could overthink it, he stuck out his hand.

"Troye with an 'e,' B-T-W," he said, as I tried to look beyond how much I hated acronyms used in real life.

"Kiko... with an...'o'," I replied, shaking his hand. It was soft, like *really* soft, and I felt this jolt—tiny but noticeable—run through me. His grip lingered just long enough to make me wonder if he'd felt it too.

"I haven't seen you around here before," Troye with an 'e' said. His head was tilted slightly and those brown eyes were looking me over in a way that made me both self-conscious and excited.

"Oh, uh, I live down near Culver," I said.

Troye paused, a smirk tugging at the corner of his mouth, and let out a small laugh—light, easy, but with a hint of mockery. "I meant *here*," he said, motioning toward the cafe behind me.

"Oh!" I said, heat rushing to my face. "Yeah, I just interviewed for a barista job, and it went a lot like that just did. I totally bombed it."

Troye's gaze dropped to the apron tucked under my arm, and he reached out, his fingers lightly tugging at the edge of it. The move was casual, but his hand brushing mine was anything but.

"It looks like you got the job, so it couldn't have been all bad," he said, his smirk widening. "Looks more like you nailed it."

I let out a nervous laugh, gripping the apron tighter as I tried to play it cool. "Well, I'm also not much of a coffee expert, but I guess I'm about to learn."

There was this pause—not like awkward or anything. Just one that lasted long enough for our eyes to meet. Troye's gaze was—I don't even know. Sharp? Curious? Looking straight into my soul? And that grin of his... the way it pulled to one side that made my chest tighten a little. It wasn't like Ricky's chill, easygoing energy. No, this felt... different, like flirty, for sure...and maybe even a little dangerous? But instead of freaking me out, I had this nervous excitement running through me.

"Maybe I'll be your first customer," Troye said, his tone playful, with just the right amount of teasing. "You know, to test your skills."

"Sure," I said, laughing way more confident than I felt. "But I gotta warn you—I'll probably enjoy that more than you'll enjoy your mediocre-at-best coffee."

The words were out before I could stop them, and I had to squash the urge to cringe. Did I really just say that?

But Troye didn't miss a beat. His grin stretched wider, and he gave me this slow once-over, his eyes practically buzzing with mischief. "I'll take my chances," he said, his voice low and smooth, like he knew exactly what effect it was having on me. "See you around, skater boy."

As I stepped back onto my board, I glanced over my shoulder. Troye had already slid his sunglasses back into place, but I could still feel his eyes still on me—and I wasn't mad about it. A small smile tugged at my lips as I headed home, my mind replaying the moment over and over. Whatever this stupid fluttery feeling in my chest was that I wasn't ready to unpack felt different. And for once, I didn't feel like I was stuck—I felt like something new was just starting.

I slouched back on the bus, probably grinning like an idiot, but I didn't care. Who knew one of the best things in my life would happen on an LA Metro bus? But that cookie? *Game-changer*. The chocolate chunks were gooey, the walnuts had that perfect crunch, and the edges were crispy in the just-right way. And the center? Oh man, the center was soft, melty perfection.

I closed my eyes for a sec, fully vibing with the flavors. The usual bus chaos—the hum of the engine, random conversations, the faint whiff of someone's lunch—faded into the background. It was just me and this cookie. Ricky wasn't lying when he hyped it up. If I hadn't already gotten the job, this cookie alone would've made me beg for it.

Like, where's the lifetime supply contract, and how do I sign?

I peeked down at the small paper cookie bag in my lap. Still a few bites left, and just knowing that made me smile harder. I took another bite, and yup, it was official: best cookie of my life. Period.

The bus rattled past the high school I was originally supposed to go to. Mom had really done the most to get me into a better middle school —using my aunt's address, lying on forms, basically running a whole undercover operation. She kept the address even after, just to make sure Mateo could have a shot, too. Classic Mom—always hustling to give us something better, even if it meant bending the rules a bit. In this case, it's what led me to Rafe and Avery, and… well… whatever I was doing now.

I let out a little sigh, guilt mixing in with the gratitude. Like, she worked so hard for us, and here I was, still trying to figure out what the hell I was doing. I glanced back at the cookie bag, took another bite, and let the sweetness take me back. Whatever else was going on, that cookie was proof that sometimes, it's okay to just stop and enjoy the little things. And right then, that cookie? It was *everything*.

I never really minded the extra bus ride to my high school. Sure, it meant waking up earlier and getting home later, but it kept me close to my crew. Those rides had become part of my routine anyway. Pop in my headphones, zone out to whatever playlist I was feeling that day, or just stare out the window and let my brain wander.

This other high school outside the window—one that would've meant a whole other life—was now just a signal for me on what was going to be my new routine. I reached up and hit the stop button, the little ding sounding up front. I glanced down at the cookie bag in my lap, debating whether to finish it off now or save the last bites for later. Later won. I stuffed the bag into my backpack like it was some kind of treasure and stood up as the bus rolled to a stop.

The second my shoes hit the pavement, I dropped my board and pushed off, the scrape of the grip tape and the roll of the wheels instantly grounding me. The afternoon sun hit my face as I cruised down the sidewalk, dodging cracks and letting the rhythm of skating drown out whatever stress was still lingering from the day.

Halfway down the block, my phone buzzed in my pocket. I slowed, coasting as I pulled it out and glanced at the screen.

Rafe (My BFF 👯)   Just Now
Party tomorrow night at Avery's. You in?

I smirked, already picturing Rafe hyping up whatever chaos this party was going to be. I let the phone sit in my hand for a second while I debated tucking it back into my pocket.

I hadn't seen Rafe or Avery all week. Every text, every call, I dodged with my custom blend of one-word replies and the good ol' "sorry, can't talk right now" decline button. Not because I didn't want to see them—I did—but every time my phone buzzed, it felt like too much. I couldn't explain it, so I just ghosted in a way that didn't *totally* look like full-on ghosting. Figured they'd get the hint and let it go.

I typed a quick "Maybe" and hit send, letting the text fly before I overthought it too much. Normally, a party at Avery's would've been an instant yes. Her place on the Venice Canals was basically designed for nights like that. Her parents were always out of town, and the house? Straight-up movie set material. String lights reflecting off the water, music that somehow felt cooler just because of the setting, and a mix of people who always kept things interesting.

Plus, I guess I had a reason to celebrate with the new job and all. It wasn't much yet, but it was something, right? Something worth being excited about. But the thought of seeing Rafe and Avery *together* had me hesitating. They'd been my closest friends for as long as I could remember, my ride-or-dies, but lately? Chilling with both of them at the same time felt... off. Like I didn't quite fit the way I used to. Like I was the fucked-up wheel on the shopping cart messing with their flow.

It wasn't anything they'd said or done—at least not directly. It was the small things—the inside jokes I wasn't in on anymore, the way their energy felt just a little too connected, leaving me hovering somewhere on the outside. I told myself I was imagining it, but every time I was around them, it felt like a spotlight on how much things were shifting.

I wanted to go. I wanted to feel like part of the crew again. Like nothing had changed. But at the same time, I wasn't sure if I could deal with it. So "maybe" it was.

The phone chimed again and up popped Rafe's reply at the top of the cracked screen:

Rafe (My BFF 👯)   Just Now
You've been MIA lately. Come through

And there it was: too much. Leave it to Rafe to turn a simple invite into a low-key guilt trip.

I stared at the notification, feeling that creeping wave of *ugh, not right now*. Like, I knew he didn't *mean* to make me feel bad, but he just had this way of doing it anyway. I swiped the message away into oblivion without any more hesitation and immediately opened Spotify, scrolling through my Kiko's Mix playlist until I found something to drown out the noise in my brain. Nah, chill vibes only.

I just slid my phone back into my pocket, and let out a breath. I'd deal with Rafe and all his Rafeness later—when I wasn't already maxed out. Right now, I just needed some space. Just me, my board, and a decent playlist to skate it out down National Boulevard.

4

Ma was finally home. She'd worked four overnights in a row, so I hadn't seen her since before the interview. Nurses, man—time moves different for them. The second she texted she was cooking, I bailed on the skatepark and headed straight home. I didn't even care if she brought up job stuff again—mostly because I could report I was now a genuine working man again—but I just missed her.

The smell hit me as soon as I got in the stairwell. *Mole de olla*—my favorite. No contest at all. That smell instantly made everything feel better. Wrestling with the stupid lock took forever—my brain was already halfway to the kitchen and the magic happening there.

When I finally got the door open, it was like walking into a warm cloud of pure comfort, so rich I swear I could taste it in the air. The beef, the chiles, the cilantro—yeah all of it—but the onions and garlic? Man, they were the real MVPs. This wasn't just food; it was *home*. Seriously, every bite would taste like my childhood.

Bandit sprinted over to the door to greet me, sliding across the linoleum floor and crashing into my ankles.

"Alright, alright, I'm home my crazy little Bandito," I laughed, crouching down to meet him as he jumped all over me, licking my face like I'd been gone a year instead of a couple hours.

With the smell of the stew still calling me and Bandit basically vibrating with excitement, I finally felt like I could let go of the day. Home just hit different. And tonight? It straight-up smelled like love.

Ma was in the kitchen doing her thing, her curly hair bouncing as she turned to look at me. The second her brown eyes landed on me, her whole face lit up.

"Mijo, you're back!" she said, her voice warm and excited, full of that mom vibe that makes you feel seen, even when you've had the longest day. "How did the interview go yesterday?"

I couldn't hold it in anymore—I broke into a grin. "Well, I got the job," I said. Her eyes went wide with pure joy as she got this big smile on her face. It was the same look she'd give me when I would win an award at school or something.

"Alright, Enrique!" she said. "I'm so proud of you!" She wiped her hands on her old floral apron—the faded vintage one she refuses to throw out—and pulled me in for one of her classic hugs that was tight, quick, and packed with so much love it almost knocked me over.

"Come, I'm making your favorite," she said, nodding toward the steaming pot on the stove. "Sit down, tell me everything."

I flopped into one of the old wooden chairs that squeaked whenever you moved. She got back to doing her thing at the stove, moving like a blur with pots clattering, drawers slamming—but that smell was all kinds of nostalgic.

Dad used to say mole was a celebration dish—birthdays, holidays, "just because it's Sunday" kind of thing. He'd sneak little spoonfuls from the pot like Ma didn't see—she always did. I used to try to copy him thinking it was some sort of tradition.

I sat there soaking it all in, feeling the day's stress melt away. Between the smell of mole, the sounds of the kitchen, and Ma's ridiculously proud smile, it was the first time all day I'd felt completely chill.

It wasn't just the food, though. It was all of it—Ma's humming, the telenovela theme song coming from the neighbor's window, the smell of garlic and spices and a history sometimes I don't feel apart of.

I never felt super Mexican, not like Mateo with his perfect pronunciation or my abuelo telling stories in Spanish I couldn't quite translate. But I wasn't *not* Mexican either. It was more like I lived in the in-between. I was the kind of kid who knew what mole de olla was but had to ask how to spell it. Who could follow a prayer in church but didn't know all the words.

My Spanish was shaky, mostly because we never spoke it at home. Dad only used it with his friends or on the phone with family back in Mexico—never with me. He said it was for our future.

Back then, I thought maybe he was embarrassed. But now I think he was just scared—scared people would hear his accent before anything else. That they'd hear mine too if I learned from him. He wanted to protect me—I totally get that. But still... I wish he didn't have to.

34

I wish he hadn't felt like passing down a language meant handing me a target. I wish speaking Spanish didn't feel like something dangerous, but I also wish I didn't feel like a visitor in my own culture.

He used to say, "Be American first, but never forget where we come from." Like it was such a simple thing, that I could hold both these things in my hands without something slipping out the side. I used to nod like I got it. I didn't though, and still don't.

This kitchen? *This* was where I came from. But some days it felt like I was chasing something I should've already had. Like I'd inherited the memories but not the map.

"So, tell me *everything* about the interview!" Ma said, practically bouncing as she leaned against the counter, her eyes sparkling like she was the one who'd just nailed a job.

"It was... okay, I guess," I said, trying to downplay it, but not too much. "The manager, Neil—he's pretty cool. Kinda over-the-top, though. Like, super big personality, but in a good way. I was, like, really nervous the whole time."

"But you got the job?" she pressed, her voice giving *I already know the answer, but I want to hear you say it again.*

"Yeah, I got it," I said, a small smile creeping onto my face despite myself. "I start on Monday. They're pairing me with this guy named Ricky for training."

"That's wonderful, mijo!" she said, her whole face lighting up. "I'm so happy for you." She turned back to the stove, humming this little tune she always hummed when she was in a good mood.

I sat back in my chair, letting her excitement wash over me. It was weird—half of me still felt unsure, like I was faking my way into this whole thing, but the way Ma was looking at me? Like I'd just done something big? It made me feel like I could pull this off.

It'd been a minute since she was this hyped about something I did. Mateo had been the star for the last couple years, scoring *all* the points. He was the type to study on a Friday night just because. He cranked out straight-As like it was nobody's business. His last science fair project had a full-on bibliography. Mine, when I was his age, was literally just a lime green oak tag poster about why dolphins are cool.

I wasn't bitter or anything; he deserved it. But seeing her look at me like *I* was the one to be proud of? It felt good, like I'd *finally* done something worth her buzzing around the kitchen, humming her happy tune.

I shifted in my chair, my brain drifting back to that almost-collision with Troye outside the café. The way he'd smiled, the way he said "skater boy," it was like a scene out of some rom-com—and it wouldn't get out of my head. But talking about it? Yeah, no way. Not happening. Crushes—or anything close—were never something we talked about, and *definitely* not crushes on *guys*. It felt like walking into uncharted territory with no map, and I wasn't ready for that.

Ma was busy ladling the *mole de olla* into bowls, so I got up to set the table. It was an excuse to move—you know?—to distract myself from the weird mix of excitement and nerves spinning around in my head.

"Mateo's eating at a friend's tonight," she said, not looking up, her tone super casual. "So it's just the two of us."

"Cool," I said, putting one spoon back and grabbing napkins. The idea of mentioning Troye popped into my head again. There was like this little voice that was just daring me to blurt it out. But I definitely wasn't sure how that would go.

Ma was pretty traditional, super Catholic, and I remembered how tense things got when I told her I wasn't into church anymore. It was one of the only times we ever yelled at each other—she was hella upset. She kept going on about how I was turning my back on my faith, but I just didn't feel it anymore. We didn't talk for a full week after that.

If that went that badly, how would this go over?

I opened my mouth, ready to say something, but stopped. I couldn't find the right way to start, and honestly, I wasn't sure if I wanted to risk ruining the status quo. So, I just... didn't. I stayed quiet and set the table while Ma turned around with the bowls. My brain was in mini-crisis while she was still humming like everything was totally normal.

The thought of Troye was still in the back of my mind. There was something in the way he looked at me—like he already knew who he was. Like he wasn't afraid of being seen. I didn't know if I wanted to kiss him or just borrow whatever confidence he was carrying around like it weighed nothing. Either way, he got stuck in my head like a song I didn't know the lyrics to yet. Just a secret I wasn't ready to let out yet. Maybe later—maybe never—but for now, it just felt safer to keep it to myself.

"Is everything okay, mijo?" Ma asked, her eyes narrowing slightly in that way she did when she was reading my mind. Ma always said I got her eyes—almond-shaped and a little too good at showing how you feel even when trying not to. "You've been very quiet today."

I hesitated as I stirred my spoon through my stew. "Yeah, I'm fine," I said, but the words felt heavy. I decided to just go with it almost as a test, "I, uh… met someone outside the coffee shop today. His name was Troye. He seemed… pretty cool."

Ma smiled, the kind of smile that felt polite, maybe even practiced, as she blew on a spoonful of mole. "That's nice. It's always good to make new friends."

Her tone was so breezy—so matter-of-fact—that it left me sitting there feeling a little stuck. *Friends?* That wasn't what this was. Troye wasn't just someone I could throw into the same category as Rafe or Avery. Meeting him had felt like more—way more. Something stuck with me in a way I couldn't quite explain yet. The way Ma said it—like she'd already decided what it meant—felt like the door had quietly shut before I even had a chance to step through it.

For a second, I wondered if she'd done it on purpose, if she was steering the conversation away without making it obvious. But the way she kept eating, her expression calm and unbothered, made me think maybe she was just oblivious. Maybe she hadn't even picked up on the fact that I was testing the waters, seeing if this was a thing I could talk about with her.

I nodded, eyes back on my bowl, suddenly not so hungry. "Yeah. He was, uh… interesting." The word hung in the air, but she didn't bite, didn't push. She just kept eating, humming a little tune.

I stirred my stew again. It was fine. Maybe it was better this way—less complicated. For now, I'd keep Troye to myself.

The rest of dinner was awkwardly quiet—the kind where you notice every clink of a fork and every scrape of a bowl. Ma tossed out random small talk about Mateo's soccer game or whatever, and I threw back some half-hearted "Oh, cool" type responses that didn't even sound convincing to me. My head wasn't in it. I kept drifting back to Troye—his smile, the way he said skater boy like he already knew me. I couldn't stop turning it over in my head, wondering about all the what-ifs. But for now, those thoughts stayed tucked away, little secrets I wasn't ready to let anyone in on.

After dinner, I cleared the table and once everything was done, I headed to my room. I just wanted to crash.

As soon as I hit my room, I face-planted onto my bed. I grabbed the handball I kept on my nightstand and rolled over and tossed it up at the ceiling a couple of times. It was easy, brainless, and somehow made the noise in my head feel less overwhelming. Sometimes I would squeeze it a couple times like a low-budget stress ball. My thoughts kept looping —Troye, the way Ma brushed it off, back to Troye again.

My thoughts kept circling back to the invite to Avery's party the next night, looping like a playlist on repeat. The idea of being there, watching Avery and Rafe together, made my stomach do that annoying twisty thing. Whatever was going on between them—friends, *more than friends*—it was a constant reminder of what I didn't have. I was the third wheel, hanging on the sidelines while they went on doing what they were doing? Yeah, hard pass. But staying here, alone in my room, overthinking everything for the millionth time was not exactly a vibe either. I caught the ball and bounced it off the wall a couple times.

"Enrique! Cut it out!" Ma yelled from the other room.

I sighed but I stopped.

The room felt smaller somehow, like the walls were closing in, screaming at me to stop sitting around and actually do something with my life. I glanced up at the posters on my wall of surfers catching impossible waves, skaters flying high above vert ramps, all of it looking way cooler than me sulking in my bed. They were practically daring me to get out of here and at least try to do something for once.

Maybe the party would actually be good. It'd just be loud music and plastic cups and people I didn't feel weird around. Maybe I'd forget how awkward I felt sitting at that table with Ma, spooning mole and not saying what I really wanted to say.

Sitting here wasn't gonna fix anything, and maybe being out wouldn't suck as much as I was convincing myself it would.

I sat up and tossed the ball onto my desk. Grabbing my phone, I opened Rafe's message and typed, "I'm in," and hit send before I could overthink it. I stared at the screen for a second.

A tiny flicker of… something hit me. Hope? FOMO? Who knows. Either way, at least I wouldn't be stuck here drowning in my own thoughts. Maybe this party wouldn't suck. Maybe it'd even be good. Guess I'd have to find out.

5

My wheels were clacking against the planks of the wooden bridge as I was headed toward Avery's. The faint bass thumping from the party drifted over the canals, muffled but still giving off that vibe—probably some EDM remix or some throwback pop banger. Avery always went with the kind of playlist everyone pretends not to love but absolutely goes off to.

As I hit the end of the bridge, I crouched low, lining up the jump. The spot where the ramp met the sidewalk had this janky angle. Not to mention there was this stupid pole that was supposed to stop bikes and —well, skateboarders like me. But I'd cleared it so many times it was basically second nature. I snapped an ollie, sailed off to one side, and landed clean on the cracked pavement, rolling into the familiar rhythm of the ride.

The Canals at night were their own kind of mood. The narrow waterways passed through the neighborhood, reflecting everything from string lights to the glow of open TV screens in living rooms. The air smelled faintly like damp concrete and weed—classic Venice.

Avery's house wasn't far down the cramped alley, just a few houses in. Beige stucco with a little balcony wrapped in white lattice, it wasn't flashy or anything, and in any other neighborhood it might even be affordable, but here in *this* neighborhood? Every house *screamed* money. I mean, in this neighborhood, even "kinda normal" meant a couple mill *easy*. I slowed to a stop and kicked up my board. I took a breath, looking up at the house.

Alright, let's see what kind of night this is gonna be.

I barely got my hand up to knock on the door before it flew open. Avery stood there with this cheesy-ass smile that was so big it was impossible not to give back. Before I could say anything, she threw her arms around me, pulling me into one of those hugs that's half affection, and half straight-up attack.

"Kikosaurus! You made it!" she said, her voice way louder than necessary and, yeah, with *way more* than a hint of vodka on her breath.

I just laughed, trying to catch my balance from her assault hug. She pulled back, and I took a second to really clock her whole look—head to toe. Usually, Avery was all about the typical chill surfer-skater fits like hoodies, board shorts, and Vans—stuff like that. But tonight she had on a crop top and high-waisted jeans—way more put together than usual. She had this small necklace on that caught the light just enough to tell you that the diamond was definitely real. Then there was the makeup, which was *way* out of character, even for party-edition Avery. It wasn't overdone, but it made me do a double take. She still looked like Avery, of course, but, like... leveled up somehow.

"Wouldn't miss it," I lied. Part of me already regretted coming, but as I stepped inside the bass from the music hit me. It was loud enough to feel it in my chest.

"C'mon!" she said, grabbing my wrist before I could even process the scene. "You have to say hi to everyone!" And just like that, I was being dragged into the middle of the madness, her excitement pulling me along like I didn't even have a choice.

My smile stretched wider as Avery's excitement practically spilled out of her, but I couldn't help catching the slight slur in her words. She'd definitely started the party early. Still, I couldn't stop my eyes from scanning her whole look, and it threw me a little. She looked good —like *really* good—but it hit different, and not in a chill way.

Was she dressing up for someone? The thought crept in, uninvited and super annoying, my mind immediately going to Rafe. *Was this all for him?* I tried to brush off the idea, but the question stayed in the back of my mind as I followed her into the crowd. And worse, why did it even bother me so much?

Avery grabbed my wrist and pulled me toward the living room. The bass from the music got louder, the noise of people blending into the kind of party chaos that usually got me hyped. But even with all of that, my brain wouldn't shut up.

People were sprawled across couches or leaning against walls with red cups in their hands, yelling over the music. And there, dead center, was Rafe—absolutely in his element. He was holding court with a small group like he'd been born to do it. Dylan from our English class was there, rocking his usual thrifted outfit that somehow looked like he'd walked straight out of a '70s band poster. Then there were Ariel and Halley—the twins who'd been in a bunch of our classes over the years. Despite this, Rafe still couldn't tell them apart, which I think low-key annoyed them but also kind of amused them at the same time.

Rafe spotted me and lit up with that big, easy grin of his. "Kiko!" he called, already weaving through the crowd. Before I could say anything, he threw an arm around my shoulders like we'd planned this moment.

"Guys, you know Kiko, right?" he said, sliding me into the convo without missing a beat. That was Rafe—always making you feel like you belonged, even if you weren't so sure yourself.

"You should've seen the waves today," Rafe said. He had that wild energy he got whenever he started talking about surfing. "It was so good this morning. Dude, like head-high—okay maybe chest-high, but they were clean."

I nodded, giving him this weak-ass half-smile. Rafe was definitely exaggerating. I only kind of tuned in as he launched into the story, his hands moving like he was carving the waves all over again—and spilling his beer as he did it.

"So, I was telling Ariel—" he started, pointing to Halley with the hand holding his red cup.

She giggled. "It's Halley," she corrected, but she had this flirty smile like this whole can't-tell-you-apart thing was actually working. "But keep going. I want to hear about this epic wave."

Rafe jumped right back into the story, flashing that ridiculous grin of his. The little slip-up didn't throw him at all. If anything, it just made everyone laugh harder. He had this way of just pulling you into his stories—his ridiculous, over-exaggerated stories.

It was like he was the main character in a movie and everyone else was just happy to be part of the scene. It was classic Rafe shit. I'd seen a it hundred times but still couldn't figure out how he made it look so easy.

But then he decided to switch it up. "Yo, you never seen Kiko surf yet. Let me tell ya, dude's smooth as hell out there. I swear." He elbowed me.

My face instantly went hot as everyone turned to me. I wasn't trying to hype myself up in front of everyone. Surfing's personal for me, just something I like to do. It's not some big flex like it is for him. But no, Rafe had to put me on the spot like I was some pro out there winning comps or something.

And of course, he didn't stop there. Turning to Ariel with his signature grin, he said, "Yo, Halley—next time we're out, you gotta come watch Kiko. He's unreal."

Ariel, glowing like she just got handed the best invite of the year, corrected him with a laugh. "It's Ariel. But yes, I'm in! Surfing sounds *amazing.*"

She drew out the last word and touched my arm in a way that sent me from awkward to panic in zero seconds flat.

Halley rolled her eyes so hard. "You don't even surf," she said, clearly unimpressed.

Ariel shot back, "I can learn."

Rafe clapped me on the back, way too hard, grinning like he'd just solved world peace. "There you go—it's settled."

I side-eyed him. "Oh, cool. Thanks for volunteering me, dude."

Rafe was laughing, clearly loving the chaos he'd just created. Ariel was buzzing, Halley looked like she wanted to disappear but couldn't quite help her smile, and suddenly I was the center of attention in a way I didn't ask for and high-key *hated.*

"*You* look like you need a drink," Dylan said. "What'll it be?" he asked, holding up his red cup.

"I'll come with," I said quickly, jumping at the excuse to get out of there. I wasn't even trying to hide how relieved I was.

We headed to the kitchen, dodging groups of people shouting over the music and a couple arguing way too loudly by the fridge. The keg was set up by the sink. Dylan leaned against the counter, handing me a cup. He just had this effortless vibe, like everything was just smooth and easy.

He had this way of watching people—not like he was judging them, just… watching, like he was collecting little pieces. I wondered what he thought about me—but I didn't ask.

"So," he said, shooting me this small smirk. "What are you up to this summer? Besides, you know, 'surfing gnarly waves'?" He threw in a terrible surfer accent and a hang loose sign.

I laughed awkwardly. "Not much. Just got a job at a coffee shop in Beverly Hills, so… kind of stoked about that."

Dylan raised an eyebrow, his grin shifting into something that felt more curious. "You gonna start lecturing us on the virtues of single-origin beans now?"

"More like trying not to be broke," I said, laughing as I poured my drink. "And maybe not setting the espresso machine on fire my first day."

"Good strategy," he said. "Nobody wants burnt coffee. That's how revolutions start."

I laughed, but then it hit me that something about this felt... different. I couldn't remember ever really talking to Dylan before. He was always just... around. Not in any one group. Super chill, super confident—the kind you don't really notice until suddenly you do. He had this low-key vibe, like he enjoyed watching things unfold, not really being in the action.

So why was he talking to me now?

"You commuting all the way to Beverly Hills?" he asked, his tone still casual.

"Yeah," I said, nodding. "This place called Gautier's on Wilshire. Skate to the bus, bus to the shop. Not terrible."

"Nice," he said, his smirk back. "Guess I know where to go when I need a latte or whatever."

"Cool. I'll hook you up with burnt coffee, on the house."

Dylan let out a soft laugh, lifting his cup in a casual toast. "Can't wait."

And just like that, he shifted his attention back to the room, totally smooth, like he hadn't just gotten inside my head. I watched him for a second, still trying to figure out why this was the first time we'd actually talked. Dylan had this way of being super cool but also kinda out there. It was like he was always one step ahead of everyone else or just like above it all.

He looked around the kitchen and leaned in, his voice all low and secretive. "Wanna join me outside? Granddaddy Purple is calling."

I raised an eyebrow, trying to look way more casual than I felt. I wasn't really sure what he meant until he let a preroll just peek out from his shirt pocket.

Weed wasn't really my thing. I dabbled here and there, but it never really did much for me. But, going back inside to deal with Rafe and the twin chaos? Hard pass. Besides, hanging out with Dylan felt easy in a way I wasn't ready to let go of just yet. "Yeah, sounds cool," I said, following him out onto the balcony.

The balcony was small, surrounded by this lattice privacy fence that tried its best to block out the world but didn't quite pull it off. Overhead, the sky was a crisscross of telephone wires and power lines, silhouetted against the faint glow of the streetlights.

Below us, I could hear some dudes laughing and clinking bottles, and there was a strong smell of cigarettes. The muffled bass pulsed through the sliding door, faint enough that it didn't feel like it was trying to drag me back inside.

Dylan reached into the pocket of his flannel shirt and pulled out the pre-roll, the kind that was giving "dispensary chic" with its sleek packaging. He popped open the tube and slid out the joint like he was handling some sacred relic. Then came the vintage Zippo from the coin pocket of his jeans—one flick, one flame, all muscle memory. It was the kind of move you only nail after a hundred tries. He put the flame to the end of the joint as he cupped his hand around it like he was in some old-school movie.

Honestly, it was kind of a flex, but he made it look so effortless I couldn't even hate. He took a couple of short puffs, inspecting his work lighting the end, before he took a deep, easy drag, then exhaled slow, releasing this thick cloud of smoke that lingered in the night air.

The smell hit instantly. I wasn't really into weed like that, but there was something about it that just made sense in the moment. It mixed with the crisp night air and the smell of beer that drifted up from a puddle that whoever was on the balcony before us had left. It created this mood that felt steady, almost grounding. Like the world had hit pause for a second just to let things breathe—and after the show that Rafe put on inside, I was all about it.

Dylan passed me the joint with a flick of his wrist. His eyes caught the glow of the balcony light—hazel, maybe? I took the joint, hesitating for a second longer than I probably should've before bringing it to my lips. I hit it too hard and instantly regretted it. It felt like sandpaper down my throat and I coughed like I'd just swallowed a gallon of ocean water.

"Easy there, dude," Dylan said, laughing softly. His tone wasn't mean, just that laid-back mix of amused and understanding, like he'd seen this a hundred times before. "It's not a race, you know."

I managed a weak grin between coughs, and my eyes were watering as I tried to pull myself together. My throat burned, but I leaned back like coughing up a lung was totally the plan. "Yeah, I got it," I croaked.

Yeah, totally convincing, Kiko.

Dylan and I leaned against the balcony wall. Even though it was June, the temperature had dropped to the low sixties, which didn't really feel cold when I was skating over, but standing in one spot? I was for sure starting to feel it through my hoodie. I shoved my free hand into my pocket between turns with the joint.

I took another drag off the blunt, finally managing to get the hang of it without the super-embarrassing coughing fits. It felt easier this time, like the smoke was smoother, and that slow wave of calm was starting to settle in. The party and the noise slowly faded until I was kinda floating in my own little bubble.

Out of the corner of my eye, I caught Dylan glancing at me. Before I could say anything, he looked away and sipped his beer. I let it slide, chalking it up to Dylan being Dylan, that cool but kinda mysterious thing he had going.

"So," he said, keeping it casual. "Any new music you're into?"

"Not exactly new," I said, leaning back against the porch rail. "But I've been listening to a lot of Luna Shadows lately."

He blinked. "Name sounds familiar, but I don't know her stuff."

I smiled a little. "You'd probably like it. It's got this hazy LA feel— melancholy but still kind of glittery? I skate to *Hallelujah California* or *Waves* at night sometimes. Makes the city feel different. Like a movie, but not the shiny parts."

Dylan tilted his head, curious now. "That sounds cool."

"Yeah. She's one of those artists where the lyrics hit harder the more you listen. Real layered. And she's got this whole community around her—like, full Discord server, die-hard fans, the whole thing."

He nodded, his lips curling up on one side. "Send me a link later?"

"Yeah," I said, kind of surprised he actually wanted to check it out. "For sure."

We fell into an easy back-and-forth about music, tossing out favorite bands and hidden gems. It was low-key fun, the kind of conversation where time just drifted by. We roasted the usual overplayed party songs. Dylan's laugh was deep and real, the kind that made you laugh along even when you didn't mean to.

But then the conversation shifted. Dylan's questions started to dig just a little deeper, his tone still casual, but curious in a way that made my chest tighten.

"Hey," he said, looking at me more directly this time. "I noticed earlier with Rafe and the twins... you seemed kinda, I dunno, uncomfortable? Like, you into someone else? Or relationships just not your thing?"

I froze for a second, his words hitting a little too close. My fingers tightened around the cup in my hand as I brought it to my lips, taking a slow sip to stall.

"Nah, it's not that," I said finally, my voice as steady as I could make it. "Just wasn't feeling it, you know?"

"That's cool, man," Dylan said, brushing a hand along the side of his head to push his hair back. His tone was easy, but the way he looked at me lingered for a second longer, like he was giving me space to keep talking if I wanted to—but I didn't. The question had struck a nerve I wasn't ready to touch, and I wasn't about to start unpacking it here on the balcony with him.

"The moon's just a spotlight," Dylan said suddenly, "shining on things we're too scared to see in daylight…"

I blinked, not really sure how to respond. Before I could think of something clever—or at least not totally cringe—to say, Dylan pulled a small, leather-bound notebook from his back pocket and flipped it open. There were other lines scribbled on the pages written between random doodles and quick drawings. He jotted the line down with a pen that was kept in the binding.

"What's that about?" I asked.

"Eh," Dylan said, closing the book and slipping it back into his pocket. "Just stuff I think of, you know? Little thoughts and moments I don't wanna forget. I write poems and stuff."

"That's cool," I said, and I meant it. I wasn't expecting Dylan to have this whole other layer to him. He leaned casually against the lattice, the faint glow from the patio light catching his face. His hazel eyes had this far-off look, like he was somewhere else entirely while saying those lines, but somehow, it made the words hit harder. There was this low-key thing about him—not the in-your-face kind of good looks like Rafe, but the kind that sneaks up on you. His hair alone was a whole vibe, disheveled but not messy, like it just naturally fell into place in that perfectly imperfect way that the girls at school probably lost their minds over. And then there was the dimple that appeared only on his right cheek when he smiled…

"I didn't know you were into that," I added, watching as he tucked the little memo book back into his pocket. His lips quirked up in a half-smile, but his eyes didn't fully lose that distant look, as if part of him was still caught in whatever thought had sparked the lines he just wrote down.

"Guess you wouldn't," he said, smirking a little but not in a mean way. "We've never really talked before."

"True," I admitted. "Kind of weird, though. We've been at the same school for four years. How'd that even happen?"

"It was a big school. Two thousand other kids. It also didn't help that we only had English together—*and* that I only transferred in at the start of senior year," he said, with a grin.

Dude was really gonna hide the main plot twist.

How did I not know?

"Where were you before?" I asked, curiosity creeping in.

"Nowhere actually," he said kind of cryptically. "Missed about a year, so had to do it over again. My mom and I moved here from just outside of Fresno."

His tone shifted just enough to make it feel like I shouldn't push any further. There was something there—something heavier—but I let it slide.

He gave me a half-smile and took another slow drag from the joint. "Long story."

I nodded, leaving it at that, but the whole exchange stuck with me. Dylan had this way of saying just enough to make me curious but not enough to satisfy it. And the poetry thing? That was unexpected in the best way. It was the first time I really looked at him and thought, *Maybe there's more to this guy than I ever gave him credit for.*

Before the silence could stretch too far, the balcony door slid open with a soft whoosh, cutting through the stillness of the night, as the music from the party invaded the space.

"There you are!" Rafe's voice broke in, pulling all the attention his way like it always did. "I thought I heard you hacking up a lung." He stepped outside, grinning as his eyes zeroed in on what was left of the joint in Dylan's hand. His face lit up like a kid who'd just found an unopened bag of Sour Patch Kids.

"Yo, let me hit that," Rafe begged.

Dylan didn't put up much of a fight. With a casual shrug, he handed the joint over, leaning back against the lattice as Rafe took it.

"What do we got here?" Rafe asked, already taking a deep pull before Dylan could answer. He exhaled with a big grin, a cloud of smoke rising up into the night air.

"Granddaddy Purple," Dylan replied.

"Nice," Rafe said, nodding like he was suddenly some kind of weed connoisseur. He took another pull, exhaling slowly, then turned to me, tapping me on the chest with the back of his hand. "Yo, dude! You gotta get back in there. Halley's totally into you."

I rolled my eyes, shaking my head. "Pretty sure that was Ariel. And nah, I'm good out here right now."

Rafe frowned, clearly unbothered by the mix-up. "I can never tell them apart," he admitted with a shrug, then grinned like he'd just come up with the perfect plan. "Okay, hear me out—whichever one you want, I'll take the other, and we can double date." He laughed, nudging me like this was a flawless idea.

Dylan, who'd been leaning casually against the lattice, raised an eyebrow. "Do either of *them* actually get a say in this?" he asked.

I smirked, glad Dylan beat me to it but couldn't help piling on. "Yeah, Rafe. Like, you *do* know they're both individual people, right?"

Rafe shot us both a look, his grin faltering for a second before he rolled his eyes and laughed. "Alright, alright. Chill, I was joking." He took another drag, but I could tell from the way he avoided eye contact that he didn't entirely get why it wasn't landing, but that was Rafe—good intentions wrapped in zero self-awareness.

Dylan glanced at me, his expression just this side of amused, like he was silently asking, *How do you put up with this guy?* I gave a small shrug, knowing full well I wasn't going to go into all of Rafe's Rafe-ness right now.

"Twins are weird," Rafe shot back, shrugging like he wasn't just digging the hole deeper. "I don't know how it works."

Dylan, who had been all mellow and laid-back a few minutes ago, suddenly bristled. His tone sharpened even more. "How *what* works, exactly?" he asked, eyebrows raised.

Rafe blinked, clearly not catching the shift in Dylan's vibe. "I'm just trying to be a good wingman for my boy here," he said, slinging an arm around my shoulders.

I groaned internally but managed to keep my voice light. "Appreciate it, dude, but I don't need a wingman right now." I shrugged his arm off, trying to keep the focus on him. "Besides, haven't you and Avery been getting, like, really close lately?"

Rafe froze for a half-second, then scoffed like the idea was ridiculous. "Nah, man. It's not like that. We're just chilling." His words sounded casual, but the quickness of his reply gave him away. Then his face shifted, and he squinted at me like he was piecing something together. "Wait... Is *that* why you've been acting weird?"

My stomach dropped, and I tried to force out a laugh as I shook my head. "What are you even talking about?" I cringed inside, knowing I didn't sound half as confident as I wanted to—and Rafe wasn't letting it slide.

He crossed his arms, giving me that *I'm not buying your BS* look. "Dude, you've been straight-up MIA this week. You dipped the other day barely saying anything, and you've been leaving us on read. What's up with that?"

I bit my lip. Somehow the guilt hit hard, like I guess he wasn't wrong. I *had* been ghosting. Just kinda lost in my own head, dodging their texts, and just… well, straight-up avoiding people. It wasn't on purpose exactly, but I knew it was happening.

"I dunno," I mumbled, as I looked away, trying to avoid his eyes. "It's just… been a lot going on lately, you know? Trying to figure some stuff out."

Rafe tilted his head, still staring at me like he was trying to piece together a mystery I wasn't ready to explain. Dylan shifted next to me, quiet but present. I gripped my cup tighter, staring into it like it had answers. The silence stretched, all thick and awkward. It was probably only a couple seconds but I was suddenly hyper-aware of how much I'd been shutting everyone out.

"Scored a gig at a coffee shop up on Wilshire," I said, keeping it casual like it wasn't a big deal—and probably not so subtly trying to change the topic.

"No shit," Rafe said, his face lighting up.

Before I could say anything more, he was off. He slid the glass door open with probably a bit too much force and shouted, "Yo, everyone! Shots! My boy Kiko's a workin' man!"

Of course, Rafe had to make a scene. The music dipped for half a second, and now everyone inside was looking out toward the balcony. My chest tightened. It was just a barista job—not some big break—but Rafe hyped it like I'd just gotten hired as CEO of Starbucks or something.

Cheers erupted, people raising their drinks as they crowded around the door, throwing out congrats and random jokes.

Avery was one of the first to step out onto the balcony, her energy matching Rafe's. "Kiko! Congrats!" she said, practically bouncing. "Where at?"

"Thanks," I said, rubbing the back of my neck, feeling a little overwhelmed. "It's this coffee shop in Beverly Hills."

"Oooh, fancy," she teased. "Which one?"

"Gautier's. I start there on Monday."

"Yo, Kiko," someone called out from inside—I vaguely recognized the voice from school. "Do you even know what a latte is?"

Everyone laughed, but before I could fire back, Rafe jumped in.

"Okay, okay. Laugh it up now," he said, as he put an arm around my shoulder. "Watch my boy here become the coffee king of LA."

I rolled my eyes, but a small smile broke through despite myself. Leave it to Rafe to turn my awkwardness into a full-on comedy show. It was a lot, but it wasn't bad. For the first time in a while, it actually felt nice to just vibe with everyone, even if I was the joke.

The shots were lined up on the counter—these cheap plastic shot cups with even cheaper whiskey that just smelled like instant regret.

"To Kiko!" Rafe shouted, raising his cup. The room echoed him with a chaotic chorus of "Kiko!" before we all threw the shots back.

The whiskey burned all the way down, and I had to fight the urge to cough. It left this weird warm trail in my chest that felt kind of good if you ignored the part where your throat was on fire. I winced, and of course Rafe noticed, laughing as he slapped me on the back like I wasn't already struggling.

Everyone scattered back to their spots. Some went to the living room, others to the balcony, some stayed in the kitchen. The music picked up again and I let myself get pulled into it.

All the conversations started to blur together, someone shoved another drink into my hand. The beer, the weed, the whiskey—it was all hitting in waves.

For a while, I just vibed. No overthinking, no awkward tension, no spiraling. Just... here. Part of the noise, part of the party.

The living room became straight-up chaotic when Avery broke out her dad's high-tech karaoke machine. Of course, Avery kicked things off —no surprise there. She scrolled through the song list and landed on "Misery Business" by Paramore—her go-to.

The opening riff hit, and the crowd went wild, cheering her on like she was about to headline Coachella. And honestly? She owned it. Avery didn't have Hayley Williams' pipes, but what she lacked in pitch she made up for with pure energy. She stomped around the room, practically screaming the lyrics, her purple-tipped hair flying everywhere. When she hit the chorus the whole room exploded, shouting it with her. It was messy, chaotic, and somehow so Avery.

The twins didn't take long to decide. After a quick back-and-forth, they landed on "Pink Pony Club" by Chappell Roan. It was such a random but perfect choice—completely their vibe. The song was for sure shaping up to be a summer banger. Halley took the lead, her voice light and confident, while Ariel backed her up with harmonies that were surprisingly on point. They weren't pros or anything, but the way they played off each other made it so much fun to watch. By the time they hit the big notes, people were clapping along, totally caught up in it.

Never one to be outdone, Rafe swaggered up, clearly ready to try to top everyone. He grabbed a mic, and scrolled through the songs, selecting "Under Pressure" by Queen and David Bowie. I had just begun to wonder why he picked a duet until I noticed him scanning the room dramatically—and locking eyes on me.

Fuck.

"Alright, Kiko. Let's do this. Duet time," he said as the opening riff started.

I backed away like he was holding a taser. "Nah, man. Not happening."

"Don't be lame!" he said, rolling his eyes like I was ruining his entire night. "You don't even have to be good—it's karaoke!"

"C'mon Kiko!" someone shouted, which was followed by the crowd chanting my name.

"Nope. Not doing it." I crossed my arms for emphasis, trying to run out the clock until the words began.

"Fine," Rafe sighed, acting like I'd left him no choice. "Guess I'll just have to do both parts then."

The beat dropped, and Rafe launched into it, starting strong with Bowie's part. But the second he hit Freddie Mercury's falsetto? It was epic.

Yeah right, it was an absolute trainwreck. His voice cracked, jumped an octave too high, and then wobbled so off-key that it was almost impressive how bad he fucked it up.

The room turned on him immediately as empty cups flew through the air like missiles, followed by a crushed beer can that missed him by inches.

"Boo!" someone yelled, "Make it stop!"

The laughter was louder than the boos, but Rafe powered through. I for one couldn't stop laughing. I was doubled over as Rafe dodged another cup.

"Geez. Tough crowd!" he shouted, between verses, throwing his hands up.

By the time he stumbled through the last lines the crowd had mostly forgiven him, clapping and laughing as he bowed like he'd just nailed a five-star performance. He turned and pointed at me. "This is all your fault, dude. Could've been a duet—*our* duet."

"Yeah, sure," I said, smirking. "Way to kill it, Freddie."

Rafe laughed it off, handing the mic to the next brave soul. The night carried on, but my thoughts drifted. Dylan had vanished somewhere in the chaos, and the longer I looked around, the more obvious it was that he wasn't coming back.

I scanned the faces around the room. Rafe was by the stereo, cracking up with Avery about something dumb. The twins were by the couches, chatting up some random dudes. I checked the kitchen, the balcony, even the corners where people usually ducked out for quieter convos. Nothing. Dylan was just... gone.

It felt weird, like something in the party shifted. He'd been there, keeping the vibe low-key, and now that he wasn't. The party felt louder. Messier. And I was a little less... grounded. I couldn't explain why, but it bugged me more than it probably should've.

"Yo, anyone seen Dylan?" I asked a couple of people hanging nearby. They barely even looked up, just shrugged. I kept half-expecting him to just slip back through the door and pick up the conversation right where we left off. But he didn't.

I checked my phone. The cracked screen barely held it together, but I could see it was creeping toward midnight. My social battery was approaching empty anyway.

I spotted Avery first, mid-laugh with someone, her whole energy just magnetic as usual. "Hey, Avery," I said, stepping in casually. "I'm heading out."

"Already? Well, thanks for coming, Kiko. Seriously, it means a lot."

"Of course," I said, giving her a small smile before easing my way out of the convo.

Next, I found Rafe. Obviously, he was mid-story, big gestures, huge energy, and a small crowd eating it up. I waited for a break—barely— and cut in. "Yo, Rafe, I'm out."

He spun toward me, grinning like I'd just handed him a punchline. "What? The workin' man can't hang?" He clapped me on the shoulder, all hype. "Go get that beauty sleep, barista boy. Don't spill the lattes."

I rolled my eyes but couldn't help laughing. "Yeah, yeah. Later, dude."

With that, I grabbed my board and slipped out. The breeze hit like a reset button, cutting through the leftover heat of the party. I dropped my board onto the pavement, the sound echoing in the stillness, and pushed off, letting the rhythm of the wheels calm my thoughts. The streets were empty, the canals quiet, a total 180 from the chaos I'd just left behind.

My brain kept circling back to Rafe and Avery, though. Even with Rafe's whole "it's not like that" routine, I couldn't shake the third-wheel vibes. Not jealousy exactly. Just… that weird feeling like I'd missed a memo about how everything was supposed to work now. It was annoying, and yeah, maybe I was overthinking it, but it was hard not to. I tried to shove it out of my head, focusing instead on the steady vibrations under my feet and the cool breeze brushing my face. The quiet streets felt surreal, like the whole world had gone on pause just for me.

As I cruised through the empty neighborhood, weaving around cracks in the pavement and gliding under flickering streetlights, my mind shifted to the next day. The new job. The new everything. It was kind of exciting, but also kind of terrifying. My stomach did this little flip, like it couldn't decide if it was stoked or panicking. Barista gigs aren't exactly life-changing, but still—it felt like something. Maybe a step forward instead of just standing still.

When I rolled up to my apartment, I stopped for a second, letting the board rest under my foot. For a minute, I just stood there, letting it all settle. Next week was going to be all new stuff for sure and I definitely didn't know what to expect. But right then, looking up at the moon, alone with my board and my thoughts, I felt… not lost or stuck. Just kinda moving forward—even if I still didn't know where I was going.

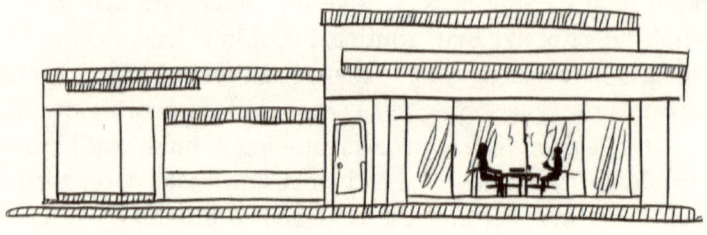

6

I was absolutely *flying* down Wilshire, trying to make up for time I didn't have. Up ahead, a guy pushing a shopping cart packed with random junk under a blue tarp veered into my path, and I swerved hard on my board to avoid him. "Sorry, dude!" I yelled, over my shoulder.

Not even two seconds later, a woman carrying a tiny fluffy dog appeared out of nowhere. I zigzagged to dodge her, nearly wiping out in the process. "My bad!" I called over my shoulder, hands up in a quick apology as I sped past.

The coffee shop finally came into view, the black-and-gold sign looking way less like a sign of relief and more like a reminder I was, once again, so late. I popped my board into my hand, not breaking stride as I sprinted through the front door that was propped open to let the breeze in.

The early lunch rush was still popping. Machines were whirring, cups were clinking, and the line stretched almost to the door. Ricky was behind the register, pulling double-duty but totally unbothered. He was just chatting with some customer while he casually rang them up. He spotted me sprinting in and grinned, already shaking his head. "Four times now, dude," he called, his voice dripping with fake disappointment. "I can only cover for you for so long. Neil's gonna start docking your pay."

"I know. My bad!" I shot back, darting past him to the back room. I tossed my skateboard and backpack into the corner as I grabbed my apron off a hook, yanking it over my head as I rushed out onto the floor.

Ricky took one look at me as he stepped away from the register. "You good, OKIK?" he said, pointing at my chest with his annoying—and perfect—smirk.

I glanced down at my name tag, and sure enough, it was upside down. I groaned as I spun it around right-side up.

"That's what happens when you're in a rush, my guy," Ricky said. He stepped away from the register to head to the espresso machine, his low-key way of telling me to take over.

There was a super impatient looking group of girls waiting at the counter. Ricky, meanwhile, was back to doing his usual magic at the espresso machine, pulling shots and steaming milk like he was starring in a TikTok video. His latte art was stupidly good—he'd flick his wrist, and boom, a perfect heart, some fancy swirl, a swan, you name it—all while chatting up customers like it was nothing. He pumped out latte art like a clown at a kid's birthday party making balloon animals.

I glanced over at him while I punched in an order, watching him move like he actually belonged here. Meanwhile, I was stuck fumbling with buttons on the touchscreen and calling out corrections to orders I put in wrong or modifications I couldn't find in the menus.

Ricky was always cool with it—dude was unshakeable. He'd come over when it slowed down to try to show me where the different options were on the touchscreen. Everyone else though... Let's just say I wasn't their favorite on the register. The problem was I was even worse at making drinks...

"You doing anything fun for the Fourth?" Ricky asked.

"Nah. Keeping it low-key," I said. I had been blowing off the invites for Thursday from Rafe and Avery—or Ravery as I started calling them. Just wasn't feeling it with the two of them acting like there wasn't something going on.

Neil burst through the front door, sweat dripping down his temples as he carried in two crates filled with milk cartons. He was wearing one of his signature floral button-up shirts, which always looked perfectly pressed. But this time it was a little wrinkled.

"Ah, the prodigal barista graces us with his presence," Neil said in that dramatic—and sarcastic—Neil way. He put the crates down near one of the undercounter fridges. "Thank you for coming to work today, *Enrique*."

I opened my mouth but couldn't decide whether to correct him or to apologize, but either way Neil waved me off before I could get the words out. "No, no," he said, standing up and brushing his hands together. "You're here now. Let's make the most of it."

Ricky tried to stifle a laugh from his corner at the espresso machine, but I caught him smirking. I glared at him and turned back to the counter, pretending to focus on the register. Meanwhile, Neil was speed-unloading the milks—whole milk, oat, almond, soy, some random brand I'd never seen before. Neil would make runs like this to Whole Foods in a pinch between deliveries. One of the morning-shift guys—some quiet dude I'd barely exchanged two words with—took over the rest of the cartons while Neil dusted off his hands and headed straight for me.

"Alright, let's see what we've got here," Neil said, sliding in behind the counter and sidling up next to me. He folded his arms, leaning slightly as his eyes scanned the register screen. "Okay, so here's the thing. You're trying to go fast, and fast is good. But speed means nothing if you're constantly fumbling, or getting the orders wrong. So let's try to slow it down, breathe, and get the orders right the first time."

I nodded, my hands hovering over the touchscreen, trying not to mess up as I could feel his eyes watching me over my shoulder. The next customer stepped up, tossing a quick "hey" my way. Neil took the lead. "Let's do this one together," he said. "Watch me."

He punched in the order, narrating as he did it, like it was some YouTube tutorial.

"Latte, almond milk, one pump of vanilla—don't go searching for the modifiers in here. The common ones are right here on the same screen off to the side. And… there we go. See?"

I nodded again, trying to absorb everything. I had to admit though that the pressure of him hovering over me made it feel like a pop quiz I wasn't ready for. Ricky was a lot more easy-going. The next customer stepped up, and Neil gestured for me to take over. "Your turn. Show me what you've got."

I moved through the steps, slower this time, making sure to follow his advice. The customer gave me a polite "thanks," and Neil nodded, a faint trace of approval crossing his face. "Not bad. You'll get there," he said before stepping back to grab a rag and wipe down the counter.

Neil's whole vibe could flip on a dime—sarcastic one minute, actually helpful the next—but I could tell he wanted us to get it right. It wasn't like he was trying to be a jerk; he just had a way of keeping everyone on their toes. It *was* his name on the place, so I mean, I got it. But I felt like I was totally screwing everything up, and really didn't want him to give up on me.

He was still wiping down the counter when he just froze mid-swipe as he spotted this woman in the corner.

She wasn't just some regular customer—that much was clear. Her vibe? Pure money. Pure power. She had this perfect designer outfit and her black hair had a gray streak that was so on point. But it was mostly her energy—this vibe like she didn't need to try to impress anyone—because she knew she did.

Meanwhile, a younger guy, maybe mid-twenties with tanned skin and platinum hair sat across from her. He looked like he was in full crisis mode the way his thumbs were flying over his iPhone, probably typing out some make-or-break email. He was definitely her assistant or something.

The woman, though? Completely unbothered as she flipped through this massive binder filled with what looked like sketches and tiny pieces of fabric, her face totally calm and expressionless. She moved like time didn't apply to her, and honestly, it kind of made everyone else in the café feel... basic.

Neil stared for a solid few seconds and sighed dramatically. He grabbed an oversized mug that Ricky had just finished doing his thing on, moving like his life depended on not spilling a drop. He paused for a second at the end of the counter, adjusted his grip, and headed toward the corner where the woman was camped out.

He finally got to her table and set the mug down super carefully, like one wrong move would ruin everything. The woman didn't even acknowledge him at first, her eyes still on the binder. When she finally looked up over the rims of her expensive looking red-framed glasses, she just gave Neil this look that was calm, but also kinda cutting. It was super unsettling—and I was pretty sure that was the exact vibe she was going for.

She picked up the mug slowly, her movements so deliberate it felt like she was judging more than just the drink. She closed her eyes for a second, breathing in the steam, then glanced back at Neil like she wasn't sure the drink was right just from the smell.

Neil looked super nervous, standing there like his job depended on this drink being right.

Finally, she took this tiny sip, paused, and pursed her lips. For a second, it looked like she might hand it back or say something, but then she gave him the tiniest little nod. Not friendly, not mean, just... this nod that I wasn't even sure I could see, before she went back talking to her assistant.

Neil nodded back way too quickly, practically stumbling over himself to get out of there. As he passed Ricky on his way to the back, he flashed a low OK sign near his chest, Ricky just nodded back not saying a word.

Neil disappeared into the back office without even glancing my way. I blinked, turning to Ricky. "Uh… what was that?" I asked, jerking my chin toward the corner.

Ricky chuckled, "Man, you don't even know." He came over and leaned on the counter with his back to the woman in the corner. "That right there is Selena Cho. Big-time fashion designer. Like, luxury brand, Paris runway, Vogue cover kinda big."

I raised an eyebrow. "And she comes here?"

"Every Tuesday," Ricky said.

"She didn't order anything though," I said.

"Doesn't need to. Same table, same vibe. Gets a hot London Fog latte —oat milk, extra foam, and just a whisper of lavender. Spends about an hour flipping through look books and swatches while her assistant tries not to combust. It's her whole routine."

I glanced back at her. She was so calm, so in control, while her assistant looked one typo away from a breakdown. "Okay, but why was Neil like… that?"

Ricky smirked but then his expression softened. "Neil moved to LA to be a fashion designer," he said, his voice lower, like he didn't want anyone overhearing. "That was his dream—designing clothes, getting his stuff on runways, the whole deal. But, you know, life happens. It didn't pan out."

I blinked, surprised. Neil? Fashion? I guess it wasn't hard to picture him being a big-time designer, but at the same time, it hadn't occurred to me. The guy did have a way of carrying himself, always dressed like he was ready to give a TED Talk on "classical elegance" or something dapper like that.

I glanced back at Selena Cho. She was casually looking over the group of girls seated at the couch on the far wall—probably judging their fashion sense, before flipping a page in her binder with this precise little motion.

"So what, seeing her reminds him of what could've been?" I asked.

Ricky nodded. "Pretty much. She's, like, peak everything he wanted. It's like a reminder of this whole life he didn't get to live." He straightened up and adjusted his apron. "But hey, what're you gonna do? Sometimes dreams don't pan out and you gotta pay the bills somehow."

I just let that sit for a second. Neil always came off as sharp and confident—definitely a little snarky—but now? It was like I was seeing this whole other side of him that I hadn't seen before.

There were a few tables and a spot on the bar that ran along the front window that needed to be wiped down so I grabbed the rag Neil left on the counter and to take advantage of the lull in customers. I went to squeeze past the morning-shift guy, who was still there for some reason, and took a half empty cappuccino to the chest as he spun from the counter towards the sink.

Awesome, I thought as I wiped at the mess that ran right down the middle of my apron. I looked over at Selena Cho, low-key worried she would be looking at me—judging me.

Instead, though, she was looking towards the door where something definitely caught her eye. She turned her head even more with one eyebrow raised, and this hint of a smile at the corner of her mouth. It was almost... approval. I followed her gaze, and there he was, just past the pastry case: Troye. Because *of course* he would walk in while I was drenched in milk froth and espresso.

It was the first time I'd seen him since the day I got the job, and he looked next-level. He was dressed perfectly, rocking a short-sleeve button-up with a bold, abstract print that somehow managed to look laid-back and high-fashion at the same time. The top button was undone, showing just a hint of a thin gold chain that caught the light when he moved. His sunglasses, oversized with a subtle tortoiseshell frame, were perched on his nose, but as he stopped in the doorway, he slid them off with one smooth motion. His bleached curls—messy in that "I spent an hour making it look effortless" kind of way—shifted as he glanced around the shop.

He scanned the cafe like he was checking the vibe, but when his eyes landed on me, man, something shifted. He like froze for a second before this smile spread on his face—nothing smug or over the top, but it seemed like one that was definitely practiced.

I walked back to the register, tossing the rag, but as he approached I just froze for a second, like hyper-aware of every detail. The designer clothes, the confidence—the sound of those boots—it was all so... fierce. Meanwhile, I was just trying to pretend I wasn't frozen in place like some NPC that hadn't finished loading in a video game.

"There you are, Skater Boy."

My brain froze for a second, still trying to decide if he was just being friendly or if this was, you know, something.

"Didn't see you last couple of times I stopped in," he added, hooking his sunglasses onto the collar of his shirt and locking those brown eyes on me, before they drifted down to my stained apron. "Thought you might've not made it." He pulled his lips back and made a cutting gesture at the side of his neck.

"Nope, still here," I said, trying for cool but probably landing closer to mildly frazzled—and also keenly aware that Ricky was watching us from the other end of the counter. "What can I get you?"

He tilted his head just enough to make it look like he was sizing me up. "Large iced half-caff dirty chai latte, two pumps of vanilla," he said, before tapping the glass of the pastry display. "And one of these cake pops—dealer's choice."

"Got it," I said, already fumbling with the register. My fingers hovered over the screen, struggling to find the modifiers for his drink. Of course, the second I started overthinking it, I could feel his eyes on me. Not in a judge-y way, but still—he was watching me.

"I didn't break you, did I?" Troye teased, leaning just a little closer. His voice wasn't mean, just playful, like he was genuinely amused at my struggle.

"I'm getting there," I said, glancing at Ricky for backup, who—thankfully—slid a cup onto the counter like some kind of wizard.

"Already made," Ricky said with zero fanfare. "Just put it in as an iced chai latte and add 3 shots of espresso. The rest doesn't matter."

"Appreciate it, hun," Troye said, flashing him a quick smile before turning his attention back to me. "Ricky's always got me covered."

Troye leaned slightly closer, pulling his phone from his pocket and said, "Apple Pay."

Everything he did, even paying for a drink, had to have a touch of flair. He tapped his phone against the contactless reader, and the soft chime felt way louder than it should have as I tried to keep my hands steady.

As I handed him the receipt, he tilted his head, still holding that easy smile. "So what days do you work, Skater Boy?"

"Oh, uh..." I fumbled for a second, my brain not fully firing. "Monday, Tuesday, Friday, and Saturday."

Troye nodded, like he was filing that information away. "Good, that means you're off Sunday," he said, his tone light but purposeful. "Come with me to LACMA."

I blinked. "LACMA?"

"Yeah," he said, leaning just enough to make me hyper-aware of the space between us. "The... LA County Museum of Art?"

"No, of course, I know," I tried to save myself. I knew what it was but my brain was short-circuiting again. Was this a hangout? A casual thing? Or was it… I mean, it couldn't be a date, right? There was no way someone like Troye was actually asking me on a date.

"Are you into art? We can do something else.."

"No that's cool," I swallowed hard and managed, "I used to draw a little, but now I just kind of mess around with photography. Nothing serious, though. Just, like, stuff for Insta."

Troye's grin widened slightly. "The Gram, huh? What's your @, I'll follow you."

"Oh, uh, it's—'@therealkikorodriguez,'" I paused, suddenly super self-conscious about my random mix of surf pics, skate clips, and blurry sunsets.

Troye tapped at his phone for a second, and then I felt the faint buzz of a notification come through my pocket. "Gotcha," he said, his tone smooth. "See you Sunday, Skater Boy. I'll message you the details."

"Cool," I managed.

He waited at the counter and nodded. I nodded along with him as the awkwardness crept all the way back in. Was I supposed to do something else? A handshake? High five? A hug was definitely not appropriate, plus the counter was in the way.

I settled on a handshake and stuck my hand out across the counter.

Troye's eyebrow raised as he gingerly took my hand. A grin spread across his face, "You forgot about the cake pop didn't you?"

Smooth, Kiko.

My head bobbed in a weird circle that was somehow a yes and no at the same time as my cheeks went on fire.

I grabbed one of the rainbow sprinkle covered vanilla cake pops and handed it to him, "Birthday cake flavor."

"Good choice," Troye said, holding it up like he was toasting before turning and strutting toward the door, leaving the faint scent of cologne and complete chaos in my head.

Ricky glanced over from the espresso machine with this shit-eating grin. "Looks like Skater Boy's got himself a date," he teased.

"Shut up," I groaned, running a hand through my hair. "It's not like that! I mean… maybe? I don't even know. Is it?"

Ricky raised both eyebrows, crossing his arms like I'd just said the dumbest thing in the world. "Bro, he asked for your schedule, invited you to LACMA, and followed your Insta. Like, what part of that isn't a date?"

I rolled my eyes. "Okay, fine, maybe it's a date, but… you're not like weirded out or anything?" I asked, suddenly realizing this was probably news to Ricky.

"Weirded out? Nah man, it's 2024. Live your life."

He stepped closer, grabbing me by the shoulders and shaking me. "Seriously, my man, chill. You're losing it, and it's not that deep. Just show up, be yourself, and you'll crush it. You've got this."

I laughed nervously, his energy making it feel a little less serious but not by much. "Thanks, man. It's just... I don't know. Never really done this type of thing before and Troye's... kind of a lot."

Ricky let go of my shoulders and leaned against the counter so I could see his face again, his vibe shifting. "Yeah, Troye can be... intense," he said. "Just—I don't know—be careful, alright? He's fun and all, but he's got this thing where he like... burns bright, you know? Like, hot and fast."

"Hot and fast?" I asked, my stomach twisting a bit.

Ricky hesitated, almost like he was choosing his words carefully. "Look, it's not my place to say. I'm just saying... take it slow. Don't fall in too deep, too fast. You're good people, Kiko. Don't let anyone mess with that."

I nodded, his words landing somewhere between totally comforting and completely nerve-wracking—so yeah, all over the place.

Ricky clapped me on the back, like the advice sesh was over. "Now get your head straight before Neil comes out here asking why those tables are dirty."

I laughed as I tried to shake off the mix of nerves and excitement as I turned back to the counter. Fun, intense, "hot and fast." I didn't know what I was walking into with Troye, but one thing was for sure...

I was about to find out.

7

I'd swerved hard on Rafe and Avery's invites for the Fourth. No rooftop parties, no sparklers, no Rafe yelling "America!" while shotgunning beers. I just couldn't deal.

And the worst part? Troye still hadn't accepted my follow-back. It had been three days now. I was starting to think he was having second thoughts.

I was waiting for my usual bus to head home, headphones in, zoning out as it pulled up with a squeal that cut through my music. The bus started to rattle down Robertson, and I made my way to my go-to seat, when the notification popped up like he was listening in my head: Troye accepted your follow request.

I told myself I was going to wait until I got home to look at his profile. Needed to play it cool... Ah, who was I kidding? As soon as I found a spot in the back corner and tucked my board against the side, I caved. My thumb tapped on Instagram, and I opened up Troye's profile.

His grid was all aesthetic and polished, like it was begging to be stared at, but his bio was peak minimalist-cool: just his name, a paintbrush emoji, and a pride flag. His profile pic was a black-and-white close-up of his face with his curly hair all wild, his eyes somehow managing to look deep even in grayscale. Classic. I hesitated, then started scrolling.

The first post was a sketch of a hand that was so detailed it looked like it could flex any second. The caption just read "Study #24" followed by a bunch of random artsy emojis.

Next was a sketch of feet from different angles. They were like dancer feet, somehow, I don't know, elegant instead of, like... gross. Who can even draw feet and make them actually look nice?

Then there was this black-and-white print of like a flamenco dancer mid-spin with her dress swirling around her. The shading made the fabric look so real, like moving even though it was still. The caption was just "Baila!" followed by a dancer and a sparkles emoji.

A little further down, there was a color painting of three abstract people in red, pink, blue, and purple. The colors were all mixed up, like blurring in some places and clashing in others. It was like chaos frozen in time. This one was apparently called "The Muses: Together/Apart."

And then the posts shifted from his art to real life. First was this black-and-white shot of him smoking in someone's backyard at night. The smoke curled into the air like it had been photoshopped in, but the way the light hit him? Yeah, it was definitely doing something.

I opened the comments.

Noah
Cute boy! ♡ 1

Ava
Looking good, Troye! ♡ 1

Alex
So artsy 🔥 ♡ 1

Isabella
Miss you Clay! ♡ 0

Who the fuck was Clay? I laughed, figuring it was a super bad autocorrect fail. Can't say I haven't been there, especially with this cracked screen.

Ah, of course, the mandatory bathroom mirror selfie was next. I guess everyone's allowed one—but Troye's was next level. Tank top, joggers, leaning casually with his phone in one hand like he hadn't spent at least ten minutes trying to get the perfect angle. It was so calculated, but damn if it didn't work.

The bus slowed for a stop, and I stared out the window, trying to take a break from overanalyzing every post. I pressed the home button to get out of Insta before I spiraled any further.

I went back to the homescreen and tapped on Spotify. My usual playlist didn't feel right. It was—I don't know—too predictable or something for the headspace I was in. I searched around for a second, then settled on *Electric Love* by BØRNS. The second the beat dropped, I was vibing, so I let the algorithm take the wheel from there. I was confident I'd be happy with whatever it thought I needed.

But by the time the chorus hit, there was no way I could sit still. My leg was bouncing and my fingers tapping on my board to the beat. My brain was doing this chaotic loop between Troye and LACMA—this was actually happening—and yet here I was, sitting on the bus with my scuffed board, wondering how I was even supposed to keep up. What I did know was that the energy I had right then was way too much to just keep sitting there.

When the bus approached the next stop, I made a gametime decision and slammed the stop button. As soon as the doors slid open, I hopped off, and dropped my board onto the pavement without thinking twice. Skating was the only thing that could burn this off.

I decided to take the long way through Beverlywood. It wasn't my usual route, definitely a little more hilly, but honestly? I needed the challenge. The second I kicked off, the wind slapped against my face, and the music in my ears somehow made it all feel even faster. Like somehow it could help me untangle all the chaos in my head.

Beverlywood was quiet. The streets were smooth but sloping, mostly uphill for the first part—no room for lazy skating here. I could feel my legs already starting to burn, but the rush was worth it. When it got too tough, I hopped off to walk it—or kind of dance it, I guess. I hopped back on when the slope leveled off.

It was just me, my board, and the music—and the algorithm was killing it. Everything else? Gone. And for the first time all day, I felt like I could breathe.

Each house I passed felt like its own little flex with perfectly mowed lawns, oversized windows, and the kind of cars that screamed comfort and money. It was totally different from the chaos and grind of the busier parts of LA—like a whole different world, really. And compared to my own cramped apartment? Yeah, it was like stepping into a dream I wasn't part of yet.

I'd always loved this neighborhood, skating through here when I needed space to think or when the noise of my own life got too loud. It wasn't just the vibe, though. It was this like quiet hope that maybe, someday, I'd actually call one of these places home. A real house, no thin walls, no freeway noise in the background. Just… peace. For now, it was enough to imagine it, letting the smooth pavement and perfect houses carry me through the dream.

I hit this spot at the top of Bagley Avenue where I knew it was all downhill from there. I paused for just a second before I gave the board one strong push.

And then I was flying.

The board rolled faster with every second, the wheels humming against the pavement with the music still blasting in my headphones. The wind was whipping past me, dragging on my hoodie like it was trying to slow me down, but I just leaned into it. The incline was steep enough that I didn't even have to push, just carving side to side to keep control, each turn sharp but smooth. Every crack and dip in the pavement sent a jolt up my legs, keeping me sharp, alive—in it.

Now this was why I skated. It was the rush, the focus. It made everything else—the noise in my head, the what-ifs, the chaos— just fade into the background, drowned out by the sound of my wheels and the music.

As I neared the bottom of the hill, I let out a breath I didn't realize I'd been holding. The adrenaline was still pumping through my veins, but the chaos of the day was left somewhere up the hill behind me.

I jogged up the side alley to the stairs that led to the apartment. I took them two at a time, super pumped.

That stupid lock. Always the same fight. I shoved the key in and jiggled it, trying to hit just the right angle to get it to catch. The scraping sound echoed louder than it should've in the stillness, and, like clockwork, Bandit went off inside. His barks were full-on chaos mode— sharp and wild, bouncing off the walls like he hadn't seen me in days rather than just this morning. It made me laugh under my breath, even though I was still wrestling with the lock.

"Okay, chill! I'm coming!" I called through the door. I twisted the key one more time and the lock finally clicked. I pushed the door open, ready for Bandit's usual assault.

As soon as I stepped in, he bolted toward me, jumping up on my legs, scratching at my pants with his tiny paws. Mateo was on the couch playing FIFA '19—yeah, I know it's like five years old, but it was the last one that works with our old-ass XBox 360. Bro paused his game almost immediately and turned to look at me. "Hey, how was work?" he asked, already walking over to the dining table like some little host-in-training.

That's Mateo for you—always polite, always put-together, like he could've been born wearing a tie or something. His glasses caught the light as he adjusted them, his dark black hair with the old-school Bieber style bangs perfectly sideswept. I dropped my board by the door, kicking my shoes off into the pile we always had near the corner.

"Not bad," I said, messing up his perfect hair. "How's FIFA going?"

He pulled away doing that head shake that seemed to magically straighten out the bangs. He gave a small shrug, like his match against the CPU didn't matter in the grand scheme of things. "Pretty good. Ma left dinner in the oven for us," he said, polite as ever, gesturing toward the kitchen. "Enchiladas."

"Nice," I said, heading toward the oven, already feeling my stomach grumble. "You eat yet?"

"No, I was waiting for you."

Ma didn't always cook Mexican meals. Sometimes it was just straight-up Hamburger Helper—Cheeseburger Macaroni, the best one of course. But every now and then she found a little time to make a dish from scratch, even when she was working crazy hours, just to show she cared.

I paused for a second, glancing back at him. He always did that—waited for me, even when he didn't have to. I always admired how steady he was, how polite and just like... thoughtful. Meanwhile, I could barely keep my emotions in check most days. He made it look so easy, and I envied him for it. I gave him a small smile and said, "Cool, lil bro. Let's eat."

I pulled the baking dish out of the oven and the smell of enchiladas hit me instantly. They were cheesy and spicy, and exactly what I needed after the day I'd had. Mateo was already setting the table, putting out the plates and one of those old cloth swirl hotplates Ma kept in the drawer. He had that focused look he always had, like even setting the table was something he wanted to get a good grade in.

Ma was working another night shift at the hospital—nurse life. She was always running herself ragged, but she still made sure we had dinner ready before she left. Even on days when she wasn't here, she made sure we were taken care of. It was just her thing.

I set the dish down on the hotplate Mateo had lined up perfectly, and he grabbed the forks and napkins, laying them out with the kind of precision only Mateo could manage. "Thanks," I said, dropping into my seat as Bandit trotted over, sniffing around like he was already plotting how to snag a bite.

"Don't even think about it, my man. Your food's over there," I told him pointing at his bowl on the linoleum floor in the kitchen. Bandit whimpered as he walked over to it.

This wasn't some big thing—just the three of us sitting down for dinner—but it had its own kind of vibe, like this tiny pocket of normal that felt steady when the rest of life got messy.

Mateo dished out an enchilada onto his plate. He adjusted his glasses with one hand while balancing the spatula in the other. "So, have you heard about Tsuchinshan-ATLAS?" he asked with that mix of nerdy excitement only Mateo could pull off.

"The what now?" It sounded like he sneezed.

"It's this comet," he said, like I should've already been in the know. "They're saying it might be visible to the naked eye in October. It's super rare—most comets aren't bright enough to see."

"October, huh?" I said, taking another bite but watching him closely. His energy was infectious, and even though I wasn't exactly a space guy, seeing him light up like that got me a little hyped too. "That's cool. You gonna camp out with your telescope or something?"

"Obviously," Mateo said, grinning. "I was already planning where to set up with Hudson and his dad. They said they'd take me to Griffith Park or maybe even farther out. It needs to be a place without a lot of light pollution, which is kind of hard in LA. But it depends on how bright the comet gets."

I nodded, his excitement pulling me in more than I expected. "Sounds like a vibe," I said. "You've been reading up on it a lot?"

"Yeah," he said, his face practically glowing. "This comet has this huge orbit, like 80,000 years. It's crazy to think we're gonna see something that hasn't been around since, like, cave man days."

"Damn," I said, leaning back in my chair. "That's kinda insane to think about."

He nodded fast, going on about the comet's trajectory and how it was discovered. I didn't catch all the details—I really tried—but the way he talked about it made me feel like this space rock was the coolest thing in the world—well the solar system, I guess. Mateo just had this way of making even random space things sound epic.

I wanted to match his energy, but my mind kept drifting to Troye and the invite to LACMA. I didn't know why I was holding back from talking to Mateo about it. It wasn't like I thought he wouldn't be cool with it. It was probably because I wanted him to see me as someone steady, someone he could look up to. Or maybe it was the whole "man of the house" thing, like I needed to keep my personal stuff in check to focus on being responsible and all that.

Both reasons felt kind of dumb, but either way, I stayed quiet, nodding along as Mateo kept going about the comet. And honestly? Watching him get so hyped about something made me forget about my own stuff for a second.

As we wrapped up dinner, I grabbed the baking dish to throw the leftovers into some foil while Mateo was over at the sink scrubbing the plates. Bandit was still lurking, tail wagging, like maybe I'd drop something his way. Spoiler alert: not happening.

"They're doing a drone show in Culver City," Mateo said, not even looking up as he rinsed a plate.

"A drone show?"

"Yeah." Mateo said kinda quietly. "Instead of the fireworks show. They said on the news that it was better for the dogs and the environment."

At least Bandit wouldn't be freaking out. The night before was the Fourth of July, and he had a rough night, even though it was just people in the neighborhood, nothing professional. I guessed Culver decided to do their show a day later to get a better crowd, it being Friday and all.

"Man, a fireworks show without fireworks. Welcome to the twenty-first century. I hate it." I deadpanned, sliding the covered dish into the fridge. "I wonder if we can still see them from the window."

Mateo just shrugged, dropping a fork into the drying rack. He was quiet—and I knew why.

"What time are they supposed to start?"

"Probably soon. It's almost nine," he said, still looking at the sink.

I leaned against the counter, wiping sauce off my thumb with a paper towel. No way we were making it and Ma would freak if I took Mateo out at this time of night. "Tell you what, kiddo. How 'bout I make some popcorn and we see if we can catch them from the bedroom window."

Mateo turned slightly, giving me a sick side-eye like he was surprised I actually had a good idea. He cracked a smile and said, "Yeah, that sounds fun."

"Bet!" I said, chucking the towel onto the counter and heading for the cabinet. "Go clear off the desk, I'll handle the popcorn."

Mateo laughed, shaking his head as he turned back to finish up at the sink. It was such a small thing, but it felt good, you know? Just us doing our thing.

A few minutes later I walked into our room with the popcorn bowl in hand, the buttery smell already taking over. Mateo had cleared off the desk between our beds, shoving aside the usual chaos—his notebooks, a tangle of chargers, and a couple of my skate mags. He had turned the lights out and perched on top of it, cross-legged in his pajamas, his glasses catching the dim light from outside as he stared out the window.

"Anything yet?" I asked, plopping the bowl down next to him and hopping up onto the desk. It wobbled a little under me, but, like always, it held.

"Nah, not yet," Mateo said, still locked on the view out over the freeway. The room was quiet except for the usual hum of the under-window AC unit, the traffic, and the crunch of popcorn as Mateo grabbed a handful.

I scanned the sky for anything even close to a spark.

"Maybe we can't see them from here," Mateo said, breaking the silence.

"They could just be running late," I said, nudging him with my elbow. He smirked, but his eyes stayed on the horizon. I kept looking too, even though nothing was happening yet. Something about the stillness felt kind of nice, like the build-up was part of it—but it also meant we weren't talking about what Mateo wanted to talk about.

My phone chimed in my pocket. I pulled it out, the screen lighting up with a DM notification. My stomach did this tiny flip as I opened it.

 Thanks for the follow-back Skater Boy 😏

Short. Flirty. Just enough to make my brain short-circuit again. I stared at the message, my thumb hovering over the keyboard like I was about to type—but nope. I locked my phone and shoved it back in my pocket instead. Right now, I was here with my brother, and that felt like the move.

Bandit jumped from Mateo's bed onto the desk with us. He sat for a moment looking out the window, probably wondering what we were looking at. When he turned around he looked at both of us before he made his move, snatching a whole mouthful of popcorn, before he bolted off the desk and out of the room like the little furry criminal he was.

And yeah—that's exactly how he got his name. Bandit. Not for the raccoon mask pattern on his face. It's because he steals *everything*—socks, food, you name it. Once, he jacked a whole slice of pizza off Mateo's plate like it was nothing.

"No!" I yelled in my deep you-did-something-bad voice. Last time he ate a half a bowl of popcorn when we weren't looking—let's just say he left a mess like all over the house. After that, I wasn't about to deal with that again.

Mateo suddenly leaned forward, practically pressing his face to the glass. "Wait, I think it's starting!" he said, pointing toward the skyline.

I followed his gaze, squinting past the trees and rooftops, and then I saw them—tiny lights rose into the air, glowing steady as they moved in sync—at least a hundred of them, floating like they were pulled by invisible strings.

"Yo, that's kinda dope," I said as I sat up straighter. The drones blinked out, then reappeared spelling Culver City in bright red and white. Mateo let out this little whoa.

The letters morphed into a waving American flag, every stripe glowing like it was caught in real wind. Then came an eagle, wings outstretched in glowing white, before that shifted into a giant red high heel. I tilted my head—confused—until it turned into a cloud, then a rainbow burst out of it.

"Oh," I said, grinning. "Wizard of Oz. Ruby slipper. Get it?"

Mateo laughed. His eyes were locked on the show. More shapes followed, like glowing faces, maybe old movie stars I didn't recognize? Then, in bright purple script, they spelled out "I Love Lucy."

Random, I thought but also kind of iconic.

The next part had all the drones coming together into a yellow-red cube that just kinda spun in the air, then turned white and dropped away row by row, like stars fading out.

"That's it?" I said, kind of surprised. It felt short—maybe ten minutes tops—but the designs were definitely clean.

"Looks like it, but it was sick," Mateo said, his face lit up. "Like, how do they even do that? The programming must be insane."

"No clue," I said, tossing a kernel of popcorn into my mouth. "But whoever's behind it? *Respect*."

Mateo went quiet after that, staring out the window like he was still hoping for an encore. Then, out of nowhere, he said, "Do you remember when Dad used to take us to see the fireworks?"

I froze for half a second, not expecting that.

"Yeah," I said, my voice softer. "I remember."

It used to be a whole thing. Dad would load us up with tacos and churros from the food trucks and find the perfect spot to spread out a blanket. There'd be live music blasting in the background, and he'd lift Mateo onto his shoulders so he could see everything. It was loud and messy and perfect.

"They canceled it in 2019," Mateo said, staring out the window. "The construction at the college."

"And then COVID," I added. "2020, 2021..."

"And then..." Mateo trailed off, but he didn't need to finish. We both knew the rest. After that, Dad was gone.

The air felt heavier, like the room was holding its breath. I wanted to say something—anything—but nothing felt right. So I just sat there next to Mateo.

After a minute, Mateo broke the silence, "Thanks for doing this with me, Kiko."

I messed with his hair again. "Of course, kiddo. I got you."

"I'm gonna go take Bandit out," Mateo said as my phone buzzed again in my pocket.

"Okay, but only right in front," I said, "Don't let him drag you on a full walk."

"I know. It's late," Mateo said in a way that had just a hint of the verbal equivalent of an eyeroll.

I grinned a little. I probably have done the same to Ma—and Dad—a million times. Now here I was on the receiving end. The kid was growing up so fast.

When my phone buzzed again, I pulled it out. Another message from Troye. He'd sent the time and details for the LACMA hangout—Sunday afternoon, the exact spot to meet, all laid out like he was already planning the perfect day. I stared at the screen for a second, my thumb hovering, as I ran through all the options for a response before typing out a quick "Sounds good" followed by a winking emoji? No, I decided to go with an upside-down smiley instead and hit send. I instantly regretted it. What even is the upside-down smiley for? Nervous energy? Mild derangement? Accidental thirst?

I sprawled out across my bed, one foot still on the floor, and rubbed my face hard with both hands.

It is what it is now.

Mateo came back in a couple minutes later.

"Think I'm gonna crash, lil bro," I said, stifling a yawn. "Trying to hit the waves early tomorrow before work."

Mateo glanced over, nodding like he was already halfway there himself. "Yeah. Probably a good call. Good night, Kiko."

"Good night, lil bro."

We both shuffled into bed. Mateo pulled his sheet up to his chin. He was already fading fast like he always did. I popped my phone on the charger that snaked out from behind my bed and placed it down on the floor.

Just as I was starting to drift, my phone lit up and gave another chime. Then another. I groaned as I reached for it, squinting at the screen and the notifications… like a ton of them… and all from Troye.

He'd gone full stalker mode, liking every single post on my feed. *Every. Single. One.* From the skate clips to my blurry sunset shots to the random photo of Bandit from last Christmas.

What the fuck? I thought, staring at the wall of heart notifications. But then again, maybe this was just how things went. Didn't have a lot of experience after all. Maybe this was just how people showed interest or started something, right? Right?

Before I could overthink it too much, another message popped up.

 Love your feed. Pics are

I laughed under my breath, rolling my eyes but smiling at the same time.

Okay, Troye, two can play this game.

Opening his profile, I went on a liking spree of my own. All the artsy prints, the stylish selfies, the random shot of him with some huge coffee cup—it all got double-tapped. The little hearts filled the screen as I scrolled, the glow of the phone lighting up the dark room.

When I finally locked my phone and set it back down, I couldn't stop smiling. Yeah, it was weird.

But maybe weird was okay.

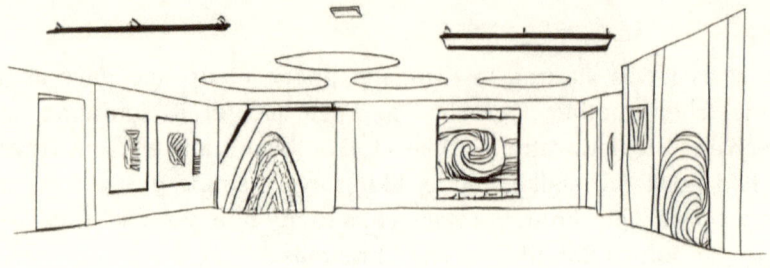

8

I was standing outside LACMA, trying not to feel like the most out-of-place person there. The whole area was buzzing—tourists everywhere, taking pics in front of that forest of street lamps. Insta gold. There were influencers striking their best *I'm-not-trying-too-hard* poses, and couples holding hands...

Meanwhile, I was low-key stressing. I'd messed with my hair for way too long this morning, and now it felt like it was doing its own thing. I tugged at my charcoal button-down, smoothing out imaginary wrinkles for the millionth time. I thought the outfit looked fire when I left—fitted shirt, good jeans—but now, looking at everyone else in oversized hoodies and comfortable fits, I felt like I'd completely misread the vibe.

I checked my phone for what had to be the seventeenth time. One fifteen. Troye said twelve thirty. Still no DM, no text, no nothing. I popped into Insta again, hoping for a clue, but nope. Just radio silence.

I told myself it was fine—this was LA after all. Traffic's a nightmare, parking's impossible, maybe he just got caught up. But that little twinge of disappointment? Yeah, it was creeping in—*fast*. I fiddled with my shirt again, trying to play it cool, but inside I was starting to feel like a clown for being this excited about something—or someone—that wasn't even showing up.

The longer I stood there, the more I couldn't help but feeling like a total idiot. I leaned against a pillar, trying to look all chill and stuff, but my eyes kept scanning the crowd. Every time someone walked through the entrance, I half-expected it to be Troye. Spoiler: it wasn't. The excitement I'd felt this morning? Yeah, that was officially running on fumes. Each minute felt like it was stretching out just to mess with me.

After checking my phone for what was probably the billionth time, I gave up and decided to wander around. I ended up at the back of the museum, where this massive rock was just floating above this path, propped up on the concrete walls. I walked under it, staring up at the thing, and yeah, it was giving me some serious main character energy.

But honestly? It hit just different. The whole "giant rock barely hanging there" vibe felt a little too relatable right then. I was fine, but also… not fine. Like, yeah, everything's good for now, but what happens if it all comes crashing down?

My phone chimed. I yanked it out of my pocket so fast you'd think it was an exploding vape pen or something.

 Hey, sorry. Running late, the Uber guy got lost.

Relief hit first, but there was still this weird knot just like sitting in my chest. I checked the time and it was one thirty seven. Okay, so he was late, and sure it was like super late, but at least he wasn't ghosting me, right?

I typed back a quick, "All good, see you soon," and shoved my phone back in my pocket. I was so trying to convince myself this was still gonna be worth it.

I passed this group of kids in matching neon camp shirts. They were climbing all over the concrete walls like it was some type of jungle gym instead of a museum until a security guard came over all, "*Off the walls, guys. Let's keep it chill.*"

The kids groaned but climbed down. A couple of them moved on to whatever chaos they could cause next—man, I wish I was that age again. I watched them for a second but not really paying attention as my brain kept spinning back to Troye.

By the time two thirty hit, I was done. My excitement was officially dead, replaced by that awful feeling where you start convincing yourself you got played. Was he even coming? Or was this one of those moments where I'd walk away feeling like the dumbest person alive?

I was like literally two seconds from calling it quits when my phone chimed. Another DM from Troye:

 Here. Sorry, took forever.

I stared at the screen, my emotions doing this weird dance between being relieved and super annoyed. Late as hell, but he was here. I shoved my phone back in my pocket, exhaled hard, and made my way to the ticket booth in the big outdoor lobby area. My thoughts were all over the place.

Troye was impossible to miss. That bleached blonde hair, styled like he had just come from the salon, practically glowed under the sunlight. He had on a camo tee that somehow looked expensive, AirPods in, and those same massive sunglasses from the other day. As I got closer, this wave of his cologne hit me, all sharp and expensive, and yeah, I hated that I didn't hate it.

He spotted me and popped out one AirPod, flashing this grin that instantly made me forget I'd been stewing over how late he was. "Hey, sorry I'm so late," he said, his voice light but legit. "Can't believe you actually waited."

I shrugged, trying to play it cool even though part of me wanted to snap. "No problem."

He adjusted this huge portfolio bag slung over his shoulder like it was just another accessory.

"Shall we?" he asked.

"Yeah, cool," I said, the irritation already fading. He was way too easygoing, and somehow it made me forget I'd been half-convinced he was gonna flake.

We walked up to the ticket booth under the big open-air lobby. "Two tickets," Troye said, smiling at me. "LA resident student rate."

"Sorry, but you gotta check that bag. It's too big for the museum," the clerk said, pointing at the giant bag slung over Troye's shoulder.

Troye's face dropped into are-you-kidding-me mode.

"I've brought this in before," he said. "Can you check with someone?"

"No large bags," the clerk replied, motioning toward the giant sign.

Troye let out a sharp breath. "How am I supposed to carry my sketch pad?"

"You can take the pad—just not the bag."

His jaw tensed, and yeah, he was two seconds from popping off.

I slid in before it got worse, touching his arm. "It's fine—I can carry it for you."

He looked at me, still annoyed, then sighed and gave in.

"Fine," he muttered, handing the bag to the clerk and the sketch pad to me like it weighed fifty pounds.

With that handled, we stuck our little visitor stickers on and started down the walkway toward the museum. I could feel Troye's mood still simmering next to me, but at least we weren't about to get into a full-blown scene over a bag. Crisis averted.

"I just need to sketch one sculpture, then we can wander around and vibe," Troye said, his tone was back to light and easy. "Half an hour tops. I'll grab some pics and finish the rest later."

The Broad Contemporary Art Museum building loomed to our left— modern and massive, all glass and clean lines. The outdoor escalator leading up to the entrance was shut down, a bright Out of Service sign parked right in front. Troye let out this exaggerated sigh, like the universe was personally out to inconvenience him.

"Guess it's the stairs," I said, nodding at the two sets of stairs climbing the side of the front of the building.

Troye stopped in his tracks, pulling off his sunglasses in mock horror. "And risk becoming a sweaty mess? Absolutely not," he said, deadpan, before flashing a wink my way.

And just like that, my face was on fire. His eyes were this warm, rich brown, lighter than mine—and way more distracting. Like, get-lost-in-them level distracting. I had to look away before my brain completely scrambled.

We moved past the stairs and into the glass-covered lobby, and got on the small line for the elevator. A security guard was trying to keep the entrance clear for those getting off.

As soon as we hit the third floor, Troye took off like he had been there a thousand times. I followed, trying to keep up while the galleries blurred around me. Paintings, sculptures, all kinds of art flashed by— some classic-looking, some super abstract, and some that just looked like someone spilled a bucket of paint and called it a day. None of it even fazed Troye. He didn't slow down or give anything a second glance.

Meanwhile, I was back here wondering why I didn't pay more attention in art history class. I'd never planned on needing it, but now? Now I wished I had something smart to say instead of just pointing and going, "That's nice."

We walked into this gallery that was practically glowing. Sunlight spilled in through the glass ceiling, lighting up everything in this golden haze. My attention went straight to this massive painting on the far wall—it was wild. It looked like an explosion frozen mid-boom, streaks of color shooting out in every direction. It was totally giving supernova vibes, and I couldn't stop staring at it.

But Troye had a mission. He took his sketchpad from me and parked himself in front of a sculpture in the middle of the room. The sculpture was... chaotic, to say the least. Twisted metal all smashed together—

industrial grays, streaks of yellow, deep blues. It looked like a junkyard and a rainbow had a fight, but it worked in this weird way. Troye started sketching, completely in the zone like the rest of the world didn't even exist.

His pencil was already moving like it had a mind of its own. Watching him work was kind of hypnotic—like he was locked into some secret rhythm that only he could hear. I couldn't help stealing glances, but I didn't want to seem like I was just standing there gawking. So, I let my attention wander, pretending to be calm while my brain was doing cartwheels.

Museums? Definitely not my usual scene. As a kid, they were just excuses to get out of school on a class trip and mess around with friends. But now? Being here with all this art—especially with him— was kind of different. The space felt heavier, like it actually meant something if you gave it a second to sink in.

I walked a slow circle around the sculpture Troye was sketching, careful not to block his view. The label read *Sweet William* by John Chamberlain. Up close, it was all chaos—twisted metal in smashed-up colors, but somehow it looked right. When I crossed to the other side, I caught Troye sneaking a glance at me. He gave this quick smile before going back to his drawing, and yeah, my brain short-circuited for a second.

I wandered back to the painting that had grabbed my attention earlier—*The Jewell* by Jay DeFeo. It hit different up close. The paint was so thick it looked like it was one of those 3D maps with mountains and valleys. Bright rays of white exploded out from the center, fading into purples, reds, and oranges that seemed to glow. It was insane. I swear it was begging me to touch it, but I wasn't about to risk being the guy who set off some alarm that would bring security running or something. Still, I just couldn't look away, because the whole thing was just… wild.

I glanced back and caught Troye watching me, his eyes clear and sharp, like he was reading something I didn't even know I was putting out. He smiled, easy and warm, and it hit me right in the chest. I smiled back, heat creeping up my neck as I stepped into the next gallery, needing a second to breathe. This stupid smile was all over my face.

The centerpiece of this room was impossible to miss—this massive wall-to-wall canvas that felt like it was about to swallow me whole. It was chaos in the best way. Machine parts twisted up with smoke, ghostly shapes of people, and flames tearing through it all. It wasn't just what was on it, though—it was the way it moved. Like the whole thing was alive and dragging me into its madness. It was heavy, like it was daring me to look deeper and feel everything at once.

I sat down on a bench in the middle of the room, letting it all sink in, trying to untangle what it was making me feel. After a while, I glanced back at the other room where Troye was still sketching, completely locked in. That's when I noticed this painting that I'd totally skipped over earlier.

It was bold as hell—this deep red canvas with two darker red rectangles sandwiching a bright white one in the middle. It was impossible to ignore, and I had no idea how I'd missed it before. Curious, I wandered back in for a closer look.

White Center by Mark Rothko, the label read. The description went on about transcendent truths and meditative responses, and I couldn't help but laugh under my breath. To me, it just looked like a giant Do Not Enter sign. Still, I stared at it longer than I meant to—like it was trying to tell me something, but whatever.

"That should do," Troye said out of nowhere, making me jump a little. He laughed, soft and teasing, and walked over to *The Jewell*, stopping right in front of it. "You seemed pretty taken with this one," he said, his voice low and smooth, like he was in on some secret.

"Yeah," I said, "it's pretty fire."

Troye tilted his head, studying the painting like he was trying to crack a code. First, he leaned in close, his eyes tracing every line and ridge of texture. Then he stepped back a few feet, arms crossed, tilting his chin up like he was sizing it up for something important.

"So what about it is pulling you in?" he asked, his voice curious, like he actually cared about my answer.

I shrugged, feeling a little self-conscious. "Not really sure," I said, trying to find the words. "I guess it's the texture of it. Like, how rough and layered it is… It kinda reminds me of a supernova."

Troye's brows furrowed, and he gave me this sideways glance. "A supernova?" he asked.

"Yeah," I said, warming up a bit. "It's like when a massive star dies. It collapses in on itself and creates this giant explosion, lighting up brighter than an entire galaxy. But only for a little while—it's like its final, epic fireworks show before it goes out for good."

Troye's lips quirked into a half-smile. "And you got all that from this painting?"

I laughed, scratching at the back of my neck. "Nah, I got all that from YouTube. But I guess this thing just kinda… brought it out of me."

Troye chuckled. "Alright, supernova boy. What about this one?" Troye asked, nodding at the sculpture he'd just been sketching. He walked up to it, tilting his head like he was waiting for it to give him some deep, hidden meaning. "What do you see?"

I paused, trying to pin down the right words. "I guess it's a bit…"

"…messy?" Troye cut in, his voice casual but a little dismissive.

"No," I said quickly. "I mean, yeah, but…"

"It looks like a car crash," Troye said, his tone this weird mix of fascination and low-key disgust.

That threw me. I hadn't expected him to just dunk on it like that. Sure, it was chaotic, but there was something more, something raw and intense that felt… important. Beautiful, even. I didn't think he'd see it that way, though.

"I don't know," I said, shifting awkwardly. He was the art guy, after all. "I think it's kind of… beautiful."

Troye looked at the sculpture again, then back at me, his brows lifting just a little, like he hadn't expected that. "Huh," he said finally, his tone neutral but maybe a little intrigued.

"I'm more into figure drawing," he added with a shrug. "My professor's making me branch out or whatever. Build my portfolio and all, but hey," he said, "you wanna wander around?"

"Sure," I said, following Troye as we doubled back through the gallery.

"So, what do you do for fun, Kiko?" Troye asked, his tone playful but genuinely curious.

Was that the first time he said my actual name?

I shrugged, trying not to sound basic. "Uh, skateboarding, surfing… I'm always listening to music, too."

"Skating *and* surfing," Troye repeated, like he was testing how it sounded in his mouth. "You're just a regular Cali boy, aren't you?"

I laughed, feeling a little called out. "Yeah, I guess so. What about you? Where are you from?"

Troye stopped walking, turning to me with this look I couldn't quite read. "What makes you think I'm not from here?" His tone wasn't sharp exactly, but there was something behind it, like a wall going up.

I hesitated, feeling like I'd struck a nerve or something. "Uh, I mean, no one from here really says 'Cali,' so I figured maybe you're from somewhere else?"

Troye's lips pulled into this half-smile that didn't quite reach his eyes. After a second, he said, "Iowa. Davenport, Iowa."

I blinked. "That's, uh… definitely a change of scene."

Troye let out a short laugh, but it was more like a scoff. "A whole other planet really. Came out here for fame and fortune. Stayed for the sunshine—and the cute surfer boys."

I grinned, rolling with his sudden mood shift. "I mean, there's a million of those out here."

"Yeah," Troye said, smirking just a little. "But most of them aren't as interesting as you."

My face heated up instantly, and I tried to play it cool, smirking at Troye like this was all normal and not completely messing with my head. "Oh, so you're saying I'm something special?"

"Very special," Troye said. His voice dropped into this low, like intimate tone that, yeah—it was doing something. "I knew it the second I saw you outside that coffee shop."

My heart did this weird little flutter thing, and I had to look away. I had this grin that I was absolutely fighting for my life to keep in check. "You're just saying that," I mumbled. I was trying to sound all casual, but my voice literally cracked.

"No, I'm serious," he said, and then I felt it—a light brush of his fingers against my arm. Barely anything, but it sent static straight up to my brain. "There's something about you, Kiko. You just feel so… real. Like you're not trying to be anyone but you."

Real. The word hit like a sucker punch. Lately, I didn't feel real at all. Everything felt like I was faking it—faking confidence, pretending I had my life together. Hell, even faking like I wasn't freaking out about standing there with Troye, who somehow thought I was worth his time. Was *he* for real? Or was this just his thing, saying all the right words to get what he wanted?

I peeked over at him, trying to read his face. His eyes—those brown eyes I couldn't stop trying to steal glances at—were steady on mine. His smile wasn't smug or forced. It was warm, like he was waiting for me to believe him. Maybe he did see something in me I couldn't even see in myself.

I bit my lip and my heart was pounding in my chest. "You really think that? Because honestly… sometimes I feel like I'm just lost, like I don't even know who I am half the time."

Troye's smile softened, and his hand stayed on my arm like he was holding me steady. "I get that," he said, his voice quieter now. "But that's what I mean. Who even says stuff like that in LA? Everyone's busy trying to look perfect, and you're just… you. That's real. It's

81

refreshing."

I glanced down, my cheeks going full red alert. "Thanks," I muttered, feeling like my voice was about two octaves lower than usual.

Troye stepped closer, closing the tiny gap between us. "Hey," he said softly, tilting my chin up with just his finger. His touch was barely there, but it sent shockwaves through me. "Don't hide."

My breath caught. The moment felt too big. I didn't know if I felt exposed or seen, but either way, it was hitting me hard. The self-doubt I'd been dragging around started to loosen its grip, replaced by this weird, overwhelming warmth spreading in my chest.

"Now," Troye said, his tone switching back to playful, "how about we keep this adventure going? There's a whole museum to get through, and I've got so much more to learn about you."

I raised an eyebrow, trying to act chill even though I definitely wasn't. "You already know way more about me than I do about you."

"Well," he said with a smirk, "why don't we save that for the second date."

"Oh, so you've got plans for me now?" I shot back, my voice only shaking a little.

Troye stepped back just enough to give me a slow, exaggerated once-over, like I was one of the sculptures or paintings that surrounded us. His mouth pulled into this thoughtful, slightly smug smile. "I think I can work with it."

I laughed nervously, shoving my hands in my back pockets to keep them from fidgeting. "Not sure if I should be excited or terrified."

Troye leaned in, his voice dropping low, right by my ear. He was so close I could feel his breath on my neck, and I swear goosebumps shot down my arm.

"Both," he whispered.

And yeah—I was officially done for.

9

The ocean breeze was cool on my face as I cruised down the boardwalk, my board humming on the concrete like it was trying to do its best to drown out the noise in my head. The place was its usual chaotic self, but I was barely paying attention. I couldn't stop dwelling on my date with Troye. Four days, and it was not just living rent-free in my brain—it felt like it evicted everything else.

It went *really* well. Troye was funny, cute, and had this effortlessly cool vibe that was impossible to ignore. But then there was that moment at the end, where we were standing in the middle of that collection of streetlamps out front. His eyes just like lingered on mine and he bit his lower lip. And me? I panicked. Full-on folded. Instead of going for it or doing literally anything cool, I went for the friendliest hug in the history of hugs and hit him with a, "See ya later," like we were gym bros.

Now every kick of my foot against the pavement was just me trying to skate away from the cringe. He was *totally* expecting a kiss. He had to be, right? And I blew it. Big time. What if he thought I wasn't into him? What if I wrecked my shot? The questions swirled in my brain louder than the guy playing *Wonderwall* on a busted guitar across from one of the tattoo parlors.

I dodged a couple holding hands and sighed, leaning into the turn. Venice was its usual mess of chaos, but all I could think about was Troye and that *almost* moment. Did I overthink the whole thing? Probably. Would I stop? Not a chance.

I rolled past one of those "Walk Your Bike" notices on the boardwalk, the ones they painted like they were supposed to be read bottom to top as you rode over them—like people were actually gonna pay attention. Except the words were way too close together, so my brain always read it as "Bike Your Walk." Classic Venice. Made me smirk, though, a little break in the endless Troye overthinking spiral.

Up ahead, the crowd thinned out, and I spotted this dude in a totally fire vintage fit—dark denim jacket, red pinstripe shirt, and olive green corduroy bell bottoms that somehow worked. Like, he looked like he walked out of a Fleetwood Mac album cover, but in the best way. He was handing out papers to anyone who'd take them.

There was only one person I knew who would dress like that at the beach in July—it had to be Dylan. No way. Of all people. I kicked off, gliding closer, low-key curious what he was doing. He handed a flyer to this lady walking her tiny dog, giving her a quick smile before moving on.

He stopped by a black construction wall, in between two rows of giant posters advertising a bunch of Las Vegas concerts, and started taping up one of his flyers.

I rolled up, slowing just enough to pop the board into my hand. "Hey," I said, feeling oddly nervous for no reason.

Dylan glanced over, giving me a small grin, like he wasn't the least bit surprised to see me. "Hey," he replied casually, his tone almost like we'd planned to meet up or something.

"Funny running into you here," I said.

"I actually saw you earlier, down by Muscle Beach, but you looked like you were… deep in thought."

My cheeks heated up a little, caught off guard. "Oh, uh… yeah," I said, scratching the back of my neck. "I've got a lot of stuff going on."

Dylan nodded, his expression impossible to read. "Figured," he said simply, like he knew exactly what was on my mind. He glanced at my board, then back at me. "How's the coffee thing going?"

I shrugged, trying to play it cool even though I suddenly felt under some weird spotlight. "It's fine. I mean, it's a job, right? Decent tips, plenty of caffeine."

Dylan smirked. "I bet," he said.

"What're your flyers for?" I asked, looking at the multicolored flyer on the wall for the first time.

Dylan tapped the stack of flyers in his hand. "I'm pushing this Open Mic Night at the thrift shop I work at next week. It's an LGBTQ+ event. All kinds of talent—poetry, music, stand-up. You should swing by."

"Oh, cool," I said, even though my brain kind of froze for a second. An LGBTQ+ event? Was Dylan…? I'd never thought about him that way, but now that he said it, I wondered how I'd missed it. Or maybe I was overthinking. Either way, the gears in my head felt jammed.

"That's cool," I added, probably a little too quickly.

Dylan nodded, peeling off a flyer from the stack and holding it out. His hand was steady, like this was just another moment for him, while I suddenly felt like I was trying to land a trick I wasn't ready for. I hesitated for half a second before taking the flyer. My hand brushed his, and it felt weirdly significant, like it shouldn't have meant anything but maybe did.

"Uh... allies are welcome, too," he said, throwing in a grin that felt both casual and confused, like he was trying to figure me out.

"Oh... no, I'm uh..." My brain scrambled for footing. "Sure, that would be cool," I finished, my voice quieter than I meant it to be. My heart was racing, but I wasn't about to unpack why with Dylan right here on the boardwalk.

Dylan raised an eyebrow, and for a moment, making it clear I wasn't the only one picking up on the awkwardness, but he just nodded and went back to his usual coolness. "Anyway," he said, flipping the tape roll into his jacket pocket, "I was about to grab a boba from that spot up on the next block. You in?"

I froze for half a second, then nodded, trying to sound casual. "Yeah, sure. Why not?"

I tucked the flyer into my pocket. As we walked toward the boba place, my head spun with questions I wasn't ready to ask, least of all to myself. But the idea that maybe if Dylan actually was... gay, or bi, or whatever... having a friend who could actually help me sort out this... whatever it was with Troye might not be so bad—but that meant actually being able to get a complete sentence out without my brain turning to mush.

Dylan stepped up to the walk-up window, the touchscreen glowing faintly in the afternoon sun. He scrolled through the menu like he worked there before tapping in his order: jasmine milk tea, boba, fifty percent sweet. "Gotta stay balanced," he joked as he hit confirm, stepping to the side.

He glanced back at me, holding up his card. "Your turn. My treat."

"Nah, it's cool. I got it," I said quickly, but Dylan gave me this look, like he wasn't about to argue. He tilted his head, this grin tugging at his lips. "Let me, Kiko. Think of it as a small poem in liquid form."

I blinked at him, caught off guard but kind of impressed. "Okay, fine," I said, sliding up to the screen and scrolling through the options. I picked a Galaxy Iced Tea, no boba—because seriously, the texture was *not* it—and stepped back to wait with him.

The boba shop wasn't busy, just a couple of tourists taking selfies with their drinks and a guy in workout gear furiously texting. Just then my phone went berserk. Chime after chime came in rapid fire. It could only be Rafe. I pulled out my phone to see, and sure enough:

	Rafe (My BFF 🛹)	Just Now
	Yo, Kiko, where you at?	

	Rafe (My BFF 🛹)	Just Now
	Zay said he saw you down by the boardwalk	

	Rafe (My BFF 🛹)	Just Now
	Still around? Let's skate	

Reading through them made my chest tighten a little. Dylan must've noticed because he asked, "Everything good?"

I glanced up at him, his expression calm but curious, and nodded quickly. "Yeah, just Rafe being Rafe," I said, holding up my phone like it explained everything. "Wants to meet up or something."

Dylan leaned against the side of the window, folding his arms and watching me with that same unreadable half-smile. "You gonna go?"

"I don't know," I admitted, tucking my phone back in my pocket. "I'm just gonna chill for a bit, you know? I'll hit him up later."

He nodded, like he got it. "Fair."

As we waited for our drinks, my eyes drifted toward the beach. Out there, bold as anything, was one of those classic lifeguard towers, but this one was painted like a giant Pride flag. Red, orange, yellow, green, blue, purple—straight-up screaming, "Here I am, deal with it." It was dope, for sure, but it also hit me in a weird way.

Like, Venice is all super chill, all about self-expression. And yet, why did it still feel impossible for me to just... say it? To stop hiding this thing that's been sitting in my chest like a fucking rock? I zoned out, letting the weight of it all press down for a second.

When I snapped to, I looked at Dylan thinking he would probably think I was bugging or something. But he was just standing there too, this little smile on his face—not like a judgy one... just like kind or something.

"Where'd you go?" Dylan said like he was just curious or checking in.

"Oh," I said, fumbling to sound normal, casual, whatever. "Nowhere. Just… got distracted."

He nodded, not pushing. "Gotcha," he said, his tone easy, like he was giving me space to breathe.

The lady inside the window slid our drinks onto the counter with a smile. Dylan's was a cream color with a layer of dark boba pearls at the bottom. Mine? A layer of purple, layer of red, and these little star-shaped mango chunks in the bottom. Dylan handed me mine with a small flourish, his grin widening. "There you go—your starry sonnet."

I couldn't help but laugh, even as I shook my head. "Just wow."

"I aim to please," he responded, and we both sipped our drinks, the moment turned into something easy and familiar like the night on Avery's balcony.

As we sipped our drinks, this dude came out of nowhere with a stack of CDs in his hand, like he was ready to drop the next big thing. He had this chill vibe, not pushy, and nodded at us like he'd known us forever.

"Yo, check out my mixtape?" he asked, holding one out toward Dylan.

Dylan gave him a polite smile. "I'm good, man. Thanks, though."

I followed Dylan's lead. "Same. Appreciate it, though."

"I'm just tryna make you better," he said, totally unbothered, then spotted a group of girls walking by and pivoted, already pitching it to them.

Dylan let out a soft laugh, shaking his head. "Gotta respect the hustle, huh?"

"For real," I said, and we started walking again.

"So," I asked after a moment, breaking the silence, "does the thrift shop have Open Mic nights a lot?"

"Nah, this is actually the first one," Dylan said, glancing at me before taking another sip. "Me and some friends started it at this coffee shop on Melrose a while back. No shade, I haven't been to your coffee shop yet. Gotta make a trip sometime."

"Of course!" I said.

"After that shop closed, I managed to talk my boss into hosting it at the thrift store."

"That's dope," I said, genuinely impressed. "So, you're like the organizer of the whole thing?"

He gave a little shrug, smirking. "Guess you could say that. I'm kind of the leader of our little band of misfits."

Dylan laughed, the kind that was light but genuine. It pulled a grin out of me too as we kept walking, the area buzzing around us. This woman sprawled out in the patchy grass next to the boardwalk caught my eye. She had a bunch of bags around her and looked like she'd had a long day—or a long life, honestly. She was probably in her 20s, but the sun and whatever else had her looking closer to fifty. She squinted up at us, like she was just waking up from a nap, and her eyes locked onto my drink.

"What is that?" she asked, pointing at it.

"Oh, it's from the boba place back there," I explained, tilting the cup so the purple and red was on full display. "Galaxy Iced Tea. Pretty good."

"Yeah, boba's funky," she said, scrunching her nose. "But *that*? That looks good."

Dylan and I laughed, and I told her, "It is. You should try it."

She gave me a thumbs up before flopping back down into the grass, done with the conversation as quickly as it started.

Dylan and I just laughed and walked on sipping our drinks like we were in some mellow indie movie where nothing actually happens but the vibes are on point. My hand brushed his once and I flinched.

It was just skin, Kiko. Chill.

Sure having Dylan as a friend would help, but as he walked a little ahead in that vintage fit, I started to think about something more. And when he turned to look at me—just a glance—and my brain being the traitor that it is, immediately went off-script.

For some reason I imagined him holding my hand. I imagined pulling him in. Not dramatic, not fireworks or whatever. Just his mouth on mine, warm and slow and easy, like we already knew how. Like we'd done it before.

I blinked and probably looked like I got something in my eye. My heart did this glitchy little flutter, and I had to check myself real quick. Because—um, hello?—I literally just went on a date with *Troye*. This actual heartthrob Troye, who was hot and confident and weirdly good at making me feel like I was those things too.

But Dylan was different. He didn't make me feel like I was things I was not. He just made me feel like I could be who I was. And who I was at this moment was having a whole-ass fantasy about kissing Dylan on this random Thursday.

He looked back again, probably wondering why I was walking like I forgot how legs work. I gave him a quick smile—too quick, probably—

and hoped he couldn't see the whole mini-movie that just played in my head. There was no way someone like Dylan could be into me.

I swear to God, my brain needs adult supervision sometimes.

"So, the Open Mic," I said, trying to recover. "Are you performing?"

Dylan grinned. "Maybe. Depends on the vibe. It's more about giving other people a space, you know? But yeah—I usually end up reading at least a poem."

"Cool," I said.

"Guess you'll have to come and find out," he said, his tone teasing. Then he slowed down, checking his watch. "I should get back to handing these out. Wanna spread the word you know? Make sure we get a decent crowd."

I nodded, feeling a little bummed the hangout was ending. "For sure. I'll definitely see you there. I'm in."

Dylan smiled, "Awesome. I'll hold you to that." We exchanged a handshake that turned into a bro hug. And with that, he veered off, heading back with his stack of posters to his own street hustle. I watched him for a second before turning back toward the direction of home, patting the flyer in my pocket to make sure it was still there.

As I cruised toward Venice Boulevard, I yanked the flyer out of my pocket, and unfolded it. "Out Loud: LGBTQ+ Open Mic Night," it read in big, artsy letters, promising "Vibes, Community, and Creativity." The thrift shop's logo was slapped in the corner. It was set for the Wednesday after next on Melrose.

Melrose. Kind of a mission without a car. I'd either have to bus it or skate a ridiculous amount of miles, and neither sounded super fun. I was working now, so I could always Uber it, but I wasn't sure if I wanted to drop that type of money just yet. Still, something about the event had me kind of hyped. The idea of being in a space where people actually got what I was going through—like, the figuring yourself out stuff—felt... right. Like maybe this could be my shot at connecting with people who wouldn't just smile and nod when I stumbled over my words. I was definitely going. It wasn't just about showing up—it was about showing up *for me.*

I folded up the flyer again but before I could stuff it back in my pocket, the low rumble of wheels on pavement caught up to me. I didn't even have to look to know it was Rafe.

"Yo, are you dodging me or what?" he asked, grinning like he'd caught me in the act.

"What? No way!" I blurted, my voice way too high-pitched and definitely too loud.

Smooth, Kiko. Totally convincing.

Rafe laughed, kicking his board to cruise right next to mine. "Relax, dude. I'm just kidding."

He nodded toward the folded paper in my hand. "What's that?"

I shoved it in my pocket, trying to look chill even though my hands felt weirdly sweaty. "Just some random flyer they were giving out up there."

Rafe raised an eyebrow, smirking. "Really? Bro, only tourists take the flyers. Kinda sus, not gonna lie. Next thing, you're gonna tell me you got one of those henna tattoos too."

"Yeah, well, I was just trying to be nice," I said.

Rafe let out a laugh. "Right. Kiko, the Good Samaritan of Venice. Love that for you." He nudged me with his shoulder, almost making me lose my balance. "So, what's it for?"

"Dude, it's nothing," I said, waving him off. "Probably some yoga class or a lame art show. I didn't even look."

"Uh-huh," he said, giving me a look that said he totally didn't believe me but wasn't about to press it, "Yo, for real, though... we never see you anymore. When's the last time you even hit the waves?"

I felt the question land like a gut punch, but I played it off, shrugging. "Work, man. It's been taking a lot out of me."

Rafe gave me this skeptical side-eye. "Work? Really? You used to hit the beach like, every day."

"Yeah, well, being a barista is, uh, surprisingly demanding," I said, laughing awkwardly. I knew he wasn't buying it, but what else was I gonna say? "It's been busy. You know how it is."

He slowed down, coasting just ahead of me. "Nah, man. What I know is you haven't been around. Feels like you're avoiding us or something."

I stumbled on my words for a second, trying to come up with something to say. "What? No, it's not like that. I've just... been tired, you know?"

Rafe stared at me for a beat longer, then shrugged, kicking off again. "Alright, Kiko. If you say so."

What I didn't say was that it had been almost a month since I'd surfed—since I'd even picked up my board. Sneaking into Rafe's backyard shed to grab the Chilli Popper while also dodging him and Avery just felt... weird.

We rolled to a stop in front of one of those tourist trap stores, the kind that's always blasting reggae and has racks of overpriced t-shirts and hoodies for tourists spilling onto the boardwalk. Right out front, there was a mannequin—well, the bottom half of one—with a bunch of women's underwear on display on different parts of the legs. Each had some wild, cringe message plastered across them, the kind of stuff you'd think was funny in middle school.

Rafe zeroed in on one that had a big red "Do Not Enter" sign slapped across the front, and nudged me with his elbow, a grin spreading across his face. "Yo, bet you see this one a lot, huh?"

I snorted, half-laughing, half-shaking my head. "Man, shut the fuck up. They made that one for you," I shot back, trying to keep it light. I even gave him a playful shove, but inside, it stung a little. I knew it was just Rafe's way of messing around—he didn't mean anything by it—but still, it hit different when it was about me.

Rafe just laughed his usual carefree laugh, and we moved on. It wasn't worth bringing up—at least not now. Banter was just banter, right? Still, I wished he'd just chill sometimes.

Rafe slowed his board, letting the wheels hum to a stop as he turned to face me. "Yo, we have the skate comp coming up in August."

"Yeah?" I asked, keeping my tone neutral even though I already had a feeling where this was going. The competition was little more than a small meetup of some locals. It was a lot more chill than some of the bigger competitions like the one that was happening at the end of July.

"Yeah," Rafe said, arms crossed. "Me, Avery, and you. We're going to crush it... but we need you, Kiko. Can't do it without you."

I hesitated, "I don't know, man. Been kinda out of practice."

"C'mon," Rafe said, his voice softening but not losing that edge of determination. "It's not just about the tricks, bro. It's us. The crew. Like old times. You in or what?"

I sighed, already knowing I'd cave. I couldn't say no to that—didn't really want to. "Alright, alright. I'll come through."

Rafe grinned, smacking the tail of his board against the pavement. "That's what I'm talking about! Gonna be legendary."

As we skated down Westminster, Rafe slowed to a stop in front of this mural I'd passed a hundred times—two astronauts chilling on a beach, one holding a surfboard and a frisbee like it was the most normal thing in the world.

Rafe popped his board up. He had paint on his shorts and his board was scratched to hell. But his eyes were lit up, that same look he got when we used to bomb hills and think we were invincible.

"That's us right there. Me and you."

I laughed, rolling my eyes. "Okay then, but where's Avery?" I asked, my tone probably a little too sharp to land the dig.

Without missing a beat, Rafe jabbed his finger at the alien in a red spacesuit, standing off to the side, its three eyes staring out from its helmet. "She's right there," he said with a big grin.

I cracked up, shaking my head. "Yeah, okay. You wouldn't be talking that smack if she was here."

Next to the astronaut mural was another one—two massive, white-furred gorillas, looking like they'd just retired from a life of chaos. I pointed at it, still laughing. "I always thought this one was supposed to be us."

Rafe took one look and burst out laughing. "Nah, man," he said, slinging an arm around my shoulder and pulling me closer. "That's gonna be us in forty years when we're old, fat, and still talking about how we totally shredded back in the day."

The mental image sent me into another round of laughter, and for a moment, everything felt easy—no stress about work, no overthinking about Troye, no dodging questions about Avery. Just me and Rafe, standing in front of some random murals, laughing like we were twelve again.

He started skating again, but then slowed down and looked back at me, his expression more serious now. "Hey, though… are you good? Like, really? You've been kinda distant lately."

I opened my mouth to answer but hesitated, my mind scrambling for something to say that wasn't a complete lie. "I'm fine," I said eventually, forcing a small laugh. "Just, you know, stuff. Work. Life. Sorry if I've been… off."

Rafe studied me for a second, his face unreadable, then nodded slowly. "Alright. If you say so. But you know I got you, right? Whatever's up."

"I know," I said quietly.

Rafe's grin returned, and he extended his fist, shifting it into the start of our old handshake—something we hadn't done in forever. I smiled and followed through with the sequence, the slap, the spin, the quick snap at the end.

For a second, it was like we were kids again, back when everything felt simpler, when the only thing we had to worry about was nailing the next trick.

"Alright, man," Rafe said, stepping back on his board. "Don't flake.

Be there."

"Yeah, yeah," I said, as I watched him skate off with that easy confidence that always seemed to surround him.

10

It was the tail end of my shift, and the café was starting to wind down. The mid-afternoon rush had fizzled out, leaving only a handful of customers scattered at tables, their conversations blending softly with the hum of the espresso machine. I was wiping down the counter when my phone buzzed in my pocket. I glanced around—Neil wasn't anywhere near—so I pulled it out for a quick check. I figured it would be a meme from Rafe or some random notification, but instead… it was a DM from Troye.

 Hey, you free tonight? Wanna meet up to talk?

I blinked at the screen. Troye. I hadn't heard from him in almost a week —not since the date at LACMA. I'd honestly assumed he'd moved on, or, you know, forgotten about me entirely.

Now "Wanna meet up to talk?" Yeah, that didn't sound chill. That sounded serious. My stomach flipped as my mind instantly went into overdrive. Was this a breakup? A just-friends talk? Was it even a thing to break up if you weren't officially together? If it was any of those things, I'd rather just save the trip and get it over with now.

I bit my lip, hesitated, and then typed back "Like… good talk or bad talk?"

I hit send and stared at the screen, my anxiety filling the silence as I waited for those three little dots to pop up. They did—finally.

 Good talk. Promise. Can you swing by after work?

I exhaled hard, relief barely edging out my nerves. Good talk. Okay, sure. I could handle that. Couldn't I? Then another DM popped up with an address on Orlando Avenue. I stared at the screen again, my mind hitting pause, before I Googled the address.

The place was up near the Beverly Center. But it wasn't a café, a park, or some fast food joint. It wasn't some neutral hang spot. The building that came up had that classic LA condo vibe—stucco walls, beige everything, these random green awnings, and these tiny balconies. It was... his apartment?

My heart started racing for an entirely different reason now. Was this going too fast? Like, was I ready for the whole come-over-to-my-place vibe? What was I even supposed to expect?

I hesitated before typing, "Uh, yeah. Sure. I get off at 5."

I sent it before I could second-guess myself. I stuffed my phone back into my pocket. My mind was all over the place as I wiped down the bar along the front window, trying not to overthink every possible scenario.

Was this just a chill hang? Something more? And why did my brain insist on turning every possibility into either a rom-com or a full-on disaster movie?

As I finished wiping down the last couple of tables, my phone buzzed again. Another message from Troye.

   Can you bring me my usual drink?

I couldn't help but smirk, because of course, Mr. Dirty-Chai-Half-Caff-Two-Pumps-Vanilla needed his fix. I messaged back a quick, "Sure thing," before heading behind the counter. Ricky was off, so it was just me, the register, and my questionable barista skills.

I stared at the menu board like it was gonna have the instructions for each drink. Half-caff? Did I even know how to do that? *Spoiler: no.* So I went with the regular version and hoped for the best. While I was at it, I decided to make one for myself, because I wanted to see what all the hype was about.

The machine whirred, steamed, and hissed as I fumbled through the process. The result? At least they looked right. Not perfect, but not a total disaster. I popped a lid on both cups and slid them into a cardboard drink carrier. There were only a few cake pops left, so I snagged one. Troye didn't ask for it, but I figured I'd surprise him.

I rang myself up, employee discount and all, and called out to Neil in the back. "Heading out, boss!"

Neil's muffled voice came back. "Got it, thanks for actually showing up on time today!"

I rolled my eyes but couldn't stop a small grin. As I grabbed my backpack and skateboard, my coworker—some guy I barely talked to who was newer than me—gave me an up-nod from the register. I nodded back, muttering a quick, "Later," before stepping out into the late afternoon.

With two drinks and a cake pop in hand, I felt the nerves creeping back. What exactly was Troye planning to say? Was this a date-date, or just some ploy to get his coffee fix while letting me down easy? Either way, I was about to find out.

The ride to Troye's place wasn't bad at all, only ten minutes from the shop on my board. The streets were pretty smooth with no major cracks to dodge—gotta love Beverly Hills. Even still, I was hyper-focused on not spilling the drinks in the carrier.

The building matched what I saw on Google: clean, modern, and kind of bougie, but in that low-key LA way. I pulled out my phone to double-check the address—unit D. The black gate at the entrance was already propped open, so I skipped the buzzer and slid right through.

The walkway was cute, lined with plants in pots that were just mismatched enough to look expensive. There were lights strung overhead. The whole place was a vibe. When I reached door D, I knocked, balancing the drinks and my board like some kind of clumsy waiter.

The door opened, and I blinked. Instead of Troye, there was this African American woman standing there, maybe mid-30s, rocking a flawless ponytail and a vibe that screamed "I have my life together." She gave me this polite-but-curious look, like, "Who is this kid, and why is he knocking on my door?"

"Can I help you?" she asked, one eyebrow slightly raised.

"Uh…" I stammered, checking the DM on my screen again just to make sure I hadn't accidentally ended up at the wrong door.

She smirked, like she totally expected that reaction. "You must be here for Troye," she said. "His room's upstairs, first door on the left."

"Oh, cool. Thanks," I said as I stepped inside juggling the drinks.

My mind was already spinning. Who was she? Roommate? Landlord? Secret family member? Troye definitely hadn't mentioned living with anyone else, so now I was just confused.

At the top of the stairs, I spotted a door slightly open with music drifting out—Lana Del Rey? Definitely. I took a deep breath and knocked on the door.

"Come in," Troye said from inside. I nudged open the door with my elbow. Troye was sitting on a full-size mattress on the far wall, a wide grin on his face. He jumped up and met me at the door, pulling me into a quick hug. "There you are," he said, his voice full of energy. Before I could even respond, he took the drink carrier out of my hands. "Come on in."

His room was small but, I don't know… cozy? It had this kinda artsy clutter—like sketch pads stacked on the floor, a Polaroid camera on the nightstand, and fairy lights strung across the wall above his bed.

Troye flopped onto the bed. He was wearing a t-shirt and some basketball shorts, a totally different fit than I expected. He motioned for me to sit. I eyed the room for a second before settling on this rickety wooden stool that was giving Jenga vibes, but it definitely seemed to be a more comfortable option for me than his bed, which was the only other place to sit.

Troye grabbed his drink, popping the straw through the lid before taking a sip. "Look at you, making yourself a dirty chai too," he teased, smirking. "That's what's up."

I shrugged, holding up my cup. "Figured I'd see what all the hype's about."

Troye took another sip, and I swear I saw the tiniest flicker of hesitation in his expression. It was subtle, but I could tell he knew it wasn't half-caff. Still, he didn't say anything, just nodded like it was all good.

Before the awkwardness could settle in, I reached into my bag and pulled out the cake pop. "Almost forgot—got this for you too," I said, holding it up like it was a rose.

His eyes lit up, genuine this time. "Aww, you didn't have to!" he said, grabbing it like it was the best thing he'd seen all day. "You're seriously the best."

I leaned back a little, sipping my drink to hide the fact that his reaction made my stomach do a weird little flip. Totally normal to get cake pops for someone you're into, right?

Keep it chill, Kiko.

"So, who let you in?" he asked, sipping the drink again.

"Uh… I didn't catch her name," I admitted, shrugging. "She seemed nice, though."

Troye smirked. "Oh, that was Maya then. Kendra's the other one, and trust me, nobody has ever described her as nice."

I laughed a little. "Roommates, huh? How long have you been here?"

"Like a few weeks," Troye said, leaning back against the bedframe. "It's not bad. Maya's cool, and Kendra mostly keeps to herself unless it's to complain about something stupid. Keeps the rent down, though, so..." He made a what-can-you-do kind of gesture. "Just a stepping stone, you know?"

"Yeah, I get that," I said, even though I really didn't. I couldn't imagine living with strangers.

Troye set his drink down and pushed himself up from the bed. "Alright, let's grab food. I'm starving."

"Oh, nice. Where you thinking?"

"Thai, maybe? I just need to get ready real quick." He gave me this grin that was half charming and half mischievous, before disappearing into the hallway.

I heard the bathroom door click shut, and the room felt like it belonged to a stranger again. As I sat on the wobbly stool, I let my eyes wander around Troye's room. I mean, it's not like I knew all that much about him yet. This felt like my chance to piece together the puzzle—at least some of it.

On a bookcase against the wall, there was a picture of him from when he was younger—darker hair, less of that cool, styled vibe he rocks now. The frame had little painted Eiffel Towers and "Bonjour" scrawled on it in cursive. I wondered if he'd been to Paris or if it was just one of those random touristy things people end up with. Then there was another photo, this one on the dresser. Troye was decked out in a marching band uniform, holding a clarinet with a red hat sitting beside it. A band kid? That one threw me for a loop.

I spotted a few sketches taped to the wall above the bookcase—ones I recognized from his Instagram, including that flamenco dancer. They looked even better up close, with all the fine details popping out. The clothes rack in the corner was packed with designer outfits, jackets and shirts in every bold pattern and color you could think of. Definitely too many to fit in his closet, which was struggling to stay closed with clothes practically sticking out from both doors.

Then, out of the corner of my eye, I noticed the prescription bottles on the dresser. I figured they were probably antibiotics or some headache stuff. Either way, I felt like it wasn't really my business, so I didn't linger on them too long.

There was the stack of unopened mail on the nightstand. One

envelope on top caught my eye because of the bold red lettering: "Important: Open Upon Receipt." The name on it read Clayton T. McCosh. I furrowed my brows, glancing toward the bathroom door. Clayton?

My brain kind of tripped over it. I tilted my head like reading it again might make it make more sense, but before I could spiral, I decided it was probably a roommate thing or maybe a landlord. Maybe a family member? "Clayton" sounded kind of older. Yeah, that made sense.

I heard the sink going so I grabbed a magazine from the bed—one of those artsy ones with the fashion spreads and pictures of weird sculptures that definitely cost more than my mom's car. I flipped through it, trying to look super casual, like I hadn't been sitting here snooping and overanalyzing his entire life.

Chill, Kiko. You're literally just here to hang out.

I plastered on a smile, ready to play it cool as Troye came back into the room, and took a sip of my dirty chai, while still flipping aimlessly through the magazine. I looked up as Troye passed by on the way to the rack of clothes—but he wasn't wearing his basketball shorts or T-shirt anymore. Nope. Just an expensive pair of Calvins that hugged him in *all* the right ways.

And yep. The chai went down the wrong pipe, and before I could stop it, I was choking. Of course, some of it shot up my nose because the universe has no chill. I scrambled to grab a napkin from my backpack, trying to play it off like I wasn't having a full-blown crisis.

Troye glanced over his shoulder, totally catching me mid-meltdown, and flashed this smile that told me he knew *exactly* what he was doing. But he didn't say a word.

As I tried to recover, he casually pulled a sleek black button-up and some tailored jeans off the rack, slipping them on with confidence. Once he was dressed, he grabbed his drink from the bed and finally spoke.

"The spot's over on Fairfax. It's like the oldest Thai place in LA or something like that," he said, like nothing just happened. "We've got time to finish these on the walk. Ready?"

I nodded, trying to keep my voice steady. "Cool. Let's go." My face was probably still red, but at least I didn't choke again.

The place felt like it was trying to be low-key but was totally curated for Instagram. The wood-paneled walls and concrete floors screamed trendy without overdoing it, and the black chairs and booths along the side made it feel kind of homey. There were these bright bird ornaments hanging from the exposed beam ceiling, swaying a little in the AC. They were random as hell, but honestly kind of cool. The walls were covered in old-school photos in vintage frames, like they raided someone's grandma's attic but made it artsy.

I sat across from Troye, who was lounging casually in the booth like he'd been here a hundred times. Meanwhile, my brain was ping-ponging between admiring the vibe and wondering if those bird things ever fell on anyone. Honestly, the whole place felt like a spot people would gatekeep so they didn't have to wait for a table.

The twenty-minute walk had been chill. Troye had kept the convo light, asking about my day at work and laughing at my lame stories about messed-up drink orders and Neil being Neil. But now that we were sitting across from each other, I knew I had to flip the script if I was gonna find out anything about him.

I glanced over the top of my menu at him. He was scrolling through his phone, probably checking Instagram or whatever, but he looked so put together, even in this laid-back spot. The black button-up he'd thrown on earlier somehow looked like it was tailored specifically for this moment.

"So," I said, lowering my menu and leaning my elbows on the table, "you know a ton about me, but I feel like I don't know anything about you."

Troye looked up, tilting his head with a smirk. "Oh, come on. You've seen my Instagram. That's basically a crash course in Troye."

"Yeah, but like… your actual life, not just the highlight reel," I pressed. "Where you're from, what you're into when you're not sketching or flexing on the 'Gram."

He set his phone down and leaned back in the booth, his smirk softening into something more thoughtful. "You really wanna know?"

"Yeah." I nodded. "Tell me about *you*, like who *is* Troye?"

Troye laughed quietly, running a hand through his bleach-blonde curls. "Alright. Let's see… I'm from Iowa, but you already know that. Nothing exciting, just cornfields and county fairs. Came out to LA about a year ago. You know, chasing the dream…"

"What dream?" I asked.

"To not be stuck in Iowa," he laughed, but there was something heavier there. "But seriously, art, design, maybe fashion. I've always wanted to create stuff that makes people feel… something. You know?"

I nodded, trying to picture him back in Iowa with cornfields and a clarinet. It didn't add up. "That's cool," I said. "So, what's the story with your roommates?"

Troye chuckled, "Oh, Maya and Kendra? Yeah, Maya's chill. She's like my unofficial life coach. Kendra... let's just say we steer clear of each other. Found them on an LA Roommates Facebook group. It's a temporary thing until I can figure out something better."

I didn't push further, feeling like there was more to the story he wasn't ready to share. The server came by to take our order, giving me a moment to regroup. As Troye ordered his Pad Thai, I couldn't help but wonder what else he was keeping in that mystery box. And for some reason, I couldn't wait to find out.

"And you?" the server asked.

"Uh," I stalled, trying to decide between two dishes. "I'll go with the... Chicken Pad Gra Pow."

"And two Thai iced teas," Troye added, before looking at me for an objection.

"That sounds cool," I said.

As soon as the server left, I leaned forward, picking at the corner of my napkin. "So, what about your family?" I asked, trying to keep the tone casual. It felt like the next logical step in getting to know Troye, but I wasn't ready for the way his face shifted. He leaned back in the booth, crossing his arms.

"Well...My parents are... a lot," he said, his voice quieter but sharp. "Super religious. Like, Bible-themed-board-games-for-family-game-night kind of religious. Like, the I'm-going-to-hell-for-my-unnatural-desires kind of religious."

"Oh." I froze, my stomach twisting. I was definitely rethinking asking so many questions.

The Thai iced teas arrived while we sat in silence. He looked down at his drink, spinning the straw in slow circles. "They sent me to one of those camps when I was 15. You know, the ones that claim they can, like, 'fix' you. Spoiler alert: they don't work. Just messed me up more." His words were bitter, but he kept his voice mostly level, like he was used to telling this story without breaking.

I totally didn't know what to say. I'd seen shit like that on TV but like knowing someone who went through it was totally different. The idea of someone doing that to their own kid made my chest tighten. "That's... really messed up. I'm sorry."

He shrugged, but the way he avoided eye contact made it clear it wasn't just a shrug-it-off situation. "I haven't spoken to them since I came out here. Figured if I wasn't good enough for them then, they don't deserve me now." He tried to sound tough, but I could tell that it bothered him.

I just nodded. I did *not* trust myself to not say something stupid or cliché, so I figured the silence was better. Troye had been through some real shit, but here he was, just sitting there across from me and somehow holding it together. And that just made me want to know him more.

"So, uh... you were in the marching band, huh?" I asked, aiming for casual.

The corners of his mouth pulled up into a small, almost amused smile. "You really were snooping, huh?"

I laughed nervously, holding my hands up. "Hey, the hat was just sitting there on the dresser with the clarinet pic—how could I not ask?"

He leaned back in the booth, relaxing just a bit. "Yeah, clarinet. Sophomore through senior year. I hated it at first, but then I got good, and suddenly it was kinda fun. Plus, the uniforms gave me an excuse to hide my terrible style back then."

I grinned. "Terrible style? You? I find that hard to believe."

"Oh, I had zero drip back then, trust me. It was all graphic tees from Kmart and off-brand sneakers. The band uniform was probably the best thing I wore in high school."

I laughed, picturing him awkwardly holding a clarinet in a stiff marching band get-up. "Okay, but did you actually like marching, or were you just in it for the free football game tickets?"

"Well," Troye said with a grin, "I *was* in it for the free trips. Band competitions out of state? Basically a mini vacation."

I laughed, "And here I thought it was all about the music."

Troye rolled his eyes dramatically. "It's *always* about the free stuff."

The conversation just finally felt lighter, the tension lifting. I could see Troye's shoulders relax as we bantered back and forth. For the first time since we'd sat down, I felt like this was less of a first date and more like hanging out with someone I'd known forever. It wasn't perfect, but it was good. And I'd take that.

He leaned in going full send on the Cheshire grin, "Also... let's just say Friday night lights weren't the only thing worth showing up for."

I blinked, not immediately catching on. "What do you—" Then it hit me. "Wait, no. You mean...?"

"What can I say? Some of the football team weren't as straight as they acted in front of their bros."

I choked on my iced tea, laughing. "You're telling me clarinet boy over here was secretly pulling quarterbacks?"

"Okay, well not quarterbacks," Troye admitted. "But a couple linebackers, maybe a tight end or two."

I couldn't stop laughing, the mental image was both wild and I had to admit, kind of impressive.

Troye leaned forward, his voice dropping to a whisper. "And band camp was... let's just say, a lot of team-building happened."

"Oh my god," I laughed. "You're ridiculous."

He just leaned back in the booth, completely unbothered and clearly enjoying my reaction. "What can I say? Clarinet opened doors."

I rolled my eyes but couldn't help smiling. This version of Troye— playful, confident, unapologetic—was magnetic. For the first time that night, I forgot about my nerves entirely and just let myself enjoy the moment.

Dinner was so good. Like, I wasn't even ready for how good. The pad gra pow I ordered was next-level spicy, with the perfect mix of heat and savory, and I could barely put my chopsticks down. Troye reached over with his fork at one point, giving me this playful "Can I?" look, and I let him grab a bite. He took one taste, raised his eyebrows, and said, "Okay, Mr. Spicy. I see you."

In return, I snagged some of his Pad Thai. It was mild, with just the right hit of lime. Sharing food felt... weirdly intimate but, like, in a fun way. We laughed, we traded bites, and I wasn't stressing over what he thought of me.

When the server dropped off the bill, I went for it immediately, ready to flex my newfound "working man" energy. Troye didn't even pretend to reach for it, though, which kind of threw me off. Like, not even the fake wallet grab? Nothing?

I cleared my throat and tried not to overthink it. "I got this," I said, pulling out my debit card.

Troye smiled, leaning back in his chair like a prince. "You sure? Aw thanks."

I laughed, but inside I was like... hmm. He didn't even put up a fight —not even waiting for a response to the "you sure?" I paid anyway, because whatever. I'm out here making my own money now, and it felt good to treat someone. Still, I couldn't shake this little voice in the back of my head whispering that he gave up on that way too easy.

The second we stepped outside, the air just hit different, like cool and crisp. The streetlights gave this kind of glow that made everything feel a little unreal. It wasn't totally dark yet, but the sky had that moody, in-between vibe, like the city was just gearing up for the night.

Troye turned to me, and oh... my... God..., the look he gave me? Full-on heart attack material. He had this little smirk, like he knew every thought running through my head, and his eyes practically dared me to make a move.

That's when it hit me: this was it. My chance. No bailing this time.

My hands were sweating like crazy, and my heart was going so hard I was half-worried he could hear it. Everything in me was tense and alive in the worst and best way.

I took this tiny step closer. Before my brain could catch up, I went for it and leaned in.

The kiss was... just wow.

It wasn't like fireworks or some dramatic movie moment. It was soft —a little awkward at first, that's for damn sure—but then it just clicked.

He kissed me back like it wasn't even a question, like it was the most obvious thing in the world. And for a second, I let myself believe it could be.

When we pulled apart, Troye's smirk had gone full smug. My face was low-key on fire and I started laughing for no reason.

"Took you long enough," he said, teasing. But there was a warmth behind it that made me feel like I'd just won something big.

"Well, I had to make sure the timing was right," I shot back, trying to sound smooth. Pretty sure I failed.

Troye just grinned and grabbed my hand like it was the most natural thing in the world. We started walking back to his place, and honestly, I don't even remember the actual walk because my brain was stuck on replaying that kiss over and over. I was trying to play it cool, but I'm pretty sure the giant, goofy grin on my face gave me away.

When we got to his place, he unlocked the door, and we headed up to his room. My board and backpack were right where I'd left them, leaning against the wall. I picked up the board, fully ready to dip, but Troye stepped in front of the door frame, leaning against it all casual-like, arms crossed, giving me that look. You know, *the* look.

"So," he said, dragging the word out like he was testing me. He walked his fingers up my chest. "You don't *have* to leave, you know."

I froze mid-move, my backpack still hanging off one shoulder. "Oh?" My voice came out way higher than I wanted, and I immediately cringed. Troye didn't even flinch—just stepped a little closer, brushing his hand against mine.

"Yeah," he said, grinning now, full Troye-mode. "It's late. Busses are terrible this time of night. I mean there's a bed right here, and…" He shrugged, like it was the most obvious thing in the world.

My brain was back to short-circuiting, running a million miles an hour. Was this a bad idea? Almost certainly. Did I care? Not even a little. The way Troye was looking at me, like he was daring me to just go with it, made it impossible to even think straight.

I typed out a quick text to my mom. It was short and simple: "Staying at Rafe's. Movie marathon. Don't wait up." It wasn't great, but it was good enough. Mateo was fine—Ma was home, and honestly, he was more responsible than I was half the time.

But still, my brain wouldn't stop spinning. *You could leave*, I thought. *You don't have to stay*. My thumb stayed frozen, like I could actually talk myself into bolting if I waited long enough.

Then Troye stepped closer. His hands found my sides, gentle at first, but enough to pull me back to the moment. Before I could even react, he leaned in, and his lips landed on my neck. It wasn't rushed; it was slow and deliberate, like he knew exactly what he was doing. And just like that, my brain left the chat. Whatever doubts I had completely disappeared.

I looked down at my phone, the screen still glowing in my hand. Troye didn't stop, his lips brushing against my jaw until they found this spot on my neck. I let out a shaky breath as my mind went blank and I hit send. The whoosh of the message disappearing felt like I was sealing a deal I didn't even know I was making.

I dropped my backpack onto the floor and tossed my phone on top. And maybe I was in way over my head. But for once… I didn't care.

11

Did we go all the way? No. But where we did go was definitely further than I'd ever been. Clothes came off. Hands wandered. There were a few moments where I thought I might actually combust from how close everything felt—skin, breath, heartbeat, all of it.

It was new and exciting and nerve-wracking and... kind of incredible. Messy, but in a way that made me want more. Like my body had known what to do long before my brain caught up. The next day, though, Ricky wasted no time calling me out.

I'd shown up to work wearing clothes that weren't mine—designer pieces from Troye's closet, that on me were... a little too tight... in all the wrong places. Ricky had taken one look at me, smirked, and said, "Raiding the boyfriend's closet?"

My face went red, and I tried to play it cool, but totally failed. I just mumbled something about not having time to go home before my shift.

Lesson learned: I started carrying at a minimum a spare shirt, socks, and underwear in my backpack. I mean, you never know, right? And... it came in handy the next time I stayed over—and the time after that. Yeah, I know, three times in a week and a half. I was still figuring out what we were even doing. Were we a thing? Just hooking up? Something in between? I didn't have a clue.

Right now, though, I was on the bus heading up La Brea toward Melrose, with the flyer for Dylan's Open Mic Night tucked into my pocket. I couldn't stop glancing out the window with a mix of excitement and nervousness that I'd been getting a little too used to lately. Dylan had been cool to invite me, and I was actually looking forward to the chance to make some friends who might actually get what I was going through.

Trying to figure out all these emotions and the whole relationship thing without any real experience—well… it was a lot. But not having anyone to talk to about it? Yeah, that made it harder. So, this Open Mic Night felt like more than just a casual thing. It felt like a chance to breathe, to connect with other people in the same situation, and maybe even to figure some things out.

The bus screeched to a stop at Melrose, jolting me forward in my seat. I hopped off, immediately hit with the late afternoon LA heat and the faint scent of burritos wafting from the Chipotle on the opposite corner. My stomach growled, reminding me I hadn't eaten lunch. I wondered if Dylan's Open Mic thing would at least have snacks—chips or cookies, something to hold me over.

Mental note: stop skipping meals.

I dropped my board to the pavement and pushed off, cruising across the intersection and weaving through the light foot traffic along the sidewalk. As I approached this ramen place, my eyes snagged on this sick dragon mural—and the cracked sidewalk in the driveway snagged my wheels.

My board jerked to a dead stop, and I felt myself lurch forward, arms flailing like I was about to faceplant. Somehow, though, I managed to regain my balance, landing on my feet but definitely leaving my pride a little shaken. I glanced around, hoping no one saw that near wipeout. A couple walking their dog gave me a quick look but kept moving. Crisis averted.

Grabbing my board, I stepped off to the side for a moment to catch my breath and laugh it off. "Nice one, Kiko," I muttered under my breath. Shaking my head, I set the board back down and pushed off again, this time paying more attention.

The thrift shop was only about a five-minute ride down Melrose, past the usual mix of cafes, nail salons, boutiques, and trendy restaurants with menus written in chalk. I coasted along, my wheels humming against the sidewalk, and rolled to a stop outside the thrift shop.

I looked through one of the big front windows. Inside, it looked like they'd moved a lot of racks to the back of the shop to make room at the front for some seating. Clothes still hung along the walls, but the center space was wide open. Against one wall, a microphone stood next to a simple PA speaker, wires snaking across the floor. A group of mismatched chairs had been set up for the audience—some metal, some plastic, and one that looked a little too suspiciously like it had been snagged from a kitchen table.

Right near the entrance, Dylan was bouncing between greeting people and adjusting some equipment, his usual chill vibe mixed with just enough hustle to show he cared about the setup. The guy had layers, no doubt.

I picked up my board, tucking it under my arm as I pushed open the door. A bell above jingled, announcing my arrival, and I took a deep breath. The smell of secondhand fabric and maybe lavender-scented cleaner filled the air. I caught Dylan's eye when he glanced up, and he threw me a quick grin.

"Kiko! Glad you made it! Welcome!" he called. His grin was easy, genuine—real. It was the kind of smile that made you feel like you actually belonged. I gave him a small wave and stepped further inside.

Dylan stepped up to the mic, tapping it lightly to get everyone's attention. The slight squeak of feedback made a few people cringe, but he quickly adjusted. "Alright, folks," he said, his voice smooth and welcoming, "we're gonna get started in just a minute, so find yourselves a seat. And if you're planning to perform, make sure your name's on the list up here." He gestured to a clipboard sitting on a stool near the mic stand.

There were maybe twenty people scattered around the shop. Mostly young, mid-20s or younger, with a couple of older people mixed in, giving off that artsy, I've-lived-a-life vibe. Everyone was chatting quietly.

I picked a seat in the back row—low-key, out of sight, perfect for just soaking it all in. The chair creaked as I sat down, and I slid my board under the seat to keep it out of the way. I was scrolling on my phone, just passing time, when I heard the sharp click of boots against the concrete floor.

Looking up, I saw someone about my age walking toward the seat next to me. They had an androgynous look and a cool vibe—wearing a black-and-white striped sweater with these too-long sleeves, skinny black jeans, and ankle boots that clicked with every step. Their eyeliner was sharp, and their black hair was short, but longer on the top and just tousled enough to scream *this probably took hours to get just right*. They dropped into the chair beside me like they'd claimed it, crossing one leg over the other with this casual energy that was giving, I'm not trying, I just exist like this.

"Hey," they said, barely turning to me with a shy smile.

"Hey," I said back, trying to play it cool but definitely feeling a little shy myself.

I put my phone away as Dylan went up to the mic again. He tapped the mic again, flashing that chill grin he always had, and said, "Alright, everyone, thanks for showing up tonight. Welcome to Out Loud. It's been a minute since we did one of these—like, the café's gone but the vibes live on, right? Big thanks to Juan and Melissa for letting us invade their shop and do our thing. Make sure to check out the racks after the show, yeah? Got some killer threads here."

A small round of applause rippled through the room as Dylan stepped back, scanning the clipboard on the stool. "Okay, kicking things off tonight is Indianna. Come on up here and do your thing!"

Indianna walked up to the mic, adjusting it with a bit of a struggle. "Hi, y'all. I'm Indianna, friends call me Indie, and yes, I *am* in fact a lesbian. Thank you for noticing."

The crowd laughed.

"The uniform gave it away, didn't it?" She gestured down to her black jeans, combat boots, and oversized flannel. "It was either this or the 'I heart Lowe's t-shirt, and honestly, it was a toss-up tonight."

The crowd broke into laughter, and she grinned. "You know, people think being a lesbian means I'm good at building stuff. And yeah, I do have a toolbox, but that doesn't mean I know how to use it. My IKEA bookshelf is hanging on by a thread. It's basically a metaphor for my love life."

More laughter rippled through the room.

"Yeah, dating as a lesbian is wild, though. You either U-Haul on date three or ghost after date two. It's like, 'Are we getting matching tattoos or never speaking again? The suspense is *killing* me.'"

Someone in the crowd let out a loud whoop, and Indianna pointed at them.

"You get it!" She gestured like she was making a phone call and whispered "Call me" with a wink.

She had the crowd roaring as she continued her set, a mix of stereotypes and jokes about modern dating, but she just had this energy. Indianna leaned into the mic one last time. "But really, I'm living my best life... Sure, my best life is eating cold pizza in bed at two in the morning, but it's mine, and that's what counts."

She stepped back with a mock bow, and the crowd burst into applause. Even Dylan looked impressed as he grabbed the mic. "Give it up for Indie, everyone! And remember, if you need your bookshelf fixed... err... probably call someone else."

That was definitely a solid start to the night. Dylan stepped up to the mic again, scanning the room with that easy grin of his. "Alright, next up, we've got someone who's no stranger to this stage—our very own Ace of Hearts, Ethan Katz,"

The crowd clapped, and I just sat there, low-key confused. Ace of hearts? What did that even mean? Was it like a compliment? A nickname? Before the questions piled up too much, the person who had been sitting next to me got up, brushing a hand through their short, choppy hair as they headed toward the mic.

"They're gonna blow us away with some magic, as always," Dylan continued.

I caught the "they." It wasn't something Dylan emphasized, just dropped into his intro as casually as everything else he said. But it landed, clicking into place as Ethan stepped forward, their black-and-white sweater catching the light in a way that made the stripes look like they were shifting.

Ethan picked up an acoustic guitar that was on a stand off to the side and adjusted the strap. It was a vintage-looking thing with scuffs on the edges that made it look like it had some stories. Dylan looked a bit confused as the room quieted.

"Sorry to disappoint, everyone. No magic tricks tonight. Instead I'm going to sing a song that means something to me. This one's called 'For Judas,'" Ethan said, their voice cool but soft. "It's by Adeem the Artist, but tonight, it's for all of you."

Ethan strummed the guitar, playing a slow melody. Their voice cut through the air, smooth but heavy with this straight-up raw kind of sadness. It wasn't just a performance; it was like they were telling a story with every note and chord.

The chorus hit, building up with a kind of power, and I could feel the emotion in it. It wasn't loud or showy, but it just like... stuck in your chest. Ethan's voice, that was all soft and quiet just a moment ago, now had that old-soul vibe, the kind that makes you stop whatever you're doing just to listen. You could no joke hear a pin drop in the shop.

I glanced around, and the whole room was locked in. There were people swaying, and some were mouthing along like they already knew the words. Even I was caught up in it. It was the way the guitar and their voice just wove together. It wasn't just music. It was like they were just pulling me into their world for a few minutes.

Ethan barely let the last chord fade before the room exploded into claps and cheers, with a few people instantly popping up for a standing ovation. Even I was clapping way harder than I thought I would, feeling like I'd just been let in on something that really mattered. Dylan pulled Ethan in for a hug and whispered something to them. When he let them go, Ethan leaned back towards the mic and gave this small, super-shy smile and just gave a quiet, "Thanks," before heading back to their seat.

"Just wow," Dylan said, stepping back up to the mic, laughing like he couldn't believe what just happened. "Let's give it up one more time for Ethan!" The applause came back with full energy, like everyone just wanted to keep hyping them up. Dylan held his hands out to calm the room. "Okay, okay. Next up, we've got something a bit different, but trust me... It's going to be just as good. Please welcome to the stage Lori!"

An older woman, probably in her late-50s, walked up to the mic. She had curly salt-and-pepper hair, big round glasses, dressed in what I could only describe as "retired hippie chic"—a flowy top, loose pants, Birkenstocks...the whole fit. She carried a beat-up paperback like it was a treasure.

"This passage is from *Oranges Are Not the Only Fruit* by Jeanette Winterson," Lori said. Her voice was chill but it low-key had that dramatic flair, like she knew how to pull people in. She opened the book and started reading, her tone shifting to something deeper, something that immediately had everyone locked in.

The words hit different. Lori made the story feel alive. She paused in all the right spots, letting the lines land before moving on.

Even though the book seemed like it was from way back, it also felt like it could've been written last week. It was raw, real, and said all the things I feel like a lot of people are too scared to say out loud.

When she finished, Lori closed the book slowly. She lifted it up and held it to her chest like it was something sacred. The applause started almost immediately—not as wild as Ethan's set, but definitely filled with this deep respect. A couple of people whistled, and someone even yelled, "You're a legend, Lori!" She smiled, gave a little bow, and stepped to the side like a total pro.

Dylan leaned back into the mic with a grin. "Wow, tonight is undefeated so far. Big, big thanks to Lori for that. Okay everyone, let's keep it rolling! Next up..."

The rest of the acts rolled through, and I stayed glued to my seat, low-key amazed at how different everyone's energy was. Some people killed it, like full-on "wow, they could do this for real" vibes, and others... well, they were trying. But honestly, even the ones who weren't that great got props from everyone, because just stepping up there? That's something I couldn't imagine doing. I clapped for every single one, hoping they felt at least half as cool as they looked up there.

When the last act wrapped up, Dylan strolled back up to the mic, his clipboard in hand. He flipped through the pages, giving this over-the-top "hmm" like he was about to announce something huge. "Alright, looks like we're at the end of the list," he said, dragging out the words and scanning the room like he was expecting someone to suddenly jump up there.

A few people shuffled awkwardly in their seats, but no one moved.

His eyes settled on me and I quickly looked away, hoping he wasn't gonna go all Rafe on me and call me out, but somehow I knew that wasn't his vibe.

I glanced back at him as he raised an eyebrow, smirking like he knew exactly how this was gonna go down. "No takers?" he asked, and when the silence stretched a bit longer, he shrugged. "Cool, cool. Guess I'll share something I've been working on."

That got my attention. He had been hyping up everyone else all night, but I'd never actually seen him put himself out there. He adjusted the mic stand, his usual chill confidence came down just a notch, like he was bracing himself. "It's a poem I wrote... uh...last week. Kinda raw—definitely needs work—but... uh... well, here it goes."

The room went dead quiet, and for a second, it felt like everyone in the thrift shop was holding their breath. I sat up a little straighter, suddenly curious, suddenly invested.

"Um," he started. "This is called 'Under the Spotlight' and uh... well here it is:

"The moon's just a spotlight,
shining on things we're too scared to see in daylight.
Secrets bloom like night-blooming flowers,
petals curling under the weight of unsaid words.
I've built cathedrals in my chest,
but the echoes inside are prayers I never speak.
A name whispered in the dark feels safer
than shouting it in the sun.
Every silence is a choice,
but every silence feels like a lie."

And... uh, yeah... That's... uh... what I've got." Dylan stammered, looking only at the microphone in front of him before his eyes briefly flicked up at the crowd who were dead silent. He turned to walk off to the side before everyone burst out in applause. Lori ran up and gave him a big hug before taking his face in her hands and obviously telling him how beautiful the poem was. She was crying as she kissed him on the forehead—and I only realized then that a tear ran down one of my own cheeks. I recognized the line from that night at Avery's, the one he scribbled down in that notebook and I was completely blown away at what that single line had grown into.

The chairs scraped on the concrete floor as everyone got up and started moving around the shop. The vibe shifted to something more relaxed. I decided to make my move and walked up to the front where Dylan was talking to Indianna and Ethan.

"That was insane," I said, giving them all a quick nod. "You guys were seriously amazing."

Indianna smirked, crossing her arms. "Damn right we were. But you gotta admit, my stand-up stole the show." She let out a raspy laugh that made it hard to tell if she was serious or just messing with me.

Ethan gave me a small, shy smile, brushing a strand of hair out of their face. "Thanks," they said softly. "I was, uh, kind of nervous."

"Ethan's never sung at one of these before," Dylan explained. "They usually do magic tricks."

"Really? You killed it," I said to Ethan. "For real. That song? Straight fire."

Dylan grinned, clearly proud of his crew. "Kiko, meet the dream team," he said, gesturing between them. "Indie, our chaotic comedy queen, and Ethan, our new resident heartbreak balladeer."

"Pleasure to meet you, Kiko," Indianna said, extending a hand dramatically like we were at some fancy gala. I played along, shaking it with exaggerated politeness.

"You too," I said, laughing. I turned to Ethan. "And dude, you gotta teach me how to play guitar like that."

"Oh, um, it's really not that hard…" they stammered.

Dylan clapped Ethan on the shoulder with this wide grin. "Don't let them fool you, Kiko. They're a freakin' prodigy. I'm just glad they decided to finally share it with the rest of the world."

Indianna rolled her eyes. "Okay, enough of the Ethan appreciation hour. Dylan, you promised food, and I'm starving."

Dylan's eyes lit up. "Pinks?"

"*Yessss,*" Indianna said immediately, stretching out the word like it was its own paragraph. "Ethan, you're in. You have no choice."

Ethan nodded sheepishly. "Yeah, okay."

Dylan turned to me. "What about you, Kiko? You down?"

I shrugged. "I've actually never been. Is it good?"

Dylan's jaw dropped, his hand flying to his chest like I'd just personally offended him. "Wait, hold up... You're telling me you've lived in LA your whole life and you've never been to Pinks? Are you even real right now?"

Indianna chimed in. "Oh my god, we've found the unicorn. Someone call the news."

"Alright, alright," I said, laughing. "Guess it's about time, huh?"

Dylan grinned. "Damn right. Let's go educate this man on one of the finest culinary experiences the City of Angels has to offer."

The cardboard tray with all our hot dogs slid across the counter, the guy calling out like he was announcing winners at an award show: "Sixty-seven!Stretch Chili Cheese, Mario Lopez, Rosie O'Donnell, and a Patt Morrison! Side of rings, side of fries, Steak-a-Molee fries, cup of jalapeños!"

Dylan grabbed the tray with all the dogs, while I picked up the side dishes, balancing everything as we made our way to the table. The red-and-white umbrellas gave off major retro vibes, and the palm plants surrounding the patio made it feel like we were chilling in someone's backyard rather than a famous hot dog spot. The line had been wild when we got here, winding around into the parking lot, but I was shocked how fast it moved. They had some crazy system that worked.

We lucked out with a table and Dylan sat the tray down with a little too much enthusiasm. "Alright, newbie," he said, sliding me my chili cheese dog. "You can't come to Pinks and not start with the classic. It's a rite of passage."

I grabbed the cup of jalapeños and popped a few on top, just to add a little kick. "Guess I'm going all in, then," I said, trying to play it cool, but secretly, I was pumped.

Indianna wasted no time claiming her Rosie O'Donnell dog, grinning as she picked it up. It had mustard, onions, sauerkraut, and chili.

"Of course I picked this one. Big, bold, lesbian, and too much for some people? Yeah, sounds about right."

Dylan snorted, taking his Mario Lopez dog. "You're not wrong. But this guy right here? Never disappoints." He bit into it with zero hesitation as guacamole and chopped tomatoes dropped off the back. He licked off some sour cream from the corner of his mouth.

Ethan quietly reached for their Patt Morrison, neatly peeling back the foil. They nodded after the first bite. Dylan had explained that Ethan was vegetarian, so the veggie Patt Morrison dog was their go-to.

The sides were all community property, except for the jalapeños. I'd claimed those. But the Steak-a-Molee fries were the main attraction. Everyone dove in except Ethan, who obviously stuck with the regular fries. Indianna dipped an onion ring into the guac on the fries, and I swear Dylan looked at her like she'd just unlocked a new life hack.

"This was so worth the wait," Dylan said between bites, his Mario Lopez dog half gone already.

It wasn't anything fancy—just hot dogs and fries under some old-school umbrellas—but it felt like one of those moments you'd look back on later and realize it was exactly what you needed.

It hit me then how easily Indianna and Ethan had just... let me in. No weird vibes, no questions about why I was there or if I belonged. It just felt natural. It had been a minute since I felt like that. Back in the day, things with Rafe and Avery had been like this, easy and fun, before everything started to shift. Now, with Indianna cracking jokes and Ethan's low-key vibe, it felt like maybe I'd found that kind of crew again.

I glanced over at Ethan, who was quietly working through their fries like they were in some kind of meditation.

"So Dylan mentioned before that you're into magic tricks."

"Yeah," they said. "Started doing them when I was younger. Normally I do a few at these open-mic nights."

"Is that where you got the nickname?" I asked.

Ethan looked kind of puzzled at me and just gave a quiet, "huh?"

"Before..." I said, "Dylan called you the 'Ace of Hearts' or something."

Ethan nodded slowly, like they weren't sure if I was joking. "Yeah. That's actually an ace thing."

"An ace thing?" I said.

Ethan smiled, "As in *ace*-exual. I'm asexual but romantic. Like, I want connection, just not sex. Other aces aren't into sex or romance. They would be an Ace of Spades. Of course there's others who are more fluid."

I blinked, surprised at how direct they were about it and high-key worried that I made this conversation awkward.

"That's... cool," I said, and meant it. "I didn't know that was a thing."

And awkwarder still...

Ethan just shrugged, not defensive, just matter-of-fact. "It's okay.

Most people don't. But that's me."

Indianna, lounging back in her chair said, "So glad Biden dropped out. Like, he was cool and all, but let's be real—it's time for a California girl to be in charge."

Dylan nodded, fully onboard. "Facts."

Ethan was quiet but nodding in agreement. They gave a little "Mmmhmm" through a mouthful of fries.

I wasn't exactly up on politics, but the idea of a female president? I could get behind that. "That'd be cool," I added, keeping it casual.

Indianna turned her attention to me, her eyes lighting up with curiosity. "So Kiko, tell us about your mysterious self." She waved her hand in a circle in kind of an "all this" gesture.

So much for chill vibes and no questions.

"Uh, not much to say, really," I said as I scratched the back of my neck. "I skate, surf… work at a coffee shop on Wilshire. That's about it. I'm just… y'know, figuring stuff out."

Indianna raised an eyebrow, clearly unimpressed with my bare-minimum answer. "Alright, but like, what's your deal? Are you single?"

Her tone was playful, but my stomach dropped. Before I could even think of a response, Dylan shifted in his seat and Indianna flinched. "Ow!" she muttered, glaring at him. "What was that for?"

Dylan raised a hand casually, stopping Indianna mid-grumble. "Sorry about her," he said, turning to me. "She can be a little forward sometimes."

Indianna let out an exaggerated gasp, clutching her chest like she'd just been mortally offended. "Forward? Me? We're just having a conversation. Kiko doesn't have to answer, but I mean, are you?" She leaned in, raising her eyebrows for emphasis. "Single?"

Dylan shot her a sharp glare, his eyes saying *Seriously, Indie?* She held her hands up, surrendering, but there was still this mischievous grin on her face.

I appreciated Dylan trying to make sure I wasn't uncomfortable, looking out for me, but… I was suddenly hyperaware of every movement, every glance, but I figured I might as well just answer. What was the harm?

"Actually… I've been seeing someone," I said, my voice casual even though my pulse wasn't. I felt all three of them turn their attention to me.

Indianna's eyebrows shot up, clearly intrigued. "Oh? Who's the lucky person?"

I hesitated, feeling like my mouth had suddenly gone dry. "His name's Troye," I said finally, glancing down at my tray for no real reason. "It's, uh... kind of new, but it might be getting a little serious."

There was a moment of silence, not quite awkward but not quite *not-*awkward, but Indianna broke the pause first, an unreadable expression on her face. "Troye, huh?"

Dylan gave a little nod, his expression also hard to read. "That's cool."

Ethan stayed quiet, focused on their fries.

Indianna straightened up in her chair, flashing a grin that was almost too bright. "Anyway, Kiko, you ever think about performing at one of these open-mic nights? We could use some skater-kid flair."

I laughed, shaking my head. "Yeah, no. It's illegal in like fifteen states for me to sing, and I'm not exactly much of a poet."

"Then do a dramatic reading like Lori," Indianna countered. "Bring the room to its knees with your sheer... gravitas."

That word alone made me snort. "Indianna, I don't think I've ever had 'gravitas' in my life. I can barely make my own coffee without screwing it up."

"First of all," Indianna responded, "Call me Indie. That's pretty much it, I don't really have a second thing..."

The table laughed, but out of the corner of my eye, I noticed Dylan wasn't joining in. He gave a faint smile, but it didn't quite reach his eyes, and something about his energy felt... different. Distant, almost. Like he'd suddenly checked out of the moment. I couldn't shake the feeling that maybe Indie's earlier question had bothered him more than I thought. I wondered if he was really upset about her being a little nosy? It didn't seem like him.

"Lori was really cool," I said. "I could listen to her read that whole book."

Dylan gave a faint smile, still distant.

"Lori is *everything*," Indie said, picking up her drink again. "Like, the supreme. The queen. Also—side note—*Dylan's mom*."

"Wow," I said. "Really?"

"Uh..." Indie said, "Yeah."

Dylan had pulled his notebook out of his back pocket and flipped to a blank page. He didn't say a word, just pressed his pen to the paper and scribbled something down. He wasn't rushing, but it was like he needed to get the words out before they slipped away. I caught a glimpse of his face while he was writing—focused, sure, but there was this vibe of something else. Like a quiet sadness had crept in when no one was looking.

I wanted to ask if he was okay, but it felt... I don't know, like delicate or something. Like whatever he was writing wasn't something I could just barge into. Still, the shift had me wondering what I missed, and why it felt like things changed when I wasn't paying attention.

Ethan leaned in, which drew me back into the conversation that had apparently continued on without me while I was off in my head.

"It doesn't matter if it's poetry or singing or, like, what Lori was doing," they said, glancing my way. "Everyone needs something. A way to get their feelings out. It doesn't have to be deep; it just has to be yours."

I blinked, chewing on that for a sec. "I guess I've always liked photography," I said, feeling a little exposed admitting it. "Never thought about it like... as an outlet or whatever. But yeah, being one of those photographers who travels the world and captures crazy sights or epic events? That's honestly the dream right there."

Dylan looked up from his notebook, and there was something in his face, like he actually saw me. And honestly, it made me a little twitchy for no reason.

I shrugged, trying not to make it a thing. "I mean, I mess around on my phone. Post a few things on Insta. Nothing crazy."

"Doesn't have to be crazy," Ethan said. Their smile was small but there was something beneath it. "It just has to be yours."

Something about that hit different. It wasn't just about photography. It felt bigger, like they'd just dropped a key into my lap for a door I didn't even know I needed to unlock.

Indie leaned back in her chair, crossing her arms with a smirk that said she was ready to make things less serious.

"What's your handle by the way?" she asked.

"It's @therealkikorodriguez," I replied.

"Alright, so what I'm hearing is: Kiko's gonna be the next big thing. We'll all be name-dropping him in a couple of years. 'Oh, yeah, we knew him back when he was just Insta-famous.'"

I laughed, even though my face was heating up. "Yeah, okay, sure," I said, brushing it off because I didn't know what else to do. "Not exactly holding my breath on that one."

Dylan wasn't letting it slide, though. "It's not about that. It's about having somewhere to start. A space to be, you know, you."

He didn't say it like it was some life-changing advice, but it still hit like one of those lines in a movie where the whole vibe shifts. I looked at them. Ethan giving me this quiet, encouraging nod, Indie smirking like she was proud of herself, and Dylan… just looking at me like maybe he saw more in me than I'd ever given myself credit for.

I grabbed the last chili-drenched fry from the tray and tossed it in my mouth, chewing like I wasn't suddenly a little choked up. "Yeah," I said finally. "I think I get that."

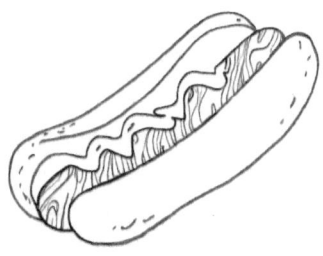

12

The sun was doing its thing, making everything look like it belonged in a movie, and Bandit was living his best life on our walk, wagging his tail like he owned the whole block. I was just vibing, enjoying the quiet, when this bright orange FJ Cruiser pulled up, roof rack loaded with two surfboards. My brain buffered for a sec when I saw the mint green Chilli Popper on top—exactly like mine. It was only when the window rolled down, and I saw Rafe in the driver's seat that I realized it *was* mine.

Bandit lost his entire mind, barking and wagging so hard it looked like his back half might take off.

"Yo, Kiko!" Rafe called, his voice setting off Bandit, who started jumping around like Rafe had just announced free steak.

Rafe didn't even bother fully parking. The FJ was half in a spot, half in the street, but that was on brand for him—big energy, zero chill. He hopped out, leaving the door wide open, and came over, Bandit immediately gluing himself to Rafe like they were long-lost besties—and they kind of were.

"Sup, dude?" Rafe said, scratching Bandit behind the ears and giving him the kind of attention that made me jealous for like half a second. "Thought I'd find you out here."

"Half the street's waiting on you to figure out parking," I said, but I was already smiling. Rafe had that effect—it was hard to stay mad at him for anything. "Whose wheels did you borrow, anyway?"

"Do you like it?" he said, standing up and giving Bandit one last pat. "Wanted to show off my new ride and drag you out to the water."

My eyes flicked to the FJ, and, yeah, I had to admit it was kinda sick. "Wait, this is yours? Since when?"

"Since this morning," he said, with his signature grin. "Big things for this summer, y'know?"

"Yeah, sure," I said, crossing my arms. "So this is, what, an elaborate flex to guilt me into surfing?"

Rafe gave me a look that was all mischief. "Nah, it's a flex and an invite. Two-for-one. So, what do you say? You gonna let that board collect dust, or are we catching some waves?"

I glanced at the FJ again, then at Bandit, who looked like he was fully team Rafe.

Little traitor.

"I don't know, man. I've got stuff—," I started.

Rafe cut me off with a mock gasp. "Stuff? Like, important stuff? C'mon, Kiko, don't make me go solo on my first surf trip with the new whip. That'd be plain tragic."

"I have to watch Mateo," I added.

"Bring him along!" Rafe replied.

I groaned, but deep down, I knew I was already caving. "Fine," I said, rolling my eyes for dramatic effect. "But only because Bandit's clearly on your side."

"Obviously," Rafe said, throwing an arm around my shoulders. "Let's hit it."

After grabbing my wetsuit, towel, and the essentials for the beach, I threw everything into a bag. Mateo was already waiting by the door in his swim trunks and one of his nerdy space shirts, holding Bandit's leash in one hand and a snorkel mask in the other.

"Bandit's coming too, I guess?"

Mateo nodded with the confidence of someone who had already decided the answer was yes. "Of course. He loves the beach."

Bandit wagged his tail like he'd heard the whole conversation and fully agreed. I sighed but grabbed an extra towel for him because there was no winning against that combo.

As we walked down the alley towards the street, Rafe honked impatiently from his FJ Cruiser. Mateo bolted down the steps, Bandit trotting after him, tail wagging like a windshield wiper on high speed. I followed, less in a rush because the second I saw Rafe's FJ still parked half in the street and half in a spot, my brain screamed, *What am I doing?*

Was putting my little brother and our hyperactive dog in a car driven by Rafe a terrible idea? Probably. But Bandit had already jumped into the backseat and Mateo was geeking out over the FJ's roof rack and asking Rafe a million questions about it.

"C'mon, Kiko, there's room for one more!" Rafe called, smirking like this was some big adventure.

I climbed into the passenger seat and shot Rafe a side-eye that basically said, *If you crash this car, I will haunt you forever.*

"Relax, dude," Rafe said with a grin. "I've got VIPs on board—plus Bandit would never forgive me if I messed this up."

That actually got a laugh out of me. "You're not wrong."

Mateo buckled himself in next to Bandit, who had already claimed the middle of the backseat and looked ridiculously happy about it. "Let's gooo!" Mateo yelled, throwing a fist in the air.

Rafe shifted into drive with an exaggerated "Here we go!" as we pulled out. And that's when it hit me. Despite his questionable parking skills, Rafe was... actually driving well. No sudden stops, no swerving, no chaotic vibes. Just smooth turns and careful stops. I relaxed a little, glancing back to see Mateo laughing at Bandit, who had his nose pressed to the window like he was trying to smell the whole city.

"Alright, Rafe," I said, leaning back in my seat. "Maybe I won't revoke your license after all."

Rafe smirked, glancing over. "Told you, man. Precious cargo. Bandit wouldn't let me live it down."

"Let's hit Santa Monica," I suggested.

Rafe raised an eyebrow. "Santa Monica? Really? I know it's been a while since you've been out on the waves but do we have to go *that* beginner?"

I shrugged. "It's got the pier, snacks, shops, stuff for Mateo later. Plus, Bandit can chill there too."

"Alright, alright," Rafe conceded with a grin, throwing the car into gear. "Santa Monica it is."

The drive wasn't bad. Rafe hopped on the 10, rolling the windows down, Bandit's ears flapping in the breeze as he poked his head out the backseat window. Mateo was scrolling through his phone, occasionally showing me random memes, and Rafe had some indie playlist blasting that I didn't hate. About twenty minutes later, we were pulling into the parking lot near the Santa Monica Pier.

We unloaded everything—surfboards, bags, towels—and made our way onto the beach. Mateo was juggling a snorkel, a boogie board, and Bandit's leash, while Bandit was already trying to dig into the sand.

"Alright, Mateo," I said, stopping near a lifeguard tower. "This is our spot. Stay in the area, alright? If you go in the water, only to your knees. Got it?"

Mateo gave me the most dramatic eye-roll I'd ever seen. "I'm not a little kid, Kiko. I know how to not drown."

Rafe stepped in between us. His tone was all chill. "We're not saying that, little man. We just want to make sure you're safe, that's all."

Mateo shrugged, a little calmer. "Yeah, okay. I'll stay close."

Bandit, meanwhile, was already trying to make friends with a group of seagulls nearby. "And keep an eye on Bandit," I added, handing him a tennis ball for distractions. Mateo saluted like he was on a mission, grabbing the ball and leading Bandit toward the shore.

With Mateo and Bandit settled, Rafe and I grabbed our boards and started paddling out. The waves were mellow—nothing crazy, which was the norm here. As we paddled past the break, Rafe nudged me with his board.

"Think Mateo's gonna keep Bandit outta trouble?" he asked, grinning.

I laughed glancing back at Mateo setting up his spot on the sand. "Probably not, but he'll try. I just hope Bandit doesn't decide to go full lifeguard and follow us out here."

We caught a few waves. They were nothing huge, just enough to feel the rush and settle into a rhythm. I paddled back out after a decent one and waited for Rafe to catch up. He was grinning like a total goof, clearly stoked, and it made me laugh.

"Man, this is the life," Rafe said, flipping water off his hair as he floated next to me. "Nothing but waves, sun, and best buds."

"Yeah, it's good," I agreed, leaning on my board. "Also, I gotta say, the truck's pretty sick."

Rafe smirked. "Right? Thanks, dude. Figured I needed something reliable for the drive back and forth to Santa Barbara once school starts. It beats Amtrak."

That hit harder than I expected. I'd almost forgotten—or maybe I'd been avoiding thinking about it. Summer wasn't going to last forever. By mid September, Rafe would be heading off to UC Santa Barbara, and Avery would be starting at Stanford. The three of us, the crew, wouldn't be the same—even more so than now.

"Santa Barbara, huh…" I said, trying to keep my tone light, even though my chest felt a little tight. "Guess the FJ's got the perfect beach vibes for it."

Rafe nodded, his grin widening. "*Exactly.* Plus, it's got room for boards, Bandit, you know, all your other essentials."

I laughed, shaking my head. "Essentials like Bandit? You're wild."

"Gotta have priorities, bro," he shot back with a wink before paddling out to catch the next wave.

"I swear that dog respects you more."

As I sat on my board, staring out at the horizon, with the ocean just seeming endless, the reality of their plans just kinda sank in. July would be over in just a few days, and all I could think about was how fast summer was slipping away.

After a solid session in the water, my arms were jelly, and the lineup was getting crowded with tourists who had no clue what they were doing. We paddled back to shore, unstrapped the leashes from our ankles, and ditched the boards in the sand.

Mateo was tossing a neon-yellow tennis ball into the shallow surf for Bandit, who was straight-up living his best life. Every time Mateo chucked the ball, Bandit bolted after it like a rocket, splashing through the water and kicking up spray. The ball would bounce awkwardly on the surface, and Bandit would pounce on it, tail wagging like a propeller. Mateo's laugh carried over the sound of the waves. Both of them were having way too much fun.

As we trudged up the beach, Mateo and Bandit ran over to meet us, Mateo holding the soggy tennis ball triumphantly. "Bandit's got more energy than you two combined," he teased.

"Yeah, but can he surf?" Rafe shot back, smirking as he tossed his board down onto the sand.

I dropped my board and sank onto the towel, letting the sun warm my skin as I stared out at the waves. Bandit, still hyped, flopped down next to me with his tongue hanging out.

Rafe shook out his hair dramatically like he was in a shampoo commercial. "Not bad out there. For Santa Monica, anyway."

"Yeah, decent," I said, pulling at the sleeves of my wetsuit. "Definitely not worth getting dropped in on five times, though."

Rafe kicked back on the towel, throwing on his shades and stretching out like some chill Instagram model. Mateo eventually plopped down too, stretching out next to Rafe. For a while, we just sat there, the three of us vibing in the sun, letting the beach noises fill the gaps in our silence.

After a bit, I sat up and scanned the scene. "Yo," I said, grabbing the frisbee from the bag. "Who's down for some frisbee?"

Rafe peeked over his shades, one eyebrow raised. "You really want to get destroyed?"

"Man, you're about to get schooled and you don't even know it," I shot back, spinning the frisbee in my hands like I was born to do this.

Mateo's eyes lit up as he jumped to his feet. "Let's gooooo!"

I tossed Mateo the frisbee to kick things off. Bandit barked like he was ready for his Super Bowl moment. Mateo launched the frisbee. He actually had a decent arm, but Rafe couldn't resist showing off, catching the frisbee behind his back or pulling unnecessary spins like he was auditioning for some commercial. Bandit, naturally, stole the show though, chasing every throw, and sometimes he actually intercepted it. The sun was still high, the vibe was immaculate, and life just felt stupidly good. It was one of those moments you wish you could freeze.

"Can we go up to the pier and get ice cream?" Mateo asked, eyes wide like he'd already decided the answer was yes.

I shook my head, leaning down to pack up the towels and stash them in the bag. "We should grab lunch first. Actual food before dessert, remember?"

"But ice cream is food," Mateo countered, flashing this annoyingly innocent smile he always pulled when he was trying to get his way. He turned to Rafe, clearly looking for backup.

Rafe didn't even hesitate. "I mean… he's got a point. It's not like it's gonna spoil our appetite or anything."

I shot Rafe a look. "Dude, you're not helping."

He just shrugged, grinning. "C'mon, Kiko. Let the kid live a little."

I groaned, zipping up the bag and giving Bandit a quick pat. "Fine, but if he's bouncing off the walls later, I'm blaming you."

Mateo fist-pumped. "Victory!"

We packed up all our stuff and lugged the boards back to the FJ. By the time we got to the pier, the smell of churros, funnel cake, and saltwater filled the air, Mateo was so excited. Scoops had a line snaking away from the window, but that didn't faze him. He was already talking a mile a minute about which flavor he was going to get.

"I'm getting the Cookie Monster," Mateo declared, holding Bandit's leash while we waited. "It's blue. And blue's the best color."

"Cookie Monster? Really?" I teased, raising an eyebrow. "You're not five anymore, dude."

Mateo rolled his eyes. "Just because you get Sea Salt Caramel every single time, doesn't mean the rest of us can't live a little."

Rafe was clearly rubbing off on him and not in a good way.

"But Sea Salt Caramel is the best." I crossed my arms.

Rafe chimed in, leaning against the railing like he had all the time in the world. "And I'm sticking with my Mint Chip. It's a classic. It's refreshing. And most important, it's green, and I gotta stay on brand."

He held up the green t-shirt he had over one of his shoulders.

I laughed. "Okay, Mr. Mint Chip. Let's see how long this line takes before we all change our minds about waiting."

Mateo stood on his tiptoes, trying to peek up front. "It's worth the wait. Ice cream always is."

Bandit barked, like he agreed, and I couldn't help but smile.

"Sorry little guy, no pup cups here," I said, petting his head, as he let out a whine.

Then my phone chimed in my pocket. I pulled it out, squinting against the glare of the sun, and there he was.

Troye   Just Now
Hey, you free later? Wanna meet up?

I felt that stupid little smile creep up, totally uninvited. I tried to lock my phone and put it away like nothing happened, but nope, Rafe was already on it.

"Yo, who was *that*?" he asked, grinning like he'd just found dirt.

"Uh, nobody," I said, way too fast, shoving the phone back into my pocket. Smooth.

"Nobody?" Rafe's grin widened like a cat about to pounce. "Bro, you don't make that face for nobody. What's her name?"

"I'm telling you, it's nothing—"

But then Mateo turned around, hearing just enough to ruin my life. "Kiko's got a girlfriend! Kiko's got a girlfriend!" he sang, way too loud. People in line glanced over. Bandit barked like he was in on it.

Perfect.

"Shut up, Mateo!" I hissed. "You're both so wrong, it's painful."

"Sure, totally wrong," Rafe teased. He was doing that smug side-smirk thing he always did. Mateo just kept giggling. Even Bandit was howling, wagging his tail like he was laughing his ass off too.

Traitors.

Finally, we got to the counter and put in our order. The guy handed us our cones, and we headed further out on the pier dodging the tourists who were in full chaos mode. Cameras flashing, kids yelling, someone arguing about churros—it was the vibe.

We were weaving through the crowd on the pier, dodging strollers, selfie sticks, and that one guy selling knockoff sunglasses. Rafe had his mint chip cone in one hand, looking way too at ease for someone stirring the pot. He slowed his pace, glancing over at me with this serious look that didn't match the ice cream dribble on his hand.

"You know. We never hang out anymore," he said.

I raised an eyebrow. "We're literally hanging out right now."

"Nah, man, I mean like actually hanging out. It's been, what, weeks?" He shook his head, acting all disappointed. "I don't even know what's up with you anymore."

Mateo, still working on turning his tongue blue, slowed down and looked between us.

I glanced back at Rafe, trying to figure out why he was making this a thing. "It's not that deep," I said, trying to brush it off, "I've just been busy."

"I just... miss you, man," he said, and his voice was serious now, and I don't know if I can recall the last time that was the case. But then he continued, "Like, for real, dude. Avery does too."

I froze mid-lick, my cone starting to melt down my fingers, because of course, he brought *her* up. The second her name came out of his mouth, it was like this weight dropped on my chest, and the chill vibe of the day just left the chat.

"Rafe," I said, trying to keep it casual, but my tone probably gave me away. "We've been hanging out all day. What are you even talking about?"

"It's not the same, Kiko," he pressed, like he had some right to call me out. "You've been distant, dude. Like, you don't even hit us up anymore. Avery keeps asking what's going on with you, and honestly, I don't know what to tell her."

There it was again—the two of them. I wondered what else about me they discussed with each other without me around. I tried to ignore this feeling in my stomach and just kept walking. Bandit trotted beside me, completely unbothered, but my brain? It was spiraling.

"I've been busy," I said, shrugging like it wasn't a big deal. "Work, life... you know how it is."

"Yeah, I get it," Rafe said, not letting it go. "But it's not just that. It's like you're keeping stuff from us."

My jaw clenched. He wasn't wrong, but the way he said it, like he was entitled to know everything about me, while the two of them were doing whatever, pissed me off. He didn't know half the stuff I was dealing with. And yeah, maybe that was my fault for not telling him, but still—it wasn't like he made it easy. Every time I thought about opening up, the image of him and Avery, all smiles and their new inside jokes, would creep into my head, and I'd just shut down.

"I'm not keeping anything from you," I lied. My voice was a little too sharp.

Rafe stopped walking, forcing me to stop too. Mateo kept going ahead, tossing Bandit's ball into the air, completely unaware of the tension building, or maybe that was why he kept walking.

"Come on, Kiko," Rafe said, his voice softer now, like he was trying to reach me. "You've always been real with me. If something's up, you can tell me."

I looked at him, at the guy who had been my best friend for so long. And yeah, he knew me better than almost anyone. But lately, it felt like there was this huge gap between us, this invisible wall that kept getting higher every time he brought up Avery or tried to pull me back into the way things used to be. He didn't get it—how could he? There was so much about me he didn't know, and maybe couldn't ever know.

"I'm fine," I said finally, my voice flat, shutting it down before it could go any further.

Rafe didn't look convinced, but he didn't push. He just sighed and gave me a quick, "Aight," as we started walking again. And somehow that seemed worse.

The day had started off easy, fun even. But now? It just felt heavy, like the crash after a perfect ride—salt in your throat, sand in your teeth, and no clue how you ended up here. Needless to say, the chill was gone.

The car ride back to my place was quiet—like, *way too* quiet. Rafe glanced over at me a few times, his eyes saying something like, *What's up with you*? But I wasn't about to open up in the middle of an FJ Cruiser ride. Bandit was drooling in the backseat and Mateo humming some random tune. So I just stared out the window instead, pretending I didn't notice Rafe's glances as I counted the palm trees as they blurred by.

When we pulled up in front of my apartment building, Rafe parked with his usual "this looks close enough" style, half in a spot, half out. Mateo hopped out with Bandit, who was wagging his tail like this whole day hadn't taken a weird turn. I grabbed the bags and slung them over my shoulder, heading towards the door.

"Hey," Rafe said, stopping me just before I could step away. His voice was quieter, almost unsure. "We're good, right?"

I forced a smile, but I knew it seemed weak. "Yeah, man, of course. We're good. It's just... you know, life," the lie rolled off my tongue too easily.

Rafe nodded, but it was clear he didn't buy it. "Alright," he said, giving me a half-smile back. "Take care of yourself, okay?"

"Always," I replied.

He watched as Mateo, Bandit, and I headed inside. I didn't look back, but I could feel his eyes on me the whole way.

We headed up the stairs to fight with the lock. The second the door clicked shut behind us, Bandit bolted toward his water bowl, his tail wagging at full speed. Mateo kicked his shoes off, and I headed straight for our room. I just wanted to collapse on my bed and forget about the whole day, and I was halfway to our room to do just that when Mateo called me from the front door.

"Hey, Kiko?"

He still had one hand on the knob, like he wasn't sure if he should've said anything.

"What's up?" I asked.

He hesitated before asking, "If you haven't been hanging out with Rafe and Avery, whose house have you been staying at?"

Well, fuck.

13

I rolled up to Troye's apartment, the late afternoon light hitting just right. I couldn't resist crossing the street to snap a quick pic of the sky with one of the giant palm trees in front.

And yeah, I had successfully dodged Mateo's little interrogation. I told him the truth... mostly. I said I'd been staying at Troye's, but I kinda smoothed it over by calling him "a friend" like it wasn't a whole thing. Mateo didn't totally buy it, though. He did that thing where he nods but his eyes are all, "yeah, sure." I tacked on that I didn't want Ma to worry because she didn't know Troye so it was just easier to say I was with Rafe. He held out until I told him I would owe him one before he let it slide—classic little brother move.

Even still, I had laid low for the week. Met up with Troye on Wednesday to walk around the La Brea tar pits, but didn't stay over. I figured it was long enough to let it blow over.

I got to the building, kicked up my board, and grabbed it under my arm. The side gate was open again—Troye's neighbors were really about that zero security life. My stomach was doing backflips as I walked to his door, which was dumb because it wasn't like this was my first time here. Still, something about Troye just made me feel like a seventh-grader with a crush all over again.

I knocked, and the door opened almost immediately. There he was, leaning casually on the doorframe, his gray tank showing off his stupidly perfect shoulders and his messy frosted curls looked effortlessly cool.

"Hey," he said with that grin of his. His eyes looked darker than usual, like deeper, but also a little... feral?

"Hey," I said with a stupid grin as I stepped inside. I was mostly just trying not to trip over my own feet, but I jumped a little when a door down the first floor hallway slammed shut.

Troye just laughed. "And that," he said with a dramatic eye roll, "is Kendra. Don't mind her."

"Umm... Okay...," I said, as Troye leaned in and greeted me with a kiss. Just a quick one, but it was the one I was definitely getting kinda used to.

"C'mon," he said, grabbing my hand and leading me up the stairs. When we got into his room, Troye closed the door behind us with what I could only describe as impatience. The door barely clicked shut before Troye spun around to kiss me again, but this time? I was ready for him. I slid my arms around his waist and pulled him in tight, making him stumble a step backward until his back hit the door. He let out this little gasp against my lips, and I couldn't help but smirk into the kiss.

It wasn't rushed or messy—just...electric. His hands found their way to my chest, then my shoulders, but I wasn't planning on letting him get too comfortable. Yeah, I was definitely feeling myself, but I didn't second-guess it. It felt good, natural, like I was exactly where I was supposed to be.

When I finally pulled back, I traced my thumb along his jawline. His eyes weren't just darker, his pupils were blown wide. His cheeks were flushed, and yeah, I could tell I'd thrown him off his game a little. I leaned in close, and made sure my lips brushed his ear—two can play his game.

"Careful," I said low, playful, "you're gonna make me think you can't keep up."

Troye blinked like he was rebooting—for once— and then he gave a little grin. "I don't know where *this* all came from, but trust me I *can* keep up," he shot back, "But... we can't get too carried away. Maya's coming back with wine."

I chuckled, stepping back to let him breathe. "Of course she is." My voice was cool, but inside, I was buzzing. He adjusted his shirt, tousled his hair and tried to play it cool. The look he gave me, though? Yeah, I knew I had him weak. And to be honest? I kinda loved it.

Troye sat cross-legged on his bed, "Maya wants me to draw her—like a full-on portrait or something. She's been bugging me about it for weeks. And a few of my friends from my program are coming over too. It's kinda like... a creative hangout, I guess." He tilted his head, giving me this hopeful smile like he wanted me to be excited.

I shifted a little, pulling my legs up onto the bed. I was trying to act chill. "Oh, cool," I said, leaning back against the headboard. "That sounds fun." Except my brain was already racing. His *art friends*? Like, talented people who probably talk about deep, artsy stuff and know things I'd never even thought about? I was sure I was going to say something dumb. What if I didn't vibe with them? Friends could be make or break in a relationship.

But, at the same time, I was kinda excited. Meeting Troye's friends felt like a big deal, like it was definitely this next step in...whatever this was. I felt Troye shift closer, and I put my arm around him automatically, pulling him in like this was second nature now. He put his head on my chest, and just like that, everything calmed just a little.

My mind wandered as he started scrolling through TikTok. Meeting his friends felt big, but what about my own. Dylan, Indie, Ethan—yeah, I could see Troye getting along with them, especially Dylan with his own unique style. They'd probably end up scouring the thrift shop scene, and maybe become besties or something. But Rafe and Avery? Yeah. Hard pass. Just imagining that mashup felt messy, like two different parts of my life that weren't meant to overlap. But when did they stop being the first people I thought about when I pictured stuff like this?

I gotta say, though, it hit me harder than I expected. Dylan, Emily, and Ethan had pretty much filled the space Rafe and Avery once occupied, and I couldn't decide if I'd let that happen or if it just... happened. Either way, it felt like a door was closing behind me. And now, entering Troye's orbit, I wasn't sure I even belonged in my own.

I brushed it off before I could spiral too far, as Troye laughed at some TikTok of a cat freaking out over cucumbers.

"Look at this," he said, holding the phone up for me to see. I leaned in closer, laughing with him, our heads almost touching. The sound of his laughter and the warmth of his body next to mine made everything else fade. For now, I didn't need to overthink. We could just sit here, laugh at dumb videos, and enjoy the moment.

A couple of minutes later, we heard the front door slam shut, followed by the shuffle of footsteps. "That'd be Maya," Troye said with a smirk, glancing at me. Sure enough, a minute later, there was a knock at the door.

"Come in!" Troye called out, leaning back on the bed like he was expecting royalty.

Maya pushed the door open with her elbow, balancing two bottles of wine in one hand and three wine glasses in the other like a multitasking pro. "Y'all better be decent," Maya warned. "I'm not trying to walk in on some... *situation*."

Troye rolled his eyes. "Relax. You think I'd yell 'come in' mid-action?"

"I don't know, Troye. You're bold sometimes," Maya teased.

She held up the bottles. "Anyway, here's what I got: cab for me, and a Bordeaux for your bougie ass." She held up the bottle dramatically before setting the clinking glasses on the dresser.

Troye jumped up out of bed and reached for the Bordeaux. He eyed the label like he knew exactly what he was doing. "Damn, girl, you're really out here making me look good. This one's fancy-fancy."

"Obviously," she said, sitting on the creaky stool. "You think I'm about to show up with the cheap stuff? Please. I have standards. Only the best for my Troye-boy."

I couldn't help but laugh at the nickname. I mentally filed that one away for later. I sat up a little straighter and tried to pretend that I wasn't *completely* clueless about wine. "I've never had a Bordeaux, but it looks fancy, so good call," I joked.

"Exactly," Troye said, still checking out the Chateau-something label. "Maya never disappoints. Always a woman of taste."

Maya grinned and leaned back dramatically, kicking off her shoes. "Duh. Y'all should be honored to even share this space with me."

Their easy vibe was kinda contagious. Watching them banter, I didn't feel like an outsider—at least, not completely. This was the first time I'd actually got to hang out with Maya and not just see her in passing. I had to admit, the more I got to know her, the more I thought she was actually pretty chill.

"Hey," Maya's voice cut in, her face was full of concern. "You're bleeding." She pointed at Troye's face.

Troye put a hand to his nose which had a flow of bright red blood coming from it. He pinched it and tilted his head back as he got up and ran for the bathroom. Maya and I just exchanged a quick yikes expression and made small talk until he came back.

After the sink turned off, Troye reentered the room.

"All better," Troye said. "It happens some times. My genes weren't designed for these dry SoCal summers."

It wasn't long before Troye's friends started showing up. First up was Alex, who I've gotta say—a total showstopper... in an, uh... objective sort of way of course. Dude was rocking overalls with no shirt underneath, like he was a model for some trendy brand. Drew followed, all red curls and long beard with like an indie folk-band vibe. Lisa was next with this electric vibe and her fire-engine-red pixie cut. They wasted no time in pouring drinks and joking with me like they'd known me forever.

And me? I was just focused on trying to remember everyone's names, but with this many new faces at once, it was kind of a toss-up. I stayed close to Troye, sipping my wine in this crowd of artsy people who seemed so cool. These were Troye's people, but I felt like I might actually have a chance at fitting into this part of his world.

It wasn't long before Maya was sitting cross-legged at the foot of the bed like she was holding court. She clinked her wine glass to get everyone's attention. "Alright, y'all," she announced, her voice playful but commanding. "I've been pestering Troye for weeks to draw me, and tonight's the night."

Troye clearly knew where this was going. "Yeah, yeah, Maya, I get it. I'm on it," he said, waving his hand as if to dismiss her.

Maya stood up and set her glass down on the desk. She held her hand up all dramatic like she was about to drop some announcement. "I said I want to be drawn," she declared. "But I want to do this the *right* way..."

Her words hung in the air for a second, and then she added with a smirk, "Nude."

I almost spit my drink. I managed to hold it together, but my eyebrows shot up so fast I was pretty sure I looked like a cartoon character. Did she seriously just say...?

The room burst into chaos as she pulled her shirt over her head— cheering, clapping, and laughter all at once. Drew raised his bourbon like she'd just proposed a toast. Lisa was scrambling for her art supplies. "Yes! Finally, someone who gets it," she said, beaming.

Troye, of course, just grinned. "Alright, alright, calm down," he said, waving a hand. "I'll grab my pencils."

Meanwhile, I was sitting there trying not to look like the only guy in the room losing his mind over this. Like, this was just... normal for them. I glanced around at everyone pulling out their sketch pads and supplies, hyped to get started, and realized, yeah, it probably was.

"You good?" Troye's voice broke through my spiral. He leaned over, his voice soft, barely audible over the commotion. "You look a little... overwhelmed. Sure you can... *keep up*?"

I hated that he threw my own line right back at me, but gave a cool, "I'm good." My voice was way too casual for how much I was panicking inside. "Just wasn't expecting this, that's all."

Troye's smile widened, but he didn't push it. "You're cute when you're flustered, you know that?"

I rolled my eyes but couldn't stop the grin tugging at my lips. "Shut up."

Maya, meanwhile, was already unhooking her bra.

I sipped my wine and watched as everyone shifted into full-on artist mode. Their sketch pads were propped on their knees or flat on the floor, and their pencils or charcoal were ready to move. Troye grabbed his pad and found a spot near the desk. He was so focused, I was actually shocked he glanced back at me.

"Grab a pad," he said. "Give it a go!"

I leaned back, letting out a slow breath. *Alright, Kiko*, I thought. *Time to go with the flow. Welcome to Troye's world.*

Alex clapped his hands and found a spot near the dresser. "Alright, people, one-minute sketches. Let's warm up. Quick and messy, don't overthink it."

Maya, fully nude and fully unbothered, struck a pose that was pure drama. One hand on her hip, the other stretched above her head like she was some Greek statue. "Sketch me like one of your European ladies," she joked.

Troye, already dragging his pencil across the page, rolled his eyes. "That's not even the line, Maya."

"Whatever, close enough," Maya shot back, holding her pose. Her skin was this flawless mocha color and was super smooth.

The others didn't even react, like this was an everyday event for them. They were all just focused on their drawings as their pencils scratched away on their sketchpads. Meanwhile, I just stared at my paper, pencil hovering, absolutely clueless. The pressure of trying to draw someone who was actually standing right there was *way* too much. I glanced at Maya, then back at my page and the disconnect was... just wow. What I ended up with looked like some mutilated stick figure. Her head was too big, one arm looked like a bent noodle, and I somehow made one of her feet way too big.

Troye noticed. *Of course, he did.* He leaned over, his knee brushing against mine, and whispered, "You're thinking too much. Don't draw the whole thing. Just break her down into shapes. See her torso? That's, like, peanut-shaped. Start there."

So, I gave it a shot, squinting at Maya and trying to peanut-shell her torso. It wasn't perfect, but at least it looked less like a horror movie extra. Troye peeked over my shoulder again. "See? That's way better. Just keep going."

Alex's obnoxious alarm cut through the quiet. "Time!" he called out, setting down his pencil and looking smug.

Maya dropped her pose. She rolled her shoulders and shook out her arms.

Everyone started flipping their sketchpads around, showing off their work and hyping each other up. I looked down at mine, still kinda embarrassed, but it wasn't as bad as I thought. Definitely *not* good, but also not the flaming disaster I expected it to be. Troye reached over to grab my pad, his fingers brushing mine. "Not bad for a first-timer," he said, flashing me this soft smile that felt way more encouraging than it had any right to.

And yeah, okay. Maybe I wasn't a prodigy or whatever, but hearing that from him made me feel like I could at least fake it for the next round.

"Alright, two-minute drill. Let's go!" Alex called out as he flipped to a new page in his sketchpad. Maya struck a new pose. This time she was seated on the edge of the bed with her legs crossed, one hand resting on her knee while the other propped her up behind her.

I flipped to a new page, ready to redeem myself. Two minutes didn't feel quite as impossible as one. It was still fast, but at least now I could breathe a little while trying to figure out how to make Maya look less like an alien giraffe.

Troye leaned in close again, glancing at my page. "Okay, you've got the basic shape down, but see how her arm bends? The curve there? Try to exaggerate that a bit."

I squinted at Maya's arm, then back at my sketch. "Like... make it all wavy?"

"No," he said, biting back a laugh. "Just follow the flow. Think of her body like it's made of connected lines. Don't focus on her hand or her face right now. Get the flow right first."

I nodded and adjusted my pencil. I was just trying to sketch out the curve of her arm in one long motion. And honestly? I had to say it actually didn't look terrible. For the first time since I started drawing, I started to feel this tiny bit of confidence creeping in.

"That's it," Troye said quietly. His voice was low and kinda encouraging. "Now just add in the angles of her legs, and don't worry about the details yet."

The room stayed chill, everyone in their own zone. Lisa looked like she was doing quick lines like she was trying to capture Maya's energy more than her shape, while Alex and Drew were super focused, their brows furrowed like they were in deep concentration. Troye kept his sketchpad tilted away from me, but I caught glimpses of his page—clean, smooth lines that somehow already looked incredible even in the roughest form.

The two minutes went by way faster than I expected, and Alex's alarm went off again. "Time!" he called out.

Maya stood up and stretched, too, giving a little twirl. "How'd I do?" she teased.

I stared at my page, and for the first time tonight, I wasn't horrified. It *definitely* wasn't a masterpiece or anything, but it was a step up from my one-minute attempt. Troye looked over, giving me a small nod of approval. "Told you. You're getting it," he said, and yeah, that felt kinda nice.

Alex unhooked his overalls with the smirk of someone who absolutely knew he was the moment. "Okay, everyone, five-minute pose. But let's make it spicy," he said, grinning like this was the most normal thing in the world. And then—boom—his overalls just hit the floor. No boxers, no briefs, just… *him*.

I froze. My pencil hovered in midair as my brain scrambled to process. Like, what? I didn't even know where to look. And then the panic hit—what if Troye caught me staring? I darted a quick glance at him to see if I was busted.

Instead, Troye was full-on laughing. "You're good. This isn't a test," he said, his tone light but reassuring. He gestured toward Alex, like this was some casual art school normalcy. "Go ahead and look. That's kind of the point. Try sketching him—it's good practice."

"Yeah, practice," I mumbled, already feeling my face heat up. I tried to focus on my sketchpad, but the whole situation was throwing me off. Like, everyone else was completely chill, and I was over here trying not to combust.

Alex struck a new pose, with his back to me leaning one hand on the wall with his hip popped just enough to… well, you get the point. "Don't hold back, y'all. I expect greatness," he teased, tossing a glance over his shoulder at Lisa, who was already in the zone, her pencil flying across the page.

Troye leaned in close to take another look.

"Don't overthink it," he said, his voice low enough that only I could hear. "Focus on the movement, the energy. It's not about perfection—it's about capturing the vibe."

"Sure. Capture the vibe," I muttered, like it was that simple. I glanced back at Alex, forcing myself to focus on his stance—and not specific parts of his body. There was this way his weight shifted from one leg to the other, and the way his shoulders angled. I let my pencil move, keeping my strokes loose like Troye had suggested.

And it actually started to kinda work. My drawing wasn't great, but it felt less like a cringey stick figure and more like, I don't know, a person. I could hear the scratch of pencils around the room, everyone locked into their own zones.

"How's it going back there, Kiko?" Alex called out, his voice full of playful confidence. "Getting my best angles?"

I nearly dropped my pencil. "Uh, yeah," I managed, my voice cracking just enough to make me want to disappear.

Troye chuckled beside me, leaning closer with that amused glint in his eye. "Relax," he whispered, like he could tell exactly how flustered I was. For some reason, that made it a little easier. I refocused on the page, letting my lines flow a little more freely.

I zeroed in on Alex's stance, trying to ignore the absolute chaos happening in my brain. His pose was bold—hip shifted, legs slightly apart, weight balanced just right. My pencil hovered over the page, unsure where to start. My gaze landed on his legs and, okay, his butt—because, like, how could it not? The guy looked like a freaking sculpture.

"Start with the biggest shapes," Troye said. "See how his legs form almost a triangle? Get that down first, then work in the details."

I nodded, swallowing the lump in my throat as I started sketching the curve of Alex's thigh and the angle of his calves. My lines were shaky, but Troye didn't say anything about it. Instead, he pointed at my page.

"Don't be afraid to exaggerate it a bit," he said, his tone low and encouraging. "Like, look at the way his quads pop out from this angle. Highlight that—push the shadow there."

I stole a quick glance at Alex, who was holding his pose like it was nothing. I tried to follow Troye's advice, darkening the lines on the underside of Alex's leg and shading where his stance caught the light.

"And his glutes," Troye added, a teasing smile playing on his lips. "Don't skip those—they're kinda the star of the show."

I nearly choked as I gripped the pencil tighter, trying to keep it steady. "Yeah, thanks for that," I muttered, trying to ignore how red my face probably was. But I added a curve to the sketch.

"You're doing good," Troye said before he leaned back.

By the time Alex adjusted his pose slightly, I had something that almost resembled a human figure—legs, shadows, and, yes, a decent attempt at the glutes. It wasn't perfect, but for my skill level, I felt kinda proud.

Maybe I wasn't going to be the next big thing in figure drawing, but at least I wasn't totally embarrassing myself. Well, not yet, anyway.

Troye and Lisa exchanged a quick glance, then both shrugged like it was the most casual thing in the world before peeling off their clothes. Lisa kicked off her Converse high-tops and slid out of her skinny jeans, while Troye stood with this exaggerated flourish, tossing his shirt onto the bed and then slipping out of his pants with way too much flair. He was now standing there, fully nude, hands on his hips.

Drew smirked, catching my awkward shuffle. "It's up to you, dude."

I hesitated for a second and fiddled with the edge of my shirt. This whole situation was already *way* out of my comfort zone, but I for damn sure didn't want to be the odd man out. With a deep breath, I pulled my shirt over my head and slid out of my jeans, leaving me in just my boxer briefs. Drew, for his part, only took off his shirt, his chest covered in a mess of red hair that matched his beard.

Everyone else was already trying different poses, laughing with each other, and sketching like this was just any normal Saturday. I settled on the bed with my sketchpad, trying not to look too overwhelmed. Troye caught my eye and gave me this reassuring smile—just a flicker, but it was enough.

I decided to stick with Alex for now. His pose had one leg bent and his hands were resting on his hips. I started sketching his legs, finding the shapes easier this time, and adding details to the curve of his muscles. My lines felt more intentional, less like a mess of squiggles.

Out of the corner of my eye, I saw Troye settle into a chair with his sketchpad. He was totally focused on Maya. His body was lean and there was this one little curl that fell slightly onto his forehead as he sketched.

My pencil was moving again, before I realized it. This time it was creating rough lines that I told myself were "artistic," but really, it was just me trying to capture how good he looked. I didn't have time to obsess over the details, so it ended up being more of a doodle than an actual drawing. Still, it was kinda dope to see something resembling Troye take shape on the page.

The room buzzed with laughter and the soft scratching of pencils against paper. The weirdness of the nudity started to fade into the background. Everyone was just... existing, no walls up, no judgment. I found myself relaxing a little, caught up in the flow of it all. For the first time in what felt like forever, I wasn't overthinking everything. I was just here. Present. And honestly, it felt kind of freeing.

Lisa's phone chimed on the nightstand.

"Oh, Brandon's here," she said excitedly.

Drew smirked, tossing his pencil onto his sketchpad. "Guess I'm the most presentable one here. Be right back," he said, grabbing his shirt and pulling it over his head before heading out the door.

While Drew went downstairs, Troye leaned back in his chair, his pencil still dangling between his fingers. "Brandon? Like... *Brandon Brandon*? Like my *cousin* Brandon?"

Lisa rolled her eyes but there was this shy smile tugging at the corner of her mouth. "Yes, your *cousin* Brandon. Don't make it weird."

"Not making it weird," Troye said, holding his hands up in mock innocence. "Just saying, you two have been 'hitting it off' for, what, a week?"

"Try a month," Lisa shot back, her tone defensive but playful. "And for your information, we're official now."

"Whoa, okay," Troye said, leaning forward like this was breaking news. "That was fast. Didn't realize we were working on express shipping with relationships now."

Lisa narrowed her eyes at him. "Don't make it sound so cheap. Brandon's great."

"Of course, of course," Troye said, waving his hand as if to brush off any offense. Then, with a sly grin, he turned to me. "Maybe Kiko and I should do the same, huh?"

My cheeks immediately flushed, and I couldn't tell if it was from embarrassment or excitement—or both. "Uh... that's—um—kind of out of nowhere." I stammered, glancing around the room like someone was gonna throw me a lifeline.

Troye just kept looking at me. His expression was calm, but there was this look of straight-up trouble in his eyes.

Yeah, no big deal. Easy for him to say. Meanwhile, I was the one sitting there feeling like my heart was about to escape my chest.

Brandon walked in looking all calm until his brain caught up with the fact that the room was basically a no-clothes zone. And when he saw Lisa—completely naked—his jaw tightened.

"Uh, babe," Brandon said, his voice low but sharp. "You wanna maybe, like, put your clothes on?"

Lisa's smile dropped. "It's for *art*, Brandon. Chill," she said. But she was already reaching for her hoodie that she had draped over the chair. The energy in the room, which had been all jokes and fun a minute ago, nosedived into awkward silence.

Alex, unbothered as ever—still completely naked—walked straight over to Brandon with his hand out like this was some corporate networking event. "Hey, it's all good, man," he said, grinning. "We're just vibing."

Brandon glanced at Alex—or tried to, because he immediately turned away. He did *not* take Alex's hand. "Right," he muttered, clearly totally uncomfortable.

Troye hopped off the bed and stepped in, his smooth, mediator energy kicking in. "Brandon, chill. It's fine," he said, throwing an arm over my shoulder like it was nothing. "I wouldn't let anything happen, Cuz. Alex and Drew? They've got girlfriends. Total safe zone."

Brandon's expression didn't shift much, but his eyes stayed glued to Lisa, now drowning in her oversized hoodie as she pulled on her bright pink boyshorts.

"And Kiko's my boyfriend, so no need to worry there."

Troye dropped it so casually I almost missed it. *Kiko's my boyfriend.* My heart stuttered. *Boyfriend*? Before I could process, Brandon's attention locked on me like I'd suddenly become the most interesting person in the room.

He squinted at me. "Do I know you from somewhere?"

I blinked, trying to figure out if I'd ever met this dude before. "Uh… I don't think so?"

"You've only been in LA for like a month, where could you possibly have met him?"

Brandon stared like he was mentally scrolling through every face he'd ever seen before finally shrugging. "Huh. Must be someone else you remind me of."

The vibe thawed slightly after that, but it still wasn't back to normal. Brandon leaned against the wall, not even trying to engage, while Lisa awkwardly packed her stuff. Troye threw out a joke about Brandon modeling for the next session, which landed somewhere between only mildly funny and "please don't make it worse."

When Lisa announced they were leaving, Brandon didn't bother with handshakes. Instead, he gave this half-hearted two-finger salute. "Later," he said, and they were gone.

As the door slammed behind Brandon and Lisa, the room exhaled. But it wasn't the same buzz as before. The ease, the rhythm—it all felt off. Like his discomfort just lingered and no one wanted to acknowledge it.

Troye turned to me with that trademark Troye smirk. He was clearly expecting a reaction. But all I could think about was one word that was echoing in my head.

Boyfriend.

Like… wait, was that official now? Did I just level up in this relationship without even knowing? Just like that? My chest tightened, and I felt Troye's arm brush mine as he sat back on the bed, grounding me before I could spiral. And maybe I wasn't ready to say it out loud, but sitting here—fully out of my depth and still somehow steady in Troye's orbit—I realized I wanted to be.

14

A month and a half on the job, and I finally had the POS system down without needing to triple-check every button. Progress, right? I even managed to make most drinks without turning them into liquid disasters—though latte art was still totally Ricky's territory. That guy could pour a heart into a cup of foam like it was nobody's business. Me? I still had a fifty-fifty shot at making something that didn't look like a sad blob.

"Medium iced matcha latte, oat milk," I called out. The girl tapped her card while I moved over to grab the blueberry scone she ordered. My hands were kinda on autopilot at this point. My brain, though? Yeah, that was stuck somewhere else.

Troye. *Of course*, Troye.

He'd been dropping some *not-too-subtle* hints over the past three days, practically begging to meet my friends. Well, Dylan and his crew, at least. Troye and I talked about Rafe and Avery—and by "talked," I mean I told him it wasn't happening. He acted like he got it, but the way he said, "It's just frustrating dating someone who's... closeted," kinda hit me in the chest. Like, bro, I'm trying here.

I shook the thought off, snapping back to the moment, handing the little bag with the scone and directing her to the other end of the counter to grab the drink. The customer thanked me as I handed them their drink, and I even managed a smile before moving on to the next person in line.

"Medium Americano with hazelnut and a large caramel macchiato, *extra* caramel," a guy in a graphic tee said, and I punched it in while grabbing two cups.

"Name?" I asked.

"Sam," he said.

The thing was, it wasn't that I didn't want Troye to meet people in my life—I *did*. Kind of at least. Dylan and his crew? They'd get it. They were cool, open, and honestly the first group of people I'd ever felt comfortable being myself around. But Ravery? That was a whole other story. They weren't just my friends; they were my history. They knew me before I even started figuring myself out. The idea of them meeting Troye felt like throwing a live grenade into something that I wasn't ready to blow up quite yet.

I finished the macchiato—extra caramel drizzle on point—and started on the Americano.

I sighed, pumping the hazelnut syrup into the bottom of the cup. Maybe I was overthinking it. Maybe Troye was right. But still... the thought of blending those two worlds? Yeah, that was a hill I wasn't ready to climb yet.

"Medium 'Cano hazy, and large extra caramel mac for Sam!" I called, sliding the two drinks onto the counter, before returning to the register.

As I headed back to the register, my phone buzzed in my pocket. No customers were in line, so I figured I'd check it real quick.

Mamadukes: Just Now
Are you coming home after work?

I started typing, "Staying at Rafe's"—the usual excuse since I was planning to stay over at Troye's.

But then Ricky walked past, wiping down the counter.

"Can't believe it's August already," he said, shaking his head.

My stomach dropped. August. I glanced at my lock screen, and sure enough: August 6th. My chest tightened. Three years. How *the hell* could I forget?

I quickly went back to delete the draft text and typed back: "Yeah, I'll be there" and hit send. Then I switched over to Troye's chat and typed out: "Hey, I gotta bail tonight. Family stuff. Sorry."

I stared at it for a second before hitting send. I didn't need to get into the whole thing. Not about today. Not about Dad. Just... no.

Locking my phone, I shoved it back in my pocket and tried to steady my breathing, but the date kept playing on repeat in my head. Three years. It wasn't even that long, but it still felt fresh, like a wound that never fully healed. Some part of me thought it'd hurt less by now, but nope. That was grief I guess, at least that's what my guidance counselor

144

told me. Even when I thought I was ready for it. Three years later now, and it still hit like a wave, dragging me under when I least expected it.

Ricky passed by again, giving me a once-over. "You good?" he asked, wiping his hands on a rag.

"Yeah, totally," I lied, forcing a shrug. My chest still felt tight, but I wasn't about to unload all that here.

"Good," Ricky said with a sly grin. He tossed the rag onto the counter. "'Cause you're about to graduate to the next level."

"Um… What does that even mean?"

He leaned closer, lowering his voice. "Hot London Fog with oat milk, extra foam, and a whisper of lavender."

I laughed, waiting for the punchline. "You're kidding, right?"

"Nope." Ricky smirked, leaning back and crossing his arms.

My stomach dropped as I glanced over at Selena Cho in her usual corner, her assistant frantic as ever. My eyes widened. "Wait, like… *her* drink? You're joking."

Ricky chuckled. "Nope. I'm dead serious. You gotta learn sometime."

"But no one makes her drink except you," I protested. "And Neil that one time. You literally told me that."

"True," Ricky admitted, grabbing a fresh cup. "But relax, dude. I'll walk you through it."

I stared at him, on the verge of full-on panic. I totally did not need this at that moment. Messing up her drink wasn't just a mistake—it was a career-ender.

"Okay," I said, taking a deep breath and squaring up to the espresso machine like it was a final boss in a video game. "Let's do this."

Ricky grinned. "That's the spirit. Step one: don't freak out." He stood next to me like a coach on the sidelines, calmly giving directions while I fumbled my way through making *the* drink.

"Steam the oat milk a little smoother—less air," he said, tapping the milk pitcher with a finger. "You're not making a cappuccino."

"Got it," I muttered, trying not to stress over every tiny swirl in the pitcher.

"Foam's looking good. Now, just a whisper of lavender."

What does that even mean? I thought to myself. I shot him a look, but his lopsided grin somehow made me feel less life-or-death. I reached for the lavender syrup, before Ricky stopped me.

"Nope. That's the everybody-else-syrup," he said, pulling a tiny bottle from his apron pocket. "We use *this* for her drink. Neil grows the lavender in his backyard and makes this infusion with agave. But we're only using two drops."

Carefully, I added the lavender using this little eyedropper, the scent subtle but present. Ricky nodded, giving me a rare look of approval as I assembled the drink.

When it was done, Ricky picked up the cup like it was a priceless artifact and gave me a quick wink. "Not bad. Let's see if she agrees."

I watched as he carried the mug over to Selena Cho's table. She was sitting in her usual spot, flipping through her latest stack of lookbooks and fabric samples. Ricky set the cup down in front of her with practiced care. His movements were deliberate. I debated just going to get my stuff and leaving. No way was I at this level.

She didn't even look up at first. I watched from behind the counter, holding my breath as she finally picked up the mug. She brought it to her lips and took a small, tiny little sip. She paused and my heart dropped. *Oh no, this is it. She hates it. I'm fired. I'll never work in this town again or something like that.*

Then, she gave the faintest nod. Just a slight tilt of her head, but Ricky didn't miss it. He gave her a small smile and backed away, but not before I swear I saw her glance in my direction for the briefest moment. Or maybe I imagined it—I was too busy hiding behind the espresso machine like I'd just survived a near-death experience.

Ricky came back, his grin smug as ever. "Congrats, you passed," he said, leaning casually against the counter.

I crouched down and let out a long, shaky exhale. "So I still have a job?"

"For now," Ricky teased, but I could feel his pride in his little protege as he grabbed my shoulder to shake me. "Good work, Kiko. Welcome to the big leagues."

After about an hour, the shop had finally quieted down after the chaos of the lunch rush. I'd been pretending I was fine, throwing on my best customer-service smile, but the guilt of not being home with Ma and Mateo was eating at me. It felt like this weight in my chest that just kept getting heavier.

I wiped my hands on my apron and glanced over at Ricky, who was taking inventory in one of the lowboy refrigerators.

"Hey, Ricky?" I started, my voice came out quieter than usual. "Think it'd be okay if I dipped out early? I, uh... I kinda forgot I had this family thing."

He stopped what he was doing, looking at me with this knowing expression. Ricky wasn't the type to pry, but it was like he could see straight through my excuses. "Yeah, sure, man," he said after a beat, his tone softer than normal. "I got it from here. Go handle your business."

"Thanks," I muttered, untying my apron and grabbing my board and backpack. As I headed for the door, Ricky called out, "Hey, Kiko—Great job today!" I nodded, not trusting myself to say anything back without choking up.

Outside, the sun felt too bright for how I was feeling. Like the sky was all blue and all. Where were the clouds? Where was the rain? How could this day be all happy and bright. I hopped on the bus, sliding into my usual seat in the back. I popped in my headphones, and scrolled through my playlists until I landed on "Dad's Music." I never really listened to this one except today... or when things got too much.

The soft horns and smooth vocals of Chicago's *If You Leave Me Now* started playing, and suddenly I was eight years old again, sitting on the curb outside our apartment, watching my dad work on his '85 Camaro. Cherry red, gold stripes along the bottom—a car that turned heads even when it was parked. He'd always have music blasting from this ancient RadioShack CD player boombox that was older than me while he tinkered under the hood, singing along with his thick accent and *completely* off-key.

Especially this song with the "Ooh ooh" part. The man couldn't hit a note to save his life, but he didn't care. I used to cover my ears and groan all dramatic, telling him he was ruining the song, but inside I loved it. I loved him. And right now, I'd give anything to hear his terrible singing one more time.

I leaned my head against the window as the bus rolled along, watching the houses blur past. My chest felt tight, the kind of tight that makes it hard to breathe, but the music made it feel like he was still here —in some way at least.

The playlist was peak Dad vibes—heavy on Chicago and Peter Cetera, with a couple of Bryan Adams and Journey tracks. Every song pulled me back to those days.

A text message came in:

 **Rafe (My BFF 🤙)**   Just Now
Hey man. Just thinking of your pops. Call me if
you want to talk

I typed out a quick "Thanks."

When the bus finally rolled up to my stop, I grabbed my board and hopped off. The ride home felt longer than usual, and when I finally got to the door, I spent way too long messing with the stupid lock.

Bandit greeted me at the door, but he was weirdly chill. Just a slow tail wag and this kinda sad look, like he just knew what today was. He always knows.

The apartment was so quiet I could hear the clock on the kitchen wall ticking. No Mateo yelling at FIFA, none of Ma's telenovelas blasting. Just quiet. I kicked off my shoes and set my board against the wall, already feeling the weight of the day pressing down.

Ma stepped out of her room, mascara wand in hand, mid-makeup routine. She looked up and paused, surprised. "Mijo, you're home early," she said.

"Yeah," I mumbled, trying to play it off. "Slow day. I got out early."

She nodded but didn't say anything right away. I could tell she was working something over in her head, and when she finally spoke, her voice was softer. "Mateo wants to go to the cemetery," she said. "I think it would… mean a lot to him… if you came, too."

The cemetery. I hadn't been back since the funeral. Every year, I found some excuse to avoid it. Too busy. Too tired. Too something. But Mateo? He never missed it. He was only ten when Dad passed, and I can't even imagine how much of that weight he's been carrying alone.

I glanced down at Bandit, who had plopped down next to me, his head resting against my leg. Then back at Ma. "Yeah," I said, my voice quieter than I intended. "I'll go."

Her expression softened, and she gave me this small, almost sad smile. "It'll mean a lot to him," she said. "To both of us."

I nodded, stuffing my hands into my hoodie pocket. I couldn't undo the last three years. I couldn't take back all the little ways I'd let them down. But maybe showing up now was at least a start. For Mateo. For Ma. And maybe even for me.

I changed quick out of my clothes that stunk of coffee and grabbed a pair of oversized aviators—just in case. We climbed into Ma's totally ancient Toyota Corolla, the car that refused to die. Twenty-plus years of LA streets, fender benders, and questionable mechanics, and it still somehow held on. The AC was weak, the radio only worked when it felt like it, and the passenger-side window would roll down, but it wasn't guaranteed to go back up. But the car was a tank, and it got us where we needed to go.

The drive to Covina took over forty-five minutes—LA traffic never takes a day off. Nobody really talked. Ma had both hands locked on the wheel, her stare straight ahead like she was just on autopilot. I kept my phone in my lap and my headphones in my ears, letting my "Dad's Music" playlist fill the silence.

A new text message interrupted the playlist:

Wave Whisperer 🏄   Just Now

♥

It was simple but conveyed a lot. I liked the text and went back to staring out the window.

At some point in the stop-and-go of the 10 as we were passing downtown, I glanced back at Mateo. He was leaning against the door, one earbud in, staring out the window. His glasses had slid down his nose a little, but he didn't push them up. I couldn't really make out his expression—it wasn't sadness, or frustration, just... blank. Like he was somewhere else entirely.

I leaned my head against the window as *Livin' on a Prayer* blasted in my ears, and suddenly, I was twelve again, riding shotgun in Dad's Camaro, T-tops off, ocean breeze whipping through my hair as we flew up the PCH past Malibu.

That drive was the farthest I'd ever been from home—at least until the next summer when we camped in Joshua Tree. The volume was cranked way past reasonable, and Dad was absolutely *murdering* the lyrics. I was right there with him though, screaming the chorus at the top of my lungs, with my hands in the air like the whole world belonged to us.

I tapped my fingers against my knee as the song played on, but it didn't hit the same way. Dad wasn't here. The Camaro was gone. And the wind in my face? Just the Corolla's struggling AC blowing lukewarm air. I let out a slow breath, gripping my phone tighter.

The car door felt like it weighed a hundred pounds as I pushed it open, like the universe was giving me one last chance to just... *not*. I thought about staying put, letting Ma and Mateo go ahead without me. I could've just sat there, and scrolled mindlessly, but then Mateo turned back, his eyes meeting mine. He didn't say anything, didn't have to. There was just this tiny little smile like he was glad I was there. That look was enough.

I sighed and got out.

The walk wasn't far, but it felt like miles. Every step heavier than the last. It was the first time I'd been there since the funeral. By the time we reached the headstone, my chest was tight, and my hands were stuffed so deep in my pockets I thought they might rip.

Enrique Guerrero Perez 1935-2003. Grandpa. The man I was named after. I'd heard a hundred stories about him but never knew him. But right below his name—*Francisco Rodriguez Soto 1982-2021.* Dad.

Even after three years, seeing it like that, etched in stone, still hit different. Too real. Too final.

Ma barely had the money for a funeral, and I knew she had to pull every string she had to make it happen. Abuela insisted he be buried here, in the plot meant for her. Said it was better this way.

She never liked that she had a burial spot waiting for her. Always said she didn't care where her body ended up—it didn't need to be with Grandpa Enrique.

Throw me in a ditch, she would say. *My spirit will find him and that's all that matters.*

I don't know what I believe about all that, but the way she said it—so sure, like it was an unshakable fact—made the whole thing feel less terrifying. Like there was definitely something after all this.

The headstone, though, just... sat there. It was cold... impersonal... like a placeholder for something way too big to fit into a couple of words and dates. It didn't feel like him. It didn't feel like anything. Just a slab of rock in the ground.

Ma had a bouquet of flowers in her hand—when did she even grab that? Had she brought it from home? Was it already in the car? I honestly couldn't even remember. She pulled out two flowers, handing one to me and one to Mateo. I took mine, twirling it by the stem in my fingers like I was waiting for it to mean something.

Mateo placed his down first, all slow and careful in his Mateo-like fashion. I went next, dropping mine next to his. Even then the whole thing felt kinda pointless. Like, what was this supposed to do? Dad was gone. He wasn't here.

Ma knelt down in front of the headstone and placed the rest of the flowers above it. She had a rosary wrapped tight around her fingers, and was quietly praying in Spanish. Mateo knelt beside her, head bowed, hands clasped.

I just stayed standing behind them.

I hadn't prayed in years, hadn't set foot in a church more than a couple times since the funeral. I knew Ma wished I would, but every time I tried, it felt forced. Like I was just saying empty words to someone who didn't seem to be listening.

So I just stood there, hands in my pockets, staring at the headstone, feeling weirdly numb. Like I was supposed to be thinking something profound, but all I could do was exist in the moment, not really knowing what to do with it.

Mateo stood up first, dusting off his jeans. He stood next to me, real quiet, like he was still lost in his thoughts. I snuck a glance at him, but he was staring at the headstone, and I wondered what he was thinking.

Ma stayed kneeling a little longer, as she traced her fingers over Dad's name, in this ritual kind of way. When she finished she sighed, deep and shaky, before standing up. I let her slide an arm around my waist, even though my hands stayed firmly in my pockets.

Mateo looked up at me from my other side. "Thanks for coming," he said quietly.

It was simple, but it landed. I just nodded, swallowing down the lump in my throat.

The three of us stood there, letting the quiet stretch. The only sounds were the breeze and the freeway traffic not too far in the distance. No one said we should go. No one broke the moment.

For once, just being here felt like enough.

I wished more than anything that my dad was with us. Not just in some poetic, "he's always with you" kind of way, but actually with us—sitting in the driver's seat, blasting classic rock from the busted speakers, cracking a dumb joke that'd make Ma roll her eyes but still smile. I wished he was there telling me to stop overthinking everything, that life sorts itself out. I wished that he'd tell me he loved me no matter what—I wanted that so bad it hurt.

But instead, all I got was a headstone and a bunch of questions with no answers.

Would he be proud of me? Of who I'm becoming—whoever the fuck that even is? Would he look at me the same way if he knew the full picture? If I told him about Troye? Would it have changed things?

I felt like it wouldn't. That he'd still be my dad, still be the guy who let me steer the Camaro from his lap when I was a kid, who taught me how to throw a punch but also how to know when not to use it. That he wouldn't pull that "I love you, but..." bullshit. That it wouldn't even be a thing.

But I'll never know for sure. And that? That's what gets me.

As we turned back toward the car, I kept my head down, watching my shoes press into the gravel. I didn't want Ma or Mateo to see whatever was going on with my face. My throat felt tight, my chest heavier than it had been in a long time. I didn't even remember when I'd slipped on my aviators, but I was glad I had. At least they could hide some of it. At least for now.

Except... I felt it. A single tear slipping past the edge of my sunglasses, tracing down my cheek before I could do anything about it.

I sucked in a sharp breath, trying to pull it together, but the second I dropped into the passenger seat, everything came crashing down.

The first sob hit out of nowhere, hard and ugly. Then another. Then another.

And suddenly, I wasn't just crying. I was unraveling. Three years of holding everything in, of trying to be fine, of dodging conversations and pushing down every complicated thought—just gone. I was sobbing so hard I could barely breathe, my whole body shaking.

"*Mijo*, it's okay," Ma kept saying, over and over, her voice soft but urgent, like she didn't know how else to help. Like she was maybe trying to convince herself too as she started crying. I felt her hand on my back, rubbing slow circles, like she used to when I was little and sick in bed.

And then I heard it. Mateo. Sniffling, then straight-up crying in the back seat—and that made it worse.

It was like a dam had finally broken, flooding the whole damn car with years of things we never said, all the grief we ignored, all the moments we had smiled and moved on even though we weren't okay. And now, here we were. Just three people sitting in a beat-up Toyota, crying together because we didn't know what else to do.

The ride home was quiet, but not the kind that felt awkward or heavy —just... necessary. Like we all needed space to sit with what we were feeling. My head leaned against the window, watching the city blur past. Ma had a hand on the wheel, the other resting in her lap, rosary beads still wrapped around her fingers. Mateo was in the back, earbuds in, staring out the window like he was somewhere else entirely. And me? I just sat there, feeling emptied out, like I had wrung every last drop of emotion from my chest. But maybe that was okay. Maybe I needed this. To let myself break down, to not be the one holding it together for once. I didn't have any answers, not about my dad, not about myself, not about anything really. But for the first time in a long time, I didn't feel like I had to pretend I did.

15

The Uber smelled like a cross of pine air freshener and old takeout. I sat there, drumming my fingers against my knee to the driver's playlist of old Hoobastank songs. We were on our way to some Korean barbecue spot in K-town. Normally, I'd be hyped to eat, but right now? My stomach was in knots.

Troye was next to me, legs crossed, fully locked into his phone, scrolling like I was not even there. He was probably liking some aesthetic shots of overpriced cocktails or some fashion inspo. Meanwhile, I was over here, spiraling.

I pulled out my phone, checked the GPS—seven minutes to go. Seven minutes until I had to introduce my *boyfriend*—which was still weird to say a week and a half later—to my new friends for the first time ever. Dylan, Indie, and Ethan were chill, but what if they didn't vibe? What if Troye said something wild? What if I was out here trying to merge two completely different worlds, and it ended in disaster?

I shifted, the leather seat making that awkward squeak. Still, Troye didn't even glance up. Dude was unbothered, living his best life.

"Hey," I said, trying to sound casual.

"Mmm?" He barely looked up, still double-tapping.

I hesitated, feeling dumb for even bringing it up. "You excited to meet my friends?"

He glanced up, brows slightly raised. "Yeah, of course." Then, like he just knew what was going on in my head, he smirked. "Why? You nervous?"

My eyes caught the Uber driver's in the rearview mirror as he glanced back at us. I lowered my voice. "No."

Troye gave me a look. "You so are."

I rolled my eyes but my leg was still bouncing, so, okay—maybe he wasn't wrong. "I just want it to go well."

Troye finally locked his phone and turned toward me. "Relax, Skater Boy. They're gonna love me."

I shot him a look. "Are they now?"

He grinned. "What's not to love?"

I snorted, shaking my head. "You're actually a pain to deal with."

"Maybe," he said, reaching over to fix my hair. "But you're still here."

I swatted his hand away, but the little moment did make me feel slightly less like I was about to throw up. The car slowed as we pulled up to the restaurant, and I took a deep breath.

I slid out of the Uber, rolling my shoulders like that would somehow shake off the nerves sitting heavy in my chest. Dylan and Indie were already standing near the front door. I gave them a quick wave, but before I could even get a word out, Troye was strutting up like he was walking a damn red carpet.

He hit Dylan first, gripping his hand in this weirdly formal handshake. Dylan paused just long enough to look mildly confused before playing along. Then Troye turned to Indie, grabbing her hand like he was about to kiss it.

Yeah, okay. Time to step in.

"So, uh… where's Ethan?" I asked, cutting through whatever the hell Troye thought he was doing.

Indie scoffed, flicking her hair over her shoulder like I'd just said the dumbest thing imaginable. "You really thought we were bringing poor Ethan to Korean barbecue? That's like taking a nun to a strip club."

"Okay, okay, so are we actually gonna eat, or are we just gonna roast each other all night?" I asked, nudging Indie toward the entrance.

Indie side-eyed me. "Oh, we can multitask."

Troye hummed in approval. "I like her."

Dylan grinned, looking between us. "Yeah, this is gonna be fun."

Inside, the smell was straight-up delicious. The whole place was a sensory overload: metal tongs clanking, flames flaring up from the grills, people talking over each other while flipping thin slices of meat. The floor was weirdly slippery, but a server in a black apron barely glanced up before waving us toward a booth in the back.

We all grabbed our seats, the grill in the middle of the table throwing off a warm glow that made the table feel extra cozy even though we were in the middle of the room. Troye slid in next to me with Dylan and Indie taking the other side.

"Nice to finally meet the crew," Troye said, flashing that smile that's way too good at smoothing over any awkwardness.

"Well most of us anyway," Indie said, eyeing Troye with that kind of skeptical curiosity you give someone you've heard a ton about but never met. "Kiko's told us *a lot* about you," she said, flipping open her menu.

"Oh, *has* he?" Troye replied. "All good things, I hope?"

I shook my head, "Okay, relax. Not *that* much."

Dylan stayed leaned back in the booth, looking at the menu.

"So how's the *boyfriend* life treating the two of you?" Indie asked.

Troye tilted his head towards me with this pouty expression and took my hand. I leaned in and gave him a quick peck.

"Oh, so you're *all* up in that honeymoon shit," Indie blurted, all of us laughing, except Dylan who was pretty invested in the menu.

Indie elbowed him, "You don't know that thing by heart? We come here often enough."

"Just trying to make a plan," Dylan said, still focused on the menu.

"Forget it," Indie said, yanking the menu out of Dylan's hand, "Your fates are all in my hands tonight!"

That didn't sound good...

"Don't worry. I'll stay away from the weird stuff... Okay, *most* of the weird stuff," she said with a wink.

When the server came up behind Indie, she used the menu to hide her mouth like she was a football coach on the sideline calling a play. She eyed Troye for a second, then me, like she was sizing us up or something.

"Hope y'all brought your appetite," she said returning to the rest of us.

"So Dylan," Troye said, "what do you do?" His voice had this kind of edge that suddenly jolted me.

"I uh..." Dylan said snapping back to the conversation. "I work at a consignment shop on Melrose."

"Oh nice, I should stop in. I have sooo many clothes I need to get rid of," Troye replied. I gave him the benefit of the doubt but it totally came off like a brag.

"Yeah," Dylan said, "We can definitely take a look. Your clothes are super-stylish."

"Thanks," Troye replied, "Your whole vibe is pretty cool too. Not really my thing, but somehow you make it work.

Help, I screamed in my head so loud I thought that Indie heard me, because she jumped in as the server brought drinks I didn't remember ordering.

"Well, that's enough about fashion," she interrupted, "No trip for Korean barbecue is complete without soju. I took the liberty of picking out the flavors I thought y'all would like the best. Let's see if I still got it…"

The server placed glasses of ice in front of each of us, before holding up the first bottle.

"Apple mango?" the server asked.

"That'd be me," Indie said.

"Lychee?" the server continued, carefully rebalancing the tray as he pulled each one off.

"That would be right there," Indie said gesturing to Troye.

"I love lychee!" Troye shouted, clapping his hands as his bottle was placed in front of him.

"And peach," the server said passing one to me and the other to Dylan.

"Peach is my favorite too," I said, trying to match Troye's energy.

"Four for four!" Indie slapped the table. "I still got it."

"You're really gonna give yourself credit for mine *and* your own?" Dylan said, giving her a sick side-eye. "Like we don't get the same thing every time?"

Now Troye was the one who was dead silent. I glanced over, expecting him to be vibing or at least doing that thing where he pretends to be above the conversation while still soaking up every second of attention. But nah. His eyes were locked onto Dylan's bottle of peach soju like it personally offended him.

I frowned. "Dude… you good?"

Troye turned to me with a forced smile. "Yeah, yeah. Just—peach isn't really my thing." He poured his own bottle of lychee soju into his glass of ice.

Dylan shrugged, taking a sip. "More for me then."

Indie, never one to let a moment linger, clapped her hands. "Alright, before this turns into a full-blown soju debate, apple mango is the best flavor. Let's get to grilling."

The server arrived with a tray loaded up with meats, laying everything out on the table while Indie started cracking her knuckles like she was about to perform surgery. "Y'all just sit back," she announced, picking up the tongs like a weapon. "I got this."

I shot Dylan a look, and he just shook his head like, "Yeah, we're at her mercy now."

Troye leaned back, watching Indie and laughing at her jokes, but I still caught him glancing at Dylan every now and then. Something about it felt off, but I couldn't tell if I was reading too much into it. Either way, I knew the vibe was off and I was *really* trying not to let it ruin the night.

But the tension between Troye and Dylan only got worse as the night went on. It was the kind of thing where no one was outright beefing, but you could feel the energy shift. Like when the air gets thick before a storm.

I kept my head down, stacking up lettuce wrap after lettuce wrap, but I wasn't missing anything. Troye had been watching Dylan way too closely all night, like he was trying to size him up. Meanwhile, Dylan had his usual quiet withdrawal going on, answering questions with just enough words to not seem rude. I was sure that neither of them was saying what they actually wanted to say, but every exchange felt like a chess move.

"So, Dylan," Troye said, swirling his soju like he was plotting something, the ice clinking on the side of the glass. "What do you do when you're not curating Melrose's finest secondhand treasures?"

I swear I saw Dylan's jaw clench before he spoke. "Ah, you know. This and that." He didn't even bother looking up, just reached for a piece of grilled pork belly like he was trying not to take the bait.

I grabbed Troye's hand and tried giving him this big smile to make him chill out but his glare went right back to Dylan. I knew this night was going nowhere good.

He let out this fake little way-too-amused laugh, "Mysterious. Love that."

Indie, the real MVP, was laser-focused on the grill, flipping slices of bulgogi and adding more meat, completely ignoring the passive-aggressive showdown happening two feet away. I, on the other hand, had little to distract me from it. My appetite wasn't gone exactly, but the longer this went on, the harder it was to focus on eating.

Dylan finally met Troye's gaze. "What about you? Besides, like, shopping. What do you do?"

I froze mid-bite. I wasn't sure if that was an actual question or a dig— who am I kidding, it was *definitely* a dig.

Troye's smile stayed like frozen. I could tell he was annoyed. "I create, actually. Art, fashion, moments." He did this vague little hand gesture, like the concept of his entire existence should be self-explanatory.

Dylan raised an eyebrow. "Moments?"

"Yeah," Troye said, tilting his head like Dylan had just asked if water was wet. "I mean, obviously not *everyone* gets it."

Okay, this was way past off the rails.

Before I could do anything to jump in, Indie slammed the tongs down onto the edge of the metal grill, making me and half the restaurant jump. "Okay, can we not turn this into a reality TV reunion episode? Eat your meat and drink your soju before I take both for myself."

I did my best to defuse the situation, "C'mon guys, seriously. We are not wasting perfectly good short rib on bad vibes."

Dylan sighed, leaning back in his seat, breaking eye contact with Troye. "Fair enough."

Troye shot me a look, I could tell we were gonna be "talking" about this later. *Great, our first argument.*

I shook my head. So much for a chill dinner.

Indie flipped a piece of pork belly onto the grill. "So anyway, I've been seeing this German girl—or maybe she's Austrian? Honestly, I still can't tell, and at this point, it feels rude to ask."

Dylan snorted. "That's a strong foundation for a relationship."

"Relax, it's only been one-and-a-half dates."

"One and a half..." Dylan said, raising his eyebrows and nodding along.

"She's at UCLA for the summer, studying architecture. Super smart, super sophisticated. Basically, the German version of me."

I smirked. "So, when's the wedding?"

Indie waved me off. "It's just a summer thing. No stress, no strings." She took a sip of her soju, then leaned forward like she was about to drop some drama. "Best part?...She's *older*."

I popped a piece of beef into my mouth, chewing before side-eyeing her, "Define older."

Indie hesitated just long enough to be suspicious, "Two years."

"Twenty four whole months? How ever do you relate?" Dylan deadpanned.

She had the nerve to look unbothered. "What? In spirit, we are the exact same age. My dad always says I'm an old soul."

"This is ridiculous," Troye said under his breath, chewing on his thumbnail as he scrolled through his feed. The phone was, like, three inches from his face.

I was pretty sure no one else heard him—or at least they didn't react.

Dylan gave Indie a look. "So, you just lied about your age?"

"Adjusted," Indie corrected, like that was somehow better. "It's a perfect summer fling. She's only here 'til September, then she goes back to, like, Oktoberfest or whatever. No reason for her to ever know."

I laughed. "Okay, but when she finds out, she's gonna be screaming at you in angry German."

Dylan clinked his soju bottle against mine. "Is there any other kind?"

Indie rolled her eyes. "Oh, please. If I get caught, I'll just say it was a miscommunication. Lost in translation. It'll be fine."

Dylan let out a short laugh. "She'll turn the whole experience into a podcast called *Why You Should Never Date a Lying American*."

I grinned, but the whole time, I kept flicking glances at Troye. He hadn't said a word. Just sat there, scrolling through his phone, fingers moving way too fast, like he was trying not to be here.

The shift was jarring. One second, he was going toe-to-toe with Dylan, and now? Full-on *silent* mode.

I tried to ignore the way my stomach knotted. Maybe he was just checking something real quick. Maybe I was overthinking it—that was kinda my brand after all—but the longer he stayed quiet, the more uneasy I felt.

The server came back and asked if we wanted dessert. Troye didn't even look up. I shook my head, ready to go and deal with whatever argument I was about to have that night.

"No no no," Indie said. "Kiko, you have to try the matcha green tea ice cream."

Dylan nodded like it was law. "Yeah, no excuses. It slaps."

"Okay, I guess," I said. "If it's really that good."

Dylan eyed Troye, scrolling away. I thought the passive aggressiveness from earlier was about to open right back up. But instead? Something softened.

"Four, then?" he asked Troye in this, like, totally genuine way.

Troye didn't even look up from his phone. "I'm good." It came out way too sharp, and he totally knew it because he threw in this, "Gotta keep my figure, you know?" with this half-assed smile.

Dylan just gave a polite smile and turned back to the server, "Three matcha green tea ice creams."

And damn, they weren't lying—the ice cream was elite. The energy at the table was at least starting to feel normal again, Dylan and Indie debating the best desserts in LA, me just vibing in the conversation. Then the check landed, and we all tossed in our debit cards—easiest way to handle it.

Except it wasn't.

The server came back, holding onto one card instead of handing it back. "This one got declined."

Indie's spoon stopped halfway to her mouth. Dylan just blinked. And me? I froze

Troye gave that fake overly polite smile, I'd been seeing too much of all night. "Run it again."

The server shook his head. "Already did."

It was like the universe hit pause for a sec. Not in a dramatic movie way, but in that awkward, secondhand embarrassment way where you just know everyone at the table clocked it but is pretending they didn't.

Troye just pulled out his wallet and handed over a platinum American Express card. Totally casual, like everyone our age just has one buried in our wallets.

"Whoa, baller," Indie said, while Dylan and I both just kinda looked at each other.

I mean I knew Troye had to have some kinda money. That was obvious from the jump—the designer fits, the way he never seemed to check prices on anything. But this? A declined debit card? And then the casual flex with an Amex Platinum? That wasn't just rich kid energy. That was… something else.

And what that was? I had no clue. I dug my spoon into my ice cream, hyper-focused on not making a big deal out of it. But my brain wouldn't shut up.

Once we got outside, though that weird energy came right back—like everyone knew the vibe had been off, but no one wanted to be the first to call it.

Indie stretched her arms over her head, in this a little too fake yawn. "Alright, y'all, this was fun," she said, dragging out the last word just enough to make me wonder if she meant it. "We gotta do it again."

Dylan nodded, shifting his weight like he was debating something. Finally, he looked at Troye. "Hey, man. I know tonight was kinda… I dunno, weird? I got my own stuff going on, and I think we got off on the wrong foot. Hope we can try again sometime."

His tone was actually sincere, which made it worse when Troye plastered on that fake smile again. "Yeah, totally," he said, voice all smooth and detached. "Real soon."

Dylan's face barely shifted, but I caught it—that little bit of disappointment before it turned back into that polite smile. He nodded once at me, then turned, heading toward the parking lot with Indie.

I watched them go, part of me wanting to call out, fix whatever just happened, but the other part too tired to try. Instead Troye and I stood there in silence, waiting for our Uber. I shoved my hands in my pockets and kept my eyes on the sidewalk below me.

This whole night was supposed to be a major step forward. Instead, it felt like I'd just put my foot in two different worlds, and I had no clue which one was gonna collapse first.

When we got in the Uber, I just stayed looking outside my window. Maybe if I focused hard enough, I could pretend I wasn't sitting in the middle of whatever this was about to be. The Uber was dead silent as we rode down Olympic Boulevard. The tension? Heavy as hell.

Then Troye sighed in this super dramatic way. The kind of sigh meant to be heard.

But I ignored it.

Then came another one. Louder this time.

Still ignored it. I thought I just might kick the can down the road long enough to get back to Troye's apartment—and maybe let him chill out in the meantime.

Then came a sharp exhale through his nose, matched with a little shift in his seat. Like he was physically containing whatever storm was about to be released on me. Even the driver glanced at us in the rearview, probably debating if he needed to up the volume on his music.

Troye let it build a few more seconds before turning to me, voice all fake sweet, the kind that had warning signs flashing in my brain. His whole body was tense, like he was holding in a scream. I knew what was coming. I just didn't know how bad it would be.

"So…," he said.

I looked back at him, doing my best to telepathically beg him to not do what I knew he was about to right there.

"I really can't believe you just let Dylan talk to me like that?"

And there it was. My stomach dropped, the way it always did when I knew I was about to be pulled into something I wasn't sure how to handle. I rubbed my hand over my jeans, trying to ground myself, trying to figure out what version of Troye I was dealing with right now.

I turned to him, keeping my voice steady. "I don't think he was trying to be disrespectful. I told you he can get a little withdrawn sometimes."

Troye scoffed, shaking his head like I was missing something so obvious. "Oh, please. He was acting like he was *soooo* above everything.

Like I'm some joke."

I sighed, already feeling the exhaustion creeping in. "You weren't exactly nice to him either."

Troye's jaw tightened. "Oh, so this is my fault?"

"This was supposed to be a chill night, meeting my friends," I said.

Troye interrupted me with this laugh that was totally over the top.

"Oh the two friends I'm actually allowed to meet?" he said. "This is why I don't date closeted guys."

The Uber driver glanced at me in the rearview again—and I debated jumping out of the moving car.

"Oh stop! It's LA babe, nobody gives a shit!" he yelled, before turning on the driver. "Sir, do you give a shit if my boyfriend here is gay?"

"Troye!" I tried to yell, but it came out as more of a plea.

"Oh no, I said the 'g' word!" Troye said, covering his mouth in mock horror. "But seriously, sir," he continued, "Do you give a fuck if he gives it to me *all* night?"

"Hey man," the driver interrupted. "It's all cool. Everybody's cool. I'm not trying to get in the middle. We're almost there."

I could see from his GPS as we pulled up to the light at San Vincente that we weren't. We had seven minutes left. Seven minutes in *hell*. There was no way I was lasting seven more minutes.

"That's not a five-star response," Troye shot back.

"Okay. I'm getting out here," I said grabbing the door handle a couple of times before the driver finally unlocked the door.

I heard Troye ask, "Really?" before I slammed the door behind me.

I hated that my board was at his place like it was some type of prisoner of war. I walked fast, hands jammed deep in my pockets like I could physically keep myself from falling apart. My face was burning, my chest felt tight, and my stomach—just hollow.

Troye really did *that*. Just threw it out there, in front of some random ass Uber driver, like it was his to say. Like it wasn't *mine*. It wasn't like I was ashamed or something. I mean, at the end of the day it was just some dude I'd never see again, but having it ripped out of my hands like that? Weaponized just to win some stupid argument? That shit stung in a way I definitely wasn't ready for. The part that bothered me the most, though? It was how absolutely savage Troye just got out of nowhere. It was a totally new side of him that I hadn't seen before—and I definitely didn't like it.

I hit the bus stop, running a hand down my face. The streetlight overhead flickered, throwing weird, stretched-out shadows onto the sidewalk. I let out a slow breath, tilting my head back. The stars barely cut through the city haze, but they were there. As distant and as untouchable as ever.

I just needed to get home. Get to my own bed... my own space. I needed to sit in the quiet and figure out if this was something I could even come back from.

16

Bandit's tongue was everywhere—my cheek, my ear, my actual freakin' eyeball. I groaned, trying to push him away, but he just wiggled closer, paws pressing into my stomach like he was not giving up on physically forcing me to wake up.

"Dude, chill," I mumbled, rubbing my face as I sat up. My body felt heavy, like I hadn't slept at all, like the weight of last night had settled right into my chest and wasn't going anywhere.

Mateo's bed was already made—of course. He was probably up at the crack of dawn, doing whatever normal, responsible people did in the morning. Meanwhile, I was waking up to dried spit on my face and the very real feeling that I had no idea where I stood with my own boyfriend. If I even still had one.

I glanced over at the corner where my board and backpack should be —where they *always* were. Except today, that corner was empty, except for an old issue of *Thrasher* half-buried under one of my hoodies.

Yeah. Not a dream.

The argument, the Uber, the way Troye had looked at me before I slammed the door—it all really happened. My stomach twisted just thinking about it.

I grabbed my phone off the nightstand, swiping at the screen, half-hoping, half-dreading what I'd see. But it was empty. No texts. No missed calls. Just a low battery warning, because apparently, I'd been too exhausted to even plug in my phone before knocking out.

I flopped back onto the bed, phone slipping from my hand onto the sheets. The space between me and Troye right now, the silence, the not knowing... it all felt worse than the actual fight. At least then I had something to push against. Now? There was just this weird, hollow feeling, like I was waiting for a text that might never come.

Bandit let out a little sigh and rested his head on my leg, his tail thumping once, like he could feel it too. Like he knew.

I stared at the ceiling, exhaling slowly.

I dragged myself out of bed, every muscle in my body feeling like it weighed twice as much as usual. My feet barely lifted off the floor as I shuffled toward the bathroom, rubbing my eyes, trying to shake off the fog of sleep and everything else clinging to me.

After I did my thing, I took a look at my reflection. The mirror wasn't kind. My hair was a mess, my eyes puffy, skin just off—basically, I looked *exactly* how I felt. I splashed some cold water on my face, leaning my elbows on the sink for a second, like I was trying to hold myself together. Bandit sat outside the door, waiting for me like he always did. Like I was gonna disappear if he wasn't keeping tabs on me.

When I came out, he followed me to the kitchen, his nails clicking against the linoleum as I opened the cabinet and scanned the shelves, hoping for anything decent. Just that off-brand raisin bran Ma always bought when it was on sale. The kind where the raisins were *too* raisiny, like they'd been sitting in some warehouse for five years just waiting for their unsuspecting victim.

I sighed and grabbed the box, pouring a bowl anyway. It was either this or nothing.

The apartment was quiet—definitely too quiet. No TV, no music. Just Bandit's tail thumping lazily against the tile as he lay at my feet, and the faint sound of the late morning traffic on the freeway.

I didn't like it. But I wasn't exactly interested in hearing anything either.

My phone chimed from the bedroom. For a second, I just sat there with the spoon halfway to my mouth. My stomach was twisting up like I'd just dropped in on a wave way too big for me. It *had* to be Troye. No one else would be texting me this early—if you could even call it early. I glanced over at the kitchen clock. Almost noon. Okay, so definitely *not* early.

But I just knew it was Troye.

Maybe he was apologizing. Maybe he wanted to talk, to fix things—or maybe he was about to tell me to lose his number. The idea made everything feel tight. I swallowed, forcing myself to look at the sad bowl of raisin bran in front of me. My stomach was too messed up to even continue eating, but I took a bite anyway, chewing like that would somehow push the anxiety down.

It didn't.

I had to check my phone—just rip the bandage off. But that would mean actually knowing. It would mean an answer, and part of me wasn't sure I wanted one yet. If I didn't look, I could stay in this weird in-between space where anything was still possible. Where Troye wasn't gone for good. Where I hadn't just completely nuked my first real relationship because I freaked out, overreacted and bailed on him in the middle of an Uber.

My hand tightened around the spoon. I hated this. The quiet. The waiting. The not knowing. I exhaled, pressing my palms into the edge of the table like *that* would somehow ground me. The phone wasn't going anywhere, but the longer I avoided it, the heavier my chest got.

The phone chimed again, not with another message but with that annoying chime that calls you out for not looking at the notification the first time, like it *knows* you heard it, and it *knows* you were ignoring it.

Enough. I pushed back from the table, the chair scraping against the floor. My hands were sweating. Like I was about to drop in on a set that was way too big, but it was time to face it. Time to get my answer.

But it wasn't Troye.

It was Rafe.

 **Rafe (My BFF 🤙)**   4m ago
Yo, let's hit the skatepark. You need to get some reps in. Comp's less than two weeks out.

I stared at the screen, trying to mentally force it to turn into something else. Something from Troye—*anything* from Troye. But nope. Just Rafe, acting like everything was fine, oblivious to the fact that I was currently spiraling.

I sighed, rubbing my eyes. Of course, I should be practicing. I'd said I'd be in the competition. I knew that. But how much more shit could I pile on top of everything else right now? I felt like I was balancing on a railing, about to eat pavement, and all I could do was brace for impact.

"Would love to, man, but I don't have a board right now." I typed, hoping that'd be the end of it.

But there they were.

Those three dots of doom popped up damn near immediately to show he was typing.

Thu Aug 15 at 12:02 PM

   ...

Rafe (My BFF)

   Why not?

I didn't really want to explain. How could I? *Sorry, man, I lost my board in a nasty breakup with my ex-boyfriend, who I've been hiding from you.* Yeah. Not happening. And I had zero energy to come up with some other excuse. Before I could stress over it though, another text came in.

Rafe (My BFF)

   Don't sweat it. You can borrow my old one

   The blue one

   I'll scoop you up. omw

I exhaled through my nose, feeling like a deflated balloon. I could say no. But saying no meant more questions, more back and forth, and I just didn't have it in me. Not today.

I typed out a quick "Ok" and tossed my phone onto the bed.

One more thing to deal with. One more thing to pretend I had under control.

I dragged myself to the bathroom, staring at the shower like it was some impossible task. Just turning the knob felt like too much effort. The idea of standing there, letting the water hit me, actually moving— nah. Not happening.

Instead, I caught my reflection in the mirror, running a hand through my hair. It was a mess, but I wasn't about to deal with that either. I went back into my room, grabbed my Dodgers hat off the hook behind the door and threw it on backwards. Problem solved. Mostly, I guess.

I swiped on some deodorant, because I wasn't a complete grimeball, then peeled off my shirt and grabbed a fresh one. Same with my underwear—bare minimum effort to not be disgusting. I picked up a pair of pants from the desk chair, gave them a quick sniff test, and called it good.

By the time I actually made it out of my room, I heard the beep of a car horn.

Rafe was already outside.

Guess I took longer than I thought. I sighed, giving Bandit a quick scratch behind the ears before grabbing my phone and wallet and heading out. I didn't even have my headphones, which were still in my backpack being held as a prisoner of war.

Rafe's orange FJ Cruiser was parked with his usual parallel park skill —half up on the curb, nose practically in the street. I slid into the passenger seat, barely managing a halfhearted handshake before slumping back against the headrest. The AC was blasting, but it didn't do much for the weird knot in my chest.

Rafe studied me for a second, like he was trying to clock whatever was off about me. "Yo, you hyped to hit the park? Been a minute."

I forced a half-smile. "Yeah, man. For sure."

He pulled out, not bothering to check for traffic, because apparently, the FJ made him invincible. As he weaved onto the road, he launched straight into the latest skatepark drama: Javi was beefing with this new guy because of a stolen trick or something equally ridiculous. Apparently, it was getting serious enough that people were picking sides. I half-listened, nodding when it seemed appropriate, but my head was somewhere else.

Then Rafe glanced at me mid-story and casually threw it out there. "By the way, what happened to your board? Did it finally give up on you?"

My fingers twitched in my lap. For a second, I debated lying—saying it broke or got jacked.

"Something like that..." I said staring out the window.

"Something like that..." he repeated. Eying me and almost running the light at Palms and Overland. A blue Santa Monica bus blared its horn.

"My bad!" he yelled out the window.

We went back to being quiet for a little while. Rafe drummed his hands on the steering wheel as we cruised down Venice Boulevard. He kept his eyes on the road, but I could feel him thinking about something, like he was debating whether to say it or let it slide.

"So, how you been?" he finally asked. "What you been up to?"

I shrugged, keeping my eyes on the palm trees passing by. "Just work."

He didn't press, which I appreciated. I knew I wasn't giving him much, but I also definitely wasn't getting into everything.

After a while, Rafe broke the silence again. "Went to Universal with my cousin last weekend. That new Jurassic World ride's pretty sick. Like the original, just updated."

I glanced over, surprised. "Wow. I've still never been there."

"Yeah, dude, I hit you up about it," Rafe said, throwing a look at me before switching lanes. "Never heard back."

Guilt twisted in my stomach. I vaguely remembered seeing his texts —maybe even opening them—but I never got around to replying. "Shit, man. Sorry. Been busy." It felt like a weak excuse, but it was all I had.

Rafe didn't say anything for a bit, just nodded like he was letting it go, but the air between us felt heavier. He turned off onto Pacific and then onto Horizon. Somehow, we lucked out with an open parking space without having to throw it in one of the paid lots. Rafe swung the FJ into it, doing his absolute best to get it in clean, but still ended up with one wheel slightly up on the curb.

"Eh, good enough," he said, throwing it in park and cutting the engine.

I smirked, shaking my head. "One day, man. One day, you're gonna park like a normal human."

He grinned, unbuckling his seatbelt. "And on that day, I'll be boring as hell."

We pushed off toward the skatepark, but from the second I stepped on Rafe's board, I knew it wasn't gonna feel right. The deck was too stiff, and the trucks weren't loosened the way I liked them. Every time I kicked off, it felt like I had to fight the board to move with me instead of just reacting naturally. My own board was basically an extension of my body—this? This felt like borrowing someone else's shoes that were just slightly the wrong size.

We cut across the boardwalk, dodging tourists, and hopped onto the Strand, weaving through the winding path that followed the beach. The ocean breeze cut through the late-morning heat, the air thick with salt and sunscreen. I should've been enjoying it, but every time I tried to ollie or just carve along the turns, the unfamiliar stiffness of the board threw me off.

When we got to the skatepark, we dismounted to climb the steps leading down into the sand, circling around to the entrance. The place was already buzzing. The street section was packed, skaters throwing themselves down the stairs and rails, some killing it, some eating pavement. Over at the snake run, a couple of dudes were taking turns effortlessly cruising the curves, moving like they had the whole place mapped in their heads—because they *did*. Tourists were leaning up along the railings with their phones out, getting their "Venice Skatepark" content for the Gram. A few photographers with long lenses hung around to snap shots of the local legends who might drop by.

And then... there was Avery. Sitting right near the entrance, perched on the railing, kicking her feet casually like she had all the time in the world. She had her signature checkerboard deck with the purple wheels. She had it custom made with her name spelled out in the grip tape with a wave design.

My stomach twisted a little. It had been weeks, but here she was, same old Avery. Her hair was tucked into her snapback, tips still purple, and she was tan from a summer spent chasing waves and dodging tourists on the boardwalk. Her Vans were totally thrashed, like she'd been skating nonstop since June—which, knowing her, she probably had. But seeing her now, out of nowhere, threw me off. The easy energy I had tried to fake all morning slipped. I wasn't ready for this.

Rafe nudged me as we got closer. "You good?"

I swallowed and nodded, tightening my grip on the board. "Yeah. Just... wasn't expecting her to be here."

Rafe sighed. "Dude, it's Avery. Of course she's here."

Right. Of course she was.

She hopped off the railing the second we got close, all smiles, like nothing had changed.

"Look who finally decided to show up!" she grinned, clapping me on the shoulder like we were best friends and hadn't gone weeks without talking.

I forced a half-smile, feeling how extra the whole thing was. It was *too* nice, like she was overcompensating, like if she acted like nothing had changed, then maybe I wouldn't notice how weird things had gotten.

Rafe fist-bumped her, which also seemed unnecessarily casual. They were already swapping stories, but I just stood there, gripping the board that wasn't mine, feeling like an outsider to something I used to be in the center of.

"Ready to run?" Avery asked, nodding toward the snake run.

"Yeah, let's do it," Rafe said, already hyped.

Avery dropped in first, smooth as ever, her board carving up the curves. Her movements were fluid and second nature. She kept it pretty lowkey but still a respectable run. Rafe followed next, his style less technical but still solid, pumping through the run like he'd been practicing. He looped once more around the deep end and finished with an over-the-top move, launching himself up from the shallow end and over the railing that Avery had been sitting on a minute ago, sending a couple tourists running.

Then it was my turn.

I took a deep breath, trying to shake the discomfort of the stiff board under my feet. This was muscle memory. I *knew* how to do this. But the second I pushed off, I felt the difference. Too stiff. Too tight. My board would've flexed, adjusted to how I moved. This one was still fighting me.

I hit the first dip wrong, wobbled, overcorrected, and—

Bam.

Laid out.

The impact rattled through my bones, my hip taking most of it, my board shooting off to the side. I scraped an elbow, but my pride? That's where the real injury was. A couple of skaters looked over, some tourists by the rail pointing their phones like they'd just caught premium fail content.

"You good?" Rafe called, already skating back toward me.

I sat up, exhaling sharp. "Yeah," I muttered.

Avery skated over, offering a hand. "Not used to eating pavement, huh?" she teased, her tone light but with… something else there.

I let her help me up, brushing off my arms. "Not used to this board," I said, but the excuse felt weak. It wasn't just the board. It was everything.

We skated out of the snake run to let everyone else get a go at it. Avery rolled up to her bag and started rummaging through it before tossing me a skate tool. "You should loosen up the trucks," she said. "I don't know how you're even riding that thing. Rafe's setups always feel like they're made for a damn robot."

Rafe scoffed, kicking his board up into his hands. "Excuse me for liking stability."

"Stability?" Avery shot back. "More like cement blocks."

I smirked, rolling the board over and getting to work. The trucks really were tight as hell. No wonder I wiped out. Loosening them would help, but something about this whole situation still felt stiff.

Avery's joke was the kind of thing she used to say to both of us, back when it was just us—our trio, unshaken. But now, the way she said it, the way she nudged Rafe, laughing, felt different. More like the way a girlfriend roasts her boyfriend, not like two friends clowning a mutual third.

I twisted the tool a little harder than I needed to, jaw tightening. Maybe I was overthinking it. Maybe it was just how things were now. Either way, I hated the way it made me feel. Like something had shifted, and no one told me. I wished they would just be open about it, and stop acting like nothing was going on.

My phone chimed in my pocket, and for a second, my heart jumped into my throat. Maybe Troye finally wanted to talk and fix things—or maybe this was it…

I fumbled to pull my phone out, nearly dropping it in the process. But the second I saw the name on my screen, my stomach sank.

It was Dylan. The other thing I probably needed to fix.

I hovered over the notification, hesitating before unlocking it. Part of me wanted to just shove the phone back in my pocket and deal with it later, but my thumb was already swiping as two more messages came through.

Thu Aug 15 at 2:26 PM

Dylan

 Hey, man. Sorry about last night. To both of you.

 I don't know what was up with me, but I feel like I made things weird

 Hope we can all hang out again sometime. On me. No bad vibes this time, I promise

I stared at the messages, my thumb hovering over the keyboard. My brain was still catching up, still tangled in the disappointment that it wasn't Troye. At least Dylan cared enough to reach out, I guess. But after how tense dinner was, after all the shade and the little digs, I wasn't sure how I felt about setting up round two, at least before I knew if my relationship survived round one.

Avery's voice snapped me back. "Yo, you good?"

I looked up. Her and Rafe were both watching me, Rafe with this weird look of curiosity, Avery with that same over-friendly expression that was meant to make me comfortable but only made me feel like more of an outsider in my own crew.

"Yeah," I muttered, locking my phone and shoving it back in my pocket. "Just thought it was someone else."

Rafe shrugged and dropped his board onto the pavement. "C'mon, man. Let's see if you still remember how to skate."

I forced a smirk, but my head was still all over the place.

After I finished adjusting the trucks, I made my way over to the ledge I normally started from.

I rolled my shoulders back, exhaling as I set the board down. My stance still felt off, but I wasn't about to let it win. I waited as one of the regulars finished his run, landing a clean kickflip over one of the hips before cruising out to some applause from the out-of-towners.

My turn now. No excuses.

I pushed off, dropping in with a little less confidence than usual, but at least I didn't immediately bail. The stiffness of the board threw me, every carve feeling just a little too sharp, every pump in the transitions needing more effort than I was used to. But I made it through, rolling out at the bottom, chest heaving but still upright.

From the railing, Rafe and Avery whooped, clapping like I'd just landed a competition-winning trick.

"That's the Kiko we remember!" Avery called out, grinning.

Rafe smirked, nodding. "Maybe we actually have a shot at this comp after all."

I let out a short laugh, shaking out my arms like I was totally chill and not still trying to shake off the nerves. "Yeah, yeah. Just give me like five more runs and maybe I won't look like I forgot how to skate."

Rafe slung an arm around my shoulders, giving me a rough shake. "You're good, bro. Just gotta shake the rust off."

And hopefully get my own board back.

I let out a short laugh, playing along. But as I looked between them, the truth was sitting right there, unspoken but loud as hell. The way they stood just a little closer than before, the way Rafe bumped her arm and she smiled but didn't look at me—like they were in on some inside joke I wasn't a part of.

And maybe I could've handled it, maybe it wouldn't have bugged me so much, if they just told me straight up. But they weren't. They were pretending like nothing had changed, like I was still in the same spot I'd always been. Like I wouldn't notice.

I crouched down, adjusting my trucks again just for something to do, something to focus on that wasn't them. "So, you guys been practicing much without me?" I asked, keeping my tone easy, testing the waters.

Avery ran a hand through her hair. "A little," she said, too vague.

Rafe kicked a loose pebble with the edge of his board. "Yeah, been keeping sharp. You know how it is."

I nodded slowly, pressing my tongue to the inside of my cheek. Yeah. I knew exactly how it was.

They weren't gonna say it. Not today.

I exhaled hard, gripping my board, pushing everything down. "Alright," I said, standing back up, shaking out my legs. "Let's hit another run."

And just like that, we went back to skating. Like everything was normal. Like nothing had changed. I was so over this, but what was I gonna do? They were not going to let me in.

I took out my phone and texted a quick message back to Dylan: "No worries man. Let's meet up."

17

Ma pulled up at the dead end on North Fuller near the park gates and threw the car into park.

"I don't think I've ever seen you go anywhere without your skateboard," she said, glancing at my empty hands like she was waiting for an explanation.

I gripped the strap of my backpack, giving a half-shrug. "It's not exactly the best terrain for it." The excuse felt weak even as I said it, but I wasn't about to tell her where my board actually was—or why I hadn't gone back to get it.

She hummed. It was the kind of noise that meant she wasn't buying it but was too tired to push. Her scrubs were slightly wrinkled, her hair pulled into a tight bun. She was probably running on nothing but coffee and a power nap before heading into another long shift.

I reached for the door handle, but the locks stayed put.

"Aren't you forgetting something, *mijo*?" she said, giving me a disappointed side-eye. I caught the ride with her to avoid the hour-plus trip on public transit or the forty-dollar Uber. It was only slightly out of her way into work, so I figured it would work out.

I sighed, already knowing where this was going. "Thanks for the ride."

She raised a brow and leaned her cheek out.

I leaned over and kissed her cheek, the same way I had since I was a kid. I knew she wouldn't let me out of the car without doing it. "Love you, Ma."

"Drink water," she said as she finally clicked the locks. "You don't hike."

I smirked, pushing the door open. "I'll try not to die."

"I don't need you visiting me at work."

She pulled off down Fuller, leaving me standing at the trail entrance. It wasn't that I didn't want to talk with her. It wasn't even that I didn't want her to ask questions. It was that I didn't have any answers.

I pulled my phone out of my pocket, thumb hovering over the screen like I was expecting something. Nothing. No texts. No notifications. Just the same blank silence I'd been getting for four days.

Troye still hadn't reached out.

I shoved the phone back before I could think too much about it. Whatever. It wasn't like I was waiting around, right? I was here. I was doing something. I was—

"Hey, man."

I didn't even notice Dylan strolling up, with his casual way that made it seem like he had nowhere to be, like we weren't about to climb through a whole-ass canyon for some reason. He was wearing these retro hiking boots with these red laces. I had never seen him in a tank top or shorts before but he at least had one of his signature flannels tied around his waist.

"You ready for this?" he asked, smirking like he already knew I wasn't.

I exhaled, tilting my head back to look at the trail ahead. "Yeah. Let's do it."

Because what else was there to do?

The dirt on the trail crunched under my Vans as Dylan and I made our way up toward Runyon Canyon Road. The sun was already working overtime, turning the back of my neck into a slow roast situation, but it wasn't unbearable yet. The whole vibe up here was different—less honking, more birds chirping, and a bunch of Lululemon-clad people either power-walking their tiny dogs or jogging like they had somewhere to be.

Dylan was easy company. No pressure to overtalk or fill the space with awkward noise. Just…chill. He was telling me some story about Ethan completely crushing a karaoke performance last night.

"They've got some serious range," I said, wiping sweat off my forehead.

"Oh, for sure," Dylan smirked. "It's great seeing him get out of his shell. A year ago he'd barely talk to even me."

I snorted. "Damn, that's wild."

The trail wasn't as bad as I expected. A slow incline, nothing that had me reconsidering my life choices. But when we came up on a bench about fifteen minutes in, Dylan tilted his water bottle toward it like he already knew I needed the break.

I dropped onto the bench with zero hesitation, stretching my legs out. "Not bad so far."

"Yeah," Dylan said, sitting next to me, taking a long sip from his bottle.

For a minute, we just sat there. The shrub-covered canyon stretched out below, with a slice of the city visible at one end, all hazy and endless, like something out of a video game. From up here, all the traffic, stress, and general bullshit felt distant. Like it couldn't quite reach me.

Dylan didn't say anything, and I liked that. Some people got weird with silence, like they had to fill it with whatever popped into their head. But not Dylan. He just let it be, like he understood that sometimes, just existing in the same space was enough.

We sat there for a while, just letting the view do its thing. The heat, the city stretched out below, the faint breeze that wasn't doing much but at least pretending to cool us off—it all just made the silence feel kinda…nice.

But eventually, Dylan shifted, elbows on his knees, rubbing a hand over his face before exhaling like he was about to step on a landmine.

"About the other night," he said, staring ahead at the canyon. "I don't know how else to describe it other than to say I was a dick."

I blinked, caught off guard by how blunt he was about it. I turned toward him, but he was still focused on the canyon, like the shrubs were easier to talk to than me.

"I dunno, man," he continued, shaking his head. "I got in my own head. I was already dealing with some stuff, and I guess I let that bleed into everything. I'm not even sure how things between me and Troye went so off the rails. It's like, one second we're just… not vibing, and the next, I'm acting like an asshole for no real reason."

I didn't know what to say. I'd been replaying that night over and over in my head, wondering if I'd done something wrong, if maybe I should've stepped in earlier or said something to calm it down before it got messy.

Dylan finally looked at me. "If Troye's still down to meet up again, I wanna try again. Be more respectful, actually give him a fair shot." His expression was open, honest in a way that made me realize just how much he meant it.

"Well…" I started, "I'm not exactly sure that Troye wants to meet up with me, let alone you guys again."

Dylan shot up from the bench, running a hand through his hair as he started pacing in front of me. His jaw was tight, shoulders stiff like he was gearing up for a fight with himself.

"Shit, Kiko," he muttered. "I didn't realize... I thought you guys just needed space after that night. I didn't think—" He cut himself off, shaking his head, frustration rolling off him in waves. "I might've actually screwed this up for you."

I stood up fast and grabbed his elbow, stopping him mid-step. "Nah, it's not like that," I said, voice firm but low. "It's a long-ass story, but I swear, you're not the reason."

His eyes caught mine, like he was trying to judge whether I was telling the truth or not, but I swear there was something else there.

I sighed, letting go of his arm and stepping back. "C'mon," I said, nodding toward the trail. "I'll explain."

We started walking again, the incline barely registering with how heavy everything felt. The sounds of other hikers faded into the background as I pieced together the words.

I told him about the Uber. How Troye had basically outed me to the driver like it was some kind of power move. How I'd bailed because I couldn't sit there and let him make me feel small. How I hadn't heard from him since.

Dylan didn't say anything at first, just kept walking. It was like he was fighting his own expressions that kept slipping through. Finally, he let out this slow exhale, shaking his head. "Damn," he said. "That's... yeah, that's messed up."

I nodded, kicking a stray rock off the path. "Yeah. So, y'know... I don't even know if he wants to talk to me. Let alone meet up with my friends again."

Dylan ran a hand through his hair again, still looking like he wanted to fight someone. "Still," he said, "I don't want to be the thing that makes things harder for you."

I glanced at him, the way his brows were pulled in together, the way he looked so *genuinely* upset about it. And for the first time in a while, I wasn't just stuck in my own head about Troye.

This was Dylan. And Dylan actually *gave a shit*.

We kept walking, the road getting steeper as it doubled back up the hill. I stopped, catching a shot in my head before I even pulled my phone out. It was this perfect mix of joggers, dogs, and hikers against the grasses, shrubs, and trees. The kind of shot that just felt right, the way the road just kinda swooped through the shot.

As I framed it up, this one jogger in particular caught my eye—dude was giving full-on TikTok fitness model vibes. Tanned skin, no shirt, short navy running shorts that barely counted as clothing, a backwards cap, sunglasses. The whole package. Right as I was about to snap the photo, he clocked me. Like, full eye contact through the shades.

Without missing a beat, he threw his hands behind his head, flexed, and stuck his tongue out in this ridiculously suggestive pose—like he was making a thirst trap just for me.

Dylan and I both just froze for a second as the dude kept jogging down the hill, laughing to himself like he knew exactly what he was doing.

Dylan turned to me, mouth slightly open. "Did that just—"

I nodded, still processing.

"No way that just happened," Dylan said, eyes wide.

I finally remembered to check my phone and sure enough, I caught it. The timing was on point. I turned the screen toward Dylan, and he leaned in close, our faces inches apart as we tried to see past the glare from the bright-ass sun.

He smelled like sunscreen and something… nice. Was that cologne? For half a second, I forgot what we were even looking at. His lashes were stupid long. Like unfairly long. And there was this tiny scar on his jaw I hadn't noticed before, like a faded slash of light.

My heart did this annoying stutter thing, and I looked back at the screen before my brain could make it weird.

We both stared at the photo, then at each other, and just lost it.

Dylan was shaking his head and leaned in to look at my phone again, our shoulders touching. "Nah, that was calculated as hell. He's got a mental folder of these poses ready to go."

"Probably thought we were tourists and wanted to give us something to remember LA by," I laughed.

I swallowed, suddenly very aware of how close we were, of the way his breath hitched just slightly. The moment stretched, just enough for my brain to notice before he cleared his throat and pulled back, shoving his hands into his pockets like nothing happened.

"Welp, this is going on my story," I tapped a few times, acting way too invested in cropping.

Dylan smirked. "You should run after him to get his handle," he said. "I bet he's got a whole highlight reel of these."

I snorted, slipping my phone in my pocket. "Dude's an icon."

Dylan chuckled, as we started walking again, but my heart was doing something weird. Something I definitely didn't have time to figure out.

We climbed a bit more, not really saying much to each other. I followed him off the road down a dirt trail, the dry dust kicking up behind us as we walked.

Finally we reached this spot that had a sick view. I mean the whole hike had some awesome views, but this? Straight up fire. Like there wasn't a part of the city I couldn't see, all at once. From the Hollywood sign to downtown to the high-rise buildings on Wilshire near the coffee shop, and even the taller ones in Century City. It was a little hazy, but I could actually make out Catalina Island out in the ocean.

"Uh…wow," I said, not really knowing what else *to* say.

"I know right," Dylan said, staring out at the city.

My phone chimed and I scrambled to get it out of my pocket.

224-555-3034   Just Now

[Amazon] Surprise! As a valued customer, You've received a gift card worth $200. Redeem it in…

I sighed, kicking a loose rock off the path and watching it tumble down the dry hillside.

"Guessing that wasn't Mr. Skimpy-Blue-Jogging-Shorts."

"No…" I said. "Be real with me for a sec. Putting everything from the other night aside… what do you actually think about Troye?"

Dylan's whole body tensed, like I just asked him to rank his own family members or something like that. He scratched the back of his neck, staring out over the city for a second like the answer might be written somewhere in the haze. "That's… I mean, it's not really my place, is it?"

I frowned. "C'mon dude, I'm asking you. I trust you."

He shifted uncomfortably, adjusting the strap of his bag like it was suddenly too tight. "I don't know, Kiko. It's your first real thing, right? You're figuring it out. That's all that really matters."

That wasn't an answer. Not really. And the way he said "figuring it out" like I was navigating some doomed experiment didn't sit right.

I eyed him. "So, you don't like him."

Dylan let out a sharp breath, looking like he wanted to disappear into the dirt. "I didn't say that."

"You kinda did."

He turned, giving me a look, but it softened almost immediately.

"Listen, man, I just don't wanna be the guy that plants shit in your head. You want an outside opinion? Ask Indie. She'll give it to you direct. She doesn't really know any other way…"

I nodded, but I was pretty sure there was more he wasn't saying.

We made our way down this trail which couldn't be more different than the road we took up. This one was rough, all dirt and rock, except where these wooden beams made these step things. I had to say, going down the trail was probably harder than coming up the road.

We got to this one spot where this rusty fence with barbed wire on the top blocked off the area to the left of the trail. Someone really didn't want random hikers on their land. The fence was covered in locks—hundreds of them like that bridge in Paris all the influencers have to take pictures in front of.

Dylan slowed down next to me as I crouched, angling my phone to frame the shot just right. The rusted locks, the skyline blurred in the background, one little cluster shaped like a heart—it was kinda perfect. Something about it felt poetic in a way I couldn't put into words, but I was pretty sure Dylan could.

"You ever think about what people were feeling when they put these here?" he asked, kinda quiet, like he was actually wondering.

I exhaled through my nose, lining up my next shot of a Buddha-head lock that someone drew a jester makeup on.

"Probably some promise to love each other forever. Then they break up six months later and pretend they never came up here."

Dylan gave a short laugh, "Not much faith in love?"

"My present situation," I said, "isn't really helping my long-term outlook on love."

He gave me this little *touché* look but didn't seem convinced. "Fair… but some of them had to stick it out."

I tilted my head, "I guess."

He gave a small shrug, his fingers grazing over a lock with initials scratched into the metal. "I dunno, man. Love's weird. Messy. But if it doesn't last, does that make it not real? Feels like maybe it's still worth something, even if it doesn't go the distance."

I thought about it, staring at the locks again. The past few weeks—hell, the past few months—had me questioning what *real* even meant. Troye's hot and cold moods, the way he made me feel like I was the only person in the room one second and completely alone the next. Was that love? Was it supposed to feel like that?

"Maybe," I muttered, not sure if I believed it.

Dylan watched me for a second before interrupting my thoughts. "You good?"

I forced a smirk. "Yeah. Just thinking."

"That's a dangerous habit," he teased, but his eyes lingered, like he wanted to say something else. He just pulled out his leatherbound notebook and scribbled something down.

One of these days I swore I was going to have to convince him to let me read what he writes down.

We kept moving down the trail, the decline forcing us to slow our pace. Then my phone buzzed. My hand shot to my pocket before I even realized what I was doing. I fumbled it out, heart kicking up. Maybe it was Troye. Maybe he finally—

Nope. Just Ma.

Mamadukes	Just Now
Working a double. Make sure you and Mateo eat something decent. Love you.	

I let a long breath out my nose, thumbs already hovering over the keyboard.

Dylan chuckled under his breath. "You never respond to my texts that fast…"

I shot him a look. "What? It coulda been important."

He side-eyed me. "Uh-huh."

I scoffed, shoving my phone back into my pocket. "I don't—"

Dylan gave me a look. The kind that shut me up immediately.

I sighed, rubbing the back of my neck. "I keep hoping it's him."

Dylan let it sit for a second before speaking. "Uh-huh. I get it."

I stayed quiet. The trail twisted ahead of us, the barbed wire fence disappearing as the hill evened out into another lookout point as it twisted back on itself down the canyon. There was this Insta-worthy bench that I had to snap a pic of.

A couple about our age was coming up the trail from the other direction and they were *struggling.* I totally got it. If we had come up this way I definitely would be in the same condition. I mean it wasn't Mount Everest or something, but I wasn't in the same shape as Mr. Skimpy-Blue-Shorts, and neither were they. They held each other's hand, though, like they were gonna conquer this together.

"You ever notice how some people just keep moving forward," Dylan interrupted, kicking a stray rock. "Even when it sucks."

I shot a glance at him before turning back toward the couple. The guy slipped on a loose patch of dirt, but his girlfriend kept him upright as they laughed.

"Just one foot in front of the other, even when they slip," Dylan said.

I looked back at him, "Is this the scenic route to you telling me to just call him?"

A wide grin spread on Dylan's face, but it stopped just short of his eyes.

"I'm saying," he continued, "Waiting at the bottom of the hill doesn't make the climb any easier…"

He slapped my shoulder and continued down the trail.

That one landed harder than I wanted it to. I looked across the canyon at the bottom where we started and saw a group of joggers just starting up. I hated that he wasn't wrong.

I had to jog to catch up to him. "Do you always come out with these profound pieces of wisdom?"

Dylan just shrugged, "I guess you just bring it out in me."

We laughed for a moment as we walked, but I stayed mostly quiet until we reached the gate, running through my thoughts.

When we stopped at the *frutero* cart outside the gate, I decided it was time to stop waiting for things to happen to me, and start doing something about it.

I didn't wait this time. I pulled out my phone, opened the text, and typed like I already knew what I needed to say.

18

"Thanks," I said, barely paying attention, as the server poured me a water.

Troye had agreed to meet me at this Mexican spot in the Farmers Market. The place had that bright, polished look that made it feel more like an Instagram backdrop than a restaurant but the reviews looked good. The whole Grove kinda had that vibe—shiny, curated, like a theme park version of LA where everything was almost too put together. Not like the city that I grew up in.

I was sitting outside under the canopy, half-watching shoppers weave in and out of stores, juggling bags in one hand and overpriced coffees—that were probably even worse than if I made them—in the other. It was the kind of place you were supposed to enjoy, and I usually did—but right now… I wasn't feeling it.

I swirled my paper straw around in my water, watching the ice melt. My stomach was a whole-ass battlefield, twisting itself up like I was about to take a final I didn't study for. Food? Yeah, not happening—at least not yet. I was too deep in my own head, waiting. Waiting for him.

The patio was loud—margaritas clinking, people laughing, sizzling fajita plates being brought out that would usually make me hungry. Right now, the smell of carne asada and fresh tortillas just sat in the air. I took another sip of my water, trying to act like I wasn't watching every single person who walked by, half-expecting one of them to be him.

My phone sat next to me, screen-down, because I already knew. No "on my way," no "almost there," nothing. Just me, waiting for him. Again.

I leaned back in my chair, exhaling hard, fingers tapping against the table. *Any minute now.*

The server dropped a basket of chips and salsa onto the table and barely paused before asking, "Would you like to put anything in while you wait?"

I shook my head. "Nah, he'll be here any minute." I said it like I believed it. Like I wasn't already spiraling a little.

The server nodded and walked off, leaving me alone with the chips... and my thoughts. I grabbed one, not because I was hungry, but because sitting there doing nothing felt worse. The crunch was weirdly loud in the silence, like it didn't belong. Like *I* didn't belong sitting here... waiting... hoping this wouldn't be the final talk.

Then, finally, Troye appeared. He was carrying my backpack and skateboard like they were bricks, his whole body screaming *struggling* even though his face was way too cheerful underneath those oversized sunglasses. Like, *aggressively* cheerful. Like overcompensating-for-something cheerful. He dumped my stuff onto one of the chairs with this dramatic sigh and wiped sweat off his forehead. Before he said anything, he grabbed the other water glass and chugged the whole thing, slammed it back down, and shot me this oops, "my bad" kinda grin.

I just stared with this half smile trying to figure out where this was going.

Troye exhaled and stretched his hand across the table, palm up, like he was asking for a truce. His voice was softer than I expected. "I missed you, Skater Boy."

I hesitated for half a second before reaching out too, my fingers brushing against his. "Yeah," I admitted. "I missed you too, Troye-boy."

He did that cute little thing where he pulls in his shoulders and coos like some type of Pokemon. I felt a smile spread across my face as my body relaxed. It was comfortable. Chill. Like nothing even happened.

The waiter returned to refill Troye's glass. "Anything else to drink besides water?"

Troye leaned back in his chair. "Just *all* the water you have. I had to lug all that"—he gestured dramatically at my backpack and skateboard like they were boulders—"across half of LA I might actually die of dehydration."

The waiter, clearly unfazed, just set the whole pitcher down on the table like *here, have at it*, then pulled out his notepad. "You guys ready to order?"

Troye barely took a glance at the menu before rattling off his order at light speed. "Yeah, I'll do the nachos with steak, a side of salsa verde, oh, and the queso fundido, and the Vampiro Tacos. No, wait, actually, scratch that, make it the California Steak Burrito Supreme, and a side of rice."

I just blinked.

"What? I'm starving."

The waiter looked at me, pen still hovering over the pad. "And for you?"

I shrugged, flipping a chip between my fingers my stomach was still not settled—not even a quarter as settled as Troye's was.

"Just uh.. guac. Thanks"

"Oh wait, add two orders of Flamin' Hot Cheetos," Troye said, before turning to me. "They were the whole reason I picked this place."

The waiter gave a quick nod and disappeared toward the kitchen, leaving us in this weird, charged silence. I tapped my fingers against the table, my stomach twisting up like it was bracing for impact.

I exhaled. "Look, I'm sorry about everything that happened that night." The words felt heavy coming out, like they'd been stuck in my chest for the past eight days, waiting to be said. "I didn't mean to just —"

Troye cut me off before I could even get into it, shaking his head. "No, I'm sorry." His voice was softer than I expected, less defensive than I braced for. "I never should've acted like that in the Uber."

I sighed, rolling my thumb over the back of Troye's hand as we held hands together across the table. The contact was such a rush, I mean yeah we kissed that one time outside the Thai restaurant, but other than that, we never really did much PDA—and this seemed so... intimate.

"I think we both could've handled it better," I admitted. No point in pretending like I didn't jump out of that Uber like it was on fire rather than trying to work things out.

"So... Dylan," I started carefully, keeping my tone light. "He actually apologized. Said he wants to try again. I really think you just caught him at a bad time." I hesitated before adding, "He's actually pretty cool once you get to know him."

Troye's mouth pressed into a thin line, and he glanced down at our hands, like he was thinking about it. "I get it," he said finally, "I just don't trust him."

"Trust him?" I asked. "You barely know him. Just give him a chance..."

Troye shifted in his seat, his hands pulling away so he could drum his fingers lightly against the table. He looked impatient, like he was already over this conversation, like talking about Dylan was draining whatever we'd built back up. My stomach twisted. I'd finally started to relax, to believe we were fixing this, and now I felt like I was blowing it.

Troye didn't seem to care about any of that. He just wanted to move on, to get back to how things were before the fight, before the awkwardness. I let it go, but that *I don't trust him* comment still lingered in my head. Like what did that even mean? But instead of pushing, I shifted to something lighter.

"I went skating with Rafe and Avery the other day," I said, grabbing a chip and breaking it in half.

Troye raised an eyebrow as he downed another glass of water.

"Oh? *The* Rafe and Avery?"

"Yeah." I nodded, glancing down at my guac like it had the answers to all my problems. "It was... fine. Just felt kinda off, y'know? I don't know if it's them or me, but I don't think it'll ever be the same."

"I mean," he said, "it's pretty obvious they're together now, right?"

I exhaled, rubbing my forehead. "Yeah, well... they haven't told me."

Troye scoffed. "And that's why it feels off. It's not you, it's them. They're acting like you're stupid or like you can't handle it, and that's messed up." He popped a chip into his mouth. "Honestly, maybe it's for the best that things aren't the same. People grow out of each other."

I frowned, feeling like that might be true, but I just didn't want it to be. Before I could say anything, though, the waiter came back, balancing a tray of plates. He set down the nachos, the queso, the side of salsa verde in front of Troye and my guac in front of me. The smell hit instantly, but my stomach still wasn't sure it could handle anything. I grabbed another chip anyway, just to have something to do. Then the waiter put down two bags of actual Flamin' Hot Cheetos cut open at the top with nacho cheese, onions, and cilantro inside.

"I thought you were kidding," I said, studying the bags.

Troye slid one of the bags toward me. "C'mon, try it," he said, nudging it closer.

I hesitated for a second before picking one up. The cheese stretched as I pulled it out, dripping onto the foil-lined bag. I popped it into my mouth, and the mix of textures hit immediately—the crunch, the heat, the gooeyness of the cheese. The spice punched through first, the kind that made my tongue tingle and warming up the back of my throat, but then the cheese balanced it out, smooth and salty. The cilantro and onions added this fresh bite at the end. It was weird but really good.

Troye, meanwhile, was all over the place. One second, he was digging into his nachos, then bouncing to his queso, then back to his own bag of Cheetos. He was eating like he hadn't had a meal in days, barely finishing a bite of one thing before moving onto the next. His knee bounced under the table, and his fingers drummed against the edge between picking up more food.

He wasn't saying much, just focused on inhaling his food like it was a race. Meanwhile, I took my time, scooping up bites of guac with a tortilla chip, half-watching the people walking past, half-watching Troye bounce between his apps like he couldn't stick to one thing. His energy was off—not bad, necessarily, just… different.

The table was a mess of half-eaten food when the waiter showed up again, this time with the burrito. I had honestly forgotten Troye even ordered it. The thing was huge, wrapped tight in foil, steaming hot as the waiter set it down.

Troye immediately started shuffling plates around, stacking empty ones, pushing his nachos to the side, sliding my guac closer to me. It took a few tries, but he finally made enough space for the burrito in front of him. He clapped his hands together like he was about to dig into some life-changing meal.

I just watched him, chewing on the inside of my cheek. Maybe I was overthinking it, but something about the way he was acting felt… off. Not in a way I could put my finger on, just a weird sort of restlessness. But whatever. He was probably just hungry.

It was like that for most of the meal. When it came time to settle the check, Troye had half-eaten plates all over the table, but at least he insisted on paying since I only ordered the guac.

There was a weird silence as Troye pulled out that Platinum Amex again, all casual like it wasn't a big deal. Like we were two grown-ass adults who regularly threw down metal credit cards at bougie restaurants. I watched him slide it across the table to the waiter, who took it with a nod, no hesitation, no second glance. Meanwhile, I was sitting there thinking—where the hell does someone our age get one of those?

I let it go, at first. We were still finding our way back to normal, no need to stir up something new. But when the waiter came back and dropped off the receipt, my curiosity got the best of me.

"So… the Amex," I said, keeping my voice light, testing the waters. "Kinda fancy. How'd you get one of those?"

Troye hesitated. Just for a second, but long enough for me to notice. "A friend set me up as an authorized user. Helps him with the points or something," he said, not meeting my eyes as he signed the receipt.

"A friend?" I pressed.

His grip on the pen tightened just a little. "Yeah. Just… some older guy. He likes buying me stuff."

I blinked and just stared at him, my stomach twisting up in knots. Like did he really just casually throw that out there?

"So he just *buys* you stuff? Like, for… *no* reason?" My voice came out super skeptical, but I couldn't help it. This wasn't normal. This wasn't *nothing*.

Troye rolled his eyes, exhaling like I was being dramatic. "Relax, babe. It's not like that." He leaned back, throwing his arm over the back of the other chair, way too casual. "He's just an older guy, a little lonely. We get dinner sometimes, he buys me things, gave me the Amex. That's all. It's not like we have sex or anything."

I felt my jaw tighten. That "anything" was doing a whole lot of work in that sentence. It didn't make me feel better. If *anything*, it made it worse.

I shifted in my seat, something nagging at the back of my brain. The name. That envelope I saw at his place.

"Wait," I said slowly, the pieces clicking together in the worst possible way. "Is that the guy? Clayton?"

Troye blinked. "What?"

"I saw mail at your place once, addressed to someone named Clayton. Is that him?"

For a second, he looked genuinely confused—like I'd asked him what year it was. Then something dawned across his face, and he let out a sharp laugh, borderline unhinged.

"Oh my god," he said, grinning wide. "No, babe. That's me."

I stared.

He leaned in, like he was letting me in on a secret. "Clayton Troy McCosh. That's my full name. Legal name. But like… obviously I don't go by that anymore."

I just blinked at him.

"Your name is Clayton?"

He dropped his voice, mock-serious. "'Clayton' sounds like a real estate agent in Glendale. Troye is a vibe, especially with the 'e'."

"And the 'e'?"

He smiled wider. "Branding. Just look at what it did for Troye Sivan"

"Yeah but that's like his actual name…"

But before I could press him on it any further, Troye stood up from the table, stretching from the big meal he actually seemed to enjoy.

"C'mon," he said, flashing me a grin. "Let's hit Gucci. I gotta grab a couple things."I didn't move right away. My brain was still catching up, still tripping over the whole "some older guy" situation. But Troye was already heading towards the stores, so I had no choice but to follow.

I slung my backpack over one shoulder, gripping my board as I trailed after Troye through the maze of designer stores. The Grove was always kind of surreal—like this weird, artificial little city where everything was too clean and too expensive. But stepping into *Gucci*? Whole different level.

The second I walked in, I felt it. That *you don't belong here* kind of vibe. The lighting was bright and dramatic, like every handbag and shoe on display was some sacred artifact in a museum. Even the air smelled expensive—like leather, floral perfume, and straight-up wealth. Troye, of course, waltzed in like he had owned the place, heading straight for a perfume display without hesitation.

I hesitated at the entrance, taking it all in. What the hell am I even doing here? Troye was in his element, picking up expensive bottles and spritzing them on these little pieces of cardstock paper. Meanwhile, I was just trying not to breathe too hard on anything that looked like it cost more than a year's pay.

I wandered over to the accessories, running my fingers over a multicolored handbag that was probably worth more than Ma's car. I imagined what it would be like to just... buy her something like this. No hesitation. No checking the price tag first—and at over four grand for that one... yeah. Just being able to walk up to the counter and say, *She deserves this.* But that wasn't my life. Probably never would be.

I glanced up to see a security guard—big dude, black suit, definitely ex-military vibes—watching me like I had "thief" written across my forehead. Not exactly subtle about it either.

Alright then. If they wanted a reason to watch me, I might as well give them something to do.

I picked up a random wallet, inspected it like I was really considering a purchase, then put it back. Then a belt. Then a pair of sunglasses. Each time, moving just slow enough to make it obvious, smirking to myself as I caught the guard shifting his stance.

Yeah, this was gonna be fun.

But before I could have too much fun with him, Troye breezed past me toward the door like nothing happened, tossing a casual, "Ready, babe?" over his shoulder. I smirked at the security guard one last time, just to be petty, then followed after Troye.

But something was off. He was walking fast, even for him. Like, borderline speed-walking, weaving through shoppers like he was in some type of spy movie. I jogged a little to catch up.

"Thought you had to pick up a few things?" I asked, glancing at his very empty hands.

Troye stopped just long enough to pull a sleek black box from his waistband, holding it up with a smug grin. The label practically screamed this costs more than your whole paycheck.

"I did."

My stomach dropped. "Troye, what the f—"

Before I could even finish, I glanced back at the store entrance. The dude in the black suit was there talking to a uniformed security guard, and pointing straight at us.

Troye's head snapped in their direction.

"Yeah, so… definitely time to go," he said. And then?

He ran.

Like, full-on sprinting… and not looking back.

Oh. *Hell no.*

The second Troye took off, I had no choice but to follow. Security was already moving, and I was not about to go down for this.

I yanked my backpack off, flinging it toward the plants near the entrance of Sephora. Not like it had anything worth getting arrested over—just clothes, random receipts, and a half-melted granola bar—but it was dead weight, just gonna slow me down. My skateboard, though? Non-negotiable. I tightened my grip and booked it after Troye.

We barreled into the parking lot, dodging between slow-moving SUVs and moms juggling shopping bags. A dude in a Buick honked like that was gonna stop us. A group of girls in matching Erewhon hoodies gasped and stepped back, clutching their overpriced smoothies.

Troye cut left between two parked cars, barely missing a side mirror. I hurdled a planter and sprinted after him, my heart slamming against my ribs.

Behind us, I heard shouting. "Hey! Stop!"

Not happening.

We hit the sidewalk on Fairfax and we nearly collided with a guy on a Lime scooter. He swerved last second, cursing us out as we ran into the street, straight into traffic.

The second my feet hit the street, I knew I'd made a huge mistake.

Troye was already halfway across, weaving through the gaps in traffic like this was some kind of game. I hesitated for half a second—just enough time for a black Tesla to scream its horn at me as I barely managed to dodge the front bumper. The driver threw up his hands, yelling something I didn't stick around to hear. My legs moved before my brain could catch up, and somehow, I made it to the other side, my pulse pounding in my ears.

We tore past the Thai place, and my brain barely registered it—the spot where we first kissed—less than six weeks ago. Now, here I was, getting chased by security over a bottle of perfume.

Troye didn't slow down, cutting hard between the Wells Fargo and Box Depot. I followed, my lungs burning. The pavement turned to cracked asphalt, in the alley behind the buildings. The smell of hot garbage hit me, but I didn't care.

I glanced back. No security guards. No one chasing us. Pretty sure they gave up after I almost got unalived crossing Fairfax, but I wasn't about to try my theory by stopping. Troye was still running, so I kept running.

We turned left into the alley that ran parallel to Beverly Boulevard, passing the gas station on the corner. We got a half a block more before Troye gave up running. He bent over, hands on his knees, laughing like this was the funniest thing that had ever happened. Like we hadn't just almost gotten arrested. Like I hadn't almost gotten turned into street art by a Tesla.

I stopped a few feet away, chest heaving, trying to catch my breath. My whole body was buzzing with adrenaline, but I wasn't feeling the high like he was. I was feeling *pissed.*

"What the actual *fuck* was that?" I snapped, voice sharp between gasps.

Troye just kept laughing, like this was some kind of inside joke I wasn't in on.

Troye straightened up, still grinning. "Relax, babe," he said, like that was supposed to make everything fine.

I was *not* fine. "Don't give me that *babe* shit," I shot back, still breathing hard. "I almost died back there."

Troye rolled his eyes, waving me off like I was being so dramatic. "Oh my god, those cars stop themselves. You're still on that?"

I stepped closer, my hands shaking, but not from the run anymore. "Yeah, I'm still *on that.* That, and the fact that you've got some old dude buying you shit, and now you're shoplifting? How the hell am I supposed to trust you?"

"You're overreacting...again," Troye said, approaching me with this seductive look. "It's not like that."

"So what's it like then?" I shot back.

"Let's just go back to my place and talk about it," he said before he slipped a hand under my shirt. "And then we can do other things..."

His eyes were wild, with that dark and glassy look, and I realized for the first time what that look actually was—or at least let myself admit what it was.

"Are you high right now?" I asked.

Troye smirked as he moved closer, leaning in like he was going to kiss me.

I jumped back. "You are. Aren't you?!"

"What? Are you pissed I didn't share or something?" he said, pulling a small bag of multicolored pills from his pocket. "Take one so you can chill the fuck out."

"Fuck outta here," I said. "I have no idea what is going on right now, I don't even know who you are. Clayton? Troye? What I do know is I'm over it."

That wiped the smirk off his face. He crossed his arms, tilting his head. "So what're you gonna do, Skater Boy? Run away again?"

I stared at him for a long moment. My legs didn't want to move. But I did. One step. Then another. Then I brushed past him, and said, "No. I'm gonna *walk* away."

Troye's voice followed me down the alley, each insult more desperate than the last. "You always do this, Kiko! You just run away instead of facing shit! No wonder you're still in the closet!"

I kept walking.

"Yeah, just keep avoiding everything! It's what you're best at, right?"

The words stung, but not in the way he wanted them to. It wasn't the first time someone had thrown that at me—hell, I'd thrown it at myself enough times. But this time, I wasn't running. I was making a *choice*.

Troye's voice cracked with something pathetic now. He knew I wasn't turning back. "No one else is gonna put up with you like I did, you know that, right?"

That made me pause for half a second. Not because I believed it... but because I *had* believed it. And that was the worst part. I had put up with so much, let so much slide, all because he was the first guy—the only guy—who ever wanted me.

But there *had* to be more than this. There *had* to be something better.

I tightened my grip on my skateboard and kept walking.

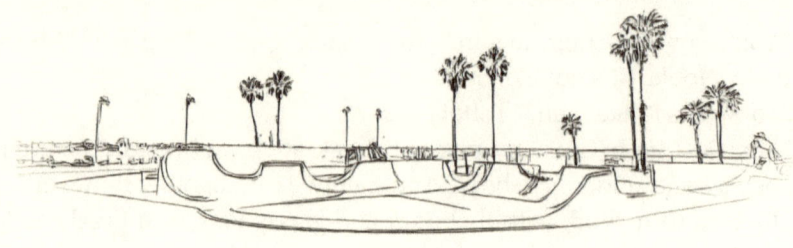

19

I stared at my phone. The cracked screen was making it hard as ever to see in the sunlight, but my message to Dylan was blunt as hell:

> Broke up with Troye. Shit was a mess.

Delivered

I sighed, my thumb hesitating over the send button. Did I even *want* to talk about it? Dylan would get it. He never liked Troye anyway. But that was the problem, wasn't it? I didn't want an "I told you so," even though I couldn't see Dylan doing that. I didn't want sympathy either. I just wanted to move on.

I held down backspace and watched the words disappear. Probably for the best.

I glanced up at Rafe. Man, I wished I could talk to him. Like *really* talk to him.

He was right there, messing around on his board, hyping up some younger skater who just landed a decent tre flip. Just doing his thing, same as always. And I was just sitting here, watching, stuck in my own head—and it sucked.

He'd always been my go-to when things got heavy, but with this? My whole relationship, the breakup, the fact that I'd been wrapped up in Troye for weeks and barely around? I hadn't told him a damn thing. And it wasn't like I didn't want to. I just… didn't know how.

Would he care? Would he get weird about it? Would it change shit between us? I hated how I didn't know the answer. How there was this part of me, this whole side of my life, that I couldn't just drop into a conversation with him the way I used to.

Maybe that's just how it was now. It felt like this wall was going up between us and it was only getting higher.

My phone buzzed in my pocket, pulling me out of my spiral. For a brief second I worried it might be Troye. But nah, it was an email.

Neil's Annual Labor Day Party - Staff & Guests the title read. I opened it up. It was one of those electronic invites with the RSVP buttons and way too much clipart confetti.

I scanned the details: the address for Neil's house in Silver Lake... an open invite to all staff next weekend. Ricky had mentioned it before. Apparently Neil threw this big party for the staff every summer, but I hadn't really thought about it. Part of me had a hard time believing I would get an invite. But now that I did? It actually sounded good. I was starting to vibe with my coworkers—not just Ricky, but even the quiet guy from the morning shift, who I learned actually had some hilarious takes when he did talk.

I clicked yes to RSVP.

I locked my phone and looked back up. Rafe landed a clean kickflip over the hip, throwing a fist in the air like he just won gold at the X Games. Avery whistled, Mateo cheered from the sideline, and I sat there feeling like an outsider to my own life.

Rafe clapped a hand on my shoulder as he rolled up next to me, all grins and easy confidence. "You ready for this?"

Avery was right behind him, adjusting the straps on her knee pads. She gave me a quick once-over, raising an eyebrow. "You don't look ready."

I forced a smirk, but I was pretty sure I wasn't fooling anyone. "I'm good."

I wasn't. Not really. My stomach was doing kickflips of its own, and my head felt too full and too empty at the same time. I was trying to hype myself up, but it would've been a hell of a lot easier if I had my music. Only realized later—like an idiot—that my headphones had been in the bag I ditched when we were running from security at The Grove. Another casualty in the great Troye disaster.

Mateo stood off to the side, arms crossed like he was the official judge of this whole thing. He had insisted on coming, hyped as hell to watch the competition. "No backing out now," he said, real serious. "I told Ma I'd record your runs."

I rolled my shoulders, stretching out the tension. "Yeah, yeah. I got this."

Avery shot me a skeptical look, but didn't push it. Rafe, on the other hand, grinned. "Good. 'Cause I already cleared a spot on my wall for one of those hand-painted boards."

"Dude," I groaned. "Don't jinx it!"

"I'm not jinxing, I'm manifesting," he said, tapping his temple.

I exhaled, shaking my arms out. The competition was starting soon. Whether I was ready or not didn't matter anymore. I had to just go for it.

The judges stood in a line near the edge of the park, each holding a mic or clipboard. One of them was an old-school Venice skater with deep crow's feet and a sun-faded snapback. He leaned into the mic. "Alright, listen up! Y'all know the deal, but let's run through it anyway."

He gestured to the other two judges—a local skateshop owner with her arms crossed over her chest like she was born unimpressed, and another OG who looked like he'd been skating since the Dogtown days. They ran through the rules: Three different events. Four teams of three to four skaters. Best combined team score takes the win. Style and creativity mattered just as much as tricks. And, of course, keep it clean —no fighting, no snaking runs, no reckless bullshit.

Then came the team intros.

First up needed no introduction. Well, because it was us.

The second team got called up: Isaiah Brown—just Zay to us—and his crew. I liked those guys. We weren't close, but they were solid skaters, always chill. No beef, no drama. Zay shot me a quick nod from across the park, and I returned it.

The third group was made up of some regulars I didn't know all that well. They were always at the park, but we never really talked. One of them, a kid with bleach-blonde hair and knee pads way too fresh to belong to a seasoned skater, bounced on his toes like he was itching to go first. Taking them should be easy.

Then came the fourth team... and that's when my stomach dropped.

I recognized them right away—another crew of Venice locals. But one skater in particular stood out... Brandon.

Troye's cousin.

That's why he looked familiar. I'd seen him around, probably a bunch of times, but now that I knew who he was, it hit different. And if Brandon was here, that meant...

I scanned the crowd. No sign of him—yet—but so much for keeping my head clear.

Brandon rolled up like he owned the place, his crew following close behind, all cocky grins and shitty energy. I clocked him the second he started heading our way, but I stayed still, hoping maybe he'd just skate past.

Not that lucky.

He stopped right in front of me, eyeing me up and down like he was sizing me up. Then, with the smuggest smirk, he hit me with: "I almost didn't recognize you with your clothes on."

His crew erupted, laughing like it was the funniest thing they'd ever heard. My stomach dropped. My ears went hot. I felt like the ground under me wasn't solid anymore.

Rafe and Avery were confused as hell, but not standing for it.

Rafe narrowed his eyes. "Dumbest shit I've ever heard. You good, bro? You need new material. That shit's whack."

Avery, arms crossed, deadpan. "Ignore him. They're just trying to mess with your head."

He was. And well... it was working.

I could still hear Brandon laughing as he skated away. His douchebag crew was trailing behind, all smirks and cocky little grins. My hands clenched into fists at my sides, but I forced them open, like flexing my fingers would stop the rush of panic creeping in.

I had to shake this off. I had a comp to focus on. But damn, that dude was not about to make this easy.

The first event kicked off, the judges calling everyone over to the street section. The energy shifted—less shit-talking, more focus. The comp was on.

Avery went first, cool and calculated, hitting a clean kickflip up the euro gap and locking into a frontside 50-50 on the ledge. She wasn't flashy, but she was consistent, landing everything clean. Rafe followed up, going for a little more style—tre flip onto the bank, back tail down the ledge. He hyped up the crowd, played into it, and stuck the landing every time.

Then it was my turn.

I rolled in, heart pounding but steady, going through the motions like I'd done a thousand times before. First trick? Clean. Second? Smooth. But then—stupid, stupid, stupid—I bailed on a simple shove-it off the kicker. A shove-it. A trick I could land half-asleep.

I kicked my board away, biting back frustration, but I didn't have time to dwell. I had to keep moving, clean up the rest of my run. And I did—landed a solid backside flip, hit the rail with a board slide—but that one stupid mistake was all I could think about.

As I skated off, Brandon snickered from his spot, loud enough for me to hear but not loud enough to call him out. My jaw clenched.

From the sidelines, Mateo cupped his hands around his mouth. "You still killed it, Kiko! Shake it off!"

I forced a nod, but I wasn't feeling it.

The other teams took their turns—some solid runs, some complete wipeouts. Zay's team did decent, but nothing that would put them ahead. Then came Brandon's crew—and they killed it. I hated to admit it, but they did. Clean tricks, technical lines, not a single major mess-up. When the judges tallied up the points, Brandon's team was ahead—by one point.

That *one* stupid little mistake cost us. I huffed out through my nose, shaking out my arms. Whatever. The comp wasn't over, and there was plenty of time to make a comeback.

But if Brandon was gonna keep running his mouth? I *really* needed to make sure I shut him up.

Brandon skated over, smugness just oozing off of him. "Man, Kiko," he said, tilting his head, eyes dragging over me in a way that made my skin crawl. "Didn't know you were into competitions like this. Thought you preferred, I dunno... *private* sessions."

I clenched my jaw, doing my best to keep my face neutral.

Rafe scoffed, "What's that even supposed to mean?"

Brandon grinned, like he just proved his point. "Nothing, man. Just saying... not everyone likes to be on display like this. Some guys do their best work, you know, when no one's watching." His gaze fixed on me again as he spoke, slow and deliberate. "You feel me?"

"Buzz off," Avery said, but I could feel her studying me.

I shook it off. Focus. Next event was the snake run, and I needed to get my head in the game. I took a deep breath and rolled my shoulders, tuning everything else out.

Until I saw him—Troye—standing just beyond the crowd, off to the side, watching.

Brandon noticed too. "Yo, Troye!" he called, waving him over like this was some kind of reunion. "Glad you could make it, cuz."

Mateo's head snapped up at the name. I saw him studying his clothes, those oversized sunglasses, the boots with the heel—who even wears shit like that to the beach. Either way I turned away when Mateo looked back at me and I felt his stare.

I glanced back and saw him looking at Troye again, his face shifting—

confused, then suspicious, like pieces were clicking together in real time. My stomach knotted.

I forced myself to breathe. Focus on the comp. Just focus on the comp. But it was too late.

I pushed off, dropping into the snake run, but my head was a mess. The turns felt off. My balance was off. I was off. Before I even knew what was happening, my wheels slipped out from under me, and I went down hard, sliding sideways down the concrete on my knees. The pain was instant—sharp, burning—but it barely registered because I could already hear Brandon laughing before I even stopped moving.

"Hey, Kiko," he called, just loud enough for me to hear. "I know you like being on your knees, but *damn* even here?."

Rage flared in my chest, but before I could even process it, Rafe was already yelling. "Hey, why don't you shut the fuck up, dude!"

Avery looked between us, finally catching on that this was more than just casual trash talk. Mateo was still staring at me. Troye was still there. Troye and Rafe and Avery and Mateo—all in the same place.

And me?

I just wanted to disappear.

"This guy's pissing me off," Rafe said, pacing back and forth.

"Just let it go," I pleaded with him, trying to grab his elbow.

He shook me off, eyes locked on Brandon like he was some final boss. "Nah, man. I'm not just gonna let him run his mouth like that. Who even is this guy? He doesn't know you. He doesn't know us."

Except he *did*. At least one of us.

Rafe rolled across towards Brandon, letting his board continue as he squared up with Brandon.

"Hey guys take it easy," one of the judges said into the microphone.

"So dude," Rafe said, "What's with all the gay jokes, huh? You got a crush on my boy or something?"

Brandon just laughed over his shoulder to his friends.

"No seriously, you got a lot to say about him being on his knees—sounds kinda like you'd like that, bro."

Brandon's smirk barely twitched. "Nah man, I don't sleep with my cousin's exes."

Rafe blinked. "What are you talking about?"

Brandon grinned wider, eyes flicking between me and Troye. "Oh, you didn't know? Your boy over here was banging my cousin."

It was like the ground got ripped out from under me. My whole body went cold, but somehow I was burning up at the same time. My ears started ringing, drowning out the sounds of the skatepark—the wheels grinding, the cheers, the music blasting from someone's speaker. All of it faded into this suffocating silence as every set of eyes turned toward me. My chest tightened, my breath got stuck somewhere between my lungs and my throat, and for a second, I swore I forgot how to exist.

My eyes went to Troye, trying to telepathically convince him to deny it, to do anything else then... what he was already doing. He was leaning against the railing like this was all some big joke, giving this little wave of his fingers.

Rafe's eyes locked onto mine, and for a second, everything else disappeared and the world blurred at the edges. It was just me, standing in the wreckage of whatever *this* was, waiting for the impact.

"Kiko?" His voice wasn't loud, but it hit like a punch to the gut. There was something raw in it—confusion or maybe hurt? It was like he was trying to put together a puzzle that suddenly didn't make sense.

And then, all at once, the noise crashed back in. The murmurs, the whispers, the damn phone's pointed in my direction. My stomach twisted. My mouth opened, but nothing came out. I couldn't explain. I couldn't move. I was stuck.

That's when Rafe turned. Not to me—but to Brandon—and just like that, he stepped forward and swung. The crack of his knuckles against Brandon's face echoed like a firework.

There were gasps as Brandon stumbled back. A couple of people turned their phones towards him. Someone shouted, "Yo, chill!" but it was already done.

Rafe didn't even flinch. His face was stone.

Then he looked at me again. His face changed, like something inside him clicked into place. Whatever confusion was in his eyes before—it was gone now. It was just pain now, and—something else... Disgust? He shook his head and grabbed his board, walking toward me. For a second, I thought he was going to punch me too. Avery called his name, her voice edged with warning, but he didn't stop.

"I can't believe you," he said, not even pausing as he brushed past me.

And just like that, the ground beneath me caved in. The weight of every stare, every phone recording, every goddamn whisper pressed down on me all at once. I wanted to disappear, to rewind time, to be anywhere but here—but I wasn't. I was here. And there was no undoing this.

I looked over at Avery—not making eye contact—but enough to see her shaking her head as she ran after Rafe, calling for him to wait up.

For a second, my legs didn't feel like they belonged to me. My knees threatened to buckle, my stomach continued to twist itself into a knot I thought would never get undone. I scanned the crowd again, faces blurring together, all watching, all knowing. My friendships were burnt down in real time, and I couldn't do anything but stand there—and try not to vomit.

And then—I saw Mateo.

The realization hit that Mateo was still here. I had been so caught up in Rafe, in the whispers, in my own unraveling, that I hadn't even thought about him.

He wasn't filming, wasn't gawking like the others. He just stood there, staring at me, his face unreadable.

I swallowed hard, but my throat felt tight. "Mateo, I—"

He shook his head, cutting me off before I could even try to explain. No anger, no accusations. Just... quiet. He stepped forward, close enough that I could see his mouth curl up on one side with some unreadable expression.

"Come on," he said, voice low, steady. "Let's get out of here."

I grabbed my board, barely feeling the grip tape under my fingers. My legs moved on autopilot as I walked off the skatepark, my ears ringing, drowning out everything but the distant call of the judges moving on like my entire world hadn't just imploded.

Zay skated up beside me, his expression unreadable at first. Then he clapped me on the shoulder, solid, like an anchor in the chaos. "This changes nothing, my dude," he said, voice steady.

I barely nodded, still locked in that daze, but before I could process it, another skater—some dude I barely knew—called out, "Keep your head up, bro."

Then I heard his voice.

"Babe."

I froze.

Troye was suddenly right there, just off to the side like he'd been waiting for the perfect entrance. His sunglasses were pushed up into his curls, and his lips parted like he was about to say something. His pupils were way too blown out for broad daylight, and worst of all, he looked way too calm for the level of destruction he'd just helped unleash.

"I mean," he said with this little shrug, "the closet's open now. That was dramatic, huh? So why don't we just—start over? No more secrets. No more hiding. We were good together, Kiko."

My mouth went dry. Mateo turned, stepping slightly in front of me without even thinking about it.

Troye didn't even seem to notice. "You're finally being honest. So maybe now… you're ready to really love me back."

I couldn't even tell if he believed it. Maybe he did—and maybe that was the scariest part.

Mateo's voice was like steel. "Fuck off."

I couldn't remember him ever cursing.

Troye laughed dismissively, like the whole thing was adorable. "Relax, little man. I'm just saying—this is a big day for him. He's free now. He can finally stop pretending."

And for a second, I wanted to scream. Because this—this twisted version of the truth—was what he saw. Not heartbreak. Not betrayal. Just opportunity.

I stepped back. "Troye… or whatever you want to call yourself… leave me the fuck alone. Never speak to me again."

He tilted his head, eyes glassy and wide. "You don't mean that."

But I did. God, I really did.

Mateo didn't wait. He grabbed my arm. "Come on."

And this time, I let him lead me.

People in the crowd murmured, a few offering quiet reassurances, words that barely made it through the static in my brain. I could hear them, but I couldn't feel them. My body moved forward, following Mateo, but my mind stayed frozen back there, stuck in the total disaster.

I had tunnel vision, focused on the pavement that turned to sand, and Mateo's sneakers moving in front of me, step by step. Everything else blurred out. I just needed to get out.

I had no idea how long we'd been walking. The sound of the waves was just this constant roar in the background, but my brain was too scrambled to process anything except the way the sand felt under my shoes—too soft, too unsteady, like everything else in my life now.

When I finally looked up, we were near the water, somehow in a spot that wasn't packed with tourists or kids screaming over boogie boards. Just open sand and the ocean stretching out forever. Mateo didn't say anything, just sat down first, and I followed, dropping down beside him, my legs stretched out toward the tide.

I stared at the waves, watching them crash and pull back, over and over. The lump in my throat got tighter. My chest ached like I'd just sprinted for miles. I blinked fast, trying to keep it together, but it was useless. The tears just came. Silent at first, then not so much. My shoulders shook, and I tried to hold in this choked, pathetic sound, but it slipped out anyway.

Mateo stayed quiet. I had no idea what he was thinking. If he was judging me. If he was mad. If he thought I was weak.

Then, after what felt like forever, he reached out, put a hand on my shoulder, and said, "Fuck that guy."

That *broke* me. It just cracked through everything—all the weight, all the noise in my head. I don't think I ever heard him curse before.

That laugh that came out was a *whole* mess. It was all broken and weird, like my body couldn't decide if I was actually laughing or just fully falling apart. It was a mess of tears and snot and weird-ass fucking sounds. If I wasn't already a disaster, that laugh made it official.

He went on, "And if Rafe's gonna be mad at you for this, then he definitely wasn't really your friend to begin with."

I sniffed hard, rubbing at my face with the sleeve of my hoodie. "It's not just Rafe," I muttered—though that was a big part of it.

My voice was rough, like I'd been screaming all day. "It's everything. It's—" I gestured vaguely, like this was supposed to explain all of it. The skate comp. The stares. The fact that my entire life just cracked open in front of half of Venice Beach. "It's all of it, little bro."

Mateo sighed, picking up a handful of sand and letting it run through his fingers. "It was gonna happen eventually though, right?"

I turned to him, brows pulling together. "What's that supposed to mean?"

He shrugged. "The amount of time you were staying over Troye's?" He gave me a sideways look. "Or that Ma's been stressing about you... because she knows something's up but doesn't want to push you?"

Guilt twisted in my stomach.

Mateo shook his head. "I just don't get why you thought you had to go through it alone."

I stared at him, stunned. Because he was right. And that sucked.

"I guess... I didn't know how," I admitted. My voice barely made it over the crash of the waves.

Mateo exhaled through his nose, like he was holding back some kind of duh response, but he let it go. Instead, he just nudged my shoulder, all casual. "Well, now you don't have to."

And somehow, that hit harder than anything else.

I exhaled, long and slow, wiping at my face again. The adrenaline was wearing off, and the reality of everything was settling in.

I let my head drop back, staring up at the sky, like maybe the answer was somewhere up there. "What do you think Dad would've thought?" I asked, voice quieter than I meant it to be.

Mateo didn't even hesitate. "Dad would've been cool with it."

I blinked at him. "Yeah?"

Mateo shrugged like it was obvious. "Yeah."

Something about the certainty in his voice made me feel like maybe I hadn't even realized how much I needed to hear that.

I swallowed, glancing down at the sand. "What about Ma?"

That made Mateo pause. We both knew it was different. Dad was easy to picture, still cracking dumb jokes, still treating me the same. But Ma?

"She's super Catholic," Mateo admitted. "But she also loves us more than anything."

That was the problem. It could go either way.

"She'd probably freak out at first," Mateo continued, picking at the hem of his shorts. "Not because she'd stop loving you or anything—just because she'd be worried. Like she knows how people can be." He tilted his head, side-eyeing me. "But there's only one way to find out."

My stomach twisted.

Mateo must've noticed, because he nudged me again. "If you want to tell her, I can be there. So you don't have to do it alone."

I stared at the waves, trying to get my breathing steady, trying to wrap my head around it.

Yeah, definitely not yet.

Mateo nudged me, then pointed further up the beach. "C'mon, let's go up to the lifeguard tower."

I followed his gaze to the one painted in rainbow stripes.

"For the aesthetic?" I asked, forcing a smirk.

Mateo rolled his eyes. "For a selfie. My cool older brother deserves at least one solid pic after today."

I huffed out a laugh, shaking my head, but I stood up anyway. He hopped up beside me, brushing the sand off his legs.

We walked over, side by side, the air feeling lighter than before. Maybe not perfect. Maybe still tangled with all the shit I needed to deal with. But lighter.

I pulled out my phone when we reached the tower, trying to frame the two of us with the lifeguard tower. Mateo threw an arm around my shoulder.

"Alright, smile or whatever."

I took the picture, the rainbow-painted wood behind us, the beach stretching off towards the pier behind it.

And as I looked at the screen, at me standing there with my little brother in front of something so bold, so *out there*, I realized there was no hiding anymore. The two versions of me weren't separate anymore. They collided—in pretty spectacular fashion—and I had no idea what that was gonna look like when everything settled.

Everything felt raw, exposed. But it was real. And for once I wasn't pretending.

20

I stared out the window as Ricky's car wound through Silver Lake. The sights of the city passed by like they always did. There were people walking their dogs, couples pushing strollers, a dude on a racing bike flying past like he was the main character in an indie film. But everything felt distant, like I was watching it all through a screen. I couldn't shake this feeling, the numbness that had settled in since the skate comp last weekend.

At least Brandon's team got disqualified. Zay's crew and the other team made sure of that. They told the judges that if they didn't get kicked out, they weren't gonna compete. The judges agreed. One small victory on a day that had otherwise wrecked me.

And somehow, despite all the phones out, all the people watching, the videos never took off. I didn't go viral. I didn't show up on the trending list. There were just a handful of blurry clips with barely any views that I really had to search for. Maybe people had second thoughts after they watched it again, or maybe they all did rally around me after Zay took a stand—or maybe the universe was cutting me some slack for once.

But it still didn't change the fact that I didn't get to come out on my own terms—that that had been taken from me.

I could feel Ricky staring at me as he tapped his fingers on the steering wheel. "You good, man? You've barely said two words all day."

I shifted in my seat, debating whether to hit him with the default *yeah, I'm good* lie or actually be real about it.

I went with the easy answer. "Yeah, I'm good."

Ricky gave me a look, the *you're-so-full-of-shit* kind, but at least he didn't call me on it. He just nodded. That was definitely one of my favorite things about him. Ricky just knew when to talk and when to leave things alone. He just let me sit in whatever I was feeling without making it a whole thing unless I wanted to.

So I went back to my thoughts, which were now on Rafe and Avery. Or, I guess, the hole they left. I hadn't heard a word from either of them since the competition. Seven years of friendship, just... gone. Mateo had tried to reassure me, said if they weren't cool with me being gay, then they were never real friends to begin with. Maybe he was right. But knowing that didn't make it hurt any less.

We used to be inseparable. A trio that didn't break, didn't change. Or at least, that's what I thought we were. Yeah right. It turns out, all it took was one summer for all of that to fall apart.

Walking into Neil's house felt like stepping into an entirely different world. The place was straight out of one of those aesthetic Instagram accounts—sleek, modern, walls of glass that had a crazy view of the city. Definitely way out of my price range, or really, anyone's price range except people who somehow always knew the right people. It was the kind of house that didn't just cost money but felt expensive, like you had to be born into a certain tax bracket just to exist comfortably inside. I looked out at the view from the living room window.

"In the winter you can actually see the Hollywood sign and the Griffith Observatory beyond those trees," Neil said, putting an arm around my shoulder in a half hug that left his other hand free to balance his martini. It was a way more friendly gesture than Neil usually showed. "Welcome, gentlemen. Make yourselves at home. There's food out back and drinks in the kitchen."

I looked at Ricky and he just shrugged.

"Non-alcoholic for you, Mr. Enrique," Neil called back from the next group he was talking to.

"Damn," I whispered to Ricky as we made our way to the kitchen that opened up to the backyard, the large sliding doors all the way open.

The party was already in full swing. Music bumped from hidden speakers, drinks flowed, people were deep in their conversations. And sure enough, Ricky had already become the center of attention—like he always did. People just gravitated to him the second we walked into the kitchen. They were trading inside jokes and talking about work drama like it was one of Ma's telenovelas. He just had that effortlessly cool way about him, like he was just suave without even trying. Meanwhile, I was standing there with no idea what to do with my hands.

I grabbed a Dr. Pepper off the drink table, cracked it open, and poured it into a red plastic cup—just to do something. I was still feeling too drained to even fake the whole social thing. I was here, sure, but I wasn't here. Everything with Rafe and Avery, with Troye, with... everything, was still sitting heavy in my chest.

I leaned against the counter and watched the party around me. It felt more like I was just floating on the edges of it than being actually part of it. I used to be much better at blending in and being easygoing. But right now? Nah, I just felt like an intruder in my own life.

My phone chose that moment to save me from my little pity party with a chime.

Sat Aug 31 at 4:27 PM

Dylan

 Hey! Long time no talk. Hope all is well

Yeah. Sorry I've been kinda MIA recently. A lot going on.

We should talk soon

Delivered

Before I could go on, a guy walked up to me—tall, chiseled jawline, crow's feet with these piercing blue eyes. He was the kind of older guy who just radiated money but in an unbothered way. His graying hair made him look even more put together, like he had this whole distinguished thing going for him.

"Hi there, I'm Mark," he said, offering his hand. "Neil's partner."

Nice catch, Neil.

I shook his hand, nodding. "Nice to meet you. I'm Kiko."

"Have you been out back yet? You have to try the ribs," he added. "Just came out of the smoker. And don't miss Neil's famous potato salad."

I laughed. "Alright, you sold me."

The backyard was just as nice as the house—not huge, but that's standard for the neighborhood. There were these string lights that crisscrossed overhead, and the grill smelled awesome. People were gathered in different corners of the yard, some from the shop and others I didn't know.

I piled my plate high—ribs, a hot dog, some grilled veggies to make myself feel like I was being healthy, and, of course, Neil's famous potato salad. The second I took a bite, I got why it had a reputation. Creamy, just the right amount of tang, and whatever seasoning Neil used made it hit way harder than any store-bought stuff.

As I made my way over to where Ricky was posted up, I caught bits of conversation. One table was arguing about the best burger spot in LA, while another was debating whether it was okay to bring outside coffee into a coffee shop—obviously a serious moral dilemma for baristas. A couple of people from work nodded in acknowledgment, making small talk about the party, how good the food was, or how nice Neil's house was. The general vibe was chill, easy, the kind of work event that didn't feel like a work event.

I finally found a seat. Ricky was holding court with a group, drink in hand, as he told some dramatic story about a customer losing their mind over a botched oat milk latte—not one that he made of course. The group laughed, but Ricky's eyes flicked over to me for a second—just a quick check-in. He didn't say anything, but I could tell he was still clocking whatever energy I was giving off.

I had to say, though, it was nice, just being around people who weren't making things complicated, who didn't have these expectations of me other than just being here and eating some good food.

As it got later, the energy started to shift. The music got quieter—no doubt from Neil turning it lower. The big bursts of laughter were happening less often, and people were starting to check the time, especially the morning crew, obviously thinking about their early shift the next morning.

The party had thinned out, just a few stragglers left lounging around, finishing drinks, and laughing in low, tired voices. Me and Ricky were posted up at this little table off to the side, just vibing, when Mark walked over. Ricky had said Mark was some movie executive at one of the studios. He had that whole salt-and-pepper, well-groomed, probably-wears-tailored-suits-on-a-Tuesday vibe. He had a cigar in one hand and a wooden box in the other.

He pulled up a chair, exhaling a slow stream of smoke before popping open the box. "You boys smoke?"

Ricky didn't hesitate, reaching for one right away. "Don't mind if I do."

I grabbed one too, but turned it over in my fingers, trying to act like I knew what I was doing. "Uh… never actually had one before."

Mark smirked. "Well, you're about to be spoiled. These aren't just any cigars—these are Davidoff box-pressed Nicaraguans."

Ricky lit his up smoothly, letting out a slow, practiced puff. "First rule, it's not a cigarette. Don't inhale. Just take a draw, hold it, let it chill, and let it out."

I nodded, like I totally got it and brought the cigar to my lips. Ricky flicked the torch lighter, the flame caught the end, and I took my first pull—except instinct betrayed me, and I inhaled deep.

Instant regret.

The smoke hit my lungs like a freight train, and I doubled over, coughing like I'd swallowed fire.

Mark and Ricky immediately lost it. Mark shook his head, amused, while Ricky smacked my back between wheezes. "I said don't inhale!" He laughed, "It's okay, dude, everyone does that the first time."

Mark took a slow drag, looking unbothered. "Rite of passage."

I wiped my watering eyes, still coughing. "Sick. Love this for me."

Neil stepped out of the house, pausing when he spotted us with cigars in hand. He sighed dramatically, shaking his head as he walked over.

"Mark, are you corrupting my employees with your terrible habits?" he teased, though he didn't look all that mad about it.

Mark just grinned, exhaling smoke. "They're grown men, dear. Let them live a little."

Neil rolled his eyes but didn't argue. Instead, he pulled out a chair and dropped into it with the weight of someone who had officially given up on hosting for the night. His tie was loose, his blazer long abandoned, and he had the slightly glassy look of someone a few drinks deep.

He glanced over his shoulder at the house, then waved a dismissive hand. "You know what? I was gonna start cleaning up, but I've decided I just don't care. That's tomorrow Neil's problem."

Neil took another slow sip of whatever was left in his glass, then looked over at me. "So what's been going on, Enrique?"

I shrugged, exhaling a little smoke just to prove to myself that I could do it without coughing this time. "Nothing much."

Neil gave me a knowing look, one eyebrow raised like he wasn't buying it.

"Darling can you bring out the Eagle Rare," he said to Mark. "We may be here a while."

Mark leaned over and gave him a kiss before disappearing into the house.

"Well, I'm glad you came tonight," he said, turning back to me. "I noticed you've been a little distant this week."

I hesitated. Usually, I would've just brushed it off, said I was just preoccupied or whatever. But something about sitting there with Ricky who always had my back, and Neil and Mark being, like, everything I wanted for myself—it made me feel like I could actually talk about it. Like I wanted to.

So I did. I told him everything. About Troye and the breakup. About the competition, Brandon, and the whole thing blowing up in my face. The words spilled out before I could second-guess myself.

"So this Troye guy," Neil said to Ricky, "this is half-caff dirty chai latte guy?"

Ricky nodded and for the first time I saw him pissed off.

"Well he needs to find another coffee shop," Neil said.

Neil let out a long breath, shaking his head. "Damn, kid. I'm really sorry you had to go through that." He swirled the drink in his glass like he was thinking of what to say next. "Getting outed like that... having your first real relationship blow up in your face—it's a lot. And it's not fair."

I just stared at the glowing tip of the cigar, watching these tiny wisps of smoke swirl up. I knew it wasn't fair, but hearing it said out loud just hit different.

Neil sat forward, resting his elbows on the table as Mark returned with the bottle of bourbon. "I know people love to say it gets better like it's some magic spell, but the truth is... it does. Just not all at once."

I nodded, but I didn't really feel it. Not yet.

Neil sighed. "And yeah, coming out now is different than when I was your age. Way better in a lot of ways. But that doesn't mean it's easy. People act like just because things have changed, it's supposed to be simple. Like you're supposed to just say 'Hey, I'm gay' and suddenly life's perfect."

He shook his head. "Doesn't work like that. It's still complicated. It's still messy. And you still gotta figure out where you fit in it all."

I swallowed hard. That part hit. Because that was exactly it—I didn't know where I fit. Not with Rafe and Avery. Not with Troye. Not even with Dylan and Indie, not really.

Neil watched me for a second, then leaned back again. "But you're figuring it out. And you're not alone in it."

"What was it like for you?" I said, quickly following it up with, "If you don't mind me asking."

Neil took a deep breath. His eyes got this distant look, like he was staring at something way off in the distance. The ice clinked as he spun it around the glass.

"It was a long time ago," he finally said. "1979—and don't even think about trying to calculate my age. I grew up in Georgia. My family was... real religious, like fire-and-brimstone types. I knew from pretty early on they'd never accept me." He let out a soft chuckle, but there was no humor in it. "They weren't too happy when I said I wanted to be a fashion designer when I grew up. So, I did what a lot of us did back then—I left."

I sat up a little, listening closer.

"Didn't even have enough to get all the way to LA like I wanted. I only made it as far as New Orleans." He shook his head, smiling to himself. "That's where I met Blake."

There was something in his eyes when he said his name. Happiness? But there was something else there. Sadness maybe?

"And Blake... well, this little blue-eyed, long haired bayou boy convinced me to at least try. To go back. To give them a chance to understand."

I already knew how this story was gonna end, but I still had hope for him, even now.

Neil sighed. "Needless to say it didn't go well. They wanted to send me to some camp to 'fix this.' There was a lot of this 'no son of mine' talk. When I refused to go away to the camp, they told me I wasn't welcome home anymore."

I felt something heavy settle in my stomach.

"So, I left again," he said simply. "And they stuck to their word." He took another sip, then glanced at me. "That was the last time I ever saw them."

"Wow..." I said. "How did you, like, make it on your own?"

Neil reached over and took a pull of Mark's cigar. He exhaled a slow stream of smoke, watching it curl in the night air. "Now you're all corrupting me." He laughed.

"You see the truth is, I wasn't alone," he said, shaking his head. "Sure I had lost my family, but I had my chosen family. Blake—for a time— and all the friends I made along the way. We looked out for each other, even when we didn't have much to give."

I stared at the flickering candle on the table. *Chosen* family. Those words kinda stuck with me.

I thought about Dylan, Indie, and Ethan, and how easily they'd brought me in, no questions asked. How Dylan showed up when I needed someone, even when I didn't realize I did. Were they *my* chosen family?

Was Ricky? The dude who always knew when to push me to open up and when to back off and leave me alone. And Neil, sitting across from me now, giving me this whole story like it was a map he probably wished he'd had.

I was starting to think that maybe I wasn't as alone as I thought.

"I didn't achieve all my dreams. I wanted to be a fashion designer. I had all these big plans. But life…" He trailed off, shaking his head.

I didn't say anything, just let him speak.

"A lot of my chosen family didn't make it," he said, voice quieter now. "The '80s were brutal—AIDS, drugs… it felt like every time you turned around, someone else was gone. Even Blake." His fingers tightened around the glass of bourbon in front of him, as Mark put a hand on his back. "I barely made it myself."

I swallowed, unsure what to say. There was nothing *to* say, really.

Then he looked over at Mark, and just like that, the weight in his voice softened. Mark reached over, laced his fingers with Neil's, and they just sat there for a moment, not saying anything.

"But it gets better," Neil finally said, his gaze still locked on Mark's. "It really does. You just have to keep pushing."

Mark squeezed Neil's hand, then clapped him on the back. "Alright, enough of this sad shit. You made it, and look at you now. Fancy house, handsome husband who is corrupting the future of our America with cigars."

Neil laughed, shaking his head. "Yeah, yeah. I'm a real cautionary tale." He turned back to me. "But really, kiddo, I'm glad you told me. And I know it's hard now, but trust me—it won't always be."

Ricky exhaled a slow stream of smoke. "Kiko's already got people in his corner," he said. "Just gotta let 'em in."

I nodded, not trusting myself to say much. Ricky wasn't wrong. I thought about Dylan, Indie, Ethan. Even Mateo. They weren't going anywhere, even if Rafe and Avery were.

Neil leaned back in his chair, swirling the drink in his hand before turning to me. "Do you know *why* I hired you, Enrique?"

"Uh… no?" I shrugged. "Honestly, I thought I bombed that interview."

Neil let out a chuckle, shaking his head. "You did."

I sat up straighter. "Wait, what? So… I actually did bomb?"

"Oh, absolutely," Neil said, nodding. "As soon as I met you, I knew your resume was a total fabrication—and then there was the customer service boiling down to 'smiling at people and stuff.' That was perhaps my favorite part."

I groaned, rubbing my face. "I knew that sounded dumb as soon as I said it."

Neil waved a hand. "Look, it wasn't a great interview, but I hired you anyway."

I hesitated. "…Why?"

Neil stared out at the backyard for a moment before looking back at me. "You reminded me of myself when I was your age—a little lost, trying to figure things out, but still pushing forward. I saw something in you. So, I took a chance."

I sat with that for a second. I had been sure I got the job out of pure luck, that Neil had just been desperate for staff or something. But knowing that he'd *chosen* me, even when I'd totally botched my interview, hit different.

"Well I'm glad you did," I said.

"Me too," Neil said.

"Me three," Ricky jumped in giving me a fist bump.

Mark stretched, letting out a satisfied sigh. "Well, this has been a surprisingly deep end to the night, but I gotta say, it was great having you both here." He smirked at me. "And hey, first heartbreak, first cigar… pretty big milestones, kid."

I huffed a laugh, shaking my head. "Yeah, what a flex."

Neil gave me a knowing look. "You're gonna be alright."

I wanted to believe him. As Ricky and I stood up, saying our goodbyes, I glanced around Neil's house—his life. He had been through worse than I could even imagine, and he still built something for himself. Found love. Found family.

If he could make it through *that*, then I could face what I had to.

21

My phone chimed, yanking me out of a deep sleep. I looked over and saw that even Mateo was still knocked out, which meant it was *disrespectfully* early. I groaned, rolling over, fully prepared to ignore it. Probably just some random notification or a scam text telling me my tolls weren't paid. But then it chimed again.

I sighed, rubbing my eyes as I rolled back over to grab my phone off the nightstand. The screen was aggressively bright. I blinked a few times before the name on the screen actually registered.

Wave Whisperer—it was Avery.

I sat up so fast my blanket slid off me. My heart was already going wild, my fingers hovering over the screen like opening the message was some kind of irreversible decision.

I hadn't heard from her or Rafe since *that* day. Now, out of nowhere—

I exhaled sharply and tapped the screen.

Wave Whisperer 🏄   2m ago
I don't even know where to begin. I'm so so sorry

Wave Whisperer 🏄   Just Now
Can we meet for brunch? Just us, if you're open to it.

My stomach twisted. I didn't know what I expected, but seeing sorry in there just made everything feel heavier. Like she actually got how bad it was. Or at least, was trying to.

For a second, I thought about just locking my phone and rolling back over. Sleeping through it. Pretending like I never saw it.

But I couldn't ignore her forever.

I chewed the inside of my cheek as I stared at the keyboard. *Where?* I typed, then deleted it. *When?* Deleted that too.

Finally, I just went with: *Yeah. When and where?*

I hit send before I could change my mind.

Wave Whisperer 🏄   Just Now
Ashland Hill? 11AM?

Of course. One of her go-to spots. Felt like in all the times we grabbed food, if she was picking the place, half the time it was there. I stared at the message for a second, then just typed back: Cool. See you then.

No emojis. No extra words. Just… enough.

I put my phone back on the nightstand and rolled over, staring at the ceiling. My brain was still too wired, thoughts spinning too fast, but eventually, I was able to drift back to sleep.

As I rolled up Main Street toward the restaurant, I spotted Avery before she saw me.

It was stupid hot—like ninety seven degrees and not even a breeze. I really just wanted to be at home in the AC, but here I was.

Avery was standing just outside the entrance, shifting her weight like she couldn't decide if she wanted to be there or not. Her hands fidgeted at her sides, pulling at the hem of her shirt, messing with the strap of her backpack.

For a second, I just stood there, holding the straps of my new backpack as I watched her. It was weird seeing her like this. Like, this was *Avery*. The same Avery I used to skate with for hours, who would roast me and Rafe like it was her full-time job. Now she looked like she was standing in front of a firing squad in her pink Powell Peralta skeleton t-shirt.

Once she saw me, she just hesitated, like she hadn't been sure I'd actually show up. Then, slowly, she gave me a small half-smile and a wave—like this hesitant, careful kind of wave. She looked like she was half-expecting me to turn around and skate away.

But I didn't. I hopped off, kicked my board up into my hands. I walked the rest of the way all slow, stalling since I was still not really sure how to play this.

Avery gave me a quiet "hey," her voice softer than usual, like she didn't know how to play this either.

And for a second, we just stood there, both of us not sure what to do. Were we supposed to go with a handshake? A nod? A hug? It was stupid—this was Avery—but it felt like we were strangers figuring out how to act around each other for the first time.

She made the call for me and stepped in to wrap her arms around me. It wasn't the usual quick, casual hug we used to do. She held on a second longer, like she wasn't sure if she'd get another chance.

She pulled back, pushing a loose strand of hair out of her eyes and tucking it behind her ear. "It's really good to see you," she said, voice heavy with something real. "And... thanks. For giving me a chance."

I just nodded, not really sure what to say.

We walked through to the back patio. The string lights, the wooden tables, and, most importantly, the shade—it was all the same. And yet, it wasn't.

The server handed us menus, but we barely looked. We'd been here enough times to have our orders locked in. "I'm gonna do the Breakfast Burrito, please," she said, barely waiting before setting the menu aside.

I smirked, "Ashland Hill Burger with bacon."

"And we're getting the pretzel?" she added, more like a question than an order.

I still wasn't sure if I wanted to commit to an appetizer too, as I still didn't know where this was going, but I just shrugged.

Avery nodded at the server and let out a small nervous laugh. "Just like old times."

Yeah. Just like old times. Except for the part where things still felt... off. Like we were playing pretend, stepping back into an old routine without knowing if it still fit.

Avery reached for her water, like she needed a second before diving in. Then she looked up at me, eyes kinda soft but heavy. "I'm sorry. For everything. What happened at the skatepark... that was just awful. And I hate that you had to go through that—" she paused, "—alone."

That word hit hard. I blinked, and before I even fully thought it through, I snapped back, "I wasn't alone. Mateo was there—he *always* is."

Her shoulders flinched like I'd slapped her. She nodded slowly, lips pressed together, and looked down at the table. "Yeah," she said quietly. "I guess I deserved that."

I just stared at her. Didn't say anything, didn't blink, just let the silence sit there between us. She fidgeted with the corner of her napkin, then looked back at me.

"You have every right to be mad," she said, voice low. "I just... I had to make a choice in that moment. Between you and Rafe—"

I cut her off, not even trying to hide the bite in my voice. "And you chose him?" I scoffed. "I mean... I guess that tracks. Whole summer's been the two of you anyway. If y'all wanted to kick me to the curb, you should've just said it straight up."

Avery's face froze like I'd just hit pause on her whole system. She blinked a couple times, opened her mouth, then closed it again. The silence hit different this time—louder somehow.

"Neither of us ever wanted to 'kick you to the curb,'" she finally said, voice barely above a whisper.

I leaned back in my chair, arms crossed. "Then why's it felt like that all summer?"

She shook her head. "We've been trying, Kiko. You've just been... I don't know, kinda distant. Hard to reach."

My jaw tightened. "Because the vibes are totally off around you guys. You're really still gonna sit there and pretend there's *not* something going on between you two?"

That shut her up. Just... silence. No excuse. No denial. Just the truth sitting there between us, quiet but loud as hell.

Avery looked away for a second, then back at me, like she was finally deciding to just say it.

"Okay... yeah," she said quietly. "Me and Rafe are together. We have been for a while."

I blinked at her. "Then *why* have you both been acting like it was just in my head?"

She sighed. "Because it wasn't serious at first. Or at least, we didn't think it was. And then it just... happened. Things got real. And we didn't know how to tell you. We didn't wanna hurt you, Keeks."

I stared at the table. My fingers clenched around my napkin like it was the only thing grounding me. "I wish you would've just been straight up with me," I muttered.

Avery tossed her arms up, eyebrows shooting up. "Straight up with you?" she repeated. "Kiko, really? Like you've been completely open with us?"

The server showed up right on cue, like the universe was trying to kill the vibe even more. He set the giant pretzel down in the middle of the table, all golden brown and perfectly salted, with little containers of mustards and pimento cheese on the side. Normally I'd be hyped. That thing was my go-to. But my appetite had straight-up left the chat.

Avery gave a tight smile and thanked the server. We just stared at the pretzel, hanging from this metal thing. She didn't touch it either.

"I know coming out isn't easy," she said quietly, her voice barely cutting through the patio noise. "I'm not trying to act like it is. I just... I wish you'd felt comfortable enough to tell us sooner."

I looked at her like she'd just smacked me. "Why?" I said, my throat dry. "So I could find out that Rafe is a homophobic asshole?"

Avery's face dropped. "Is *that* what you think?" she asked, her voice almost cracking.

I didn't back down. "What else am I supposed to think?" I said, anger boiling up. "I got outed in front of the entire skatepark and Rafe looked at me with straight up disgust, and then he hit me with the whole 'I can't believe you' and stormed off."

Avery shook her head, eyes wide. She reached across the table and grabbed my hand. "Oh my God, Kiko. That's not how it was at all. Rafe was *hurt*. He didn't even make it to the boardwalk before he broke down crying."

I was trying to process. "Hurt?" I repeated, like the word didn't make sense.

"Yes. Hurt. He thought the two of you shared everything. Like, *literally* everything. I mean, you guys used to finish each other's sentences. And then... there's this whole part of you, something huge, and he didn't even know." She looked back up at me, soft but firm. "It wasn't that you're gay. He doesn't care about that. Neither of us do. We just want you to be happy."

I sat back a little, the words still landing.

"He's just... not great at saying how he feels," she added. "And that day? He was caught *way* off guard. He didn't handle it well, I'll admit that. But that look you saw? That wasn't disgust, Kiko. That was heartbreak."

I didn't know what to say at first. My throat felt tight, like I couldn't even swallow if I wanted to. We both just kind of stared at the pretzel, not really eating, just... sitting in silence.

Then Avery broke it. "How did we even get here?" she said quietly. "We were a trio. You, me, Rafe. And now it's like... all this space and secrets between us."

I let out a breath and kinda smiled. Not because it was funny—just that type of smile when someone says exactly what you've been thinking. "Yeah," I said. "I feel that too."

She looked up at me, eyes glassy. "I love you, Kiko. We both do. We never stopped. And I want to find a way back from this. I don't wanna leave for college with things like this between us."

I nodded slowly. The words were hitting, even if I wasn't sure what to do with them yet. But they meant something. They mattered. And for the first time in a minute, I felt like there was hope for us after all.

The server dropped the rest of the food on the table, giving a polite smile before disappearing again. The plates barely fit, all crowded together—burger, burrito, fries spilling over the edge, and the whole-ass pretzel, sitting in the middle like a third wheel.

Avery laughed. "We've got, like, enough food for four people."

I had to laugh too as I shook my head. "There's no way I'm finishing all this." Still, I reached for the pretzel, tore off a chunk, and took a bite.

She leaned over and snatched one of my fries—just like it was before all this. "So..." she said, chewing. "Your first boyfriend. I know it obviously ended like a total dumpster fire, but... do you wanna talk about it?"

I paused for a second, staring at the "AH" brand burned into the top bun of my burger.

I picked at the pretzel, not really looking at Avery but not avoiding her either. "It was... a lot," I said, kinda laughing under my breath. "At first, it was exciting, you know? Like—someone *actually* liked me. And he was hot, and confident, and said all the right things, and I guess I got caught up in it."

Avery nodded, letting me go on without jumping in, which I appreciated.

"I guess I just liked having someone," I continued. "Like, having a person who saw me that way. It felt good. But Troye—he was intense. He was always going a hundred miles an hour. I thought that was just part of his vibe, but then it started to get messy. Shoplifting, weird-ass stories that didn't add up, pills. Shit just kept escalating."

I finally looked at her. "I put up with a lot. More than I should've, I guess. I kept telling myself it was worth it because he chose *me*. But then one day I'm running from security because he stole a perfume. That was my breaking point."

She didn't say anything right away, just nodded slow. Like she was really listening. It felt kind of wild to talk about it like this—like it wasn't just all stuck inside my head.

Avery's voice softened when she spoke, like she was trying to get something through to me that I wasn't picking up on. "You know, the way you're talking, it sounds like you think *you* were the lucky one to land Troye. But honestly? It was the other way around."

I felt my chest tighten a bit, like I didn't deserve that kind of praise, but she kept going.

"You don't deserve all that mess you went through with him. You deserve someone who sees you, all of you. Not... whatever that was."

I shook my head, picking at the food. "Dylan said the same thing the other day," I muttered, staring at my plate. "But it doesn't feel like that."

Avery perked up instantly. Like, full sparkle-in-her-eyes mode. "Wait —*Dylan*? Dylan Wright? You've been hanging out with *Dylan*?"

I nodded, chewing on my bottom lip.

She grinned. "That's awesome. He's such a sweet guy. Like, actually solid." She paused, pointing her next stolen fry at me. "That's the kind of guy you should be with."

I let out a short laugh, more out of disbelief than anything. "Yeah, okay. There's no way someone like Dylan would be into me."

Avery raised an eyebrow like I'd just said the dumbest thing ever. "Kiko, be serious. You're smart, funny, emotionally available—when you're not spiraling at least—and you've got great hair. Don't sell yourself short."

I shrugged, looking down at my plate. "I don't know. Dylan's just... chill. Like, he's got this vibe like he actually has his shit together. I'm still out here trying to figure out who I even am."

"Well," she said, stealing another one of my fries, "sometimes people seem like that but inside aren't much different than where you're at."

I kinda scoffed. The whole idea seemed crazy to me.

"You're a *catch*, Kiko," she said bluntly.

I looked down, quiet for a sec. "I guess... it doesn't feel like I'm a catch when everything I've been through just feels like... I've been used," I said.

"Kiko," she said, eyes locked on mine, "you gotta stop acting like you're just some background character in everyone else's story."

I let out this weird half-laugh, half-sigh, like I didn't know what to do with that.

"I'm serious," she said. "You've been through it, for real, but that doesn't make you broken. You care hard, you show up for people, even when you're hurting. That's not something everyone does."

"I just feel like I keep getting picked last, y'know? Or probably more like not at all." I said. "It's not just relationships. Rafe's going off to college, I mean *you're* going to freakin' Stanford. And I'm working the afternoon shift in a coffee shop."

She shook her head. "Keeks, people just don't know what they're sleeping on. And yeah, maybe you're figuring stuff out, but that doesn't make you any less awesome."

I blinked a few times, trying not to tear up and get all emotional in this brunch spot.

"One day, someone's gonna look at you and just get it. No games, no BS. They'll just… see you. And you won't have to chase that feeling. It'll just be there."

I didn't know what to say, so I just nodded.

"I still think you should shoot your shot with Dylan. I'm just sayin'," she added.

I just shook my head.

We did our best to finish the food and boxed up the rest—half a burger and a sad-looking piece of pretzel in mine, and the remains of her breakfast burrito in hers. Avery flagged down the server and insisted on paying even though I half-heartedly tried to reach for my wallet. She hit me with the *I got this* glare and that was that.

Out on the sidewalk, the sun was way too bright for how emotionally drained I felt. I stuffed the leftovers in my backpack.

Avery fished her keys out of her bag. "I have my dad's car," she said, dangling them. "I can give you a lift."

I shook my head. "Nah, I think I'm gonna hit the boardwalk, clear my head. Maybe see if I can, like… show my face at the skatepark again."

Her smile faltered a little, but she didn't push. "Okay. Just—give Rafe a chance, alright? He misses you. Like, bad."

I looked down at my shoes, then back at her. "I'll think about it."

We stood there for a beat before she opened her arms. "C'mere."

We hugged—tight, like we used to—and for a second it felt like the summer hadn't wrecked everything. She smelled like that fruity shampoo she always used. Familiar. Safe.

"Text me," she said as we pulled apart.

"Yeah," I nodded. "I will."

Then she headed for her dad's car, and I turned toward the beach.

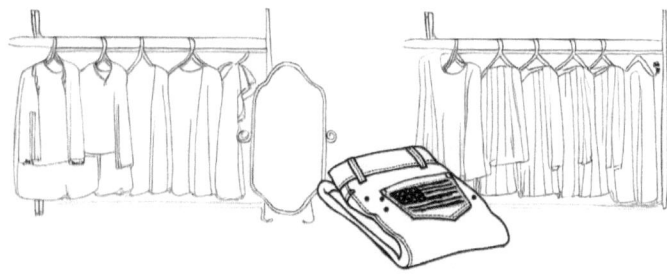

22

I looked at the jeans in the mirror. They were definitely doing something. Tight in a way I wasn't used to, but not in a bad way. I turned to check the back again, still unsure about the flashy zippers and the flag patch stitched loud and proud on the back pocket. Very "look at me," which wasn't exactly my vibe. But also… maybe could be?

"They're sick," Dylan said, lounging against one of the clothing racks with a half-empty Topo Chico in hand. "Like, annoyingly good on you."

"Yeah," Indie added, twirling a hanger around her finger. "Hot-boy thrift mode activated."

I snorted. "Okay, relax."

But I couldn't lie—hearing that made me feel kinda fire. I twisted to the side again, checking how they sat. They were way too long, like definitely-pooling-around-my-ankles long, but that could be fixed. For $39.99, they were low-key a steal. Ethan had explained that Robin's Jeans weren't cheap, and this pair still had most of the edge stitching intact.

I stepped out of the mirror space and struck a dumb little pose. "Alright, so hemmed or rolled?"

"Rolled until you find a tailor," Indie said, already digging through a rack of jackets. "But for real, you're buying those."

Dylan nodded. "Non-negotiable."

I laughed. "Is this how you make all your sales?"

"It is when something looks that good on someone," Dylan said.

I ducked back into the dressing room to change. The jeans weren't just a good fit—they felt like proof. Like I could be someone who wore weird flag-pocket jeans and actually make it work. Someone who showed up and didn't shrink back.

Maybe I was finally getting there.

I stepped out of the dressing room, back in my regular shorts, jeans folded over my arm. I gave Dylan and Indie a look like "yup, I'm doing it." They both smiled and gave this quiet nod of approval.

At the register, Ethan was already checking out. I noticed chipped nail polish on one hand, black but mostly gone, as they stacked a mix of treasures they found—a sheer button-up, a faded band tee, some high-waisted jeans, and what might've been a skirt or just really flowy pants. Hard to tell, but very them.

Indie came up from behind with this old school Miami Dolphins Starter jacket that looked like it was ripped out of someone's garage in the '90s.

"Doesn't it suck for you, Kiko, that only half the store's for you when the whole store is for me and Ethan," Indie joked.

"Ethan and I," Dylan corrected. He wasn't buying anything. Working there probably means he can pick the things he wants before they hit the racks.

Once we were done, we stepped outside. Melrose was buzzing with people everywhere, walking, skating, taking selfies in front of murals. I stopped to take some shots of sticker-covered poles and gates. The street was loud and alive, but it didn't feel overwhelming. It just felt like a great day.

Next stop was the Doc Martens store, all industrial and sleek with that smell of new leather hitting the second we stepped in. Ethan's eyes lit up like we just walked into a candy shop. They made a beeline for the display with all the different colors. Indie followed right after, holding up this shiny pair of cherry red platforms.

"Tell me these aren't *so* me," Indie said, striking a little pose with one boot under her chin.

"They're aggressively you," Ethan deadpanned.

Dylan and I hung back near the entrance, letting them do their thing. Dylan leaned over and whispered, "Ten bucks says neither of them buys anything."

I smirked. "Not taking that bet."

Next we wandered into Brooklyn Projects, and instantly I felt more in my element. Like, this was my kinda spot—decks lined up on the walls, sneakers, streetwear. The place smelled like grip tape and fresh rubber, and there was this bench by the window made entirely out of snapped skateboard decks. Pure art.

I drifted over to the sneakers, already knowing I was gonna fall in love with something I couldn't afford. Sure enough, they had the Nike SB Dunk Lows in the Escargot colorway—bright green, tan, and metallic vibes with just enough weirdness to be sick. I picked one up, turning it in my hands, imagining it on my board. Not practical right now, but damn if I didn't want 'em.

Dylan came up beside me, nodding at the Dunks. "You should get 'em," he said, casual but with that little smile he does when he's low-key hyping you up. "I could totally see you rocking those."

I hesitated for a sec, doing the mental math. Honestly? I'd been saving pretty good from the coffee shop, and I hadn't treated myself in a minute. After everything this summer threw at me, maybe I deserved to feel like I had something nice. Something fresh. Something mine.

"Yeah," I said, more to myself than him. "Screw it." I turned to the sales associate. "Do you have these in an eleven?"

I went up a half-size so they wouldn't be too snug.

Meanwhile, Indie and Ethan were completely absorbed by the little koi pond near the other window. Ethan was crouched down, taking a video, and Indie was trying to name them based on vibes.

"This one's definitely named Casper. He looks like he's got trauma."

As we left, Dylan said, "Donuts?"

Indie clapped once, loud. "Say less. I'm driving."

I kinda shrugged, confused. "Uh, donuts?"

That earned me a full dramatic spin from Indie. "Okay, first of all—what? Second of all—if you're asking that you've never had *these* donuts."

Dylan leaned in like it was serious. "You haven't *lived* until you've been to SK's."

A few minutes later, we were packed into Indie's tiny car, music blasting, with all the windows down. It was like five minutes tops before we pulled into this random corner shopping center—nothing fancy. Just a nail spot, a hair salon, some print shop... and then there it was: SK's Donuts. A little crowd gathered out front, and that smell in the air? Yeah, okay. I was starting to get it.

Inside, the place was lowkey a vibe—white tile walls, cases glowing like a jewelry store but filled with donuts instead of diamonds. And I'm not talking like your basic glazed and chocolate sprinkle situation. These were extra. There were donuts with cereal on top, donuts stuffed with like three layers of filling, even some that looked like tiny works of art. And yeah, a whole case of vegan options for Ethan, which they went straight for.

Dylan wasted no time ordering a Reese's Chunk—had to be his go-to. Indie chose the Pumpkin Spice. Ethan ordered a Vegan Oreo Blast that looked insane, and I ended up going with the Red Velvet. It just looked kinda fire sitting there with the cream cheese frosting and little crumbled bits on top. It was calling my name.

We got Thai iced teas and headed back out, sitting on the cinderblock wall next to Indie's car, kicking our feet like middle schoolers after school. Everything slowed down for a sec. Just good donuts, good drinks, and people who actually gave a shit about me. Honestly? Kinda perfect.

Dylan nudged my elbow and nodded at my donut. "Red velvet's solid, but there's no way it tops this one."

I raised an eyebrow at him. "Oh yeah?"

He held out his donut, like, right in front of my face. "Try it."

I laughed, leaning in and taking a bite. It was warm and rich and stupid good, and I chewed slowly, savoring it. Dylan was watching me the whole time, this soft little grin tugging at his lips like he already knew he was right.

"Okay," I said, swallowing. "That's criminally good."

He leaned back, smug. "Told you."

I couldn't help but smile back at him, and for a second it felt like we were in our own little pocket of the world. The buzz of traffic and the crunch of donut bags and Indie telling Ethan not to feed pigeons just blurred into background noise.

I looked at Dylan again, and something flickered in my chest. Avery's voice echoed in my head—he's the kind of guy you should be with. And I don't know, maybe she wasn't just trying to play matchmaker. Maybe she saw something I didn't.

The problem was, I've always been trash at figuring out when someone likes me back. Like, actually likes me. And right then, staring at him with chocolate on the corner of his mouth, I couldn't tell if this was just a sweet moment between friends… or something more starting to click into place.

Ethan scrolled through their phone and suddenly gasped. "Oh, Universal Studios," they said, turning the screen around to show us the ad, "We should go again soon."

Indie's eyes lit up like she'd just been dared to do something unhinged. "Why not right now?"

Everyone sorta laughed, like haha sure, wild idea. But Indie stayed dead serious.

"No, I'm not joking," she said, already standing up. "What are any of you even doing today?"

We all looked at each other and shrugged.

"I've actually never been," I said, feeling kinda sheepish.

Dylan gasped like I just admitted I'd never seen sunlight. "Well, then we *have* to go."

"Say less," Indie said, grabbing all our empty donut bags, tossing them in the trash. She pointed toward her car. "C'mon, nerds. Adventure awaits."

And just like that, we all piled into her car. No plans, no prep, just sugar highs, good vibes, and the kind of spontaneous decision you remember way longer than anything you planned.

We stepped through the gates at Universal and it was like instant sensory overload—music blasting, kids screaming, the smell of buttered popcorn and churros swirling around like some chaotic theme park perfume. I kinda just stood there for a second, soaking it in. I'd seen the front gates in movies, on Instagram, whatever—but standing there? Actually being here? It was just totally different.

"So… where to first?" I asked, turning to the crew.

Indie didn't hesitate. "Minions ride. Of course."

Ethan raised their hand like it was a group vote. "I really want to do Secret Life of Pets. Last time the wait was too long."

Dylan jumped in, "So those are right next to each other. We hit those two, then head down to the lower lot for Jurassic World—*the* best ride here—and the Studio Tour at some point of course."

I was already sweating a little, but in a good way. Like the kind of sweat you don't mind 'cause you know the day's gonna be fire. I looked around at my friends, all hyped up like little kids, and realized—this was *exactly* what I needed. Just a random day with people who actually wanted me around. No drama. No judgment. Just dumb rides, overpriced slushies, and a vibe that felt like freedom.

A little while later, we were standing in line for the Minions ride. It said fifteen minutes on the sign, which honestly felt like nothing after what I'd heard about theme park lines. Indie was way overexcited answering the questions on the quiz that was playing on the overhead TVs and repeating lines from the movie in her best Gru impression while Dylan filmed it for his story.

He swung the camera around to me and I instinctively ducked down a little. "And here we have our boy Kiko… about to ride his very first theme park ride. How's it feel, King?"

I gave a shy little laugh. "It's not my first. I did the rollercoaster at the pier."

I barely got the words out before Indie and Dylan pounced.

"That doesn't count!" they said at the same time.

Even Ethan quietly said, "It really doesn't."

I rolled my eyes but I was smiling too. Getting clowned by your friends like this was… kinda nice. It felt easy, like they accepted me. I could just exist. Even if they were roasting me. Which, let's be honest, was kinda love in its own way.

The ride itself? Total chaos. Like, I came out blinking like I'd been hit with a cartoon frying pan. My body didn't know whether it loved or hated the motion simulator. We stumbled out, all of us laughing like idiots.

"I love those little guys," Indie said, putting her sunglasses back on. "But now we need something for wholesome little Ethan." She ruffled their hair. "Let's go meet some animated pets."

The line for Secret Life of Pets didn't even feel long at all as it snaked through different apartments from the movie. Ethan was pointing out the mail slots that you can peek through to see screens playing videos. Indie's favorite part was the animatronic dachshund getting massaged by a blender. Me? I was just taking it all in with a crew that had taken me in. The actual ride was pretty cool too.

Once we got off the ride, I was one hundred percent ready to adopt some animated dogs—no offense Bandit. We were all starving, so we hit up the Despicable Delights stand.

I grabbed some popcorn—just a cup, not the forty dollar collectible car bucket despite Indie begging me to. Ethan and Dylan split some churros. And Indie? Of course she handed over her card and snagged the twenty dollar collectible Minion cup with some radioactive-looking blue slushy inside.

"Worth every penny," she said.

Dylan just shook his head. "You're so unserious."

She winked. "And yet? I slay."

And I just… smiled.

We were heading toward the Simpsons area when I paused outside the entrance to the Harry Potter section. The music was playing, the street looked straight out of the movie with the school in the background, and the whole thing just looked… magical.

"Whoa," I said, stopping in my tracks.

Indie glanced over her shoulder. "Yeah, it's cool, but we don't go there."

Dylan chimed in. "We can walk through if you wanna see it, since you've never been, but we don't buy anything from there. I love the books and movies, but J. K. Rowling still gets a cut, and she's been super anti-trans. So, yeah."

"Oh," I said, blinking. "I didn't know that."

"No stress," Dylan said, giving me a quick smile like it was no big deal.

I felt kinda dumb, like I should've known or paid attention to these type of things more, but none of them made it weird. No one lectured me or made a face. We just... moved on. And that made me feel kinda safe in a way.

Even if we weren't buying anything, it was still cool to walk through. There were kids—and adults—running around with wands and scarves of the different houses. It was like being *in* the movie.

We cut up some back path and stopped just outside a sign for the Studio Tour. Dylan was on his phone, thumbs moving fast. He showed me the app that said the wait for Jurassic World was sixty minutes. *Yikes.*

"Yeah, but this is why they made virtual queues," he said, not even looking up from his phone. "I'm gonna put us in for later."

He glanced up. "Studio Tour's only like a ten-minute wait. We can do that in the meantime."

And just like that, we were moving again and I fell into step next to him.

The tram smelled like sunscreen and metal. Indie made a dramatic little gasp when we reached our car. "We're splitting up," she said, pointing like she worked there. "You two sit in this row and Kiko you *have* to have the outside seat. It's your first time."

Before I could protest or even process what that meant, she was nudging me forward like a mom sending her kid to their first day of school.

So I climbed in. The seats were vinyl and warm. Not hot-hot, but definitely preheated by other bodies. I scooted across to the end, the side that opened up to the right side, and sat down.

Out of habit, I threw my arm across the back of the seat. Not like a suave move or anything—just instinct. Muscle memory from benches and couches.

Then Dylan sat down next to me.

And suddenly my arm was there—just hovering behind him. Not so much touching, but like… not *not* touching either.

My whole body tensed. My shoulder locked up. I stared straight ahead like maybe if I didn't move, it would be less awkward.

I thought about pulling my arm back, just dropping it in my lap like a normal person, but somehow that felt more conspicuous. Maybe even unfriendly? Like *he* didn't seem to have a problem with it. Friends do this, don't they?

So I left it. Frozen in place. Casual, but not—which I guess was my version of casual. I probably looked like a mannequin having an existential crisis.

Indie slid into the row behind us, leaned close to the railing, and flopped into the seat like she'd probably done this a million times. "I'm sitting on the right too," she announced. "It's where all the best action is."

Ethan followed her in without saying anything. I glanced over my shoulder at them and they just gave me a quick side-smile like they knew something I didn't.

The tram lurched forward. My shoulder twitched. I pretended not to notice how… intimate this felt.

I felt Indie's hand on my shoulder, my right one—the one not currently caught in this awkward, maybe-borderline-flirty, maybe-totally-neutral arm position around Dylan.

She gave my shoulder a squeeze in this firm, weirdly grounding sorta way. Just a second, maybe less. And then she pulled her hand back and started chatting with Ethan about something she saw on TikTok.

But I kept thinking about it. About *why* she'd done it.

Was that her way of saying *go for it*? Like a psychic shove toward the boy sitting next to me? Or was it just a "hey, glad you're here" kind of thing? A friend thing? Or was it an Indie-being-Indie thing, and not really having an explanation.

But then, of course, Avery popped into my head again—pointing a fry at me and saying, "He's such a sweet guy. That's the kind of guy you should be with."

I didn't know what to say then, and I still didn't.

Then out of nowhere there was Troye's voice, that day in the alley after we ran from security. "No one else is gonna put up with you like I did, you know that, right?"

That cut deeper than I liked to admit, because yeah I was kind of a mess. Would anyone have the patience to deal with me dealing with myself? No way Dylan would—would he?

I hated that I was spiraling. I hated that I could never figure these things out. That I was reading into every tiny moment like some kind of desperate teen rom-com protagonist with a crush and no chill. Which, yeah, maybe I was.

No. I definitely was. There was no way Dylan was into me like that.

But now I was sitting here, stiff as a corpse, arm stretched behind Dylan like we were on some type of date, and my heart was doing the absolute most. But Indie's handprint still kind of sat on my shoulder.

Was it a hint? Signal? Some type of comfort? No idea, but I took a deep breath and tried to relax.

"Selfie time," Dylan said holding his phone out catching all four of us in the frame.

The tram rolled along the winding road toward the lower lot, past posters of old movies—*Woody Woodpecker, Frankenstein,* stuff I'd only seen in clips. Then there were the real sound stages they used to make actual movies and TV shows like *Family Feud* with Steve Harvey—that apparently doesn't only exist in YouTube clips. The guide kept cracking jokes, the kind that made people laugh more because of how hard she committed than because they were actually funny, and the whole thing started to feel like this strange in-between space—part museum, part backstage pass—and part weird dream I hadn't woken up from.

We rolled into the backlot and passed that little town square from *Back to the Future,* the clock tower still standing like time had stopped right there in 1985. A few turns later and we were in what looked like New York City—brick buildings, fire escapes, fake steam rising from a fake manhole cover. Then we hit a tunnel, and the tram slowed as a voice came over the speakers, telling us to put on our 3D glasses.

I fumbled with mine, trying to slide them on one-handed so I didn't have to move my arm. It wasn't graceful. I almost stabbed myself in the eye, but I got them on. When I glanced sideways, Dylan was pulling his own pair into place—and somehow, in the shuffle, he felt closer. Like just an inch closer, but enough that I felt it—enough that my breath caught a little. I turned away and pretended to adjust my glasses again so I didn't have to deal with whatever that feeling was.

Suddenly we were in a jungle—like, full-on vines and fog and 3D raptors lunging out of the darkness, way too close for comfort. They started fighting a T-Rex, and then freaking King Kong came crashing in like it was his movie now. It was total chaos, the tram shaking like we were actually about to tip over. The movement causing Dylan to bounce into me.

And then, just as fast as it started, we were out of the tunnel and cruising through streets that looked like London, passing giant monster murals, and into another building.

Inside it looked like a subway station—graffiti on the walls, flickering lights. I was convinced there were probably rats lurking somewhere. All of a sudden there were flashing lights, a siren, the whole ceiling to the left dropped with a bus sliding down. A train came into the station and went off the track. Not super convincing but fun anyway.

But then a massive wave of water came rushing down the stairwell on my side. Like real-ass water—and a lot of it. I flinched hard as the cold spray hit. For as much water as there was, it wasn't a lot that actually hit me. Even still, I instinctively leaned away from it—straight into Dylan.

This time it was not just a brush or a bump—I was fully pressed against him, his shoulder to my chest, his thigh to my thigh, like my entire body forgot what personal space was. For half a second I froze there, skin buzzing, heart doing this panicked little stutter. Then I pulled back fast, pretending like I wasn't mildly short-circuiting inside. I didn't dare look at him because I didn't want to know what his face was doing.

From behind us, Indie called out, "That's why I sit on the right."

The tram rolled into this sleepy little fake town—white picket fences, boathouses, docks—and the guide announced it as Amity Island, home of Jaws. There was a pond off to the side with a shark fin slicing through it like it had somewhere to be. A second later, a fake diver went under, and the water turned red like they'd poured a bucket of food coloring in it. Super fake, super dramatic, but also kinda sick.

"Here comes Bruce!" Indie called behind me, like she was talking about an old friend.

"Bruce?" I asked.

"Bruce," Dylan confirmed. Then he leaned in, real close, holding his phone up to get a video just as this giant animatronic shark exploded out of the water.

It came up right next to our tram car—so close I could've reached out and touched it except for the whole keep arms and legs in the tram rule —and the whole Dylan's face inches from mine thing.

I tried to focus on the tour guide after that. Her voice was steady and goofy in a way that helped me latch onto it, like a lifeline. I started doing that breathing thing my old guidance counselor taught me: four in, hold for four, four out. Over and over, just trying to calm the noise in my head, the echo of Dylan's voice close to my ear, the lingering warmth where our sides had been pressed together.

We rolled through an old western town next, right as a flash flood crashed through the street, water splashing high enough to make people gasp. Then came a full-on plane crash set, with all this flaming debris like we'd landed in some post-apocalyptic fever dream.

Another small town followed, too perfect to be real, then the tram eased into another dark tunnel—this one blasting music and car engines for another 3D scene of a *Fast and the Furious* scene that felt like a video game on steroids. I kept breathing. In. Hold. Out. Just trying to be there. Just trying to stay in my own body.

When the tram finally pulled back into the loading area and the lap bars released with a little click, I felt this weird wave of relief wash over me—like I'd just survived something way more intense than a theme park ride. Not because of the earthquakes or the sharks or the very-aggressive Vin Diesel hologram, but just… all of it. The closeness. The almosts. The what-does-this-even-mean of it all.

Dylan checked his phone as we stepped off the tram like nothing happened. "We've got twenty minutes to get to Jurassic World," he said, squinting at the screen. "And we still have to make it down all those escalators."

I nodded, a little too eager to have something to do. Something that involved moving. Moving felt safe. Thinking… less so.

We borderline ran through The Simpsons section. It was straight-up trippy. Like, the show was just… there. All around us. From the fake brick buildings to that giant statue holding up a donut. I never really watched The Simpsons heavy or anything—just episodes here and there —but it was still like running through the actual cartoon.

We made our way to the massive escalators that take you down to the lower lot. The first one dropped us off at this overlook where you could see all of Universal City laid out below—studio rooftops, soundstages, and the hills in the distance. I paused for a sec and took a couple shots with my phone. The light was hitting just right, and the view was too good to pass up.

There were like three more escalators to go. It felt endless, but kinda epic too. Every level we dropped, it got louder—screams from Jurassic World, rumbling tracks, the whoosh of rides in motion. Like the energy down there was just building up.

Somehow we ended up in the front row. Indie said something low-key and charming to one of the ride attendants, and the next thing I knew, she was ushering us right to the front like we were VIPs.

"This is the only way I do this ride," Indie said as she slid into the far seat, Ethan following, leaving the middle seat wide open. I hesitated for a second before climbing in. Dylan gave one of those "after you" gestures. I don't know why it felt weird—it was just a seat. Just molded plastic. But still, it felt like a choice. Like I was taking a spot in something I wasn't sure I was ready for.

Dylan sat down next to me, his knee bumping mine for half a second before he shifted slightly. Some rando lady in a Universal shirt and a bright pink fanny pack, the kind of person who looked like she had planned this vacation six months in advance and laminated her itinerary finished the row. She gave me a polite smile. I nodded back, but all I could think about was how close Dylan's arm was again as the lap bar came down.

The ride was honestly sick. Right off the bat, we went through this tunnel where these giant screens showed that massive water dinosaur leaping out of the water to eat a shark like it was a snack. The timing was perfect too, because right as its jaws closed, we got sprayed in the face.

"Poor Bruce," Ethan said quietly.

We all laughed. They didn't talk often, but when they did it was absolute gold.

Outside, the boat drifted along this winding path surrounded by animatronic dinosaurs on both sides—long-necked ones munching on trees, raptors peeking out from behind rocks like they were definitely up to something. Everything looked real enough to make you second-guess reality for a second. Then we hit this indoor section, and it went pitch black. Like *can't-see-your-hand* dark.

I sat there, holding my breath for no reason, when I felt Indie's elbow nudge mine. Just shifting in her seat or whatever. Right?

Before I even knew what was happening, we were tipping forward—slow at first, then suddenly not—and the boat dropped, fast and hard, slamming down into the water outside with this massive splash that soaked us all over again. Then we were gliding smooth around the last bend, heading back into the station.

We climbed out of the boat, all of us laughing and talking over each other about how awesome it was. My heart was still racing, but in a good way this time. I could totally see why it was Dylan's favorite ride.

As we walked down the ramp, still dripping and kind of dazed, we passed the photo station. We all slowed down without even saying anything, like some unspoken rule demanded we check how ridiculous we looked.

The photo popped up on the screen and there we were, sitting across the front row—Ethan with their hands over their eyes, Indie full chaos mode with her arms thrown up in the air, and me right in the middle, gripping the front edge of the boat like I was bracing for impact, hair wild, and somehow looking more genuinely happy than I could ever remember feeling. It was total main character energy. And then there was Dylan—just off to the side, not looking at the camera, not even reacting to the drop—his head turned, eyes on me, with the biggest smile on his face—like I was the best part of the ride.

I scanned the QR code and had to go through the whole thing— downloading the app, making an account, attaching my debit card—but there was no way I was leaving without that picture. That photo— Dylan looking at me like that—it did something. He didn't act any different afterward, still his usual calm, slightly unreadable self, but it shifted something in *me*. Gave me this quiet, shaky kind of confidence. Like maybe there was a chance. Maybe I *wasn't* making it all up in my head.

As we walked, I glanced over at him and saw that same smile again —but this time, it wasn't at me. It was at that leather-bound journal of his, as he scribbled something down, his head tilted just slightly like whatever he was writing actually made him happy.

And I didn't know what it was—or if it even had anything to do with me. But I *wanted* it to. *God*, I wanted it to.

23

I was skating down Westminster, the kind of morning where everything felt a little too bright, too clear. It wasn't the fastest way to the beach. I knew that, but I took it anyway. Probably to stall, like I had been all week. Waiting until the very last day possible. Or maybe because I wanted to see *them*.

The murals.

I slowed down right in front of them, letting the board glide to a lazy stop. The astronauts were still there, chilling like always—surfboard, frisbee, beach vibes in full effect. I could hear Rafe in my head pointing at them and saying, "That's us right there." All proud, like we'd somehow been immortalized as cartoon space bros on some random wall in Venice.

And yeah, it made me laugh at the time. The way we could just be around each other. Messy and loud and stupid, but still good. Still *us*.

Now I stood there, staring up at it, and all I could think was how completely wrecked everything felt. Like the whole friendship had short-circuited and no one knew how to reboot it. I didn't even know if we *could* go back. But I missed it. I missed *him*.

I took a deep breath and kicked off again toward the beach. I was meeting Rafe and Avery at the skatepark—one last time before they left for college. Today. They were leaving *today*.

All summer, things had felt so off. Like we were three separate satellites drifting farther and farther from each other's orbit. Rafe and Avery had been caught up in their secret thing, which wasn't so secret anymore but still felt weird and fragile and half-addressed. And then there was me—feeling like an extra in my own friend group. Watching them pull closer while I got pushed out.

And after the whole thing at the skate comp—after that—I don't know. Something cracked. And it felt like something permanent. But after the talk with Avery, I felt like there might be a way back.

And maybe there was, but I couldn't stop thinking about how much *time* we'd wasted. How we'd had this one last summer—this final summer before they go off to college, and do college things, and make college friends… and we'd spent most of it pretending like everything was fine, like we weren't already slipping away from each other. And now here we were. Out of time.

I cut across the boardwalk, weaving through tourists, joggers, and around this tiny dog in even tinier sunglasses, then dropped down onto the Strand.

The skatepark came into view, and that's when I saw her—Avery. She was looking out in the opposite direction, hair pulled back, eyes scanning the crowd like she was looking for someone. For me, probably, expecting me to be coming from that direction.

But there was no sign of Rafe.

He didn't come.

I stood there, scanning the park one more time like maybe I missed him somehow. But no. Just Avery walking toward me, and a bunch of early skaters already dropping in. No Rafe.

That feeling crept in slow—like my stomach sinking. I kept trying to tell myself he might still show, might come flying down the path last second like he always did. But it didn't feel like one of those times.

And the more I stood there, the more it started to settle in—this might be it. This might be what it's like from now on. Me showing up. Him not. That space where he used to be—where he *should've* been—just staying empty.

If he didn't want to fix it now, if he couldn't even try when everything was about to change, maybe he wasn't going to. Maybe that hole was permanent.

Avery's face was already sad as she walked up—like she knew what I was thinking before I even said it. She pulled me into a hug, tight and warm in that Avery way that always made it harder to pretend I wasn't feeling stuff.

"Thanks for coming," she said, and for a second I thought that's it. That we were just gonna sit here and pretend Rafe never existed.

Then she added, "He's out by the Breakwater."

Relief hit me like a wave—fast and dizzying—but it didn't last long. Because now I knew he *was* here, and that meant I had to talk to him.

No more dodging, no more letting the silence do the work. And I'd already started to convince myself I wouldn't have to. That maybe this was the clean break.

Avery stepped back and gave me this look—soft, but serious. "I'll give you guys some time," she said. "Please just… let him explain. You *know* he's not always good with words. Just—give him a chance."

I nodded, even though my stomach was twisting. Because I wanted to. I did. I just wasn't sure where this would end up.

I walked out onto the sand, heading toward the Breakwater. I'd crossed this beach a hundred times—me, Rafe, and Avery lugging surfboards, arguing over who was gonna eat it first out on the waves. I used to walk it with my dad too, back when I was little and still thought he'd always be around. Sometimes I was alone, like I was today.

But today the beach didn't feel familiar. It felt stretched out, like one of those old movies with some character crossing a desert.

I spotted him sitting there, letting sand slip out of his hand to get carried by the breeze. He didn't turn around when I got closer. Didn't even move. Just sat there, all still and quiet, like I wasn't even there.

I stopped a few steps behind him, not sure if I should say something or wait.

"Remember when the beaches opened back up after lockdown?" he said, still not looking at me. "That morning we went out super early? First time we saw each other in person after, like, almost two months of just FaceTiming and those glitchy-ass Skype calls."

"Yeah," I said, and my throat felt tight as I sat down next to him.

We fell back into that silence again. Like that memory was supposed to lead to something, but neither of us knew where. Both of us were trying to say something, but the words were just… not there.

Rafe picked at the edge of his boardshorts, fingers twitchy, still staring out at the waves. When he finally spoke, his voice was low, way quieter than usual. "I just… I don't get why you didn't tell me."

I swallowed, hard.

"You're my best friend," he said, and that cracked something a little, because he wasn't saying it like a fact. He was saying it like a question. Like he wasn't sure it was still true. "You think I would've freaked out or something? Like, I *wouldn't* have—" He cut himself off, shook his head. "I could've been there. I *would've* been there. But you… like… didn't trust me."

That last part hit. I didn't know if it was fair, but I couldn't say it wasn't true, either.

"It wasn't about trust," I said, even though maybe it kinda was. "I just… wasn't ready. I didn't even really know what to say. And then after the comp, it was just—too late."

Rafe still didn't look at me, but his jaw clenched. "You think it felt any better finding out with everyone else?" His voice cracked a little on everyone. "You could've told me. You *should've*. I mean—we tell each other *everything*."

"Do we?" I said before I could stop myself. And then it was out there.

He flinched, barely, and finally turned his head just enough that I could see the side of his face.

"You didn't tell me about you and Avery," I said, quieter now. "So I don't know, man. It's not like it's just me."

He ran a hand through his hair, frustrated. "That wasn't—shit, that wasn't even supposed to be a thing. It just happened, and then we didn't know how to say it. It's not like we were trying to hide it from you."

"Still felt like it," I said. "You two had each other. And that's awesome. Like I really am happy for you. But I was just… there. Watching."

Neither of us talked after that. It still felt like there was stuff we didn't know how to say, like instead of us sitting on the same beach right next to each other we were both sitting on our own little islands, wanting to swim across but not sure how deep the water was.

Rafe hunched forward, elbows on his knees. "I'm not good at this," he muttered. "I don't know how to say shit the right way. I just—when I think about all the stuff you were dealing with, and you didn't tell me… that sucks, Kiko. It really fucking sucks."

I nodded, eyes on the horizon. "Yeah. I know."

And that was the closest either of us got to an apology.

We stood up around the same time, brushing sand off our legs. Something had shifted between us. Not fixed—not totally—but at least it was something.

When I turned to face him, Rafe finally looked at me. And I noticed his eyes were wet. He wasn't full-on crying, but it seemed like he was close.

"We gotta do better," he said, his voice rough.

"Yeah," I said. "We do."

And then we hugged. Tight. Not one of those quick guy-pats we'd always do, but a real one—the kind that says I still care, even if we suck at showing it.

"I love you, dude," Rafe said into my shoulder, quiet like he wasn't sure if I'd hear it.

"I love you too," I said back. No hesitation.

Then we pulled apart and started walking, side by side, heading back up toward the skatepark. Rafe wiped at his eyes with the back of his wrist, and I pretended not to notice.

When we got back to the skatepark, Avery was sitting on one of the railings, picking at her nails like she was trying to stay busy. She looked up when she saw us. Her eyes were moving quickly between me and Rafe, like she was looking for some type of sign as to how it went. But then Rafe threw an arm around my shoulder, easy and familiar, like nothing had ever been broken—and I swear I saw her let out this huge breath. She gave this little smile. Not a big one, but enough to say okay... *maybe we're still us.*

As Rafe passed her to pick up his board, she mouthed a quick "thank you" at me.

I just nodded and gave her a quick smile.

"So today's the day," I said, even though we all knew it.

Rafe nodded, putting an arm around Avery now. "Yep. By this time tomorrow, we'll be at Stanford."

Avery leaned in and kissed him quick. It still felt a little weird to see them like that—like my brain hadn't totally adjusted to the new layout of things. They were a *them* now. Not just Rafe and Avery, but Rafe-*and*-Avery.

"I'm excited to stop in San Luis Obispo tonight," she said, her voice soft but a little brighter. "There's this river walk that keeps popping up in my Reels I've been wanting to check out."

Rafe glanced over at her, smiling, then back at me. "I'm driving the coast after. Taking my time to get back to Santa Barbara. My classes don't start 'til next week. Gotta check out some spots up north."

He said it like it was no big deal, but it sounded like a whole other life waiting just around the corner.

"So you're bringing your board?" I asked, already kinda knowing but still needing to hear it.

Rafe snorted. "You know it! I don't even know if it's gonna fit in the dorm, but whatever. I'll sleep next to it if I have to. No way I'm missing those northwest swells up there."

Classic Rafe. Priorities in check.

I looked at the two of them and before I could stop myself, I said, "One last run?"

Rafe rolled his eyes, but he was already smiling. "Bro, don't be all dramatic. I'm only gonna be, like, two hours away. I'll be home every other weekend."

"Still," I said, shrugging, trying to play it off even though my chest felt tight. "Avery won't."

Avery gave this little nod, already stepping toward her board like that was all she needed.

So we dropped in—me, Rafe, and Avery—carving around the park like it was second nature. For a few minutes, everything else faded. It was just us, skating like nothing had changed. Like we weren't saying goodbye at all.

We skated a few more laps, not saying much, just moving, letting it be simple for a little longer. Then Avery coasted to a stop near the edge of the park, toe of her shoe dragging on the concrete.

"Alright," she said, brushing her hair from her face, "we should grab food before we hit the road and I can't leave without getting a Spicy Pepperoni square from Prime."

"Good call," Rafe said. "C'mon Kiko. It's on me."

We headed to the FJ Cruiser, parked a couple blocks away and Rafe unlocked it with a beep. The back seat was a disaster—bags, boxes, a laundry basket with random stuff jammed inside. College move-in chaos.

"Sorry," Rafe said, popping the door open. "You get the VIP seat, right next to the shower caddy and my emotional support hoodie collection."

They both started shifting stuff around to make room, and I climbed in. Avery handed me a plant that she swore she could keep alive in her dorm. It was super cramped and kinda ridiculous, but weirdly comforting too, literally surrounded by them.

The pizzeria was about twenty minutes away on Santa Monica Boulevard, the kind of chill drive where the windows were down and nobody really talked, just music playing low and wind whipping through the car. When we got there, the smell hit before we even stepped inside—cheese, garlic, pepperoni grease, all of it just right.

The Spicy Pepperoni square slice hit exactly how it always did. Crispy edges, sauce with a kick, cheese melted just enough to stretch when you pulled it apart. It wasn't fancy or anything, but it was ours. A ritual. One of those comfort things that never changed no matter how many times we did it.

Rafe bought a t-shirt from behind the counter, one with this skeleton eating a slice with a palm tree in the back. "Gotta rep the hometown," he said, holding it up with this half-smile, like he was trying to make light of it but kinda meant it too.

When we finished eating, none of us rushed to leave. We just stood around the parking lot half in the sun, half in the shade—like maybe if we stayed there long enough, the goodbye part wouldn't come. Like we could slow time down if we just stayed still.

Avery stuck out her bottom lip like she was trying to keep it together, but her eyes were already glassing over. One blink and the tears were coming. Rafe wasn't far behind—he had that misty look again, trying to blink it away.

I kept my eyes on the pavement, pretending to study a crack in the asphalt, but I felt it—this one tear slipping out before I could stop it. Just one.

Avery pulled me into a hug without saying anything, and I hugged her back. I had my face buried in her hair, just trying not to fall apart.

"I'm gonna miss you," she said.

"I'm gonna miss you too."

Then Rafe swooped in, arms wide, kinda goofy but also not— wrapping us both up in a lopsided group hug like he couldn't help himself.

We all laughed through it, even with tears on our cheeks, and for a second it felt like it used to. Like nothing had changed. But now they were leaving. And this—this was the part where we let go.

I watched them climb into the FJ Cruiser, doors slamming, engine kicking on like it was no big deal. Avery waved from the passenger seat, and Rafe gave me this dumb little salute through the window as they pulled out onto Santa Monica. The whole thing felt weirdly dramatic— me just standing there, waving like I was in the last scene of some coming-of-age movie.

And then—brakes squealed.

Rafe slammed to a stop in the middle of the road and some car behind them swerved and laid on the horn. I just blinked, confused, like *what the hell is he doing now.*

Then the FJ pulled a full U-turn, straight up whipping it back toward the parking lot like they forgot something huge.

But it was me who forgot something huge. Avery was already leaning out the window, holding up my skateboard.

"You were about to send your board to college!" she shouted, laughing.

I groaned and jogged over. "Yikes!"

But yeah. I had absolutely almost done that.

We waved again and then they pulled back out onto Santa Monica, windows down, music faint but still bumping. This time, there were no sudden stops or U-turns. This time they didn't turn back.

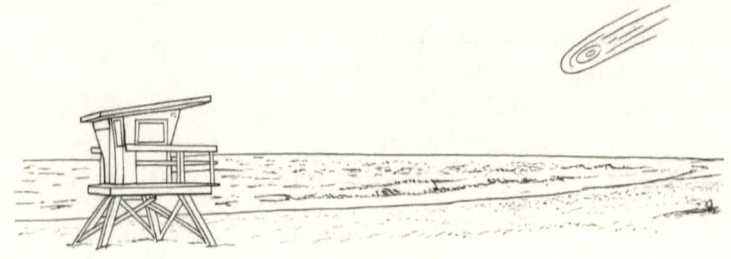

24

I walked out onto the beach from the boardwalk, still in my work shirt and everything, skateboard in one hand, and my backpack slung over my other shoulder. I was way too excited to be here. The sun was setting with the sky giving these awesome shades of orange and yellow, and the breeze was doing that perfect-not-too-cold thing.

It was three weeks since Rafe and Avery left for college, and I'd been keeping myself stupid busy—working extra shifts, skating pretty much every other chance I could get, and even helping Ma organize random boxes she swore she was "finally going to deal with." Basically anything to keep from overthinking… well, everything.

Indie had gone from soft matchmaking mode to full chaos agent. Like, straight up dropping "accidental" hints about Dylan every time we hung out, sending me memes and songs. She was *not* subtle.

Now when Dylan texted earlier "you coming tonight?" with that little smiley face—I swear I smiled like a loser for a full five minutes.

I spotted them before they spotted me. They had two large blankets laid out on the sand near the Pride Flag Lifeguard Tower, one with Indie stretched out next to Ethan sitting cross-legged, the other with Dylan sitting cross-legged next to a very obvious, very empty space. Like… painfully obvious. Like "reserved seating for someone with a crush" level obvious.

Ethan was strumming their guitar, something soft and pretty. Indie looked up first, because of course she did. It was like she'd been tracking me from the moment I stepped onto the beach.

"Kiko! You made it!" she called, already waving, with this mischievous grin on her face.

"Yeah," I said, making my way over. "The bus was taking forever, and I got stuck at work."

Dylan looked up at me and smiled, all chill and casual but somehow still... more than that. "You ready to see this comet?"

I smiled back and dropped my bag on the sand. "Yeah. My brother said the last time this comet came around was, like, caveman times."

"Wild," Dylan said, as he patted the empty space on the blanket.

I kicked off my shoes and sat down, but my brain immediately turned it into a whole event. Like, how close was *too* close? How far was *too* far? I didn't want to be weird about it, but I also didn't want to act like I was scared to sit next to him. Because I wasn't. Not *scared* scared. Just... okay yeah, maybe a little.

I sat down, trying to make it look natural, like I wasn't calculating the exact number of inches between his knee and mine. I left a little space. Not a huge space. Enough to be like, "hey, I respect boundaries," but also "hey, I am available to be emotionally wrecked by you at any time."

Yeah, I was spiraling.

He glanced over once I settled, not saying anything about the gap, just gave me a small smile.

"You've been working a lot lately," he said, in that calm, Dylan-sorta way.

"Yeah," I nodded, still hyper-aware of the space between us, and debating if I should shift closer or farther. "Couple people left for school so I picked up extra shifts. It's been kinda non-stop."

I didn't add that part of me liked the excuse, or that staying busy was easier than dealing with all the weird quiet moments in between. Like this one.

I turned toward Ethan, the soft strumming of the guitar pulling me out of my overthinking spiral. The chords were kinda dreamy, and just... did something in the back of my brain.

"That sounds familiar," I said. "What is it?"

Ethan looked up with this quiet little smile like they were happy I noticed but didn't want to make a big deal about it. "'Stargazing' by Myles Smith," they said. "But it's the acoustic version. I learned it just for tonight. Seemed... appropriate."

"That's our little Ace of Hearts," Indie said with a proud smile. "Always showing up to surprise us with their romantic bangers. Where have you been hiding this talent your whole life?"

Ethan laughed under their breath and kept playing. I know they acted like the compliments were nothing, but I could tell they were proud. And yeah, the song fit... a little too well.

Indie sat back on the blanket, phone in hand. "So when's this thing supposed to show up?" she asked, already Googling it.

Ethan didn't even look up, still playing soft chords on their guitar. "About forty-five minutes after sunset," they said. "So... about a half hour?"

I nodded like I knew that and I was sure Mateo mentioned it at some point. He was probably getting a sick view of it from Griffith Park with Hudson and his family.

Indie made a face at her phone. "Okay, there is no way I'm even trying to pronounce this."

She spun her phone around.

"What even *is* that?" she said. "Looks like someone fell asleep on their keyboard."

I had to admit, the name was ridiculous. It really just looked like letters smashed together. Mateo would totally know how to say it. Pretty sure he also told me how to say it weeks ago. If I'd just paid more attention, I could've really impressed everyone right then.

"Let's just call it Gay-ley's Comet," she said, as we all laughed.

We lost track of time after that, with everything slowing down in the best way. The sky kept darkening and we just... chilled. Talking about nothing, the way you do when you're trying not to think too hard. The way you do when everything feels kinda perfect.

Ethan had switched songs, and I didn't catch the new one at first, but then I heard the melody—"Sailor Song" by Gigi Perez. They started humming along under their breath, soft and low. It wasn't like a performance or anything, but more like they were just humming the song for themself.

Indie started giving Dylan crap about the time they all did that escape room for her birthday and he bailed halfway through. "You sat on the floor next to the fake bookshelf and said, 'I'm just gonna emotionally tap out.'"

Dylan shrugged, totally unbothered. "I was claustrophobic and there were too many keys."

Indie laughed. "You didn't even *try* the first puzzle. You just looked around and said, 'Nope.'"

"I stand by it," he said. "That room had weird energy."

It was such a Dylan move—opting out in the most polite way possible. But honestly? That was one of the things I liked about him. He didn't pretend to be chill with stuff just to go along. He just... was who he was.

246

We went back and forth like that for a while. Twenty minutes, maybe more. Long enough that the sky turned fully indigo and you could start to make out the stars. Not the comet yet, but still—something about it felt like waiting for some type of sign.

Indie sat up suddenly, looking at the sky like she was about to announce breaking news. "Comet should be here any minute," she said, brushing sand off her shorts. "I'm gonna head down to the water, see if I can get a good pic down there."

Then she gave Ethan a look, all fake chill. "Why don't you come with. I need help with the settings."

Ethan gave her a look like *seriously*? but stood up anyway, slinging their guitar over their shoulder. "Yeah, okay," they said, clearly in on whatever plan Indie thought she was being subtle about—as subtle as a sledgehammer.

And just like that, they were gone, leaving me and Dylan sitting there in this weird... vacuum. Not uncomfortable, exactly, but definitely something.

Neither of us said anything. I stared at the sky. He fiddled with a loose thread on the blanket. It was like the whole night hit pause.

My brain kicked into overdrive. Should I say something? Should I wait for him to say something? Was it already awkward or was I just making it awkward?

God, I had to do something—*anything*—or I was gonna self-destruct right there on the beach.

But we just kinda sat there.

It wasn't awkward exactly, but it was definitely a silence that I was way too aware of. I could hear Ethan's guitar down by the water, and the waves rolling in, and my heartbeat doing the absolute most for no reason. I kept thinking *say something*, like over and over in my head, but every time I tried to come up with words, they all sounded dumb.

I wanted to do something—to make a move. But I didn't know what that even looked like. What if I ruined it? What if I read the whole thing wrong? What if he didn't want me like that—not really?

And then Dylan spoke. Just... out of nowhere.

"And there she is."

I looked at him, but he didn't look back. Just pointed up.

"There," he said.

And I saw it—the comet. It was barely there—like, you could totally miss it if you weren't paying attention. Just a fuzzy blur, like someone smudged the sky with their thumb. But it was real.

And he showed it to me.

We sat there staring at the comet like it was more than just a blur in the sky. Like it meant something. It wasn't even that impressive-looking, if we were being honest. Just a smudge. A soft, pale streak against the dark. You could miss it if you weren't really looking.

"It only comes around every eighty thousand years," Dylan said, voice low. "Kinda wild, right?"

"Yeah," I said. "Like, what are the odds? Us being here right now."

"I know," he said, still looking up. "Billions of years of space garbage and fireballs and—somehow we're sitting here watching this one."

He said it so calmly, like it was just another fact. But there was something in his voice that stuck with me. The way he said "somehow."

I wanted to ask him what he meant. Wanted to say something about how hard it is to be seen at the right time. How maybe some people pass by each other again and again and still miss it. But the words felt too heavy. Too real. And I didn't want to risk ruining the quiet.

"It's kind of sad," I said instead. "That something can come all this way just to disappear again."

"Yeah," he said, barely above a whisper. "Or maybe that's what makes it worth seeing."

I didn't know what to say to that. Not without saying too much.

We went silent again, both of us watching the same tiny blur in the sky. I kept thinking about how rare it was. How random. How sometimes you only get one chance to show up. And maybe—maybe you miss it anyway. Because you don't know how to say what you mean. Or you're scared to.

I don't know. Maybe we were both scared.

Maybe we were both waiting for the other person to go first.

And maybe that's why I decided to do something.

I pulled out my phone and tried to get a photo, messing with the settings. Night mode. Exposure. Zoom. Half the shots came out like blurry nonsense, but I finally got one where you could kinda see it. Just a faint streak, like proof it was real. That we were here.

"Selfie?" I asked, before I could overthink it.

Dylan smiled at me, then nodded. "Yeah, okay."

He leaned in, casual but close, and I wrapped an arm around his shoulder, doing my best to be chill.

The photo came out *way* better than I expected. Our faces were lit up by the glow of my screen, both of us giving these smiles that were not big or forced. Just real.

I stared at it longer than I probably should've, because yeah—it was hella perfect.

Dylan's face was right there next to mine, both of us smiling like it was just… normal. My arm was still around his shoulders, and he hadn't moved away.

He was warm, solid, and so close I could feel the way his breath shifted when he laughed.

Everything in me was buzzing. Not in a dramatic, fireworks kind of way—more like this low, steady feeling I couldn't ignore anymore. The kind that made your fingers twitch and your heart race and your brain try to talk you out of doing the one thing you know you want to do. Because what if it all goes wrong? Like, not just awkward, but ruin-everything wrong?

But there we were, sitting between the waves and the stars, and for once… I didn't pull away.

And for a moment, that felt like a sign. Like this was the opening, the moment when everything shifted and I could stop wondering. My chest was tight, buzzing with nerves and adrenaline and something that felt like hope.

I looked at him—like really looked—and he met my eyes for half a second, calm and unreadable, but still he didn't pull away. So I leaned in.

I didn't rush. I moved slow, careful. My heart was hammering so hard it felt like it echoed in my throat. And just as I got close enough to feel his breath… his shoulders tensed.

I probably wouldn't have noticed it if I wasn't like hyperaware of every fucking thing at that second.

And then he pulled away.

Not harsh. Just this super small move that said way more than I wanted it to. It wasn't harsh, like he didn't push me away—that might have hurt less. But it was just enough to break something inside of me.

"Kiko," he said almost apologetically, "wait."

And that was it. That one word, and everything changed. My stomach dropped, my arm still resting where it wasn't supposed to be. The space between us that now felt way too small. Everything was wrong. I had to get away.

"Shit," I muttered, shaking my head. "Sorry. I—I thought…"

I didn't wait for him to say anything else. I didn't want to hear some kind, well-meaning explanation about feelings being complicated or bad timing or how I was still important to him. I already knew what he meant—*it's not like that*—and that was enough.

I stood up way too fast, brushing the sand off my jeans even though most of it stuck anyway. My chest felt tight and stupid and heavy, as I scrambled to get my shoes at least partly on.

"Kiko, wait—"

I heard Dylan's voice behind me.

"I've got work early," I said, cutting him off. My voice came out flat, way too practiced for how shaky I actually felt. "But we should, like... hang out again sometime. All of us."

I didn't mean it. Or maybe part of me did, but the rest of me knew I wouldn't be able to sit next to him again like nothing happened. Not after this. Not after I made it weird and crossed a line and proved every fear I'd had about liking someone like him true. Someone who was kind, and smart, and creative, in a way I probably didn't deserve.

I didn't look back as I walked across the sand. I just kept going.

Of course Dylan wasn't into me. Of course I blew it. How do you go back to being friends with someone after that? How do you sit across from them knowing they had to let you down easy?

He'd never looked at me *that* way. Not really. I was just really wishing he would and seeing stuff that wasn't there. And I should've known.

I walked up to the boardwalk fast, not stopping, not thinking, just moving. My legs felt shaky but I forced them to keep going, like if I didn't stop, maybe the feeling in my chest wouldn't catch up.

When I hit the pavement, I gave my board a running start and kicked off hard, the wheels catching with a loud rattle. I didn't know where I was going. I just needed to get away. From the beach. From the comet. From Dylan still sitting there on that blanket probably feeling sorry for me.

The wind hit my face as I picked up speed, hair blowing into my eyes, and for a second it felt like I could outrun the whole thing. Like maybe if I skated fast enough, I could pretend it didn't happen. That I didn't mess it all up.

I ended up in the Canals without even thinking about it, turning onto the narrow alleys like muscle memory. But my vision was blurry, and I couldn't see.

I wiped my eyes and my hands were wet. *Was I fucking crying? Really?*

And then I was passing Avery's house.

It was dark. Silent. No lights, no music, no Avery flinging open the door yelling for me to try some weird kombucha she just discovered.

Just quiet. I remembered her saying her dad was gonna be surfing in Australia and New Zealand for like a month. The house was basically empty.

And somehow, that made it worse. The whole place felt hollow. Like something had been removed and nothing filled the space.

Just like in me.

25

I was standing in the kitchen in my boxers, pouring myself a bowl of that same off-brand raisin bran. The sound of the flakes hitting the ceramic was too loud.

Everything felt like that lately—too loud or too quiet, nothing in between. The last couple of days had been this weird mix of too much and not enough. Like I couldn't stop thinking, but also couldn't bring myself to do anything. Just scrolling, half-assing my shifts at work, skating with no destination, pretending the silence didn't feel heavier now.

And it wasn't just me. Everything looked different. Dimmer. Like someone had turned the saturation down on the whole world. The colors were there, technically, but, like, muted. Faded. Like the sky forgot how to be blue. Like food tasted like nothing. Like I was watching my life on a screen with the brightness all the way down.

I sat at the table, staring at nothing, chewing the dry flakes mechanically. Just that same weird cardboard texture I'd somehow gotten used to.

Ma was talking… I think. Somewhere in the background, her voice was going in and out like a radio with bad reception. I caught pieces of it—something about laundry, maybe the neighbors—but none of it landed.

"KIKO."

I blinked, looked up like I'd just woken up from something. She was standing near the sink, arms crossed, looking at me like I'd grown a second head.

"You okay, mijo?" she asked. "You've been walking around like your head's in the clouds for days now. What's going on with you?"

I didn't answer right away, just gave her a shrug—the kind that's supposed to say *I'm fine, leave it alone* without actually using like... words.

Because even if I wanted to tell her the truth—*the* truth—I couldn't. Not without saying *he*... without saying Dylan. And I had no idea how that would land. Ma loved me, yeah. But love didn't always mean understanding. Not in our house, with things like this. So I kept my eyes on the table, staring at the stupid cereal flakes in the bowl.

Ma sighed, not mad, just... tired, I guess. "You've been... off lately," she said. "Like your brain's somewhere else."

She waited for me to say something, but I didn't.

She went back to rinsing a plate, shaking her head. "Just don't shut me out, mijo."

And I wanted to say *I'm not*. I wanted to say *I'm trying here*. But I couldn't even figure out how to start.

Bandit had his front paws on my thigh, but he wasn't begging for food like usual. No tilted head, no sad little dramatic eyes aimed at my cereal. He was just... watching me. Like he knew something was off. Like he was checking on me.

It made me smile, just a little. The first real one in days.

I reached down and scratched behind his ears, his fur soft and messy from sleep. "I can always count on you," I whispered, low so Ma wouldn't hear over the sound of the water. Bandit leaned into it, pressing his head into my hand like he got it.

The faucet shut off with a squeak, and the apartment went quiet again. Just the buzz of the fridge and Bandit's tail thumping softly against the leg of the table.

Ma turned from the sink, drying her hands. "Can you walk him before work?" she asked. "Mateo's been doing it all week. You need to pitch in."

I nodded, still rubbing the top of Bandit's head. "Yeah. I got it."

She gave me a look that was somewhere between "thank you," and "get it together." Then she went into her room, leaving Bandit and me alone at the table.

I pulled out my phone, even though I already knew what I'd find. No new messages. No missed calls. Nothing. Just the same screen I'd been refreshing like an idiot for the last few days, hoping it might magically change.

The last text I got from Dylan was from the morning after it happened.

Just two words.

Sun, Oct 13 at 10:02 AM

Dylan

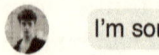 I'm sorry.

That was it. No follow-up or explanation. Just a soft little gut punch I didn't know what to do with. I stared at it way too long when it came in, and I was still staring at it. Just two words—*and a period.* You don't use a period in a text without it meaning something. Something final.

Indie had lasted three days before giving up. She'd texted the same night... and the next day... and the day after that.

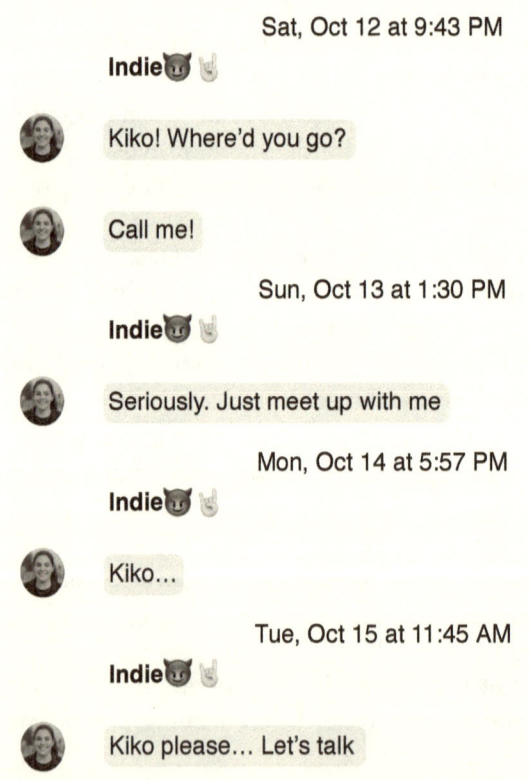

Sat, Oct 12 at 9:43 PM

Indie

Kiko! Where'd you go?

Call me!

Sun, Oct 13 at 1:30 PM

Indie

Seriously. Just meet up with me

Mon, Oct 14 at 5:57 PM

Indie

Kiko...

Tue, Oct 15 at 11:45 AM

Indie

Kiko please... Let's talk

I didn't answer any of them. Not because I didn't *want* to, but because I didn't know how. What was I supposed to say? *Hey, sorry I tried to kiss our friend and made things super weird and now I want to fall into a hole and disappear?*

Even if she was trying to smooth it over, even if she thought it wasn't that bad—*I* knew. *I* knew I'd made a fool of myself. *I* misread everything. *I* wrecked the friendship by making it super awkward—and maybe that was why it felt so alone right now.

I set my phone down on the table and just stared at it, the screen dimming like it was done with me too. Rafe and Avery were gone—off living their best college lives, sending the occasional text or pic, but it wasn't the same. They had each other—even if they were a few hours apart. Still it was a whole new world, and me? I had this apartment, this bowl of dry cereal, and Bandit watching me like he was the last one holding the line.

And now with everything that happened with Dylan—and by default, Indie and Ethan too—it felt like the circle had fully closed. Those were my people. My only people. And I'd managed to make everything weird with one half-second of hope and bad timing.

I guess I could start hanging out more at the skatepark—everyone seemed cool enough since the comp. I could try to slide into Zay's crew, maybe catch a few sessions with the guys who were always there, the ones who knew me enough to say what's up, but not enough to ask questions. They were cool—laid back, funny, talented—but it wasn't the same. It was different when you had friends who actually got you. Who could sit next to you and not need words to know something was wrong. Friends who helped you figure your shit out without making you feel broken.

At least until you tried to kiss one of them.

I leaned back in my chair, the back legs tipping slightly before settling again. Everything just felt heavy. Not dramatic, not even sad, really. Just lonely in that quiet way where you start to wonder if maybe this is just how things are now. This is what happens when you stop playing it safe —you lose people.

And that's what I'd done.

Bandit let out a low whine, followed by a sharp little bark. If subtitles were a thing in real life they would probably say, "*okay, enough emo wallowing, I need to pee.*" He started pacing in circles near the door, tail going in quick bursts, paws tapping the floor like he was counting down the seconds before losing his mind.

"Alright, alright," I mumbled, dragging myself up.

I shuffled into my room and stared at the pile of clothes on the chair —well, the chair that used to be a chair before it got absorbed by a mountain of laundry. I grabbed a t-shirt and gave it a quick sniff. Probably wearable. I found a pair of jeans in the pile too and did the same test. They passed too, barely.

"Close enough," I muttered, pulling them on.

Back in the living room, Bandit was already waiting by the door like my little soldier, paws jittery, eyes locked on me. I crouched down, clipped on his harness and leash, and gave his side a pat. "You're lucky you're cute."

I slipped on my Vans, grabbed the keys, and opened the door. We headed down the stairs, through the side alley, and out onto the sidewalk. Bandit trotted ahead, ears perked, nose twitching, totally in his element.

At least one of us knew where he was going.

We started up the hill, Bandit doing his usual zigzag pattern like the sidewalk was a puzzle he had to solve in under ten minutes. He sniffed everything—trees, poles, fire hydrants, even the tire of a parked Corolla.

"This is like your Insta feed, huh?" I said, watching him with one hand in my pocket. "Just out here sniffing everyone's posts. Seeing what everyone's up to?"

Bandit paused at a lamppost, tail wagging, clearly excited about whatever headline another dog had left behind. Then he lifted his leg like he was adding his own comment to the thread.

"Nice," I muttered. "Real original content."

It went on like that for a while. A pit stop every few feet. Bandit doing his business one carefully chosen location at a time, like it all had to be strategic. And once he was satisfied—meaning he'd peed on literally every other vertical object on the block—he circled back to me, walking a little closer now, like *oh hey, you're still here?*

I gave him a side-eye. "So now you wanna pay attention to me?"

Bandit looked up at me, tongue out, totally unbothered.

"Cool. That's fine. I love being your emotional support human when you remember I still exist."

We got to the park—well, more of a chill green wedge than an actual "park," but it had trees, some grass, and no one around. That was enough. No kids, no couples walking hand-in-hand, just me, Bandit, and the buzz of some nearby leaf blower.

I sat down under one of the trees, leaning back against the trunk. Bandit looked at me like *permission?*, and I unhooked his leash. He didn't go far, just started making loops around the grass sniffing for anything interesting.

I pulled out my phone. Stared at the screen for a second. Then I opened *that* app—the hookup one I hated, that I swore I was gonna delete a hundred times. It glared back at me like, *oh hey, back so soon?*

I rolled my eyes at myself and tapped it open anyway.

It was a grid of torsos, speedos, and bathroom mirror selfies, and a few with the default gray face—like mine still had. Three messages already popped up.

LookingNow4Fun? Hey there what's up?		Just Now
Hmu dl•• Hey		Just Now
Masc Pic?		Just Now

I wasn't even looking for a hookup—not really—no, not at all, actually. I just wanted—something. Like a distraction or a connection. Like a reminder that people still wanted to talk to each other, or maybe even to me. It sucked that the only app built for that kind of thing expected you to lead with thirst traps or some "you up?" at 2AM energy.

Why wasn't there an app like this for friends? Not like "friends" on here or friends with benefits. Just like, for genuine friends. One that didn't assume everyone was trying to smash. Just something where you could say *hey, I feel like garbage and I don't wanna be alone today but also don't wanna talk about it unless I feel like it.* That'd be cool.

I scrolled. Went into a few profiles just to do something. One guy had a backwards hat and basketball shorts pulled down just enough to show off his v-lines. Another was this Irish-looking dude in the front seat of his car, black hat, hoodie, little smirk like he was trying to look deep but mostly looked bored. Then there was this guy clearly at Runyon Canyon, shirt off, golden hour selfie locked in.

That one hit different.

Because all I could think about was the day Dylan and I went up there for that hike. More than the view it was just how we sat on that bench and didn't say much, but it still felt like one of the best days I'd had all year.

Yeah. That was enough of this app for now.

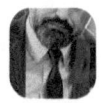

Handsome&Older Photo Received		**Just Now**

Yeah. *Definitely* enough.

I didn't even open it. Just closed the app, but for some reason, my brain went straight to Troye.

Was that the guy who'd been buying him stuff, giving him that credit card... and God knows what else? Probably not. Was it someone like that?

Before I could stop myself, I had opened Instagram. My fingers moved without thinking, like muscle memory. Troye's profile popped up. I hadn't blocked him for some reason, but I wasn't following him anymore. His profile was public though, so I didn't have to.

Only one new photo in the last few weeks.

It was dark and kind of moody, maybe taken in someone's backyard. His face was barely lit, just the faint glow of a cigarette cherry lighting up his face in this super-dim light. Same cheekbones, same bored, unreadable expression.

The caption just said: *Noire.*

I stared at it longer than I should've, letting all the old memories crawl up from wherever I'd shoved them. Before the drama. The way things started intense and somehow ended even more intense. But there was always something about him—something broken and beautiful and magnetic. Like if you could survive the chaos and the fake stuff long enough, maybe you'd find something real in the middle of it.

I wondered how it all got so messed up between us. I wondered if he ever thought about me the way I was thinking about him right now. If maybe, somehow, there was still a chance...

But then I remembered what he said the last time we saw each other —how no one was ever gonna love me or put up with me the way he did. Like I was something people had to endure and being close to me was like a favor or something.

I tapped back a bunch of times until I was on my feed. I wasn't doing that again—even if he might've been right.

The first video on my feed was one of those clips with a guy in a suit onstage, standing in front of those massive LED screens like he was about to announce the next hot tech gadget or at least sell me a crypto pyramid scheme or something. The caption: "No one is coming to save you."

I almost scrolled past it, but my thumb hesitated.

I glanced around—still just me, Bandit doing laps around me like he was training for a doggy track team. The park was quiet with no one nearby.

I tapped the screen and the video restarted with sound.

"No one is coming to save you," the guy said, all confident like he was letting the audience in on the biggest secret in the world. "You need to do the thing yourself. Whatever it is that you want to do. You need to just do it."

I rolled my eyes at first. *Do the thing* to do the thing. Like wow, why didn't I think of that? But then he kept going.

He started talking about Warren Buffett's five/twenty-five rule—how you write down the top twenty-five things you want in life, circle the five most important, and then you completely ignore the other twenty. Not because they aren't cool or meaningful, but because they're distractions. The almosts. The "maybe I could" things that keep you from going all in on what actually matters.

I just sat there, staring at the screen, letting that sink in.

Because damn. I had a whole list. Probably *more* than twenty-five. And I wasn't doing any of them, not even doing anything towards them. I was just stuck on everything I almost had. Everything that almost worked.

Sure, I'd love a relationship. It's not like I was against it. I wanted that connection, that feeling of being seen and chosen and understood. But if I was being real with myself, I knew that wasn't the thing that was gonna fix me. Not on its own.

I had to figure *me* out. Like, who I *actually* was and who I *wanted* to be —not just the guy clocking in at the coffee shop four days a week, handing out oat milk lattes with fake smiles. Yeah, it paid the bills, and I didn't hate it, but I couldn't do it forever. That couldn't be the whole story.

Surfing and skating were cool. They gave me space, gave me peace, when I wasn't completely lost in my head. But let's face it—I wasn't going pro. I wasn't pulling 900s or getting brand deals or getting flown to Australia like Avery's dad. That wasn't the path.

So what was?

I kept coming back to this one thing—photography. I'd been messing around with it for a while, just on my phone mostly, but there was something about capturing a moment, freezing it in time, making it mean something. I'd see those photographers on Instagram, the ones who travel the world for some magazine or brand or whatever, and I'd think—*damn, that could be me.* Telling stories through pictures. Being in the places people dream about.

Was that something I could actually throw all my effort into? Like *really* try?

I didn't know.

But maybe it was time to stop waiting for someone to save me.

26

I was behind the register, elbow on the counter, scrolling through camera reviews on my phone while two girls across the room tried to get the perfect shot of their pumpkin spice lattes. One was crouched low with portrait mode dialed in like she was about to submit the drink to a museum. The other was fluffing the cold foam with a straw like she was a photoshoot assistant.

It was a slow day, which meant I could zone out a little without anyone breathing down my neck. The playlist was soft and moody, the lights were warm, and for once, no one was asking for anything.

I flipped between tabs—starter cameras under $500, comparison guides, a Google search "Best Budget Camera for Broke Creatives." I didn't need anything wild, just something solid, something better than the cracked-screen, memory-maxed iPhone 7 I was still limping through life with.

Come to think of it, I probably needed a new phone too, but I had to focus on my priorities. I didn't know exactly what I was doing. Just that it felt kind of good to want something again. Something that was real— and that was mine.

I was deep into this TikTok of some dude breaking down the features of a base model DSLR, totally sucked in. He was pointing at buttons I didn't understand, talking about things like ISO and aperture, and somehow making it make sense. I had my phone on the counter just next to the register, laser-focused on it.

So I didn't even notice her until she spoke.

"Are you into photography?"

I jumped a little, nearly knocking my phone off the counter. She was standing right at the counter, smiling—an older Black woman, maybe around Ma's age, dressed sharp in a denim jacket and gold hoops that caught the light. Her voice was smooth, calm. Not like she was annoyed I hadn't noticed her, but like she actually meant the question.

"Oh—uh, yeah," I said, still lowkey scrambling to lock my phone and pretend I was doing something useful. "Sorry, I was just watching this thing about cameras. I'm thinking about getting my first one, and I'm kind of overwhelmed, honestly. There's like… a million different options. Lenses. Settings. Whole languages I don't speak."

Her smile widened, but not in a condescending way—just kind and curious.

"Well," she said, resting her hands lightly on the counter, "what are you looking to shoot?"

I scratched the back of my neck, suddenly way more self-conscious than I'd been two minutes ago watching some TikToker say "depth of field" like it was a casual word.

"I'm not totally sure yet," I said. "But like… the kind of stuff you see in travel magazines? National Geographic? That vibe. I really like photojournalism or like street photography too. Like, capturing real stuff. People, places, moments that actually mean something."

She smiled again, this time with a little more sparkle in her eyes. "I'd go with Canon. Something like the M50 Mark II. It's relatively cheap as far as the mirrorless models go, but it's pretty solid. You can use EF-M lenses now, and if you ever want to upgrade to a higher-end model later, you can just get an adapter instead of replacing your whole kit."

I raised my eyebrows. "Wow, you sound like you really know what you're talking about."

She let out a soft laugh. "I know a thing or two. Imani, by the way."

"Kiko."

"I got that," she smiled, glancing at my name tag.

We both laughed. Imani was confident, but chill. She wasn't showing off—just knowing. It made me stand up a little straighter. Maybe I was actually talking to someone who'd done what I wanted to do.

"Do you have any photos you'd like to share?" she asked, still leaning casually on the counter like she wasn't in a rush at all.

"Uh, just stuff I've shot with my phone," I said, picking it up off the counter. "Nothing, like, professional or anything."

She nodded, and I scrolled to my Instagram and handed her the phone. I was weirdly nervous, like she was gonna scroll too far and find something dumb I posted in middle school, but she kept it on the grid, tapping slowly through a few shots—skaters at the skatepark, a sticker-covered pedestrian crossing sign, the washed-out mural wall I liked skating past on my way home. Then she stopped on one from Runyon Canyon.

It was the photo I took of that Buddha head lock someone had stuck on the fence just off the trail. The sun was hitting it just right and the shadows made it feel like it was watching you. I remembered how Dylan laughed at me for crouching in the dirt to get the angle I wanted —and that hurt.

"This one," she said, tapping the screen lightly. "You've got a good eye."

I shrugged, but it meant something coming from her. "I just shoot stuff I like."

"You're good with composition," she said. "Settings and equipment is easy to teach. But skill like this? It's transferable to any camera, no matter how fancy."

"Thanks," I said.

"If you're serious, you should take a class," she added. "The community college offers some good ones. Winter session's coming up —you could start then. They've got an Associate's track for photography. And if you ever want to keep going, some of the credits transfer to UC schools."

I blinked. "Wow, really?"

She smiled. "Really. You don't have to have it all figured out today. But you've got something. You should do something with it."

And for a second, I actually believed her.

She handed my phone back, smile still easy, like she already knew the idea was gonna rattle around in my head all day, whether I wanted it to or not.

"Just think about it," she said. "And who knows—if you decide to go, you might even end up in one of my classes."

"You teach?" I asked, eyebrows raised.

She gave me a small shrug, like obviously. "Told you—I know a thing or two."

Then she ordered a pecan latte—solid fall-core choice and totally underrated. After that, she turned to take a seat... at the corner table with Selena Cho.

My heart skipped. *Crap! It's Tuesday!*

I panicked for a split second, brain scrambling—*her drink!*

But Ricky was already on it, placing her London Fog with oat milk extra foam on the counter with all the quiet ceremony it deserved. He added the whisper of lavender—the good lavender—before Neil picked it up to carry it over.

I let out a breath.

As I leaned on the counter, pretending to check inventory on the screen, I couldn't help but glance over at them—Imani scrolling through photos on her iPad Pro, showing Selena Cho something with this effortless confidence. And for the first time in a while, I didn't feel stuck. I felt... curious. Hopeful, even. Like maybe I could have that one day— my own work, my own voice, sitting across from someone who gave a damn. Maybe this thing I'd been scared to claim, this dream of photography, of telling stories with light and angles and instinct, wasn't just some random phase. Maybe it was the beginning of something real.

I was skating up toward my apartment, playlist going, sun low in the sky, and my wheels humming over the cracked sidewalk. I had just hit that perfect part of the song when the message chimed, cutting the music off mid-chorus. *The worst.*

I pulled the phone out of my pocket to see who it was.

 Rafe (My BFF 🛹)   Just Now
Hey man, how are you?

I frowned a little, dragging one foot to slow down. Rafe never texted like that. Not unless something was up. Especially not the day after Avery had sent me basically the same thing—*hey, just checking in, how've you been?*

Now I was suspicious, so I texted back.

Tue Oct 22 at 5:55 PM

Good u?

Read

Rafe (My BFF 🛹)

 I think I'm gonna come home for a long weekend next week

Rafe (My BFF 🛹)

 Got a gap in midterms. Figured I'd see what's up back in LA for Halloween

I kicked my board up into my hand and stood outside my building for a second, staring at the screen. It was chill, technically, but I felt like something was up. Rafe hadn't been home at all yet, even though he had said he'd be back every other weekend. Now I was getting these cryptic texts and all of a sudden he's rolling back into town? Nah. Something was definitely up. But there was only one way to find out what.

> Cool. We should do something

Delivered

Then I slid my phone into my pocket just as I heard barking up the block—full volume, zero chill. That was Bandit.

I looked up to see him practically flying down the sidewalk, leash stretched to its limit with Mateo trailing behind like a kid's balloon. Bandit was small, but Mateo wasn't exactly built for resistance. Scrawny arms, oversized hoodie, his sneakers barely gripping the pavement.

"Whoa, slow down, little dude," I called out, laughing as Bandit launched himself at my legs like he hadn't seen me in years.

I crouched to pet him, letting him wriggle and snort and freak out in his usual way. Mateo caught up, panting and half-annoyed. I stood and reached over to muss his hair, which earned me a shove and an exaggerated eye roll.

"Ma's home," he said, brushing his bangs back into place. "She's making chiles rellenos."

I grinned. "*Delicioso.*"

We started walking up the alley toward the apartment, Bandit finally calming down and trotting between us. Something about it felt... normal. Easy. Like maybe I was still allowed to have moments like this.

You could smell the roasted peppers and melted cheese and my stomach growled loud enough for Mateo to give me a look.

We kicked off our shoes by the door and headed into the kitchen, the two of us moving in sync without even talking. Mateo grabbed the plates, I got the silverware and napkins. Bandit circled our feet like he was waiting for someone to accidentally drop a whole entrée.

We set the table, and a minute later Ma brought over the serving dish. We all sat down together—for the first time in what felt like forever. No one rushing off, no leftovers eaten separately at weird hours. Just all of us, at the table, like how it used to be.

"This is nice," Ma said, smiling as she spooned food onto our plates. "Feels like it's been a while."

"It has," I said, and meant it.

She looked over at me as she sat down. "How was work?"

"It was chill," I said. "Actually—kinda cool. I met this lady. She teaches photography at the community college. We got to talking, and… I don't know. I've been thinking about maybe enrolling for the winter or spring semester."

Ma raised her eyebrows but didn't say anything right away. Just waited.

"Don't worry about the money," I said, totally reading the *how much is this gonna cost* look on her face. "It's really not that much and I Googled financial assistance and there's this College Promise Program or something like that from the state that makes it almost free if I get it."

"Photography sounds like a tough field to make money," she said.

"There's a ton of ways to make money—freelance stuff, editorial, brands, travel gigs, weddings if I have to." I shrugged. "She looked at some of my photos and said I had a good eye. She wasn't just being nice, either."

Ma nodded slowly, chewing, then wiped her mouth before answering. "Sounds like you've actually thought it through."

"I have," I said, more confident than I expected.

She smiled, like a full smile, and I realized I hadn't seen her smile like that in a long time—or maybe I just hadn't noticed it.

"I say go for it, mijo. It's good to see you excited about something. You've been kind of… in your head lately."

"Yeah," I said, glancing down at my plate, then back up. "I know."

Mateo looked at me from across the table. Not saying anything, just one of those quiet, sideways glances like, *if you're gonna do it, this is your shot.*

And I don't know—maybe it was the food, maybe it was the way Ma smiled when I talked about photography, maybe it was just that we were all actually sitting down together for once—but before I could talk myself out of it, I said it.

"I, uh…" I shifted in my seat, eyes flicking to Bandit, who was curled up under the table like he somehow knew this was a Moment. "I had this friend who I thought maybe wanted to be more than friends, but… apparently not."

Ma looked up from her plate. "Oh?"

Just like that. Not sharp, or surprised. Just kinda letting it hang there.

I felt my pulse in my ears. This was the last off-ramp. The moment before saying something I couldn't unsay. But Mateo was still watching me, and Ma didn't look mad or weirded out, just... listening. So I kept going.

"I *really* liked him," I said. "And I guess I've just been kind of bummed about it."

I expected something—shock, confusion, a weird silence that went too long. But there was silence, but not the heavy kind. Just a pause.

Then Ma nodded, slowly, and set her fork down.

"That sounds like it was tough," she said. "Do you want to talk about it?"

That was it. No big questions. No big moment. Just... that.

"Not really... at least not now," I said.

"Thank you for telling me. You know you can always talk to me," she said. "I just want you to be happy."

And just like that, something let go in my chest. Like I could finally exhale. Relief washed over me so fast I almost felt dizzy. I looked at Mateo, who gave me the smallest smile, before he went back to eating.

After dinner, we ended up on the couch, all three of us, with Bandit curled into a little loaf on the floor by our feet. Ma flipped on Dancing with the Stars—something I barely ever watched, but she had the DVR stacked with episodes because she's normally working.

But this one was actually live. It was Disney night. Big costumes. Big energy. Mateo made it through half the episode before he yawned loud enough for Ma to shoo him off to bed, but I stayed.

At some point, Ma started stroking my hair. Just lightly, fingers running through it like she used to when I was a kid and had nightmares. Normally, I'd pull away. I don't even know when that started—maybe middle school? High school? That dumb reflex of *I'm too old for this now*. But I didn't this time. I just let her.

This couple was talking about how difficult the samba is, because you need to do so many things at once. Honestly it sounded exhausting just hearing them describe it—until I realized that that's exactly what the last few months had become. There was so much I needed to do at the same time. Between work, relationships, friendships, family— keeping everything apart and in its own little box so they wouldn't cross paths. It was like my own personal samba—and I was clearly not getting tens from the judges.

Their dance was absolute fire. The dude was dressed like Tarzan doing these wild hip rolls, while his partner was doing these crazy spins. They both killed it.

I waited until the commercial before I spoke.

"What do you think Dad would've... you know... thought?" I asked, eyes still on the screen.

Ma didn't answer right away. Her hand paused for a second, before it continued, slow and steady.

"He loved you," she said softly. "No matter what."

Her hand kept moving gently through my hair, and I could feel her breath shift, like she was thinking about how much to say.

"You know," she said after a moment, "your dad actually had a friend who was... like you."

She didn't say the word. But I figured she was still getting used to it. I mean... so was I.

"He was the first friend your father made when he came here. When he came out... a lot of people turned their backs on him. It was a different time back then."

Her voice got quiet, not sad exactly, just careful.

"But your dad never did. He stood by him. It wasn't always easy—people said things, made assumptions—but he didn't care. He used to tell me, 'When someone's your friend, they're your friend. That's it.'" She paused, like she was seeing him in her head. "He had a good heart."

I turned to look at her.

"So when I say he loved you no matter what," she said. "I'm not guessing. I *know*."

I didn't know what to say. I just nodded, and went back to staring at the screen where the judges were giving their scores for the Tarzan dance. Damn, were they tough on them, but for me it was like the whole room shifted. Like there was this weight lifted off me, like I didn't have to carry everything alone.

I'd always wondered what my dad would've thought. If he'd still look at me the same. If I'd disappoint him just by being honest about who I was. But now I knew.

And it meant everything.

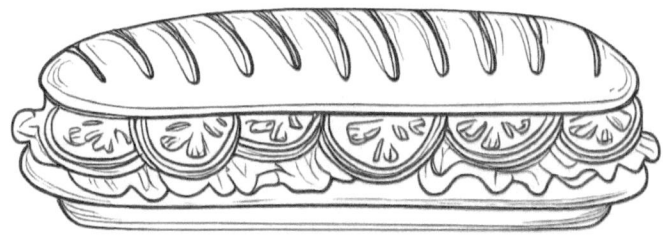

27

The orange FJ Cruiser was half parked in front of my building, on the wrong side of the street, with tires at some weird angle like Rafe had skidded into place and decided *eh, good enough*. He was behind the wheel, rapid-firing the horn, windows down, music blasting some chaotic remix that sounded like it came straight off a frat playlist. His curls were longer than before, brushing the top of his ears, and his arms were tanner than I remembered. He looked the same but different. Grown, maybe.

"Bro, chill," I called out, stepping through the gate. "My neighbors are gonna lose it."

Rafe leaned out the window, already grinning. "Let 'em! I'm just out here celebrating the glorious reunion of two long-lost besties after being tragically separated by the harrowing academic trials of UC Santa Boring!"

"Wow," I said, "'Harrowing academic trials?' Who even are you right now and what have you done with my bestie."

"I'm a college boy now," Rafe replied. "They're teaching your boy some things."

I walked around the front of the car to get into the passenger side.

"Maybe one day they can teach you how to park," I said.

"Okay, first of all, rude," he said, hopping out and slamming the door shut. "Second of all, this is an art. You don't drive so you just don't get it."

I rolled my eyes, but I was already smiling. Dude was a menace, but he was back.

Rafe looped around the corner and onto the onramp for the 10, one hand casually on the wheel, the other flipping through his playlist. The bass was thumping, and the windows cracked just enough to let in the warm afternoon air.

"So... where are we going?" I asked, watching the scene shift as we headed east.

"Fat Sal's," he said, eyes on the road like he was on a mission. "I've been *dying* for one of their sandwiches since, like, week two of school."

I blinked, confused. "Fat Sal's is the other way."

"Nah, I wanna go to the one in Hollywood," he said like it was obvious. "I like that one better."

"They're literally the same, and the one in Culver City is like five minutes away."

He shrugged. "I got a car for a reason. We should explore a little."

I stared at him, then back at the road. He was acting weird, but then again, he always did this—took the long way, made things into whole events. Even when we were just skating, he needed to try a new route— only today this route had taken us straight into midday freeway traffic.

The truth was, though, I was just glad he was back. Even if he was being extra. Even if he was making me spend my day off in traffic to get a sandwich we could've gotten ten minutes ago. It felt good to just be with him again—no pressure, no expectations. Just the familiar chaos of Rafe's brain steering us somewhere for no real reason at all.

So I let it go. Let the sights slide by the window and enjoyed the fact that someone I cared about was still here, still *choosing* to hang out with me. So Hollywood it would be—if we could get there alive...

The off-ramp for La Brea was wide open and Rafe gunned it out of the practically stopped traffic. He took the tight loop of the cloverleaf a little too fast, and I grabbed the "oh shit bar" almost positive we were gonna hit the wall. Rafe was completely unfazed though as we somehow completed the loop and continued on like nothing happened.

I was mentally preparing for thirty minutes of fighting for a parking spot once we got to Hollywood. When we reached the corner of La Brea and Melrose, I stared at this blank white building on the corner. The Chipotle that was there, next to Pinks was just... gone. Like totally gone. The signs were down, the windows empty, and even the multicolored mural was now just a blank white wall. The place was just a weird, hollow building now. Like it never existed at all.

"That's crazy," I muttered, but Rafe didn't hear me. He was too busy singing along to some '80s power ballad, trying to be all dramatic, but ending up just being wildly off key.

I kept staring at that corner as we passed it. It just felt wild, the way something that used to be so there could just vanish. Like all it took was time and some paint and now it was a ghost. A shell. Nothing.

I just kinda leaned my head against the window, watching zombie Chipotle disappear in the side mirror. Things changed so fast. One day things are all familiar and solid, and the next they're just gone, like they never mattered at all.

I never even went to that location, just passed it on the way to the Open Mic Night, so I didn't know why it hit me like that—but it did.

We cut over to Highland and pulled into an L-shaped shopping center. Fat Sal's was split between two separate storefronts with a random sushi place sandwiched—yeah, I know—in between. It was a totally cursed layout, but somehow it worked.

My stomach growled as we parked. After that unnecessarily long detour through half the city, I was more than ready to eat. Their sandwiches were *fire*—greasy, overloaded chaos on a hero, and somehow always exactly what you needed even if you might regret it after.

We walked into the side wedged into the corner of the strip mall, next to an AutoZone with a flickering sign and a guy loitering outside selling bootleg phone chargers. There was plenty of seating and no line, which was a score for this time of day. The guy behind the counter was already watching us like he was ready to take our order.

I stepped up, already reaching for my wallet when Rafe said, "Wait— let's go to the other side."

I turned. "What? What's wrong with this side?"

He shrugged, too casual. "I just like the other one better."

"It's the same place!" I said, motioning around. "I don't get it."

But he was already backing out the door. "C'mon. It's better over there."

I stared after him, frowning. Rafe was always a little extra, sure, but this was weird even for him. The whole vibe was off. First the Culver location is not good enough, now this particular side is not good enough? I couldn't wait to hear how a specific table was better than the others.

Something was up. I just didn't know what yet.

We walked up to the counter and I scanned the menu, even though I already knew what I was getting. I'd been craving something massive, but I didn't want to go overboard—not in front of Rafe, who had a photographic memory for every time I ever ate "like a raccoon" even though he eats like a pig. So I played it safe, simple italian hero nothing crazy.

"I'll do the Italiano hero," I said, "with hot peppers."

Rafe was already grinning wide. "Fat Jerry," he said with zero hesitation. "No pickles."

The Fat Jerry had ribeye, chicken fingers, mozzarella sticks, and all sorts of toppings, so yeah, like I said.

The guy behind the counter gave us our number and I turned, ready to scout out a table—when I saw someone sitting alone near the side windows right next to the counter.

Ethan.

They were half-picking at a falafel sandwich. While I stopped mid-step, brain stalling out like my body had just hit a wall. Ethan looked up, met my eyes, and gave this small, hesitant wave. Nothing big. Just a hey, I see you kind of thing.

I realized I was just standing there like an idiot, halfway to the table, staring.

Rafe slid up beside me, all fake-casual and too loud. "Oh wow, you know that guy? What a coincidence."

I turned toward him slowly, eyes narrow. "Yes," I muttered through clenched teeth. "I know them. What a coincidence."

Rafe shrugged still feigning innocence. Clearly I'd been set up, but I think what was messing me up most was I had no idea how Rafe and Ethan knew each other.

"What is this?" I whispered, sharp. "What is this actually about?"

He just shrugged, all innocent at first, but he gave up.

"Listen, just give him—"

"Them," I interrupted.

Rafe stopped before he continued, "Just give them a chance."

I looked back at Ethan, and walked over to sit down across from them, still kind of rattled, still unsure of what was even going on still. Ethan just gave me this soft, almost apologetic look.

"How've you been?" they said quietly.

I nodded, playing with the edge of a napkin. "Alright, I guess."

They tilted their head. "Indie said she tried to reach out a few times. Said she hadn't heard back."

"Yeah, I..." I trailed off, trying to find the right word. "Things got..."

"Weird," Ethan finished, without judgment.

I smiled, just barely. "Yeah. Sorry. Things got weird."

They gave this little sigh, folding their hands in their lap. "I'm not sure I should be here," they said. "But we didn't know any other way."

I looked at them, unsure what that meant until they kept going.

"Dylan's been really bummed," they said. "I've never seen him like this. Like, not even during all that stuff with his dad when he first came to LA. He won't say it out loud, but... I'm pretty sure it's you."

I stared at them, caught somewhere between disbelief and dread.

"I didn't mean to upset him," I said. "He was a really good friend and I shouldn't have made a move. I just... I don't know... like misread the situation or something."

Ethan looked at me, confused.

"I don't know what happened that night, honestly. But I don't think you misread things completely," they said.

I blinked. "Then what... happened that night?"

"I think... he just panicked or shut down," Ethan continued. "He's never really done the whole 'real-relationship' thing—at least not in LA —and I think he just... shut down. Whether it was about you, or something else, I don't know. But something scared him."

I looked down at the table, something heavy sitting on my chest, but not the same heaviness as before. This one had space in it.

"I think... maybe it's worth talking to him again. I don't know what either of you were thinking that night. But I don't think it was nothing. I think there's something there, even if it got messy."

I didn't say anything right away. I just let their words settle. Let the idea of "maybe" roll around in my head again. And for the first time in days, it didn't feel impossible.

Ethan kept nudging the crust of their sandwich with one finger. I knew the pause was intentional—not awkward, just Ethan being Ethan. Just them being precise with their words.

"Indie reached out to Avery last week," they said finally. "She got Rafe involved."

I sat back, the pieces starting to snap together in my head. The long detour. Rafe's weird behavior. The forced "coincidence" of us ending up on this side of Fat Sal's after going to the other one.

I laughed. "Well that explains him acting all sus since he got back."

Ethan nodded sheepishly. "Well yeah. This whole thing was kind of... coordinated. My job was to get you to come out to WeHo for Halloween Carnaval. Indie's working on Dylan."

"I should have known."

Ethan looked up then, their voice soft but steady. "I know it probably feels easier to stay sad, or hurt, or just... done. Like that way, you're in control. But just because something got messy doesn't mean it wasn't real. And honestly?" They paused. "Sometimes the scary stuff is just proof that it *mattered*."

I didn't say anything for a second. I just kind of sat with that... because yeah, it *had* mattered. All of it. The night on the beach, the comet, the almost-kiss, even the silence after—it was real—and I'd been trying so hard to protect myself that I hadn't even let myself miss it.

Ethan watched me carefully in that super observant Ethan way.

I let out a shaky breath. "Alright. I'll come."

Their shoulders relaxed slightly, and I could tell they were relieved because this tiny hint of a smile popped up.

"But," I added, "the only problem is I don't have a costume."

Rafe came strolling over with our sandwiches at that moment, plopping into the seat next to me like he hadn't just orchestrated a mildly manipulative emotional intervention. He took one look at my face and smirked. "So? You're going, right?"

I gave him a side-eye but nodded. "Yeah. I'm going."

"Then boom—easy. You should just do the vampire costume you wore last year. That thing went hard."

"I still have the cape," I said. Pretty sure it was somewhere in the wrinkled mess stuffed in the bottom of my closet. "But I don't have any makeup. The stuff from last year's all dried out and gross by now."

But before I could even finish the sentence, Ethan was already tapping furiously on their phone, their eyes laser-focused in that crazy way they got when they were super-excited about something. I watched them, confused, until my phone chimed a second later.

"That's your shopping list," Ethan said.

I checked the screen.

It was a list—nude lipstick, white foundation, smokey eyeshadow, black eyeliner, and glitter gel. Because of course Ethan was gonna add glitter.

"I don't know about the glitter," I said. "I was thinking more Anne Rice than *Twilight*."

Ethan grinned. "The glitter's for me. Your place tomorrow at five?"

I agreed. Looking at how excited Ethan and Rafe both were, I was starting to feel like there was a chance this might work.

"*Operation Get-My-Boy-a-Boy* is in full effect!" Rafe announced.

I wished he'd kept that level of confidence for the next part of our day.

Just a couple hours later, Rafe and I were standing in the cosmetics aisle of Target like we'd just been dropped onto Mars. We were surrounded by a wall of tiny plastic boxes and shiny tubes, and none of it made any sense. There were like fifteen different kinds of foundation —matte, dewy, full coverage, medium coverage, something with "blur" in the name—and don't even get me started on the eyeshadow palettes. Neutrals, smoky, jewel tones—whatever that meant. One of them was literally just named Chaos.

"What even is a contour? Is this bronzer?" Rafe muttered, squinting at a box trying to read the tiny print. "Face powder for dramatic cheekbones…"

"I don't know," I said, holding up a random stick thing and turning it over. "I think you use this to make shadows on your face? Or maybe it's lipstick. I have no idea. Ethan should've been the one here."

"No offense," Rafe said, "but your vampire glam needs adult supervision."

Before I could respond, he peeled off down the aisle and returned a minute later with a Target employee in tow—a woman probably in her late twenties with cool braids and a red shirt.

She looked at us for all of two seconds and smirked. "Let me guess… Halloween?"

"Is it that obvious?" Rafe asked.

"Very," she said, laughing as she scanned the mess of products in our basket. "Alright, let's make this easier."

She pointed to a drugstore foundation stick. "This one's easy to apply, doesn't cost a ton, and blends pretty well. It won't give you movie-level contour, but it'll get the job done for one night." She glanced around the shelf. "White foundation's been sold out for days, though. Sorry—you're gonna have to work with pale and dramatic."

"We'll make it work," I said, already trying to figure out if the glitter gel I picked was the one Ethan wanted.

She double-checked our basket, running down the list like a seasoned pro. "You've got lipstick, foundation, eyeliner, glitter gel… yep, you're good to go. Just maybe watch a tutorial before trying to glue anything to your face."

We both laughed, thanked her, and headed for the registers.

Somehow, it felt like we'd just passed a quest in a video game. Makeup acquired. Level: unlocked. Still no idea how to use half of it— but at least we had the gear.

As we tossed the Target bags into the back of the FJ Cruiser, Rafe leaned casually against the bumper, spinning his keys on one finger like he was trying to look cool in a teen drama. He had that look on his face

—the one that usually meant he was about to derail whatever low-key plans I thought we had—again.

"By the way," he said, catching the keys and pointing at me like he just remembered something vital. "Game five is on tonight."

"Of course," I said. There was no baseball fan in LA that wasn't aware.

"Dodgers can wrap it up tonight with one more dub."

I gave a low whistle and nodded. "Facts. You wanna watch it at my place?"

He pushed off the car and started walking toward the driver's side. "I have a better idea. We gotta be in it, you know? Crowds, yelling, overpriced nachos—vibes."

I followed him, raising an eyebrow. "Yeah vibes and IDs. You do remember we're not, like... legal to get into most places that are gonna be showing it, right?"

Rafe gave me that signature shrug, the kind that always came with confidence that you just had to trust, even if you were certain there was no backup plan. "We'll figure it out. Trust me."

So we headed over to Culver City, the sky shifting into that deep blue twilight, all golden-pink reflections in the FJ's rearview mirrors. Rafe had the windows down and the music up, blasting some classic rock ballad playlist. Those songs just made everything feel more epic than it was. He was singing along off-key, drumming on the steering wheel like he was hyping himself up for the playoffs too.

My phone chimed with a text from Ethan. It was just a link to a Youtube video. I popped an earphone in and clicked on the link. The video was of Dylan, standing at the microphone from the Open Mic Night. No—wait, it wasn't from then. It was from a different night. I thought the poem was the same, but it was different.

> "The moon's still a spotlight,
> but now it catches me alone—
> center stage in a show that never opened.
> No lines, no cues,
> just the hollow sound of what might've been.
>
> I lived an entire lifetime in my head. A life
> of road trips, and funky coffee shops,
> of pumpkin patches and Christmas markets,
> of smiles, and hands held, and stolen kisses,
> of lazy weekend mornings—and a family that would never be

I practiced smiles in the mirror
for moments that never came.
Icarus never got to soar—because this time
his wings melted while he was still on the ground,
just for daring to dream of the sky.

I don't know what hurts more—
that nothing happened,
or that I loved the nothing—
like it was everything."

If I needed any further convincing, this was it. I was *going* to fix this. Tomorrow was the day. Tonight was just figuring out how to exist with the anticipation of the next day.

We pulled into one of those parking garages near downtown just as the game was starting, the sounds of the pre-show commentary echoing from Rafe's phone as he tried to stream the first inning while we walked. The streets were already buzzing. People in Dodgers jerseys everywhere, spilling out of bars and patios, talking loud and hyped like they were already celebrating a win for the night.

I pulled on my tie-dyed blue hoodie since the temperature had dropped into the fifties. I was also hoping my lucky hoodie might bring my Dodgers some luck.

We stopped in front of this bar just off Washington with giant TVs you could see from the street, the inside glowing like a stadium. It was packed—standing room only, people halfway out the doors, beers in hand. It was perfect.

Until the bouncer gave us one look.

He didn't say anything. Just jerked his thumb to the left with a slight smirk that screamed *not tonight, kids.*

Rafe gave a dramatic sigh as we stepped aside. "We were this close to greatness."

We lingered on the sidewalk, just outside the zone of legality, watching the game through the window like a couple of street urchins. Just in time to catch Aaron Judge of the Yankees step up to the plate. One pitch, one swing, and the ball launched over the right-centerfield wall like it was nothing. The bar exploded—people jumped up, cursing, spilled beer everywhere.

"Two-zero," I muttered. "Not a great start."

Rafe didn't blink. "You gotta have faith, my dude."

I shot him a look. "You always say that."

"Yeah," he said, grinning as he shoved his hands into his hoodie pocket. "And I'm usually right."

We crossed the street to another bar. This one was smaller but just as packed, with TVs visible through the big glass windows and a crowd that looked like they'd been there since noon. The noise was spilling out onto the sidewalk, and the bouncers at the door weren't even pretending to be chill. One look at us and they just shook their heads.

Rafe tried to flash his most charming smile anyway. "Just wanna catch a few innings, promise we won't even—"

The bouncer didn't even blink back. "Keep it movin', fellas."

So we did.

We ended up on the curb a few yards down, sitting on the concrete like a couple of rejected fanboys watching the stream on Rafe's phone. By the bottom of the second, it was already 4-0 Yankees. Another run batted in, some messy defense, and the Dodgers looked like they were sleepwalking.

I groaned. "Still not good."

Rafe didn't even look away from the screen. "Faith!"

I rolled my eyes, then pointed across the street to an upscale Indian restaurant that was way less crowded than anywhere else we'd tried. The lighting was mellow, a few people scattered at tables, and—most importantly—three TVs mounted near the bar and even some on the patio all playing the game.

"Okay," I said. "Can we at least have faith in that restaurant?"

Rafe nodded. "Now that is a miracle I can get behind."

We ended up getting a table on the patio and split a couple orders of naan, which wasn't exactly ballgame food, but it hit the spot.

Sure, we weren't drinking or screaming with the crowd, but honestly? It was still fun. Just sitting there with Rafe, watching the game on a screen that didn't buffer every ten seconds, messing around, talking trash about the commentators' outfits—it felt like how things used to be. Easy.

Then Giancarlo Stanton stepped up to the plate and crushed one so hard into left-centerfield. The restaurant went quiet. Even the couple next to us—who hadn't said a word the entire time—stopped mid-bite and stared at the TV.

5-0, Yankees.

Rafe winced, but I didn't say anything. I should've felt defeated. Normally, this is where I'd shrug and say it was over, that it wasn't the

Dodgers' night. But instead, I sat there, with my eyes glued to the screen. I had this feeling that something was about to break loose. There was this tension in the air—not panic, not disappointment—anticipation. Like the story wasn't over yet.

It was weird, but the feeling was familiar. That same quiet buzz I'd been carrying around since I spoke with Ethan—and definitely since the video of Dylan's poem. That poem didn't sound like someone who didn't care. It sounded like someone trying to say what they couldn't say in another way.

Even after the awkward silence since the almost-kiss… was there still something there? Something waiting? I didn't know if it was hope or just me being stupidly stubborn, but I couldn't shake the sense that the game wasn't finished. No, not yet.

And in the top of the fifth, everything changed.

The Yankees' defense straight-up collapsed. Like, full implosion mode. A ground ball with no one covering first, a hit into centerfield that scored two more runs. Then Teoscar Hernandez hit a fly ball to centerfield, bringing in two more runs. It felt like someone changed the game difficulty setting, or turned on cheat codes. Rafe and I leaned in, laughing in disbelief as the Dodgers circled the bases.

This dude at the next table over was clearly a Yankees fan because he looked like he wanted to cry into his chicken curry. He just stared at the TV in disbelief.

The bars up and down the block erupted in cheers. It was chaos. Beautiful, unexpected chaos. And I let myself believe that maybe—just maybe—the comeback was possible. In the game…

And in everything else.

28

The night before still felt like a blur, but in the absolute best way. After my Dodgers pulled off one of the most insane comebacks anyone has ever seen, the whole damn city went and lost its mind. Cars were honking their horns, blasting music. Some had people hanging out of windows waving flags and Dodgers jerseys. Fire engines cruised past with their sirens blaring, not responding to any emergency, just out of pure celebration. You couldn't even tell where the yelling was coming from half the time—out of bars, apartments, rooftops—everywhere just exploded all at once.

Rafe and I had walked around for hours, just letting ourselves get pulled into it. He kept dancing with random people outside bars or whenever a car pulled up blasting music at a red light. Total chaos, but again, the good kind—the kind that makes you feel like you're part of something way bigger than yourself. And somewhere in all that noise, neon, and firework smoke, I felt it too. This quiet energy underneath everything—was it hope? Like maybe what happened with Dylan wasn't over. Maybe, just like my Dodgers had been down 5-0 and still came back to win the whole damn thing. Maybe I still had a shot too. Like the story wasn't finished yet and it was just getting started.

The doorbell buzzed, loud and sharp, and Bandit went absolutely nuts. He launched himself at the door like he was going to take on whatever threat decided to show up and ring the bell to ask to be let in.

"Bandit, chill!" I shouted, half-laughing as I tried to nudge him back with my foot. He dodged me, still losing his mind—that is until Rafe, who hadn't even gotten up from the couch, called out lazily, "Bandit. Stop."

Instantly, Bandit shut up and plopped his butt down with a wag of his tail like he hadn't just been aggressively barking at the top of his lungs two seconds ago.

I just stared at him for a sec.

"Traitor."

I shook my head and opened the door.

Ethan stood there, hands stuffed into the sleeves of a black hoodie with a light pink backpack slung over one shoulder. They gave me a small, kind-of-nervous smile, like they were trying to play it cool.

"Hey," I said, stepping back to let them in. "You find the place okay?"

"Yeah," they said, glancing around. I could tell they were a little hesitant, just kind of hovering near the door instead of coming in right away.

I followed their gaze to Bandit, who was still parked by my feet, staring up at Ethan like he was ready to start the chaos all over again.

"You good with dogs?" I asked, tipping my head toward Bandit. "I can throw him in my room if you want."

Ethan crouched down instead, holding out a hand. Bandit, took one sniff and immediately rolled over to demand belly rubs like they were long-lost friends.

"We're good," Ethan said. His smile was a little more genuine, and he seemed to relax a bit.

"So," Ethan said, adjusting the bag on their shoulder, "are we ready to do this?"

I nodded, but inside my brain was doing about a hundred laps.

This.

Sure, on the surface, this probably meant getting my costume together, doing the makeup, and figuring out how to look like a vampire and not a total clown in front of a crowd full of people. That part was somewhat manageable—I mean it was straight-up technical. Something you could just—I don't know—YouTube tutorial your way through or something.

But there was also the other part—the part that wasn't about picking the right eyeliner or finding the perfect placement of the fake blood.

It was the part that was about *Dylan*.

Tonight wasn't just about dressing up and chilling in West Hollywood. Tonight was about finding out if everything I felt—everything I thought *he* felt—was actually real. Or if I'd built it all up in my head like some sad movie character who didn't get the hint until it was way too late. Either it all meant something…. or I was about to go down in flames with a face full of makeup and fake vampire fangs.

And that was the worst part.

Because I didn't know.

I couldn't trust my own read on any of it.

After everything with Troye—all the mixed signals, the way things had just blown up without me even seeing it coming. I didn't believe— no, I *couldn't* believe myself anymore when it came to stuff like this. That I could tell when someone *actually* liked me, or when I was just... convenient, or safe, or a mistake they were trying to figure out how to walk away from... or someone that they weren't into at all...

So instead I was stuck relying on everyone else, on Ethan, and Indie, and even Rafe—people who seemed to know how to *human* better—to tell me what was real.

And I hated that.

I hated feeling like something was broken inside of me. I hated feeling like I couldn't just know like they all seemed to know. But still, they believed in *this*, and somewhere deep down, even through all the second-guessing and the knots in my stomach, I wanted to believe too.

I glanced at Ethan, who was waiting without rushing me, like they knew exactly how big this felt even if we hadn't said it out loud.

"Yeah," I said, voice rougher than I meant it to be. I cleared my throat and tried again. "Yeah. Let's do it."

Because even if I didn't trust myself right now, maybe it was okay to lean on the people who did.

Ethan tapped the back of the chair and motioned for me to turn around, away from the table. I shifted in my seat, nerves kicking up a little, and changed into the shiny white vampire shirt—the one with the ridiculous frilly cuffs and deep V-neck. The fabric felt slick and a little cold against my skin.

They handed me a hair tie, and I pulled my hair back as best I could. As soon as I settled, Ethan got to work. They were like, laser focused, barely blinking.

I watched them out of the corner of my eye, the little mirror set up behind me out of reach. They moved fast but precise, tapping a sponge into foundation, brushing powder along my face and neck, pulling little tubes and pencils from their bag like some kind of low-key magician. Up close, I noticed Ethan was wearing makeup too—subtle, but there. It was just a slight shimmer to their skin under the glow of the ring light. Their lashes looked darker than usual, and I wasn't sure if that was mascara or just... them. They had that kind of face that didn't need much—just a few touches and it looked like art. I never really noticed before, and I wondered if it was just a today thing or if they always wore makeup.

I had to look away as Ethan dragged a pencil along the corner of my eye. As they worked, I felt the makeup building up. It wasn't heavy... just different. Ethan finished by swiping the lipstick over my lips. They stepped back, arms crossed, head tilted, studying me.

Rafe joined them with wide eyes as they both stared at me, not saying anything.

"What?" I said, twisting a little in the chair but not daring to turn around yet. "Did it come out okay? Do I look ridiculous?"

Neither of them answered, which immediately sent my anxiety into overdrive, though a proud grin started to spread on Ethan's face.

I stood up and turned to face the mirror, and for a second, I didn't even recognize the dude staring back at me.

He was pale. His features were sharper. He was almost... haunting. But this dude was me. He looked—no, *I* looked—like someone who belonged in another world entirely, like I was someone who could walk into a room and make people stop and look. Not just background noise.

I sat there, staring at my reflection. Ethan hadn't just slapped a coat of paint on me—they *transformed* me. And for the first time all week, I had to admit, I was feeling myself.

While I was messing with the plastic fangs before deciding to give up on them, Ethan was going hard with their own costume. They cracked open the glitter gel and painted these shimmery designs across their arms and cheeks, then started sticking on these little press-on gem stones, making this whole constellation pattern across their temples. When they changed, they came out in this skimpy green outfit—like forest green crushed velvet with sparkly wings strapped to their back—and threw in these freaky black whole-eye contacts that made them look straight-up unreal. Like a forest sprite from some dark fantasy movie that definitely wasn't PG-13. They'd gone all in. No half-measures.

Rafe, though? He was a whole other story as he strolled out of my room proudly rocking a Captain America t-shirt and jeans. When Ethan and I both stared at him, he just shrugged and tried explaining that it counted, but neither of us was buying it—and even Bandit let out a little whine like he was disappointed in his chosen master—but honestly, it was peak Rafe. Once everyone was ready, we called an Uber and piled in, the three of us wedged together in the back seat, making sure Ethan's wings didn't get crushed or my cape wrinkled. With the windows cracked, the energy was already buzzing as we headed toward WeHo.

When we got to WeHo, the party was already insane. Santa Monica Boulevard was closed off so it was a full-on mob scene, like one big block party. Everyone was packed shoulder to shoulder with people in every costume you could think of. I spotted like five different Beetlejuices within thirty seconds. Two guys had these movie-quality Ghostbusters suits, complete with the light-up proton packs. Skeletons and zombies were everywhere, some with fake blood dripping down their shirts, others with makeup so good it looked like their faces were actually rotting.

One dude towered over the crowd in this neon pink cop hat. He was like seven feet tall, rocking a matching fur coat and these bedazzled platform boots that added a solid six inches easy—like this dude wasn't tall enough. He looked like he just stepped out of some chaotic fever dream, and not gonna lie, I was here for it.

Everywhere I looked, there was something wild—half the guys had twisted their costumes into the "sexy" version somehow. Sexy dark angel. Sexy cowboy. A bunch of sexy Luigis, though not a lot of sexy Marios for some reason. Shirts were clearly totally optional, and from what I could tell, generally frowned upon. It was no doubt hard to even figure out where to look without feeling completely overwhelmed.

I leaned in toward Ethan, trying to raise my voice over the noise and music blasting from scattered speakers in the crowd. "How the hell are we supposed to find Dylan in this?"

Ethan didn't even flinch, already texting like they had it under control. "Leave that to me and Indie," they said, weaving through the crowd without so much as glancing up.

As we pushed forward through all these little pockets of chaos, Rafe was getting side-eyes and laughs for his lazy-ass excuse for a costume. One dude in a full Ironman suit even pointed at him as we passed and shouted, "Assemble! But like, actually like try next time!" which made what felt like half the street burst out laughing.

Rafe just grinned and saluted him, unbothered as always.

At the intersection of N San Vicente, it was absolute chaos. A full stage was set up right there in the street, lights flashing across the crowd. A DJ was hyping everyone up, music blaring so loud it felt like it was vibrating through my ribs with every beat. The crowd was so packed it felt like we were all one, shoulder to shoulder, barely moving, just swaying in different directions, with these narrow streams of people trying to squeeze through to get to the other side.

Ethan was on their toes, scanning the crowd like a hawk, one hand holding onto my sleeve so we didn't get separated. I could tell this had to be the spot, because of course Indie would pick the loudest, most overwhelming, most impossible place in all of West Hollywood to make this happen. Absolute peak chaos.

But then I saw him. Before Ethan. Before he saw me.

Dylan.

He was standing maybe twenty feet away, just past a group of guys in matching sailor costumes, wearing this vintage hippie getup that looked like it had been thrifted straight from 1971. He probably put it together at work, though I'm sure he had most it already. He had on a tie-dyed headband, round pink-tinted sunglasses, and an old army jacket that looked perfectly worn-in. I couldn't see his pants through the crush of people, but I was willing to bet money they were bell bottoms.

But I froze.

For a second, it was like everything else muted—the crowd, the music, the lights. All of it faded out, and it was just him. And me. Separated by a sea of strangers and a mess of uncertainty I hadn't been able to shake since the beach.

He wasn't smiling. He wasn't laughing or dancing or even really engaging with the chaos around him. Dylan could usually be a little distant, sure—but this was something else. He looked like he was just floating through it. Like he'd shown up, but mentally hadn't actually arrived. It was like some spark in him was missing.

Ethan was still on their toes, scanning the sea of bodies, trying to find him. But I didn't say anything. I just stood there, tucked into a sliver of space between the crowd, and watched Dylan for a little longer.

If everything crashed and burned tonight—if I'd read this all wrong again—this would be it. The last time I'd let myself look at him and think there was a chance. It would be the last time I could believe, even for a second, that maybe all those little almost-moments between us had meant something.

I thought about the poem. About the life Dylan had written in those lines—the coffee shops, the pumpkin patches, the Christmas markets. All those small, quiet, beautiful things. The life I hadn't realized I wanted until he said it out loud.

It sounded like a life I wanted to live.

It sounded like a life I wanted to share.

But here I was, standing there with my heart pounding under my too-shiny shirt and worried I was sweating off my vampire makeup. I knew this would either be the beginning of that life—or the last breath of that dream.

And *fuck* I wasn't ready to let this one go.

But then he turned and looked straight at me, and yeah—there went my breath getting straight-up caught in my throat. It happened so fast it just felt like everything inside me slammed to a stop.

He saw me—not just glanced past me—but *for sure* saw me.

Ethan seemed like they noticed, because without saying a word they just let go of my wrist. They gave me a small grin—with those creepy all-black contacts—as they slipped back into the crowd almost like they knew they didn't belong in this moment.

At first, Dylan squinted a little, almost like I looked familiar but he couldn't quite clock me. And then, his expression just shifted—he recognized me alright. But it was like his mouth didn't know whether it was supposed to frown or smile and ended up in this weird in-between that was both and neither at the same time. He lifted a hand and gave me this tiny wave, that wasn't quite awkward but seemed—I don't know—almost weak. Tired even. It was giving "this took absolutely all of my energy."

I stepped forward without even thinking, and he was moving too. Both of us were trying to weave through the crush of people. We bumped into shoulders and did our best to dodge flailing arms and elbows of people dancing. I was not trying to get a black eye right now.

When we got to each other, both of us tried to say something, but the music was so loud my chest was vibrating—or maybe that was just my heart pounding against my ribcage.

We both laughed, uselessly shouting into the noise, and Dylan jerked his chin toward the edge of the street, signaling to get out of the crush. I nodded and followed—but before he could disappear into the moving wall of people, I reached out and grabbed his hand.

Not tight. Not pulling. Just holding on to him, because there was no way in hell I was about to let him get swept away.

We pushed through the crowd, still holding on together, until finally the bodies thinned and the noise faded enough that we could hear our own thoughts again.

Dylan stopped and turned to face me, the pink lenses of his glasses slipping down his nose just enough that I could see his eyes, clear and real, and wet with tears.

And for a second, neither of us said anything.

Dylan rubbed the back of his neck, his eyes darting around like he couldn't figure out where to start. And then the words just spilled out, fast and messy and way too honest to be rehearsed.

"I'm sorry," he said, voice rushing. "For pulling back at the beach. It wasn't that I didn't want to kiss you. I did. I wanted to so fucking bad that it freaked me out. And I wasn't sure if you were ready or if it was just some... rebound or if—" He let out a short, shaky laugh, looking down for a second. "Or if that was just me making excuses because I was scared. And you always look at me like... like I've got it all figured out. But I don't, Kiko. Like, not even close. I'm all kinds of fucked up..."

He said it like he fully believed it. Like he was already bracing for me to turn and walk away.

He was still going, "And if you saw all of it, really saw it, you wouldn't want to be with—"

But I didn't even think. I just stepped forward and kissed him.

It wasn't careful. It wasn't planned. I just grabbed the front of his vintage jacket and pulled him in, and Dylan went perfectly still for half a second—like his brain short-circuited—before he just like melted into it. ,

And it was—

God, it was *everything*.

The noise of the street, the flashing lights, the heat of the crowd—all of it blurred into nothing. It was just the press of his mouth against mine, soft and a little shaky, like he couldn't believe it was happening either. His hands found my hips, kinda careful at first but then holding them tighter, like he was just anchoring himself there.

I felt his breath catch when I deepened the kiss, and he leaned into me like it was the easiest thing in the world and he'd been waiting for this as long as I had.

And for the first time in a long, long time, everything in me went quiet. No second-guessing. No spiraling or racing thoughts. No wondering if I was reading it wrong.

Just him.

Just me.

Just *this*—perfect, real, and ours.

Like we were both in the exact spot in the universe that we were supposed to be.

I pulled back first, just enough to breathe, but not enough to let go. Our foreheads were almost touching, and for a second neither of us said anything. We just stood there, eyes locked, everything around us still loud and chaotic—music, yelling, lights flashing—but it all felt far away.

Dylan looked at me like he was still catching up to what just happened. His lips were a little parted, his cheeks flushed. I couldn't stop staring at him. And maybe I should've held it in, played it cool or whatever, but I didn't. I couldn't.

"I'm not into you because you've got it all together," I said, voice low, shaky but real. "I'm into you because you're honest—you're *real*. Because you feel stuff and don't pretend not to. You don't have to be perfect—I don't *want* perfect. I want *you*. And honestly…I never thought you could be into someone like me."

Dylan blinked, then let out this laugh and shook his head like I was ridiculous.

"Kiko," he said, smiling now, "I've been into you since that night on Avery's balcony, and if I'm being honest—or *real*—probably before that."

I laughed, a little embarrassed, but he stepped closer. His hand brushed mine again.

"You walk around like you don't even know the way you pull people in," he said. "You think I'm deep? You're the one who made me wanna feel stuff again." He paused. "You're the one who makes things *mean* something."

And yeah—maybe my heart exploded a little right then, but I held it together.

I didn't speak right away. I just stood there with Dylan, our fingers still interlocked like we were holding on to each other for dear life in the middle of all the chaos of the crowd. The music was still thumping in my chest, and the laser lights were cutting through the dark in every color imaginable. The people in the crowd were laughing and yelling and dancing. It felt like the whole city was celebrating with us.

"I kept thinking about that night on the beach," I said finally, my voice barely carrying between us. "I didn't know if it was just me."

Dylan looked me in the eyes. "It wasn't."

That was it. No dramatic poem or monologue, just the truth, in two simple words—or three? How do contractions count? Either way it hit me so hard that I just had to smile.

After a moment we both turned and started back through the crowd, still holding hands—both because we didn't want to let go but probably more because we didn't want to lose each other. This time, though, the chaos didn't feel overwhelming. The energy of the crowd was *electric*.

We spotted our friends near the edge of the street. Indie was bouncing on her toes the second she saw us. She had been shipping this for a long time. Ethan was standing beside her with a wide grin on their face. Rafe was holding up his phone, and I could already hear Avery's voice coming through before we were even close enough to make out what she was saying.

Indie couldn't contain herself anymore. "YASSSS. Okay! There they are! Look at these two!"

Ethan gave me this small, quiet smile like they'd just finished setting up the final scene of a long game of chess. They'd taken out their contacts so they didn't look too freaky anymore.

Rafe grinned wide and flipped the phone toward me. "Look who made it just in time."

Avery's face filled the screen, like she was holding the phone up to her face to get a better look. "I told you," she said. "*That's* the kind of guy you should be with."

I looked around at all of them—this messy, weird little group that somehow held me up through every second of doubt—and felt something settle in my chest like it was just all clicking into place.

Me. Dylan. All of our friends.

Right here, right now.

It felt like the end of one story—and the start of something even better.

Epilogue

The sun was still low, just kinda glowing through the haze like it wasn't even fully committed to the day yet. The water was chill—perfect for a morning session. I paddled out on my mint green Chili Popper, my head quiet—for once. There were none of my usual spirals or crazy overthinking. It was just me, the ocean, and the rhythm of it all—and Rafe, of course.

He was already out ahead.

We made it past the break, letting the sets roll through while the sun climbed higher behind us. The kind of morning where everything felt soft and easy. Rafe sat sideways on his board, kicking one foot in the water, looking like he was about to say something dumb—so, yeah, pretty much business as usual.

"So, real talk. In all the years we've been friends... did you ever have a crush on me?"

I looked over at him. "What?"

"You heard me," he said, grinning. "Like, ever. In the entire history of us, like seven years. Nothing?"

I looked over. His board rocked under him, shoulders relaxed like always, and he had this dumb smirk that said he already knew the answer. He was a good-looking guy, sure, I could admit that. But he was also... Rafe. And that kinda canceled it out.

I shook my head. "I'm not doing this."

"C'mon. No cap. I had to make the list right?"

"Not even once," I said, laughing.

Rafe immediately gasped like I'd betrayed his soul. "Bro. That's actually so rude."

"What?" I said, still laughing. "Why is that rude?"

"Because I am crush-worthy, dude! I've got charisma, I've got abs and dimples, I've got that 'future zaddy' energy."

"First of all, never say 'zaddy' again," I splashed him. "Right now, your best trait is that your car has working AC."

"That's a huge green flag in this economy!"

I wiped a bit of water off my forehead. "You used to wear those awful cargo shorts with the drawstring and insisted they were 'functional.'"

"They were! I could carry, like, a box of Fruit Roll-Ups in each of those pockets. You didn't see the vision."

I snorted, tipping my head back. "You're lucky that somehow Avery saw any vision."

"She did." He tapped his temple. "That's why she's the smart one."

We drifted quietly for a moment, the jokes settling into something easier. Rafe glanced over, a little more serious now. "Still wild, though. All this time. We've been through so much."

I nodded, eyes on the horizon. "Yeah. And somehow we're still here."

He smiled. "Always."

We gave each other a bro hug, both almost losing our balance.

"You better not wipe out," he warned, shooting me a look over his shoulder. "Gotta show off those skills."

I rolled my eyes. "Wiping out is part of surfing, dude."

"Yeah, but now you have an audience," Rafe said, grinning. "Don't want him to think he's dating a noob."

I laughed, flicking water at him.

He started paddling, turning back just long enough to shout "I still say I'm totally crush material!" Then he took off on a wave with that signature flashy style of his.

And me? I just sat up on my board and looked back toward the beach —where *he* was.

Dylan was sitting on the sand with his leather journal open and pen in hand. He looked up and spotted me, gave me this lazy little smile like he'd been waiting for me to notice. And yeah, it hit me right in the chest.

It still felt a little unreal that this was actually happening, that we made it through all the awkwardness and missed signals and doubts and ended up here. With him watching me surf and with me not freaking out about every tiny thing.

Just... *living*.

We were heading downtown after this for the Dodgers parade. Rafe was hyped and so was I. But this moment, here, right now? Sitting on my board, Dylan watching from the beach, the day just getting started— it felt like something I didn't even know I needed.

I paddled toward the next wave, ready for it—and whatever came next. Because this was the start of something good.

I caught the wave clean—paddled into it without hesitation, no second-guessing, no overthinking. I just trusted my body and let it happen. I felt the board lifting under me and I popped up fast, feet planting right where they were supposed to. For the first time in forever, it didn't feel like I was forcing it or chasing some version of who I used to be, or some version of who I felt like I *had* to be.

I dropped low, bent my knees, and started trimming down the line The wind was rushing past my face, cold and salty, but it felt good—sharp in the best way. I shifted my weight, cutting back across the face of the wave. I carved again, letting it pull me forward, then snapped back the other way, staying in the pocket.

It wasn't flashy but it felt right—fluid and natural. It was like the ocean had finally stopped fighting me...or maybe I stopped fighting it? Either way, it felt like we both made up and were good now.

I couldn't stop grinning. My heart was racing, but not in that anxious way—it was fun. It was flow. I rode it out for what felt like forever, working the board back and forth, feeling the water lift and carry me like it used to—like it still could.

The wave started to close out, and I could feel my balance start to go. But instead of trying to save it, I dropped down to my stomach and let it carry me. The board zipped forward, the water pulling me in fast and smooth—and for a second I felt like a little kid again, riding my boogie board. Just playing with no pressure, no crowd. Just joy.

Rafe was already paddling back out and I glanced up and Dylan was walking toward the shallows, his jeans rolled up to his knees and that same soft smile on his face he'd had the whole time.

I coasted as far as I could before the wave fizzed out under me. I hopped off and walked the rest of the way.

"Not bad, right?" I said.

"Not bad at all," Dylan replied. "You look good out there."

"You look good everywhere," I said back, a wide grin spreading on my face.

I reached up, slow and careful, like I didn't want to break whatever this moment was, and let my hand rest against the side of his face. His skin was warm from the sun. My thumb brushed along his cheekbone, and for a second, everything held still—like the ocean was waiting too.

Then Dylan leaned in.

The kiss was soft and sure—the kind that didn't need to prove anything. It was quiet and steady and so full of feeling I swear the rest of the world just faded out. The waves, the seagulls, even the parade waiting for us downtown—*none* of it mattered—because in that moment, there was nowhere else I wanted to be.

I had the ocean behind me, the sky above me, and *everything* in front of me.

We stood there, with the water splashing against our ankles, and I realized this wasn't just some perfect moment in someone else's story—it was mine.

I wasn't floating anymore, waiting for some wave to shift or for someone else to tell me who I was going to be. I chose this—I chose *him*. And for the first time, it felt like I was actually in control, steering my own life toward love, toward possibility… and toward whatever came next.

And yeah, maybe I didn't have all the answers—I definitely didn't. But I had something better: I had a beginning. And I couldn't wait to see where my story was going to take me.

I couldn't wait to see where it was going to take *us*.

THE ~~END~~ Beginning

If You or Someone You Know Is Struggling

The characters in this story are fictional, but the struggles they face are very real. If you or someone you love is dealing with substance use, addiction, or mental health challenges, you're not alone. Help is available—confidentially, without judgment, and often 24/7.

U.S. National Resources

Substance Abuse and Mental Health Services Administration (SAMHSA)
24/7 Helpline: **1-800-662-HELP (4357)**
www.samhsa.gov/find-help/national-helpline
Free and confidential treatment referral and information service for individuals and families.

988 Suicide & Crisis Lifeline
Call or text: **988**
www.988lifeline.org
Available 24/7 for anyone in emotional distress or suicidal crisis.

National Alliance on Mental Illness (NAMI)
Helpline: **1-800-950-NAMI (6264)**
www.nami.org
Information, support, and advocacy for people affected by mental illness.

LGBTQIA+ Specific Support

The Trevor Project (for LGBTQ+ youth)
Call: **1-866-488-7386**
Text: 'START' to **678-678**
www.thetrevorproject.org

Trans Lifeline
Call: **1-877-565-8860**
www.translifeline.org
Peer support and crisis line run by and for trans people.

You matter. Your story is still unfolding.

www.ingramcontent.com/pod-product-compliance
Lightning Source LLC
Chambersburg PA
CBHW050028120726
47903CB00006B/1958